Praise for Simon Bestwick

"Simon Bestwick's *And Cannot Come Again* shows once more why he's one of England's premiere authors of short fiction. In here you will find stories that haunt you, frighten you, and dare you to understand those parts of yourself you pray remain hidden from the rest of the world. A startling book of loss and revelation."

—Simon Strantzas, author of *Nothing is Everything*

"Simon Bestwick's stories have for quite a while now tended to be the best thing in any magazine in which they appear. '. . . And Dream of Avalon' harnesses the potency of cheap music, as Don Henley's '80s smash 'The Boys of Summer' soundtracks a deceptively bitter meditation on the dangers of nostalgia . . . robustly representative of the good solid bedrock of our field of weird fiction."

—Steve Duffy, author of
Tragic Life Stories and *The Moment of Panic*

"His swift, evocative prose, his deep humanity, his visionary insight, above all his sheer gift for telling a gripping story puts Bestwick right in the front rank of horror writers, indeed any kind of fiction writer today. And this volume is Bestwick at his best. If you have yet to read him, I can assure you *And Cannot Come Again* is a superb introduction to a superb writer."

—Reggie Oliver, author of
The Ballet of Dr. Caligari and Madder Mysteries

"Simon Bestwick is one of the best writers around of dark and genuinely scary short horror fiction. Be afraid. . . ."

—Alison Littlewood, author of
A Cold Season and *The Crow Garden*

"Simon Bestwick's fictional monsters may be supernatural but they're not exactly magical. They're the stuff of grown-up nightmares. They fester and grow from ignored trauma, casual degradation, and the cold, sickening awareness that comes after long periods of isolation or neglect. The scars we routinely hide in daylight, out of politeness or a pitiful yearning to fit in, are inevitably revealed in our darkest dreams—and in these stories, which depict the brutality of our worst natural impulses. Each tale poses an urgent question about who we are, what we want to be, and the cost of bridging the gap—both individually and as part of a supposedly civilized world. From the stunning and disturbing first tale, it is established that the author won't flinch before the most intimate and horrific of human transactions. Part of our shock comes from the knowledge that we, the readers, are not exempt from judgement. However lofty our intentions, we've inflicted harm or harm has been inflicted in our name. We are adults, capable of creating monsters. And whether we will transcend the base material from which we and our nightmares are made is debatable."

—S. P. Miskowski, author of *The Worst Is Yet to Come*

"*And Cannot Come Again*, Simon Bestwick's latest collection, confirms again his importance in contemporary horror. Each story's opening sentence takes you into a world where you walk alone through the different dark corridors of the narrative, and what you see, what you hear, what you smell, makes you feel your way with some fear through the paragraphs until you're flooded with the bright white light of each devastating final paragraph. This is how you write horror. And this is what Simon Bestwick accomplishes time and again in these tales. But the book should come with a nightlight. You'll need it after reading about Dermot's deal with the police, what moves through the grass under the trees, the father and daughter down by the duck pond, the torments of Martin Carr, and all the other horrors in this original, compelling, truly scary 100,000-word collection. Highly recommended."

—Ralph Robert Moore, author of *The Angry Red Planet*

"If you need further evidence of why Simon Bestwick is a stalwart of the British horror scene, then look no further than *And Cannot Come Again*. He gathers the northwest in his fist and charts its darkness, be it the streets of Manchester and Salford, the hillsides of the Lake District or the wooded corners of Cheshire. Simon explores brutality—murder, the myths of masculinity, abuse, the pain of adolescence and loss of innocence—but it's tempered by emotive writing and Simon's ability to bring his own social and political sensibilities to the work."

—Priya Sharma, author of *All the Fabulous Beasts*

"I love the way Simon Bestwick's stories start with a soft familiarity, setting us down among the buses and parks, city centres and quiet houses, before coalescing into such sharp depictions of deeply effective horror. The ghosts and monsters he creates are so vivid because they spring from places we know. He's a master at tying terrors to our shared reality."

—Aliya Whiteley, author of *The Beauty* and *The Loosening Skin*

"Simon Bestwick is a master of unsettling stories about people effectively haunted by themselves. While often uncomfortable or even gruesome, these tales of regret and accumulated pain are always compelling and resolutely human."

—Tim Major, author of *Machineries of Mercy* and *Snakeskins*

"The stories in Simon Bestwick's extraordinary collection *And Cannot Come Again* are revelations—uneasy, often bleak and always necessary. Bestwick reaches far and deep to illuminate the deep wounds we all share and might otherwise try to forget—terrifying and enlightening us in almost the same breath."

—David Nickle, author of *Eutopia: A Novel of Terrible Optimism* and *Volk: A Novel of Radiant Abomination*

"Simon Bestwick's *And Cannot Come Again* is a masterful exercise in turning subtle unease into genuine horror. You can't quite put your finger on the moment you slid past the point of no return, but if you're thinking about it it's already far too late. Unexpected. Painful. Truthful. Unflinching. Awful in a wondrous way. This collection sets Bestwick well on his way to standing beside the likes of M. R. James, Machen, and Poe."

—Angela Slatter, World Fantasy Award-winning author of *The Bitterwood Bible and Other Recountings*

"Simon Bestwick shines a light on the dark places in the human heart."

—Erica L. Satifka, British Fantasy Award-winning author of *Stay Crazy*

"Simon Bestwick's fiction is like a neat incision—seeds are planted, the cut is sewn up. You're very aware that something dark is still growing under the skin."

—Colleen Anderson, author of *A Body of Work*

"Simon Bestwick's stories are sharp, bleak, odd, full of grief and grace. If you only know him from his novels, this will be a treat (though you very much should read those, too). If you don't know him at all, then for God's sake, treat yourself. In a genre full of unsung treasures, his song deserves to be heard."

—Gemma Files, author of *Experimental Film*

"Simon Bestwick goes to places least travelled and brings back diamonds soaked in the blood of the psyche. His stories don't aspire to sermon; like all good fiction their integrity, their bravery command their own unique survey of the human condition. That places Bestwick in a rarefied group. This collection is a treasure."

—Usman T. Malik, British Fantasy Award- and Bram Stoker Award-winning author of *The Pauper Prince and the Eucalyptus Jinn*

AND CANNOT COME AGAIN

TALES OF CHILDHOOD, REGRET, AND INNOCENCE LOST

SIMON BESTWICK

FIRST EDITION

And Cannot Come Again © 2019 by Simon Bestwick
Introduction © 2019 by Ramsey Campbell
Cover art © 2019 by Erik Mohr
Interior & Cover design © 2019 by Jared Shapiro

Distributed in Canada by
Fitzhenry & Whiteside Limited
195 Allstate Parkway
Markham, Ontario L3R 4T8
Phone: (905) 477-9700
e-mail: bookinfo@fitzhenry.ca

Distributed in the U.S. by
Consortium Book Sales & Distribution
34 Thirteenth Avenue, NE, Suite 101
Minneapolis, MN 55413
Phone: (612) 746-2600
e-mail: sales.orders@cbsd.com

Library and Archives Canada Cataloguing in Publication

Title: And cannot come again : tales of childhood, regret, and innocence lost / Simon Bestwick.
Names: Bestwick, Simon, author.
Identifiers: Canadiana (print) 20190103582 | Canadiana (ebook) 20190103590 | ISBN 9781771484923
   (softcover) | ISBN 9781771485227 (hardcover) | ISBN 9781771484930 (PDF)
Classification: LCC PR6102.E88 A73 2019 | DDC 823/.92—dc23

CHIZINE PUBLICATIONS
Peterborough, Canada
www.chizinepub.com
info@chizinepub.com

Edited by: Greg Murphy
Copyedited and proofread by Brett Savory

Canada Council   Conseil des arts
for the Arts   du Canada

We acknowledge the support of the Canada Council for the Arts which last year invested $20.1 million in writing and publishing throughout Canada.

ONTARIO ARTS COUNCIL
CONSEIL DES ARTS DE L'ONTARIO
an Ontario government agency
un organisme du gouvernement de l'Ontario

Published with the generous assistance of the Ontario Arts Council.

Printed in Canada

And cannot come again

TABLE OF CONTENTS

THE MAN WHO PUT
THE BEST IN BESTWICK

THE TURN OF THE CENTURY SAW THE GROWTH OF SEVERAL BRITISH PROVincial horror writers, committed to their territory and to social observation. The late Joel Lane lay farthest south, reporting from Birmingham. Northwards we find folk such as Nicholas Royle (Manchester) and Gary McMahon (Sunderland), not to mention Jeremy Dyson (who cites as an inspiration the insight that you could set horror in the north) and his fellow writers of *The League of Gentlemen*. One of the most accomplished and eloquent is Simon Bestwick, and here is a feast of his work.

We Northerners don't disguise our roots. "Dermot" declares this at the outset, locating us in Manchester with great exactitude. Precision is a characteristic of Simon's prose—keen observations deftly conveyed. This thoroughly disturbing tale poses a grisly moral dilemma, suggesting how conquering monsters may require monstrousness. I'd call it allegorical horror, but its meaning only stokes its power.

"Beneath the Sun" begins more gently, dealing with grief. It shows that Simon is at home just as much in a pastoral setting as in the city streets, but the idyll swiftly changes "when you've seen what lies beneath the surface you're presented with at first." Indeed, this could define an aspect of our field—the revelatory nature of horror. Central to the tale is another dreadful choice, and even if it's inadvertent, that's little consolation. I suspect decisions we regret haunt all our lives.

"The Moraine" leads us to the edge at once, vividly conveying the kind of experiences walkers risk on the heights. The prose is as pointed—one might say spiky—as the relationship of the couple it depicts, which threatens to collapse under pressure into shards like stone. The sense of place grows more powerful as it turns uncanny, and this tale is a classic instance of the central Gothic principle, where the setting is itself a character. It gives new meaning to the notion of a killing ground.

For all the horror, a sense of humanity is central to Simon's tales. Indeed, in much of the best of our field, the two elements are inseparable. In "Comfort Your Dead" the human story only very gradually reveals what lurks behind it—in fact, in one sense it never ceases to be human. We might well hope nothing too disturbing is there, but we're at the mercy of Mr. Bestwick. What lies in wait is no less poignant than unsettling.

"The School House" evokes childhood, that most fearful place, and how it may shape the rest of our lives. Its grisly vision of a grammar school rings uncomfortably true, especially to those of us who attended one, although the tale addresses a wider educational issue—learning by rote, suppression of personality, training to conform and not to question. That's just the start of a paranoid nightmare. While hideous hospitals are a staple of our field, few are as relentlessly terrible as this.

"Left Behind" doesn't waste a moment or indeed a word in seizing the reader, though it's by no means short of felicitous turns of phrase. The story leads us into a darkness that proves to be Manchester—not too accurate a premonition of it, we must hope. Noir meets science fiction here, and ends in enigma. Often in our field—certainly here—a mystery is more satisfying and resonant than too much explanation. I have to wonder wickedly whether Simon means his title to rescue the phrase from the intermittently hilarious Nicolas Cage film about the Rapture, or indeed the book on which it's based.

Like much of Simon's work, "Hushabye" conveys his concerns about the ways too many folk have to live now. All sorts of social observations surround the central theme of child abuse, which involves the supernatural without cheating on the real thing. Indeed, uncanny as the perpetrator is, he's no more monstrous than the kind of criminal he metaphorically represents, nor any less dreadfully human.

"A Small Cold Hand" confronts the loss of childhood too. Again the tale pounces on us before we can draw much of a breath, but it's gentler than most of its companions in this volume. Both wistful and disturbing, it achieves its power by reticence, so often beneficial in our field.

"The Proving Ground" reminds us of the economic truths too many people face these days. Even the woods are invaded by the seedy presence of the run-down city. I detect echoes of the fairy tale at its darkest and most unforgiving—the child abandoned in the forest—but here even the ogre is ruthlessly urban. We may be glad its activity takes place between paragraphs.

"Angels of the Silences" takes on a task I don't believe I could—writing from the viewpoint of a goth girl. I hope it's not too presumptuous of me to hail it a success. It certainly succeeds as a thoroughly citified ghost story of a special kind—you may not look at urban crowds in the same way again. We know every crowd hides secrets, but these are of the spectral sort. We learn ghosts can cry, and this reader did.

". . . And Dream of Avalon" has a theme that's surely universal: the past that never leaves us. It may be best returned to only in our heads rather than putting the vision at risk. In its evocation of memory and loss, the tale approaches the prose poem, and it's a fine addition to the literature of the truly spectral.

"Winter's End" starts on an untypically optimistic note, but we may remember this is Bestwick. Before the end we're faced with an especially horrible haunting (and, let me say, an enviably memorable and original sign of it). "Childhood, regret, and innocence lost . . ." This tale epitomises all of them, but may the bleak coda hint at hope?

"They Wait," and so does old age. By imagining the experience while we're relatively youthful, writers may anticipate their own. When we reach it, how may it compare? If it's as vividly envisioned as Simon's sympathetic imagination manages, pretty well, I'd think. The tale has all the resonance of an urban legend, and its magical notion is uncomfortably eloquent. Alas, it may reflect the views of folk younger than the author.

What's this? Has Bulwer-Lytton joined us, or has Snoopy? Fear not—the prose of "The Children of Moloch" immediately turns more first-hand than the first line. Have we returned to Avalon again? No, only to a recurring Bestwick theme—indeed, to more than one. In some ways this collection shows the characteristics of a novel. Be warned: this may be the grimmest and most unsparing story here. Be reassured as well that you'll be rewarded by the vision that the story earns—the most intense in the book.

On one level the title of "And Cannot Come Again" is ironic, given how relentless the past can be in Simon's work. The story belongs to an established tradition of the genre, which might be named the Gang of Four—tales of a quartet of friends whose early experiences will haunt and influence their lives. Stephen King gave us *The Body*, Kim Newman *The Quorum*, Peter Straub a somewhat older bunch in *Ghost Story*, and there are other books (*Obsession*, *Thieving Fear* . . .) Simon's painfully truthful tale enriches the genre that defines it, and that's true of his work in general.

Have I anything to add? Perhaps just that, on reflection, the title of this appreciation strikes me as not quite enough. Yes, Simon put the best in here, but I believe his wife—Cate Gardner, herself a considerable writer—must be celebrated as well. A supportive partner is a writer's treasure, and I believe they both are to each other. May they continue productive and prosperous.

Ramsey Campbell
Wallasey, Merseyside
29 March 2018

FOR CATE, AS EVER, WITH ALL MY LOVE.

DERMOT

The bus turns left off Langworthy Road and onto the approach to the A6. Just before it goes under the overpass, past the old Jewish cemetery at the top of Brindleheath Road and on past Pendleton Church, it stops and Dermot gets on.

He gets a few funny looks, does Dermot, as he climbs aboard, but then he always does. It's hard for people to put their fingers on it. Maybe it's the way his bald head looks a bit too big. Or the fishy largeness of his eyes behind the jar-thick spectacles. The nervous quiver of his pale lips, perhaps.

Or perhaps it's just how pale he is. How smooth. His skin—his face, his hands—are baby-smooth and baby-soft. Like they've never known work, and hardly ever known light.

All that and he's in a suit, too. Quite an old suit, and it's not a perfect fit—maybe a size too large—but it's neat and clean and well-maintained. Pressed. Smooth.

And of course, there's the briefcase.

It's old-fashioned, like something out of the seventies, made out of plain brown leather. He doesn't carry it by the handle. He hugs it close against his chest. Like a child.

Dermot finds his way to a seat and parks himself there. His hands glide and slide smoothly over one another, as if perpetually washing themselves. His lips are slightly parted, and behind the thick glasses his pale, almost colourless eyes are fixed on some far-distant vanishing point beyond the bus's ceiling.

After a moment, the man next to him grunts and gets up. Dermot blinks, snapped rudely out of his reverie, then gets up to let the man past. He thinks the man's going to ding the bell to get off but he doesn't, just goes and finds another seat. Another, Dermot-less seat.

Dermot doesn't care.

He sidles up closer to the window and watches Salford glide past him in the thickening dusk, streetlamps glinting dully in the gathering grey of impending night.

But he gazes beyond what is there to be seen.

And licks his lips as the bus rides on.

"SPECIAL NEEDS," SLURS SHIRES, OUTSIDE THE DOOR. "SPECIAL *NEEDS* . . ."

Abbie stops tapping her pencil on the desktop and looks up at Carnegie.

They're alone in the little office, the little dusty old office that never has a proper clean and has phones and a fax machine and a desktop computer that were last updated in 1991. Well, maybe a little more recently in the computer's case, but only that.

They're the dirty little secret. They're the office in the police station that nobody wants to admit is there, nobody wants to acknowledge exists.

That nobody wants to admit there is a need for.

"Special *Needs* . . . Special fucking *Needs* . . ."

Shires is pressing himself up against the door's big frosted-glass pane with its reinforcing wire mesh. Seen through it, he's blurred but Abbie can make out enough. His arms are up, bent at the elbows and bent sharply in at the wrists, fingers splayed, a parody of some kid with cerebral palsy. He's making that stupid, that *fucking annoying* voice, by sticking his tongue down between his bottom lip and his teeth and gums. It's supposed to make him sound like a spastic.

They have to call their little office something, have to give it some kind of name, and so they call it Special Projects. Shires and the other lads and lasses in the station who know about it call it Special Needs.

It passes for humour around here.

But it's fear, nothing more. It's not the drab little out-of-date office, caught perpetually in its early-nineties time warp, that they're scared of. It's what it represents.

It's what they have to fight.

And how they have to fight it.

That's the theory, anyway. Abbie knows all about the theory. She knows all about what goes on in here, in theory. She's read all the reports, the rulebooks, the case files. She knows the score. In theory.

But this is the first time she's done it for real.

Carnegie, though, he's different. He's a big guy, solid-looking. In his forties, she thinks. Late thirties, maybe, and feeling the strain. Dirty-blond hair, washed-out watery-looking blue eyes and features that all look too closely gathered together in the middle of his face. Black jacket, long black coat, black trousers and shoes. White shirt. No tie. The washed-out watery-looking blue eyes are rolled up towards the ceiling, and each new breath is blown out through his lips. Hard. A little harder each time, it seems, Shires lets out his stupid call.

"Special fucking *Neeeeeeeeds.*"

Shires slaps and bats a splayed bent hand weakly against the frosted, wire-meshed glass, pressing his face up close against it.

Carnegie grabs the door handle, twists and slams his shoulder back into it. The door opens outwards and the impact knocks Shires flying back into the corridor, arms flailing. There's a heavy crash as he lands.

Carnegie pulls the door shut again. He turns to face Abbie and shrugs.

"Argh! Carnegie you fucking cunt!" Shires's voice is muffled.

Abbie is biting her lips hard so as not to laugh. She has to stop herself doing that because if she starts, she doesn't know if she'll stop.

Moaning, groaning and mumbling indistinct threats of revenge, Shires stumbles away down the corridor and out of earshot.

Carnegie spreads his hands in a *what-can-you-do* gesture.

Abbie can't restrain herself anymore and bursts out laughing.

Carnegie starts laughing, too.

On the frosted-glass pane behind him, around head-height, there's a splash of red on the outside of the door.

They're laughing.

And then the phone rings and they stop.

They just look at the phone, Abbie sitting at her desk, Carnegie standing by the door, and they watch it and listen to it ring and ring and ring.

DERMOT STANDS PATIENTLY BEFORE THE DESK. THE DESK SERGEANT IS trying to keep his eyes off him, but they keep straying back and every time they meet Dermot feels the thrill of contact, the hatred and the loathing and the contempt like the charge that jolts down a live wire when a connection gets made.

The desk sergeant motions with his eyes to one of the seats in the reception area. The subtext of which is, *get the fuck away from me.*

Dermot doesn't care. He'd rather sit down anyway.

He goes to the chair and he sits and waits. His hands flow over and over one another in their endless washing motions. He hugs the briefcase tightly to his chest. Like a baby.

He licks his lips.

And he waits.

THE PHONE RINGS.

"Gonna answer it?" Carnegie asks.

"No," Abbie says.

"Answer it," says Carnegie.

She looks up at him. The phone rings. She wants to say, *You answer it.* The phone rings. Or maybe, *You answer it, sir.* The phone rings. Maybe, even, *You answer it, sir. Please.* The phone rings. But she doesn't. The phone rings. Because he is her superior officer. The phone rings. And this is her first time. The phone rings. This is her test. The phone rings. This is her rite of passage. The phone rings. And if she fails it, she's out. The phone rings—

She picks it up and answers it. "Special—" She nearly says, *Special Needs,* stops herself just in time; turning tragedy into farce would just add insult to injury. "Special Projects."

"He's here," the desk sergeant says.

Send him up, she almost tells him, but she stops herself again, once more just in time. They won't sully their hands with Dermot. They'll kid themselves they're not involved, leave it to the tainted bastards in Special Needs to do the job.

"I'll be right down," she says.

THERE'S A LOUD, DEFINITE *CLICK* AS THE DESK SERGEANT PUTS DOWN THE phone. He feels Dermot's eyes on him and looks his way. "They're coming down for you," he says, managing, just about, not to grit his teeth. *Now stop fucking looking at me or I'll break your filthy fucking neck, no matter what you are to them.* That's what the subtext is.

Dermot just smiles, a mild, milky smile, and the desk sergeant looks away.

Dermot knows they hate him, but he doesn't care. In fact, he rather likes it.

Because they need him. He knows they need him and they know they need him, too.

They have to give him what he wants.

No one in the reception area is looking at him. The lift door chimes and opens. A woman approaches. Girl, really. Trouser suit. Blonde hair. Pretty, rather. If she were his type . . . but she isn't. Pity really.

But then, if she were his type, this wouldn't be all the sweeter. Because it's all the sweeter for the power, and what he can make them do.

She comes over to Dermot. She smiles and tries to look civil, but Dermot notices she doesn't offer to shake hands. There are limits even for the people in Special Projects.

"Sir?"

He nods. He bets it hurt her to call him that.

"Detective Constable Stone. If you'll just come with me?"

Without waiting for a reply, she turns and walks away. The desk sergeant steals a glance at her small, taut behind, rolling beneath the clinging fabric of her trousers, then recoils, blushing, as Dermot catches his eye and smirks.

The desk sergeant's face is red. His knuckles, of the fists clenched on the desktop, are white.

Dermot follows the girl into the lift. No one else looks at him, her, at them. No one else wants to admit they're linked or connected in any way, shape or form.

But they are.

"HAVE YOU READ MY FILE?" HE ASKS HER AS THE LIFT ASCENDS.

Abbie starts, nearly jumping, gets it under control. She's stolen a couple of quick glances at him, but that's all. She hoped he'd stay quiet, stay silent, till she'd got him to the office. Hoped Carnegie would do all the talking with him. She'd just have to make the tea. Not get involved. Not be complicit. Tell herself she wasn't responsible.

Don't talk to me, you bastard, she thinks.

But he does. He has.

And they have to cooperate with him. Have to go softly-softly. Have to give him what he wants.

Even my complicity? Even my soul?

You're kidding yourself if you think you haven't given that already, she tells herself. *You're already part of this. Carry on.*

He's looking at her, eyebrows raised, waiting politely for her answer. "Yes," she says.

He nods. "Then you know all about me," he says. It's a statement, not a question, this time. His voice is wavery and weak, with a faint Irish accent. It goes with his pale face and bland features and colourless eyes. With his soft, smooth, hairless hands that have never known honest work.

"Yes," she says. She doesn't want to reply but she has to. "Yes, I know all about you." She tries to keep her voice neutral but can't, not quite. She wishes she could, especially when she sees the look on his face.

He likes this. Making us dance to his tune. He likes this. Almost as much as the other part.

She isn't going to think about the other part. That will come later. She has to get through this one stage at a time, step by step. If she thought about the other part, she'd never be able to get this done. And she has to.

The lift chimes, and she'd never have believed that simple sound could fill her with such relief.

"We're here," she says, and steps out of the lift.

DERMOT FOLLOWS HER DOWN THE SAME PLAIN, DUSTY CORRIDOR HE'S come down how many dozens, how many hundreds, of times before? He doesn't know how many. Even he's lost count. Neither she—the pretty little Detective Constable Stone—nor whichever senior officer awaits him in the room will know.

Will it be Ryan, or McDonald? No—Carnegie, he thinks. It will be Carnegie's turn now. Carnegie won't know how many times Dermot's come down this corridor and into this room. To perform his thankless task. To receive his grudging reward. But he could find out if he wanted. It will be in a file somewhere. In this country, everything has to go on file.

DC Stone opens the door that Dermot knows so well, the one with the frosted-glass pane reinforced with its wire mesh. Odd. There's a smear of blood on it, slowly drying.

Inside, at the desk, is Carnegie.

I was right, thinks Dermot. *I always am.*

Carnegie smokes.

He doesn't offer one to Dermot. Or to Abbie, for that matter. Not that she cares. She has her own packet of Silk Cut. Carnegie favours Sovereign, a much stronger brand. High tar. There's an ashtray on the tabletop. Fuck the smoking ban.

"We know there's at least one in the city," he says. "We need you to tell us where it is."

Dermot pointedly wafts a hand in front of his face. Carnegie glowers and bashes out his half-smoked cigarette.

"What about my fee?" Dermot asks.

"Fee?" Carnegie spits the word out with loathing.

"My reward, then. For doing my bit. For being such a good boy. For saving so many lives."

Carnegie's eyes are slits. His hands are clenched, the knuckles white. His mouth looks like a half-healed scar. Then he breathes out and his face goes slack.

"Your reward's waiting downstairs," he says. "When you deliver your side of the bargain. You know what we want. Where is it?"

Dermot smiles, nods, licks his lips. It's the last that Abbie finds the worst. The anticipation in it.

He closes his eyes. Prayers his hands together. Smiles. Parts his lips oh-so-slightly and spit bubbles go *pop-pop-pop.*

He opens his eyes and his hands drop. His eyes are bright.

He speaks, rapidly. Abbie's already scribbling, transcribing it in shorthand. Then he's done and she's picking up the phone.

Sirens wail in the night, and three police vans tear up Oldham Road into an area of bleak, functional-looking sixties-era council housing and old mills and factories either abandoned or converted to new purposes. Most of the district's one big industrial estate.

At one point along the roadside, a rank of three shops. The buildings are abandoned, boarded up and covered in geological layers of flyposters. The vans screech to a halt outside them. Armed police officers pile out. Some carry shotguns, other submachine guns.

Doors are kicked in and boots thunder up the stairs.

What they're looking for is on the topmost floor.

All the upstairs rooms of the three shops have been knocked together, creating a huge open space.

Things lie on the floor. Five of them. Still asleep. Waiting to wake up. They are vast. They have long talons. Longer jaws. And worse.

Guns are aimed.

Yellow eyes open. Something wakes, leaps up, howling, screeching, clawed hands aloft.

A dozen guns fire simultaneously. The flat, thundery blasts of shotguns, the staccato splitting cracks of submachine guns. The rearing thing is danced back across the room and collapses to the bare, rotted floorboard, writhing, spurting, and then is still.

Then the guns aim down, at the other things, and they fire again.

They don't stop until nothing is left alive on the floors or walls of that upstairs room.

THE PHONE RINGS.

Dermot watches Carnegie pick it up. The big man nods and grunts. DC Stone is watching all of this, her eyes darting back and forth from one of them to the other.

Carnegie replaces the handset.

"They found them. There were five of them. Just like you said. They got them all." He doesn't want to say the next bit, but Dermot has his eyebrows raised and is demanding it, tacitly. Just like he always does. And so Carnegie says it: "Thank you."

"You're welcome," says Dermot. "Now," he strives to keep his voice level; to show excitement would be unseemly, "there's the small matter of my reward."

"Yes," says Carnegie thickly, not looking up at him, looking down at the surface of his desk instead. "Detective Constable Stone?"

"Sir?" says Stone at last.

Carnegie still doesn't look up from the top of his desk. "Take him down to the cells. It's cell number thirteen."

"Ah," says Dermot. "How apt."

Carnegie doesn't look up or reply.

Stone's face is ashen. She's even shaking slightly. "If you'll just come with me," she says.

ALL THE WAY DOWNSTAIRS IN THE LIFT, ABBIE'S THINKING *THIS CAN'T BE real*, thinking *This has to be a dream*, thinking *Please let me wake up before*—

But it is, it isn't, she can't.

The lift doors open in the basement and she heads out, Dermot following in her wake. He's trotting after her, she realises with disgust. Trying to hide his excitement and failing. Miserably.

But who's more disgusting, he or she?

The custody sergeant doesn't look up from his paper at either of them as they pass. Determinedly. He knew they were coming. And he knew, just as well, that he wasn't going to, didn't want to see them.

Abbie leads Dermot down past the row of cells. They're all empty tonight. That's been arranged.

There's a slap of paper, the sound of boots on a tiled floor. She glances round to see the custody sergeant walking out fast. Getting out before the sounds start. Well, there'll be nothing else in here demanding his attention tonight.

She puts the key in the lock and opens the cell door. Light from the corridor spills into the darkness.

"Mummy?" The voice is tiny, thin and blurred. "Daddy?"

Dermot stands at the threshold, not going in yet.

"Go on then," she says. He doesn't move.

"Mummy?"

This time she prods his shoulder. *"Go on."*

Dermot's head snaps round and for a second Abbie is afraid. But he's only smiling. Smiling and holding her with his eyes. Till she drops her gaze.

Then he's moving, tired of the game, and into the cell. Abbie pulls the door shut behind him, but not fast enough to evade a glimpse of the child's face, bewildered and afraid, or shut out the beginnings of her cry.

DERMOT HEARS STONE'S FOOTSTEPS RECEDE DOWN THE CORRIDOR. HE puts the briefcase down on the floor and loosens his tie.

The little girl has backed up against the far wall.

Dermot opens the briefcase and takes his tools out one by one. He puts them on the floor beside the case. And then he starts to undress.

In the pub, afterward, Carnegie is on his third double Scotch and Abbie's forsaken her usual white wine spritzer for a vodka tonic. She's on her third. There's been less and less tonic in each one.

"You did good today," he says. Thick and slurred, but drunkenly sincere.

"Doesn't feel like it."

"It's got to be done," he says. "They need us. Otherwise . . ."

She knows. Knows what would happen without Dermot to tell them where the latest batch of creatures are incubating, ready to wake to murderous life. Knows you do your time in Special Projects—a year, two, maybe three—and then the world's your oyster, a fast track to any job you want, or if you don't want one anymore, early retirement on a fat pension. There's a reason for that. A price you pay.

She downs her vodka, digs out her mobile, rings for a cab. She feels bad, a little, about leaving Carnegie to drink alone, but sharing the bar with him just makes her remember what she's now part of.

"What time do you need me in tomorrow?"

"Don't bother. Come in in the afternoon." His watery blue eyes are bloodshot. "You passed the test, Abbie. You're in. I'll handle the cleanup."

Normally, she'd object to being treated like the little woman. But this time around, she doesn't mind.

She weaves out the door to the waiting cab.

Alone now, Carnegie downs the last of his whisky. Without being asked, the barman brings him another.

Carnegie bolts half of it in one, feels it burn its way down. Tomorrow, he'll go to cell thirteen, like so many times before. Dermot will be lying there, naked and pallid as a grub, clothes bagged up in a Tesco plastic carrier, tools already wiped spotless and back in the briefcase.

Carnegie will wake him up and take him to the showers. Get the blood off. When he's clean and dressed, he'll drive Dermot home. But first he'll have to go back into the thirteenth cell, and before they come to hose it down, he'll have to gather the bones.

BENEATH THE SUN

It was the summer after my mother died. My father and I had moved out of our old house and to another, more memory-free, on the outer edges of suburbia, bordering on the countryside. If you walked far enough, you were lost in the green hills and woodlands of Cheshire, without even a farmer or upper-class moron—a species common in Cheshire then and still, and sadly showing no signs of extinction—to break the solitude.

That was what I needed. The atmosphere in the house was almost unbearable at this point. Grieving, in retrospect, is a process we all handle in different ways and by different means. My father's was to withdraw into his work. Mine? To wander off. To go places where my brain didn't work anymore, because there were trees and flowers and birds and hills and streams to lose all awareness in. The house suited us both. It allowed my father to make his withdrawal absolute, and it enabled me to walk away. Silences ached like wounds between us and I often thought that if I didn't come back from one of my early-morning or early-evening rambles through the woodland, it would take him about a week to notice.

I had no friends—we'd moved too far away from our old home for there to be a hope of my retaining them. So I walked alone through the woods and came back later and later. Soon I took to taking a packed lunch with me. Other times I didn't even bother with that.

The particular morning I want to tell you about was no different from any other. I was at this time twelve years of age. I went out and walked into the woods. I stood in the front doorway before going and listened to my father pounding the typewriter keys—he still regarded computers as the tool of the devil—for a few moments before leaving. I slammed the door hard. If I'd hoped for a response, I didn't get it.

Something of my numbness cracked around me that day and sobs hitched in my chest as I walked. The sunlight, sky and heat-dried yellow grass blurred together as I walked, then faded into the warm dark green, black and brown of the woodland.

I don't know exactly where it happened. All I can tell you is that when my crying fit had subsided, I was completely ignorant of where it was I'd ended up. I was on a hillside, and at its foot the pines were thick. They were the first conifers I'd seen in the area surrounding my house. I wondered how far I'd travelled. I looked up at the sky, trying to gauge east and west and north and south. The sun was close to its zenith, at any rate, and burning hot. There were clouds, but well in the distance. I felt parched and dry.

I walked down the slope instead, towards the cool piney shade promised by the trees. Mum had used to hang one of those little pine air fresheners in the family car. Dad didn't. Perhaps the memory of them was painful to him, or perhaps he just kept forgetting.

I could smell the pines as I walked, and thought of my mother. I hadn't dared do so in a long time. It occurred to me that I needn't worry about bawling here. There was no one around, nobody to see or hear. But nothing came out then. Nothing has since. That morning was the last time ever. I can't cry now. I don't know why that should be. I've never understood it.

The pines were cool and their smell was my mother's. That felt good. Then I emerged from their shelter into a broad yellow field.

I walked. The field was wild and thickly overgrown, snarled with brambles and wild tall grass. A dead black tree loomed up ahead and cast a spill of shadow over the yellow stalks. I kept walking in its general direction. There was nowhere else to go.

Then I tripped on something and went sprawling. My eyes stung. They might have been tears, but not the kind I can't cry now. I looked and found I'd tripped over a stone. Closer inspection showed it to be the broken remains of a slab. There was worn lettering on it: a name, and dates.

On my hands and knees in the long grass, I saw there were more of them, strewn about. I was lucky to have fallen only once. Most of them were only modest headstones, but here and there was a stone cross, and tumbled on her side, the remains, worn and lichened and pitted, of a stone angel.

Something moved the grasses nearby. I looked, but only glimpsed some loping shadow. Within seconds, I couldn't even be sure that it wasn't just the wind rustling at the dry hollow stems.

I stood and walked more slowly and carefully, the way you always do when you've seen what lies beneath the surface you're presented with at first. I moved towards the dark tree. A cricket somewhere nearby let out its relentless chirruping whirr.

They were under the tree.

At first I thought they were more stones, large ones; they were grey and pitted-looking, lumpy and unfinished and rough-surfaced. There were patches on them that resembled lichen in the baking summer heat. Then I began to notice things about them; there was a mottled, moist texture to them that argued against rock, that argued instead the flesh of something that wasn't meant to be in the sunlight, or spent a long time out of it. And they smelt—a bit like a tramp who hadn't washed in a long time, though there was something else that took me a moment to place—the way some pieces of chicken my father had bought had smelled after being left out too long. I felt myself gagging and clapped a hand over my mouth.

There was something else, too. They were moving.

There were, I think, about five or six of them. They had hands and feet and heads. I don't know if they used to be men and women—maybe back when they were alive—or if they were something else entirely. But they were tussling over something on the ground, in the centre of them. It was red, or a lot of it was—the pieces they picked up and lifted to their thankfully unseen faces to tear at. Flies were buzzing. The crickets had fallen silent but the flies seemed very loud. I couldn't believe I hadn't heard them before. It was burning hot. My lips and mouth were dry. They always had been. I felt giddy. I tried to breathe deeply, but breathed in the smell that was coming off them and again almost threw up. I clamped my hands back over my mouth. I didn't want them to see me. I didn't want them to know I was there. I backed slowly away, slowly and quietly, not daring to look away but tense over where each footfall might come down, in case some dry dead thing snapped to alert the feasters.

It didn't. But instead I trod on something hard and unyielding—I think it was another fragment of gravestone—that gave underfoot and buckled my ankle over. A scream at the sudden shocking insult of the pain tore out of me as my leg collapsed. I missed hitting my head on the stone angel by inches. I made a fumbling effort to stand, but even as I tried to put weight on my hurt ankle a spear of pain turned bone and muscle to liquid and I fell again.

But I could hear the crash and swish of things moving through the field towards me, large and ungainly and clumsy, of broad heavy hands swatting the grasses aside. I tried to drag myself away, wriggling like a snake, but they were too fast. There was no outpacing them. I saw their silhouettes looming around me and circling, like shadows on a bamboo screen.

As they closed in on me, they blotted out the sun. It was directly above and they made shadows of themselves against it. They smelt worse than ever. I glimpsed a part of one of them. There was an open sore on its flesh with flies crawling over it. I still couldn't see much of their faces as they bent over me. Just grey. Their eyes and mouths were red.

I was babbling—blubbering—something by this point, over and over again. I can't really remember it now, except for two words: *Not me. Not me.*

The stench, the heat, the fear—one or all of those and I passed out. When I woke up, the shadows were stretching out along the field, trailing through the grasses like weeds in the river, drawn out by the pull of the current.

I was alone, and there was no sign of anything grey and moving. I picked myself up and put some weight on my twisted ankle. It twinged but this time my leg held me up.

I made my way back to the hillside. From up there, with the height and thickness of the pines, the field was invisible, as if it had never been.

It was easier than I thought, finding my way to the familiar paths that would take me home. Perhaps I clicked into some kind of automatic pilot as I began to tell myself that what I'd seen that morning wasn't real, couldn't be real, that it was just some hot fever dream. I wanted to believe it so it wasn't hard. It was getting windy by then, and a bit cold; the sky was greying over. A dull, dark mottled grey, like stone, or something else.

I almost ran—as close to it as my bad leg would let me—down the woodland path that led to my house. When I stumbled out, I stopped. I knew my dad didn't like company—that was why we'd moved out here—so I couldn't understand why there were so many cars parked outside. And a white van, or at least what looked like one. But then I saw the little yellow-black strips of tape fencing off the house from me, the men in black uniforms around it, the red stripe around the body of the van, and the blue light on top of it.

Mrs. Green was there—she was our nearest neighbour. When she saw me she let out a cry and pointed. The policemen ran over to me. "Come on, son," I heard one of them say. "Come on."

"Where's dad?" I asked.

"Come on."

"Poor little mite . . ." I heard Mrs. Green saying. The rest was sniffles and lost in the slam of the police car door.

The sky was all grey now. A policeman started the engine. He was talking to me soothingly but I didn't listen.

Not me. I'd lie awake thinking that, over the aching but tearless nights that followed. *Not me.*

Someone else, anyone else, but not me.

Of course, I don't know what I might have said, much less why they should have listened to it. If listen they did. If they were there at all. A fever dream. I tell myself that. Most of the time I believe it. Most nights.

THE MORAINE

The mist hit us suddenly. One moment we had the peak in sight; the next, the white had swallowed up the crags and was rolling down towards us.

"Shit," I said. "Head back down."

For once, Diane didn't argue.

Trouble was, it was a very steep climb. Maybe that was why we'd read nothing about this mountain in the guidebooks. Some locals in the hotel bar the night before had told us about it. They'd warned us about the steepness, but Diane liked the idea of a challenge. All well and good, but now it meant we had to descend very slowly; one slip and you'd go down the mountainside, arse over apex.

That was when I saw the faint desire-line that led off, almost at right angles to the main path, running sideways and gently downwards.

"There, look," I said, pointing. "What do you reckon?"

Diane hesitated, glancing down the main path then up at the fast-falling mist. "Let's try it."

So we did.

"Look out," I said. Diane was lagging a good four or five yards behind me. "Faster."

"I'm going as fast as I bloody can, Steve."

I didn't rise to the bait, just turned and jogged on. The gentler slope meant we could run, but even so, we weren't fast enough. Everything went suddenly white.

"Shit," said Diane. I reached out for her hand—she was just a shadow in the wall of white vapour—and she took it and came closer. The mist was cold, wet and clinging, like damp cobwebs.

"What now?" said Diane. She kept her voice level, but I could tell it wasn't easy for her. And I couldn't blame her.

Don't be fooled by Lakeland's picture-postcard scenery; its high mountains and blue tarns, the boats on Lake Windermere, the gift shops and stone-built villages. You come here from the city to find the air's fresher and cleaner, and when you look up at night you see hundreds, thousands more stars in the sky because there's no light pollution. But by the same token, fall on a slope like this and there'll be no one around, and your mobile won't get a signal. And if a mist like this one comes down and swallows you up and you don't know which way to go—it doesn't take that long, on a cold October day, for hypothermia to set in. These fells and dales claimed lives like ours each year.

I took a deep breath. "I think . . ."

"You okay?" she asked.

"I'm fine." I was a little nettled she'd thought otherwise; she was the one who'd sounded in need of reassurance, but I wasn't going to start bickering now. It occurred to me—at the back of my head, and I'd've denied it outright if anyone had suggested it to me—that this might be a blessing in disguise; if I could stay calm and lead us to safety, I could be a hero in her eyes. "We need to get to some lower ground."

"Yes, I know." She sounded nettled, as if I'd pointed out the stupidly obvious. Well, perhaps I had. I was just trying to clarify the situation. All right, I wanted to impress her, to look good. But I wanted to do the right thing as well. Honestly.

So I pointed down the trail—the few feet of it we could see where it disappeared into the mist. "Best off keeping on. Keep our heads and go slowly."

"Yes, I worked that bit out as well." I recognised her tone of voice; it was the one she used to take cocky students down a peg. There'd been a time when I used to slip into her lectures, even though I knew nothing, then or now, about geology; I just liked hearing her talk about her favoured subject. I couldn't remember ever seeing her in any of *my* lectures—not that she was interested in music. Maybe it had never been what I'd thought it was. What either of us had thought.

Not a good thought to have right now, but unfortunately I'd been having far too many thoughts like that lately. We both had. Hence this trip, which was looking less and less like a good idea all the time. We'd spent our honeymoon here; I suppose we'd hoped to recapture something or other, but there's no magic in places. Only people, and precious little of that; less and less the older you get.

And none of that was likely to get us safely out of here. "Okay then," I said. "Come on."

DIANE CAUGHT THE BACK OF MY COAT AND PULLED. I WHEELED TO FACE her and swayed, off balance. Loose scree clattered down into the mist; the path had grown rockier underfoot. She caught my arm and steadied me. I yanked it free, thoroughly pissed off. "What?"

"Steve, we're still walking."

"I noticed. Well, actually, we're not just now, since you just grabbed me."

She folded her arms. "We've been walking nearly twenty minutes." I could see she was trying to stop her teeth chattering. "And I don't think we're much closer to ground level. I think we might be a bit off course."

I realised my teeth had started chattering, too. It was hard to be sure, but I thought she might have a point; the path didn't look like it was sloping down any longer. If it'd levelled off, we were still halfway up the damned mountain. "Shit."

I felt panic threatening, like a small hungry animal gnawing away at me inside my stomach, threatening to tear its way up through my body if I let it. I wouldn't. Couldn't. Mustn't. If we panicked we were stuffed.

At least we hadn't come completely unprepared. We each had Kendal Mint Cake and a thermos of hot tea in our backpacks, which helped, but they could only buy a little more time. We either got off this mountain soon, or we never would.

We tried our mobiles, but it was an exercise; there was no reception out here. They might as well have been bits of wood. I resisted the temptation to throw mine away.

"Should've stayed on the main path," Diane said. "If we'd taken it slow we'd have been okay."

I didn't answer. She glanced at me and rolled her eyes.

"What?"

"Steve, I wasn't having a go at you."

"Fine."

"Not everything has to be about that."

"I said, 'Fine.'"

But she wouldn't leave it. "All I said was that we should've stuck to the main path. I wasn't saying this was all your fault."

"Okay."

"I wasn't. If I'd seen that path I would've probably done the same thing. It looked like it'd get us down faster."

"Right."

"I'm just saying, looking back, we should've gone the other way."

"Okay. All right. You've made your point." I stood up. A sheep bleated faintly. "Can we just leave it now?"

"*Okay.*" I saw her do the eye roll again, but pretended not to. "So now what? If we backtrack—"

"Think we can make it?"

"If we can get back to the main path, we should be able to find our way back from there."

If we were very lucky, perhaps; our hotel was a good two miles from the foot of this particular peak, and chances were the mist would be at ground level, too. Even off the mountain we'd be a long way from home and dry, but it seemed the best choice on offer. If only we'd taken it sooner, we might not have heard the dog bark.

But we did.

We both went still. Diane brushed her dark hair back from her eyes and looked past me into the mist. I looked, too, but couldn't see much. All I could see was the rocky path for a few feet ahead before it vanished into the whiteout.

The sheep bleated again. A few seconds later, the dog barked.

I looked at Diane. She looked back at me. A sheep on its own meant nothing—most likely lost and astray, like us. But a dog—a dog, most likely, had an owner. . . .

"Hello?" I called into the mist. "Hello?"

"Anybody down there?" Diane called.

"Hello?" A voice called back.

"Thank God for that," Diane whispered.

We started along the rattling path, into the mist. "Hello?" called the voice. "Hello?"

"Keep shouting," I called back, and it occurred to me that we were the ones who sounded like rescuers. Maybe we'd found another fell-walker, caught out in the mists like us. I hoped not. What with the dog barking as well, I was pinning my hopes on a shepherd out here rounding up a lost sheep, preferably a generously disposed one with a warm, nearby cottage complete with a fire and a kettle providing hot cups of tea.

Scree squeaked and rattled underfoot as we went. I realised the surface of the path had turned almost entirely into loose rock. Not only that, but it was angling sharply down after all. Diane caught my arm. "Careful."

"Yeah, okay, I know." I tugged my arm free and tried to ignore the long sigh she let out behind me.

The mist cleared somewhat as we reached the bottom. We could see between twenty-five and thirty yards ahead, which was a vast improvement, although the whiteout still completely hid everything beyond that point. The path led down into a sort of shallow ravine between our peak and its neighbour. The bases of the two steep hillsides sloped gently downwards to a floor about ten yards wide. It was hard to be certain as both the floor and those lower slopes were covered in a thick layer of loose stone fragments.

The path we'd followed petered out, or more accurately disappeared into that treacherous surface. Two big flat-topped boulders jutted out of the scree, one about twenty yards down the ravine floor, the other about fifteen yards on from that, at the mouth of a gully that gaped in the side of our peak.

The mist drifted. I couldn't see any sign of man or beast. "Hello?" I called.

After a moment, there was a click and rattle somewhere in the ravine. Rock, pebbles, sliding over one another, knocking together.

"Bollocks," I said.

"Easy," said Diane. "Looks like we've found some low ground anyway."

"That doesn't mean much. We've lost our bearings."

"There's somebody around here. We heard them. Hello?" She shouted the last—right down my earhole, it felt like.

"Ow."

"Sorry."

"Forget it."

There was another click and rattle of stone. And the voice called out, "Hello?" again.

"There," said Diane. "See?"

"Yeah. Okay."

There was a bleat, up and to our left. I looked and sure enough there was the sheep we'd heard, except it was more of a lamb, picking its unsteady way over the rocks on the lower slopes of the neighbouring peak.

"Aw," said Diane. "Poor little thing." She's one of those who goes all gooey over small furry animals. Not that it stops her eating them; I was nearly tempted to mention the rack of lamb in red wine jus she'd enjoyed so much the night before. Nearly.

The lamb saw us, blinked huge dark eyes, bleated plaintively again.

In answer, there were more clicks and rattles, and an answering bleat from farther down the ravine. The lamb shifted a bit on its hooves, moving sideways, and bleated again.

After a moment, I heard the rocks click again, but softly this time. It lasted longer, too, this time. Almost as if something was moving slowly, as stealthily as the noisy terrain allowed. The lamb was still, looking silently up the ravine. I looked, too, trying to see past where the scree faded into the mist.

The rocks clicked softly, then were silent. And then a dog barked, twice. The lamb tensed but was still.

Click click click, went the rocks, and the dog barked again.

The lamb bleated. A long silence.

Diane's fingers had closed round my arm. I felt her draw breath to speak, but I turned and shushed her, fingers to her lips. She frowned; I touched my finger back to my own lips and turned to look at the lamb again.

I didn't know why I'd done all that, but somehow knew I'd had to. A moment later we were both glad of it.

The click of shifting rocks got louder and faster, almost a rustle, like grass parting as something slid through it. The lamb bleated and took a few tottering steps back along the slope. Pebbles clattered down.

The rock sounds stopped. I peered into the mist, but I couldn't see anything. Then the dog barked again. It sounded very close now. More than close enough to see, but the ravine floor was empty. I looked back at the lamb. It was still. It cocked its head.

A click of rocks, and something bleated.

The lamb bleated back.

Rocks clattered again, deafeningly loud, and Diane made a strangled gasp that might have been my name, her hand clutching my arm painfully, and pointed with her free hand.

The ravine floor was moving. Something was humped up beneath the rocks, pushing them up as it went so they clicked and rattled in its wake. It was like watching something move underwater. It raced forward, arrowing towards the lamb.

The lamb let out a single terrified bleat and tried to turn away, but it never stood a chance. The humped shape under the scree hurtled towards it, scree rattling like dice in a shaken cup, and then rocks sprayed upwards like so much kicked sand where the lamb stood. Its bleat became a horrible squealing noise—I'd no idea sheep could make sounds like that. The shower of rubble fell back to earth. The lamb kept squealing. I could only see its head and front legs; the rest was buried under the rock. The front legs kicked frantically and the head jerked about, to and fro, the lips splaying back horribly from the teeth as it squealed out its pain. And then a sudden, shocking spray of blood spewed out from under the collapsing shroud of rocks like a scarlet fan. Diane clapped a hand to her mouth with a short, shocked cry. I think I might have croaked, "Jesus," or something along those lines, myself.

The lamb's squeals hit a new, jarring crescendo that hurt the ears, like nails on a blackboard, then choked and cut off. Scree clattered and hissed down the slope and came to rest. The lamb lay still. Its fur was speckled red with blood; its eyes already looked fixed and unblinking, glazing over. The rocks above and around it glistened.

With any luck it was beyond pain. I hoped so, because in the next moment the lamb's forequarters were yanked violently, jerked deeper under the rubble, and in the same moment the scree seemed to surge over it. The heaped loose rock jerked and shifted a few times, rippled slightly and was still. Even the stones splashed with blood were gone, rolled under the surface and out of sight. A few glistening patches remained, farthest out from where the lamb had been, but otherwise there was no sign that it'd even existed.

"Jesus." I definitely said it this time. "Jesus fucking Christ."

There was a moment of silence; I could hear Diane drawing breath again to speak. And then there was that now-familiar click and rattle as something moved under the scree. And from where the lamb had been a voice, a low, hollow voice, called, "Hello?"

DIANE PUT HER HAND OVER MY MOUTH. "STAY QUIET," SHE WHISPERED.

"I know that," I whispered back, muffled by her hand.

"It hunts by sound," she whispered. "Must do. Vibration through the rocks."

There was a slight, low hump where the lamb had been killed, and you had to look hard to see it, and know what it was you were trying to spot. A soft clicking sound came from it. Rock on rock.

"It's under the rocks," she whispered.

"I can *see* that."

"So if we can get back up onto solid ground, we should be okay."

"Should."

She gave me an irritated look. "Got any better ideas?"

"Okay. So we head back?"

"Hello?" called the voice again.

"Yes," whispered Diane. "And very, very slowly, and carefully, and quietly."

I nodded.

The rocks clicked and shifted, softly. Diane raised one foot, moved it upslope, set it slowly, gently down again. Then the other foot. She turned and looked at me, then reached out and took my hand. Or I took hers, as you prefer.

I followed her up the slope. We climbed in as near silence as we could manage, up towards the ravine's entrance, towards the solidity of the footpath. Rocks slid and clicked underfoot. As if in answer, the bloodied rocks where the lamb had died clicked, too, knocking gently against one another as something shifted under them. "Hello?" I heard again as we climbed. And then again: "Hello?"

"Keep going," Diane whispered.

The rocks clicked again. With a loud rattle, a stone bounced down to the ravine floor. "John?" This time it was a woman's voice. Scottish, by the accent. "John?"

"Fucking hell," I muttered. Louder than I meant to and louder than I should've, because the voice sounded again. "John? John?"

Diane gripped my hand so tight I almost cried out. For a moment I wondered if that's what she meant—make me cry out, then let go and run, leave the unwanted partner as food for the thing beneath the rocks while she made her getaway, kill two birds with one stone. But it wasn't, of course.

"Shona?" This time the voice was a man's, likewise Scottish-accented. "Shona, where are ye?"

Neither of us answered. A cold wind blew. I clenched my teeth as they tried to start chattering again. I heard the wind whistle and moan. Shrubs flapped and fluttered in the sudden gale and the surrounding terrain became a little clearer, though not much. Then the wind dropped again, and a soft, cold whiteness began to drown the dimly glimpsed outlines of trees and higher ground again.

Stones clicked. A sheep's bleat sounded. Then a cow lowed.

Diane tugged my hand. "Come on," she said, "let's go."

The dog barked two, three times as we went, sharp and sudden, startling me a little and making me sway briefly for balance. I looked at Diane, smiled a little, let out a long breath.

We were about nine feet from the top when a deafening roar split the silence apart. I don't know what the hell it was, what kind of animal sound—but even Diane cried out, and I stumbled, sending a mini-landslide slithering back down the slope.

The broken slate heaved and rattled, and then surged as something flew across, under, *through* the ravine floor towards us.

"Run!" I heard Diane yell, and I tried, we both did, but the shape was arrowing past us. We saw that at the last moment; it was hurtling past us to the edge of the scree, the point where it gave way to the path.

Diane was already starting back down, pushing me behind her, when the ground erupted in a shower of stone shrapnel. I thought I glimpsed something, only for the briefest of moments, moving in the hail of broken stone, but when it fell back into place there was no sign of anything—except, if you looked, a low-humped shape.

Diane shot past me, still gripping my hand, pelting along the ravine. Behind us I heard the stones rattle as the thing gave chase. Diane veered towards the nearest of the boulders—it was roughly the size of a small car, and looked like pretty solid ground.

"Come on!" Diane leapt—pretty damned agile for a woman in her late thirties who didn't lead a particularly active life—onto the boulder, reached back for me. "Quick!"

The shape was hurtling towards us, slowing as it neared us. Its bow-wave of loose stones thickened, widened; it was gathering speed. I could see what was coming; I grabbed Diane and pushed her down flat on the boulder. She didn't fight, so I'm guessing she'd reached the same conclusions as me.

There was a muffled thud and the boulder shook. For a moment I thought we'd both be pitched onto the scree around it, but the boulder held, too deeply rooted to be torn loose. Rocks rained and pattered down on us; I tucked my head in.

I realised I was clinging on to Diane, and that she was doing the same to me. I opened my eyes and looked at her. She looked back. Neither of us said anything.

Behind us, there were clicks and rattles. I turned slowly, sliding off Diane. We both sat up and watched.

There was a sort of crater in the layer of loose rocks beside the boulder, where the thing had hit. The scree at the bottom was heaving, shifting, rippling. The crater walls trembled and slid. After a moment, the whole lot collapsed on itself. The uneven surface rippled and heaved some more, finally stopped when it looked as it had before—undisturbed, except of course for the low-humped shape beneath it.

Click went the stones as it shifted in its tracks, taking stock. Click click, as it moved and began inching its way round the boulder. "John? Shona? Hello?" All emerged from the shifting rocks, each of those different voices. Then the bleat. Then the roar. I swear I felt the wind of it buffet me.

"Christ," I said.

The rocks clicked, softly, as the humped shape began moving, circling slowly round the boulder. "Christ," my own voice answered me. Then another voice called, a child's: "Mummy?" Click click click. "Shona?" Click. "Oh, for God's sake, Marjorie," came a rich, fruity voice that sounded decidedly pre-Second World War. If not the First. "For God's sake."

Click. Then silence. The wind keened down the defile. Fronds of mist drifted coldly along. Click. A high, thin female voice, clear and sweet, began singing "The Ash Grove." Very slowly, almost like a dirge. "*Down yonder green valley where streamlets meander . . .*"

Diane clutched my wrist tightly.

Click, and the song stopped, as if a switch had been thrown. Click click. And then there was a slow rustling and clicking as the shape began to move away from the boulder, moving farther and farther back. Diane gripped me tighter. The mist was thickening and the shape went slowly, so that it was soon no longer possible to be sure exactly where it was. Then the last click died away and there was only the silence and the wind and the mist.

TIME PASSED.

"It's not gone far," Diane whispered. "Just far enough that we've got some freedom of movement. It wants us to make a move, try to run for it. It knows it can't get us here."

"But we can't stay here either," I pointed out in the same whisper. My teeth were already starting to chatter again, and I could see hers were, too. "We'll bloody freeze to death."

"I know. Who knows, maybe it does, too. Either way, we'll have to make a break for it, and sooner rather than later. If we leave it much longer we won't stand a chance."

"What the hell do you think it is?" I asked.

She scowled at me. "You expect me to know? I'm a geologist, not a biologist."

"Don't suppose you've got the number for a good one on your mobile?"

She stopped and stared at me. "We're a pair of fucking idiots," she said, and dug around in the pocket of her jeans. Out came her mobile. "Never even thought of it."

"There's no signal."

"There wasn't before. It's worth a try."

Hope flared briefly, but not for long; it was the same story as before.

"Okay," I said. "So we can't phone a friend. Let's think about this then. What do we know about it?"

"It lives under the rocks," Diane said. "Moves under them."

"Likes to stay under them, too," I said. "It was right up against us before. *That* far from us. It could've attacked us easily just by coming out from under, but it didn't. It'd rather play it safe and do the whole waiting game thing."

"So maybe it's weak, if we can get it out of the rocks. Vulnerable." Diane took off her glasses, rubbed her large eyes. "Maybe it's blind. It seems to hunt by sound, vibration—"

"A mimic. That's something else. It's a mimic, like a parrot."

"Only faster," she said. "It mimicked you straight away, after hearing you once."

"Got a good memory for voices, too," I whispered back. "Some of those voices . . ."

"Yes, I think so, too. And that roar it made. How long's it been since there was anything roaming wild in this country could make a noise like that?"

"Maybe a bear," I offered, "or one of the big sabre-toothed cats."

Diane looked down at the scree. "Glacial till," she said.

"What?"

"Sorry. The stones here. It's what's called glacial till—earth that's been compressed into rock by the pressure of the glaciers coming through here." She looked up and down the ravine.

"So?"

The look she gave me was equal parts hurt and anger. "So . . . nothing much, I suppose."

Wind blew.

"I'm sorry."

She shrugged. "S'okay."

"No. Really."

She gave me a smile, at least, that time. Then frowned, looked up at the way we'd come in—had it only been in the last hour? "Look at that. You can see it now."

"See what?"

She pointed. "This is a moraine."

"A what?"

"Moraine. It's the debris—till and crushed rock—a glacier leaves behind when it melts. All this would've been crushed up against the mountainsides for God knows how long. . . ."

I remembered Diane telling me about the last Ice Age, how there'd have been two miles of ice above the cities we'd grown up in. How far down would all this have been? And would—*could*—anything have lived in it?

I was willing to bet any of our colleagues in the biology department would have snorted at the idea. But even so . . . life is very tenacious, isn't it? It can cling on in places you'd never expect it to.

Maybe some creatures had survived down here in the Ice Age, crawling and slithering between the gaps in the crushed rock. And in every food chain, something's at the top—something that hunted blindly by vibration and lured by imitation. Something that had survived the glaciers' melting, even prospered from it, growing bigger and fatter on bigger, fatter prey.

The lost lamb had saved us by catching its attention. Without that, we'd have had no warning and would've followed that voice—no doubt belonging to some other long-dead victim—into the heart of the killing ground.

Click click click, went the rocks in the distance, as the creature shifted and then grew still.

And Diane leant close to me, and breathed in my ear: "We're going to have to make a move."

TO OUR LEFT WAS THE WAY WE'D COME, THE SCREE-THICK PATH SLOPING up before blending with the moraine. Twenty yards. It might as well have been ten miles.

The base of the peak was at our backs. It wasn't sheer, not quite, but it may as well have been. The only handholds were the occasional rock or root; even if the fall didn't kill you, you'd be too stunned or injured to stand a chance. The base of the opposite peak—even if we *could* have got past the creature—was no better.

To our right, the main body of the ravine led on, thick with rubble, before vanishing into the mist. Running along that would be nothing short of suicide, but there was still the gully we'd seen before. From what I could see the floor of it was thickly littered with rubble, but it definitely angled upwards, hopefully towards higher ground of solid earth and grass, where the thing from the moraine couldn't follow. Better still, there was that second boulder at the gully mouth, as big and solidly rooted-looking as this one, if not bigger. If we could make it that far—and we might, with a little luck—we had a chance to get out through the gully.

I looked at the boulder and back to Diane. She was still studying it. "What do you reckon?" I breathed.

Click click click, came softly, faintly, gently in answer.

Diane glanced sideways. "The bastard thing's fast," she whispered back. "It'll be a close thing."

"We could distract it," I suggested. "Make a noise to draw it off."

"Like what?"

I nodded at the rocks at the base of the boulder. "Pick a spot and lob a few of them at it. Hopefully it'll think it's another square meal."

She looked dubious. "S'pose it's better than nothing."

"If you've got any better ideas."

She looked hurt rather than annoyed. "Hey."

"I'm sorry." I was, too. I touched her arm. "We've just got to make that boulder."

"And what then?"

"We'll think of something. We always do."

She forced a smile.

Reaching down to pick up the bits of rubble and rock wasn't pleasant, mainly because the thing had gone completely silent and there was no knowing how close it might be now. Every time my hands touched the rocks I was convinced they'd explode in my face before something grabbed and yanked me under them.

But the most that happened was that once, nearby, the rocks clicked softly and we both went still, waiting, for several minutes before reaching down again after a suitable pause. At last we were ready with half a dozen good-sized rocks apiece.

"Where do we throw them?" Diane whispered. I pointed towards the footpath; we'd be heading, after all, in the opposite direction. She nodded.

"Ready?"

Another nod.

I threw the first rock. We threw them all, fast, within a few seconds, and they cracked and rattled on the slate. The slate nearby rattled and hissed as something moved.

"Go," Diane said. We jumped off the boulder and ran for the gully mouth.

Diane'd often commented on my being out of condition, so I was quite pleased that I managed to outpace her. I overtook easily, and was soon a good way ahead. The boulder was two more strides away, three at most, and then—

The two sounds came together; a dismayed cry from Diane, and then that hiss and click and rattle of displaced scree, rising to a rushing roar as a bow-wave of broken rocks rose up behind Diane and bore down on her.

I screamed at her to run, covering the rest of the distance to the boulder and leaping onto it, turning, holding my hands out to her, as if that were going to help. But what else could I have done? Running back to her wouldn't have speeded her up, and—

Oh. Yes. I could've tried to draw it off. Risked my own life, even sacrificed it, to save hers. Yes, I could've done that. Thanks for reminding me.

It got to her as I turned. There was an explosion of rubble, a great spray of it, and she screamed. I threw up my hands to protect my face. A piece of rock glanced off my forehead and I stumbled, swayed, losing balance, but thank God I hadn't ditched my backpack—the weight dragged me back and I fell across the boulder.

Rubble rained and pattered down about us as I stared at Diane. She'd fallen face-down on the ground, arms outstretched. Her pale hands, splayed out on the earth, were about three feet from the boulder.

I reached out a hand to her, leaning forward as far as I dared. I opened my mouth to speak her name, and then she lifted her head and looked up. Her glasses were askew on her pale face, and one lens was cracked. In another moment I might have jumped off the boulder and gone to her, but then she screamed and blood sprayed from the ground where her feet were covered by a sheet of rubble. Her back arched; a fingernail split as she clawed at the ground. Red bubbled up through the stones, like a spring.

Diane was weeping with pain; she tried to twist round to see what was being done to her, but jerked, shuddered and cried out before she could complete it. She twisted back to face me, lips trembling, still crying.

I leant forward, hands outstretched, but couldn't reach. Then I remembered the backpack and struggled out of it, loosening the straps to give the maximum possible slack, gripping one and holding the backpack as far out as I could, so that the other dangled closer to her. "Grab it," I whispered. "I'll pull you in."

She shook her head hard. "No," she managed at last. "Don't you get it?"

"What?" We weren't whispering anymore. Didn't seem much point. Besides, her voice was ragged with pain.

"It wants you to try. Don't you see? Otherwise it would've dragged me straight under by now."

I stared at her.

"Steve . . . it's using me as bait." Her face tightened. She bit at her lips and fresh tears leaked down her pale cheeks. When her green eyes squeezed open again, they were red and bloodshot. "Oh God. What's it done to my legs? My feet?"

"I don't know," I lied.

"Well, that's it, don't you see?" She was breathing deeply now, trying to get the agony under control. "I've had it. Won't get far, even if it did let me go to chase after you. Can't get at you up there. So stay put."

"But . . . but . . ." Dimly I realised I was crying, too. This was my wife. My *wife*, for Christ's sake.

Diane forced a smile. "Just stay put. Or try . . . make a getaway."

"I'm not leaving you."

"Yes, you are. It'll go after you. Might be able . . . drag myself there." She nodded at the boulder. "You could go get help. Help me. Might stand a chance."

I looked at the blood still bubbling up from the stones. She must have seen the expression on my face. "Like that, is it?"

I looked away. "I can try." My view of the gully was still constricted by my position. I could see the floor of it sloping up, but not how far it ultimately went. If nothing else, I could draw it away from her, give her a chance to get to the boulder—

And what then? If I couldn't find a way out of the gully? If there wasn't even a boulder to climb to safety on, I'd be dead and the best Diane could hope for was to bleed to death.

But I owed her a chance of survival, at least.

I put the backpack down, looked into her eyes. "Soon as it moves off, start crawling. Shout me when you're here. I'll keep making a racket, try and keep it occupied."

"Be careful."

"You too." I smiled at her and refused to look at her feet. We met at university, did I tell you? Did I mention that? A drunken discussion about politics in the student union bar. More of an argument really. We'd been on different sides but ended up falling for each other. That pretty much summed up our marriage, I supposed. "Love you," I managed to say at last.

She gave a tight, buckled smile. "You too," she said back.

That was never something either of us had said easily. Should've known it'd take something like this. "Okay then," I muttered. "Bye."

I took a deep breath, then jumped off the boulder and started to run.

I didn't look back, even when Diane let out a cry, because I could hear the rattle and rush of slate behind me as I pelted into the gully and knew the thing had let her go—let her go so that it could come after me.

The ground's upward slope petered out quite quickly and the walls all around were a good ten feet high, sheer and devoid of handholds, except for at the very back of it. There was an old stream channel—only the thinnest trickle of water made it out now, but I'm guessing it'd been stronger once, because a mix of earth and pebbles, lightly grown over, formed a slope leading up to the ground above. A couple of gnarled trees sprouted nearby, and I could see their roots breaking free of the earth—thick and twisted, easy to climb with. All I had to do was reach them.

But then I noticed something else, something that made me laugh wildly. Only a few yards from where I was now, the surface of the ground changed from a plain of rubble to bare rock. Here and there earth had accumulated and sprouted grass, but what mattered was that there was no rubble for the creature to move under.

I chanced one look behind me, no more than that. It was hurtling towards me, the huge bow-wave of rock. I ran faster, managed the last few steps, and then dived and rolled across blessed solid ground.

Rubble sprayed at me from the edge of the rubble and again I caught the briefest glimpse of something moving in there. I couldn't put any kind of name to it if I tried, and I don't think I want to.

The rubble heaved and settled. The stones clicked. I got up and started backing away. Just in case. Click click click. Had anything ever got away from it before? I couldn't imagine anything human doing so, or men would've come back here with weapons, to find and kill it. Or perhaps that survivor hadn't been believed. Click. Click click. Click click click.

Click. A sheep bleated.

Click. A dog barked.

Click. A wolf howled.

Click. A cow lowed.

Click. A bear roared.

Click. "John?"

Click. "Shona? Shona, where are ye?"

Click. "Mummy?"

Click. "Oh, for God's sake, Marjorie. For God's sake."

Click. "Down yonder green valley where streamlets meander . . ."

Click. "Christ." My voice. "Christ."

Click. "Steve? Get help. Help me." Click. "Steve. Help me."

I turned and began to run, started climbing. I looked back when I heard stones rattling. I looked back and saw something, a wide shape, moving under the stones and heading away, back towards the mouth of the gully.

"Diane?" I shouted. "Diane?"

There was no answer.

I'VE BEEN WALKING NOW, ACCORDING TO MY WRISTWATCH, FOR A GOOD half hour. My teeth are chattering and I'm tired and all I can see around me is the mist.

Still no signal on the mobile. They can trace your position from a mobile call these days. That'd be helpful. I've tried to walk in a straight line, so that if I find help I can just point back the way I came, but I doubt I've kept to one.

I tell myself that she must have passed out—passed out from the effort and pain of dragging herself onto that boulder. I tell myself that the cold must have slowed her circulation down to the point where she might still be alive.

I do not think of how much blood I saw bubbling out from under the stones.

I do not think of hypothermia. Not for her. I'm still going, so she still must have a chance there, too, surely?

I keep walking. I'll keep walking for as long as I can believe Diane might still be alive. After that, I won't be able to go on, because it won't matter anymore.

I'm crawling, now.

We came out here to see if we still worked, the two of us, under all the clutter and the mess. And it looks like we still did.

There's that cold comfort, at least.

Comfort Your Dead

You'll be all right?" I asked.

Amanda looked up at me, all big blue eyes and blonde curls. "Yes, Daddy. I'll be fine. Now go on."

She can be a right little madam, sometimes. I do my best not to spoil her, but she's all I've got; she's my little princess and she always will be, even in ten or twenty or a hundred years. Sometimes, though, she can sound so grown-up it's frightening. Like now.

"Are we going to live with Susannah and Michael?" she asked, just before I went.

I turned back and looked at her. "I don't know."

"You do like her, don't you, Daddy?"

"Yes, I do."

"More than me?"

"No. No one more than you. You know that."

She was silent for a moment or two, but I didn't turn to leave because I knew she had something else to say.

"I'd like it if we did."

"If we did what?"

"If we went to live with Susannah and Michael."

There really was no answer to that.

I SUPPOSE I SHOULD EXPLAIN.

It had all started a fortnight before; Amanda and I were walking in the park. We do that a lot.

It was early November, so we had our jumpers and coats on, but it wasn't quite cold enough for mittens and scarves yet.

It's a nice park, quite a good size. There are open green bits and a children's playground, trees and a duckpond. A very big duckpond. Big and deep.

But anyway. We were by the railings next to a wide copse of beeches and oaks. The ground was thick with fallen red-and-gold leaves and we could see the puffs of our breath in the damp air. It was quiet and the sky was grey.

I'd got hold of a bag of monkey nuts, still in their shells, and I had a bag full of bits of bread as well, for later. We threw the nuts to the squirrels. You get a lot of them in the park. Normally they go bolting off if you so much as look at them. Never mind Alice's white rabbit for being in a hurry (Amanda's favourite story *ever*); the squirrels in the park go shooting around like they've drunk fifteen cups of espresso.

But they're different around this time of year, probably because they're busy stuffing themselves ready to hibernate. They're not as nervous; they'll come quite close and you can see them properly. Amanda loves them when they're like this; she can watch them all day long.

"Do you want to go and feed the ducks now?" I asked. She nodded.

Mallards drifted on the pond's green surface, quacking. I crouched down beside Amanda, helped her throw the bread between the railings, and they all came clambering out onto dry land. After a bit, I saw pieces of crust flying in from above us, and realised someone had joined us. I looked up.

She was about twenty-eight, maybe thirty—around my age anyway—and medium tall, like me, with gold-brown hair to her shoulders, olive skin, and the kind of chin, cheekbones and nose that could get her on the cover of *Vogue*, but when she smiled—and she did that when I caught her eye—her face became something very friendly and warm. It was the kind of face you'd look forward to coming home to, the kind of face that would age well, that wouldn't look substantially different, except for a few more laugh lines and a framing of grey hairs, when she was someone's favourite grandmother. And she had the biggest, warmest brown eyes, too.

Do I sound smitten? Perhaps I was. I'm a bit old to believe in love at first sight, but there was something there. Maybe it was because we were both parents, both on our own, both out with our kids—her little boy was with her, but I'll come to him in a minute. She was a very pretty woman, well out of my league. Of course I'd thought that before, about Emily, and been wrong, but you couldn't be that lucky twice. Could you?

"Hello." I stood up, sneaking a glance as I did at her wedding hand. I know, it's a terrible habit, and I keep trying to break myself of it, but it set in not long after I lost Emily and gets stronger with the loneliness. Not that I'd felt lonely for some time, not with Amanda—looking after a child, especially with her mother gone, takes up so much of your time and fills so many gaps—but sometimes it just takes a warm and pretty smile to remind you of all you've had to do without.

(By the way, she wasn't wearing a ring.)

"Hi." She smiled again, then looked down at Amanda, bent forwards a little and waved. Amanda hid behind me. "Sorry," I said. "She's a bit shy."

"So's mine." We both looked down at her little boy—I told you we'd get to him—who was peering out from behind her leg. He didn't take after her at all—milk white with ginger hair and saucer-wide eyes the same blue as Amanda's—until he grinned up at me with his mother's smile. "Michael, say hello," she said.

"Hi." He ventured out as he spoke, and seeing him, Amanda crept into plain sight as well.

"It's nice here, isn't it?"

"Yes," I said. "We come here a lot."

She gave the railings an experimental shake, then looked embarrassed. We shared a smile over the funny little ways of parental paranoia.

"Best to be sure," she said, looking at the dark, still water. "I heard a kiddy drowned here once."

Amanda looked up at me, big-eyed; I gave her hand a squeeze. "It's all right, sweetie," I said. "It was a long time ago."

"God, I'm sorry. What am I like?" Embarrassed at herself again, she squeezed Michael's shoulder—he'd stepped nervously away from the railings.

Her name, as you'll have guessed by now, was Susannah. She was twenty-nine, divorced, and had moved to the area a month ago. Michael had just started school.

"What about you, then?" she asked later. We were sat on the bench in the playground, watching Michael and Amanda on the swings.

"What about me?" I asked.

"Come on, stop being the man of mystery. Tell me about yourself!"

So I did. Not that there was much; Amanda had been my whole life for so long.

"Come on," she said. "That's what you do, not who you are."

I laughed. She buzzed with energy, spraying it in all directions. At first, I wasn't sure I liked it; after so long spent in a quiet, doing-almost-nothing existence, it was a jolt. But after that initial shock, it was—refreshing. "Well, what *do* you want?"

"Come on, dish some dirt. Are you divorced, separated, what?"

"Widowed," I said.

Her hand went up to her mouth. "Chris, I'm sorry, I didn't mean to—"

"It's okay. It was some time ago. Nearly . . . five years now."

Susannah glanced across at Amanda, now laughing wildly as she shot down the slide, Michael only a second behind her.

"She doesn't remember," I said quietly. "She was only a few months old."

Susannah didn't say anything, not to pry and not to change the subject either. It's the best way to get someone to talk.

"It was a car accident," I said. "Emily loved to drive." God, she had as well; I remembered her in the little Fiat she'd loved so much, horn beeping. She'd always driven too fast, as if there were a stopwatch timing her. We'd actually met when she rear-ended me at a stoplight. "As soon as she'd had Amanda she wanted to get back behind the wheel. She liked doing things for herself as well." I looked down at a crumpled Coke can on the grass. "Her car'd been in the garage while she was pregnant. Anyway, the brakes hadn't been checked. And . . . they failed on a tight corner one night, and . . ." I blinked fast. "Sorry."

"Chris, I didn't—"

"I know. I haven't talked about it in ages. Thought it couldn't get to me like that now, but . . ." I looked back over at Amanda and Michael. "When you lose someone like that—so sudden—it just takes everything away from you. You know?"

She put her smile on crooked. "I'm not doing very well, am I?"

"You're doing fine."

AND SO, TWO WEEKS LATER, THAT WAS HOW I CAME TO BE WALKING DOWN one of the quiet streets near the park, in the chilly dusk of a Friday in November, on my way to the little terrace where Susannah lived.

I'd got to the florist just before it closed and bought a bunch of tulips, then to the off-licence (no worries about *that* staying open) for a bottle of wine. Red or white? I'd no idea what she was cooking, so I bought one of each.

Now I stopped outside her door and rang the bell.

Colour moved in the warm light behind frosted glass. The door opened. "Hi there."

"Hi." Awkwardly, I held out the flowers.

"Thanks."

Michael's father had picked him up for the weekend earlier on, so we had the place to ourselves. She'd made a chicken casserole with boiled rice.

The white wine went well with that. The red we drank later, on the worn but comfy living room couch. Worn but comfy about summed up the room, and the house—its old but serviceable carpets, the terracotta woodchip on the walls at least ten years old, the clumsy but bright finger paintings Michael had brought home from school. A buttery glow seeped through the lampshade and made the room look warm as well as feel it.

We talked about our jobs. Susannah worked as a paediatric nurse. We also talked about day care; before Michael had started school, she'd had trouble finding a crèche for him.

"How did you manage, with Amanda?"

"Just . . . friends, really," I said. "There's an old dear, lives round about. Friend of our family. She came in and looked after Amanda before Amanda started school. It's easier now."

"It always is. It must've been a nightmare before."

"At times. But Amanda makes up for it."

Susannah cocked her head. "You really do love her, don't you?"

I stared at her. "Well . . . *yeah*."

"Sorry. It's my job. I see a lot of kids every day. And they don't all have that. Some of them are why they get sent to me. Amanda's very lucky, is what I mean."

"Lucky?"

"To have you."

My eyes were stinging. "I think you've got a very rose-tinted view of me, Susannah."

She put a hand on my shoulder. "Do you?"

"You don't know me."

"I'd like to."

"I've not been a good father. I've let her down. When . . . when it happened—" I couldn't finish.

"Show me anyone who's as good at it as they think they should be. Especially after what happened to you. She's happy, well-cared-for, loved. . . . I don't see what more you could have done for her."

I did when I thought of where we both had to stay, but that was my shame and not to be shared. I wouldn't tell Susannah, much less show her. I wiped my eyes. "I'm sorry. I'm sorry."

"It's all right."

She held me for a while. It felt good just to let go for a time, to lean on somebody else. I don't know how long that went on for, but then we looked up at each other. Her lips were parted. She closed her eyes.

I leant forward and kissed her. Her mouth tasted of spices and wines and everything seemed to dissolve—the room, the world, everything. Only our mouths were real, and the kiss.

We didn't go any further than that. It felt like being about seventeen again, necking in the corner of some pub or club we shouldn't have been in.

Around midnight I wandered home, smiling all the way and hardly feeling the cold.

"Is Susannah going to be my mummy now, Daddy?"
  "Sh."
  "Are you and her getting married?"
  "Mind your own business."
  "Stop it! That tickles!"
  "All right."
  "Are we going to live with them?"
  "I don't know."
  "Can't they come and live with us?"
  "No, darling, they can't."
  "Why not? Daddy? Daddy? Why not?"

So it went on for two weeks more. We met in the park a lot, and would go back to Susannah's house for a hot drink after. Autumn was fading into winter; soon enough it would be scarves and mittens after all.

Just as Susannah and I were becoming close, so Amanda and Michael became inseparable playmates. One day, Amanda solemnly told us that they were going to get married, and Susannah and I both laughed and issued a joint "aw" at the cuteness of our offspring, hands touching on her kitchen table.

I had a few more dinners at Susannah's place, and one night I stayed over, with Michael at his dad's again.

"You know, I still haven't seen your place."
"You don't want to. Trust me on this."
"I *would* like to."
"Maybe," I lied.

A few days later, Susannah found a grey hair. "Getting old," she grinned, and plucked it out. It twisted between her finger and thumb; Amanda stared at it.

Afterwards, when we'd gone home, Amanda said, "Susannah isn't going to get old, is she, Daddy?"

"Everybody gets old, sweetheart."

"I'm not going to get old!" She stamped. "And you're not either! Or Michael!"

It had the tone of a royal command; I didn't know whether to laugh or cry. "Amanda, everyone does."

"No! If he gets old he won't want to play with me anymore!"

What could I tell her? That nothing goes on forever? She seemed too young, too vulnerable, to have to learn that so soon, though I knew that to me she always would.

"I won't let him get old! I won't let him!" She was crying. "Old people go away like Mummy did! I don't want them to go away! Not Michael!"

"Amanda—"

"And not Susannah either! I want her to stay! I want her to be my mummy!"

I picked her up and held her as tightly as I could. It was all I could do, everything I had. But it wasn't enough.

Everything you can do has a limit. Even for your child.

"You won't go away, will you, Daddy?"

"Never, sweetie." I kissed her hair. "Never, never, never."

She seemed fine again the next day. It was a Saturday and there was a hint of fog in the air.

We met Susannah and Michael just after lunch and walked through the park. It was very cold but the squirrels were still there; a couple of them anyway.

We threw them nuts until our packets were empty; after that they scuttled away.

"Say 'bye-bye' to the squirrels, Michael," Susannah said, the soft berry of her mouth at his pink ear.

"Why, Mummy?"

"They're going to bed now for the winter."

"Daddy, can me and Michael go and feed the ducks?"

"Michael and *I*, sweetie."

"Can we, Daddy?"

Me and Susannah exchanged grins. We both dug out small bags of bread and handed them over.

"Come on, Michael!" They held hands and ran down the path.

"Don't go too far!" We called after them. They stopped at the railings by the pond, in safe, plain sight. The fog was thickening; it was like watching them through a veil. In a minute, it'd be time to go.

"Love's young dream, eh?" Susannah laughed.

"Yeah." We walked slowly towards them. "Hey," she said. "Come here."

"Yes, ma'am," I said, turning to face her.

"That's what I like," Susannah said, hands on my shoulders. "Total obedience."

I held her waist. "Your wish . . ." Her hands met behind my neck. Somewhere in the warm haze, I realised this was the first time we'd kissed outside.

When we parted, Susannah blinked and stared about. "Jesus," she said.

In the time it took to kiss, the fog had grown thick as cream. We couldn't see much more than three or four feet ahead. And we certainly couldn't see our children.

"Michael?" called Susannah. Her hand was tight round mine. No answer. She started moving through the fog, towing me in her wake.

In the distance, there was a loud, sudden splash.

There are some sounds, if you're a parent, more terrifying than any other.

"Michael!"

And some absences, too.

"Amanda?"

No answer.

We were already running.

They weren't there by the railings, but one of the bags of bread was. The other lay beyond it, on the grass, crumbs scattered almost to the water's edge, beyond which bubbles were flying up to break on the surface near the centre of the pond.

"I can't swim," Susannah whispered. "Chris, I can't swim."

I jumped the railing, flung off my jacket and ran into the pond.

The first few yards nearest the shore aren't deep, they slope gently down, but after that the bottom of the pond just drops away. One moment I was running into the water; the next—gone.

The cold slammed into me. Silver bubbles of air flew up through the green murk. I dived down towards them—and there our children were.

Amanda's face was all grief and rage; her tiny fists were locked in Michael's t-shirt as she pulled him deeper down. The bubbles flew from his mouth as he fought and screamed. But then the bubbles stopped and he tried to breathe.

I fought with her; my own daughter, I fought with her. But the grip of her hands wouldn't break.

So I did the only thing I could do, and slapped her across the face. My own child. It was the only time I'd ever raised a hand to her. I hated it and myself. But it broke her grip. I grabbed Michael as he sank limply, and swam up towards the dim winter light; I could feel Amanda behind me, inches from my heels.

I broke the surface, gasped my way into the shallows and onto dry land. Susannah was scrambling over the railings. "Oh God! Oh God!"

I put Michael down on the grass. He wasn't breathing.

"Oh God— Oh God—"

"No," I said. "No, no, no."

I bent, spread his arms out, pushed down on his chest till water spilt from his mouth and nose. Pushed. Pinched his nose shut. Blew air into his mouth.

Push down. Blow air. Push down. Blow air.

"Oh God— Oh God—" Susannah rocked on her knees beside me.

Michael coughed, bringing up the last of the water, sucked ragged breaths, began to cry. I grabbed my jacket and wrapped him in it. "Get him to a hospital, now."

"I hate you!" I turned. Amanda was in the shallows, fists pounding dark water white. "You never let me have anything I want! I hate you! I hate you! *I hate you!*"

She whirled and stormed away from us, sinking.

Susannah was white. "Go on," I said. "Get him out of here. Now!"

"But— Amanda!" All that was left on the surface were a few last blonde curls, sinking from sight. "She's drowning!"

"No, she won't," I said. "She already has."

Time stopped, silent and dead. Susannah just stared at me. Michael whimpered.

"I'm sorry," I said. "I really am."

"What?"

"I lied to you," I said. "Emily's still alive, as far as I know. She moved away after—it happened."

"But you— What about—?" She broke off.

"It was my fault," I said. "I took my eyes off her. Only for a minute." I shook my head. "Some things you can never forgive yourself for."

Susannah backed away from me. "I never meant you any harm," I said as she lifted Michael back over the railings. "I thought I could make it work, the four of us. Others have. We've been so lonely. . . ."

She backed through the mist with Michael, became a shadow and then nothing, as if she were the ghost.

I got up; turned; looked out at the place we had to stay in; the winter-black water, empty of birds, smooth as glass. The clatter of Susannah's shoes faded as she ran towards the park gate. When they were gone, I walked slowly into the pond.

THE SCHOOL HOUSE

I was on a train, an express; I forget where from. It went straight through the station nearest the school. The neighbouring woods blurred by. When we passed the building itself, everything went into slow motion for a second. The playground was screened off from the railway tracks by a chain-link fence and nothing else. Beyond it was Drakemire.

Dozens of windows all caught the afternoon sunlight. Even then, I remember thinking they were like tiny eyes—faceted like an insect's, following us as we passed. A predator glimpsing prey, weighing the pros and cons of giving chase.

Mum poked me in the arm, smiled and said: "You're starting there next week."

I was eleven. I turned my head and watched it recede: waiting for its prey to come to it.

NOAKES WAS STRUGGLING WITH THE NEW PATIENT, TRYING TO PIN HIM down. They fought in the shadow of a willow tree, just off the gravel driveway where Dr. Petrie's car had stalled, its doors open. Petrie wasn't doing much to help, but then he rarely did. He just dithered, opening and closing his mouth.

Denholm ran in and helped Noakes pin the new patient down. Petrie snapped out of it, blinking, then knelt and gave the man an injection. The patient stopped struggling; the orderlies stood.

"What happened?" Denholm asked.

"Bloody nutjob," grunted Noakes.

"He'd been very compliant," Petrie protested. "Then as we came down the drive he just—"

"Flipped out," finished Noakes. He had a black eye already, and a fat lip, too.

Petrie's hair was dishevelled; buttons were missing from his shirt. "He managed to get out of the car—"

"The doors weren't *locked*?"

Petrie went red beneath his tan. "Thank you for your help, Mr. Denholm. Now I'm sure you—"

"Danny?"

The patient was a thin, scruffy man in dreadlocks and dirty jeans. Not what you usually saw at the Pines. But somehow familiar. Reddish hair, blue eyes, thin-lipped mouth . . . "Danny?" the patient asked again. His speech was starting to slur. "Danny Denholm?"

"Yeah," he said. "That's—"

"Grimshaw?" The man's eyes were closing. "Eddie Grimshaw . . . ?"

The last word trailed away and his head lolled to one side.

Petrie stared at Denholm. "You *know* him?"

"Sort of." Denholm shifted, uncomfortable. "We were at school together."

PETRIE LOOKED OUT OF HIS OFFICE WINDOW, FASTENING A NEW SHIRT. Denholm read from a crumpled sheet of yellow A4:

"'The School House is like a mad doctor's lab. They've still got bits of me in jars. Pickled but alive. They got to me. I am scarred. I am scarred. Kids march in; adults march out. The bits that weren't required are cut away.'"

Denholm put it aside. On the back of a flyer for an anti-war demo he read:

"'Dreamt about it again last night. Wandering through the halls. Echoes. Laughter. Shadows. Corridor on corridor. Labyrinth.'"

The happiest days of your life. Denholm put that aside too. Quickly. Before any more thoughts followed.

"Were you good friends?"

Denholm looked up. Petrie was facing him now, silver hair combed neat again, hands behind his back.

"We got on." Denholm looked down at the next piece, a drawing in charcoal and crayon. Mostly red crayon. "Not best mates or anything, even then. As for now—hadn't seen him in . . ." he considered ". . . ten years, easily."

"And you both attended"— Petrie consulted his notes—"Drakemire Grammar School in Elderham, Cheshire?"

"Yeah." Denholm studied the drawing. The building was a black, spiky silhouette, gables like shark's teeth, windows filled in red, like wounds or eyes. The train track in the foreground was smeared red, bits of stick people strewed all along it; the playground was a clean white space dotted with more stick figures, mutilated ones with blank faces staring out of the page. The trees in the woods looked like deformed, skeletal hands. Denholm tried a laugh; it came out shaky. "Don't remember it looking like this."

"Probably didn't, to you," said Petrie, knotting his tie and trying to look wise. *Berk*, Denholm thought, and shifted in his chair. Petrie stroked his chin. "Any idea why he might hate the place so much?"

"Not offhand." No one thing, just a few thousand petty cruelties built up over years. Denholm studied the drawing again. "Could be drugs."

"Mmm. Something of a chemical bin, our Mr. Grimshaw. Very foolish." Petrie shook his head, which Denholm thought was a bit rich coming from a man who couldn't medicate the patients fast enough. Didn't he know they called him "Dr. Feelgood" behind his back? "LSD, ecstasy, cannabis . . . but even so, why fixate on this in particular?"

Denholm wondered why Petrie cared. Word among the staff was he was a complete disaster as a doctor, but looked good and licked arse. So here he was: zookeeper to fucked-up rich kids. The Pines was, officially, a care home and psychiatric hospital; in reality it was a place to keep these permanent embarrassments to Mummy and Daddy out of sight and mind. Take the money, lock them up, dope them up. A cushy number, on the whole. Maybe Petrie actually wanted to do his job for a change. "I dunno," he said finally. "Don't think he was particularly happy there, but . . ."

"Were you?"

Denholm shifted in his seat. That'd been a surprisingly sharp one for Petrie. "I'm not the one ended up in a mental institution, though, am I?"

"Well, actually . . ." Petrie gestured round, then sighed. "All right. I'll be honest here. Mr Grimshaw isn't an ordinary patient."

Denholm waited.

"His father's rich and influential, as you'd expect. However, he badly wants an heir to take over the family business, and Grimshaw's the only one he's got. If we could cure him, Grimshaw senior would be very grateful. Follow me?"

"Well, yeah. But it's not exactly our usual thing, is it?"

"Grimshaw senior doesn't agree. And he's the one with the money." Petrie settled back in his chair. "Grimshaw says he'll talk about what he did, but only to you."

"I'm not a trained psychotherapist."

"You don't have to be. You were at Drakemire together; he says you'll understand. Just listen, and report back to me."

"Well—"

"Your salary will be reviewed immediately," Petrie added. "This is a great opportunity for us all."

Denholm thought of his rent and his bank balance, and after a moment, nodded.

EXCEPT FOR THE BORED-LOOKING WOMAN AT THE COUNTER, DENHOLM and Grimshaw were alone in the canteen. Grimshaw's hair had been cropped and he was wearing pyjamas and a dressing gown; most of the residents ended up looking that way. But his eyes were bright and alert; little or no medication, that meant. Good news if he was chatty; bad if he was violent.

Rain slid down the windows, made rippling patterns on the walls with the faint light from outside.

"So?" said Denholm at last.

Grimshaw shrugged.

"You were the one wanted to talk."

"Said I'd talk to you," Grimshaw said, "Didn't say I wanted to do it *now*."

Denholm waited. Grimshaw fidgeted, chewed his nails. They were bitten to the quick. He was trying to act like he didn't care, but he was frazzled and on edge.

"You wanna know why I did it?" Grimshaw looked at him. "Or why I ended up like this? Rich kid like me?" His eyebrows rose. "Yeah? Which?"

Denholm waited. Grimshaw drummed his fingers on the table.

"Come on, Danny. Lost your voice? What d'you wanna hear about?"

"What do you want to talk about?"

Grimshaw slapped the tabletop. "I don't wanna talk about fuck-all! I was happy in me room!"

They glared at each other. "All right," Denholm said at last. "The school."

Grimshaw snorted. "That fucking place."

"You seem to have a real downer on it."

"Don't you?"

"I'm not in here for setting light to the place."

Grimshaw snorted again; this time it was almost a laugh. "Not telling me you never thought of it? Are you? Not telling me you were *happy* there?

Fucking all right place if you were some cunt like Joe Coneeny or Mark Thwaites, but people like us? *Real* people? Fuck that."

"Real people?"

"Like us." Grimshaw chewed another nail. "They brainwash you there," he said at last. "Tell you what to think."

"Come on, Eddie—"

"I'm telling you. It *shapes* you. Makes you into a 'good citizen.' And if you don't fit . . . if you *can't* . . . remember Martin Berry?"

"Yes." Martin Berry. Hounded and bullied constantly for his voice and girl-ish looks. Martin Berry hanged himself in a copse near his parents' house.

Grimshaw's voice rose. "Not telling me you weren't like him or me, are you? Think you're more like Coneeny, Thwaites? Those wankers? Are you?"

"I'm not like you." It seemed vitally important, suddenly, to deny that.

"No? Why aren't you a doctor, then? If a gormless cunt like Petrie can make it any muppet can. You're what? An orderly here?"

Denholm kept his voice level with an effort. "We're not talking about me."

"Aren't we?"

"We're talking about you."

"Same thing."

"You're saying you're me?"

"Course not. But your story's my story."

"Don't be silly, Eddie."

"Shouldn't you be calling me 'Mr. Grimshaw'?"

"I looked at that folder of your stuff," Denholm said at last. Casually. He saw Grimshaw's face tighten, grow guarded. "Those scribblings of yours."

"That's private." Grimshaw spoke through his teeth.

Denholm had read them all in Petrie's office. "You keep saying in them you're scarred," he said. "Or mutilated. Same stuff keeps coming up in your sketches. Mutilation. Surgery." He recalled one sketch: three teachers in surgical gowns, wielding scalpels. And on the operating table, a boy's carcass, flayed and mutilated. Gowns flecked with dark gore.

Grimshaw smirked, but he was twitching. "It's a *metaphor*, Danny. If you could see the kids' minds, it's what *they'd* look like. The *real* truth about that place." His fingers came to his mouth again. "How they made us *conform*. If I could just get *back* . . ." He gnawed his nails once more, and began shaking his head side to side.

"Yes?" No answer. "What, Eddie? What if you could get back?"

But Grimshaw just kept shaking his head, on and on, and Denholm could get no answer out of him. Not till he got up to leave.

"We're all still here, you know," Grimshaw said, folding his hands on the tabletop. Blood welled from the edge of a fingernail, where he'd bitten down too far.

"What?"

"All of us. Even Coneeny and Thwaites. You never leave."

"What are you on about?"

"We're all still here. Here in the School House."

"This isn't Drakemire, Eddie."

The look on Grimshaw's face was almost pitying. "No?"

I DIDN'T RECOGNISE THE CORRIDOR AT FIRST. AFTER A MOMENT, WHEN I registered the walls—the trophies, the paintings, the photographs and the noticeboards—I realised it was Drakemire.

It was dark, it was night. The place was almost silent, but not quite; there was a far-off soundtrack of background noise. Some of it was just creaks and rustles and dripping sounds, the kind you'd get in any big old building, but the others were different—I could hear scraping sounds and ticking noises, stuff like that. Made me think of machines—clocks and knifegrinders. Later on, I heard someone giggling, but when I looked around there was nobody there.

Another time I saw a shadow move, but I didn't go to chase it. I just kept walking. I didn't know what I was doing there. *(You've always been here. Always, and still are.)* But I just kept walking. I knew I wasn't there to explore. I had a purpose. But I didn't know what. There was the me in the dream, knew why I was there, but the real me didn't. Does that make sense?

I crossed over a covered walkway at one point. I remember that. I remembered the walkway—it led into the bit of the building where the music rooms were. They were the only classrooms in that section. The rest was taken up with the staff room and different teachers' offices.

The walkway overlooked the playground, crossed it. Looking to my left, I saw the playground extending back to end at the tennis courts, the woods emerging behind them. To my right, I saw the other one, leading up to the wire-mesh fence overlooking the train track. Suddenly, it was daytime.

A train was rushing past. It didn't stop. It didn't end. There was neither start nor finish to it, just an endless rattling metal blur that turned the countryside beyond it into a sequence from some grainy old animation film, the kind they might've made in Czechoslovakia around 1974.

The playground was full of boys—thirty? Forty? Fifty of them?—all standing still, arms at their sides, their backs to me, watching it go by. The train just kept on rattling past. I saw their hair and clothing flicker and flutter in the breeze off it, but they didn't move.

Then, suddenly, they all turned round and looked up at me.

But I was too quick for them. Ha. I spun round and bolted back the way I'd come. I didn't see them. I was too quick. I didn't see their faces. I didn't see them.

Well, no more than a glimpse.

Not quite quick enough then . . .

I stopped running and got to a classroom door. A wooden door, painted that sickly, institutional green you get in schools and prisons. And hospitals and police stations. And here at the Pines, come to think of it. A long glass panel in it, narrow and vertical. That frosted safety glass. You know the kind, with the wire mesh embedded in it. It was still daytime. Through the door I saw a tall blurred shape.

I pushed the door open and it was night again.

The only light in the classroom was the orange glow from streetlamps, seeping through. A teacher stood beside the desk. His head was bowed, and his upper body tilted slightly sideways towards me.

The boys were all sat at their desks, faces pillowed on their folded arms. Hair in *identical* pudding-basin cuts. Even the shade didn't vary, as far as I could tell in the half-light.

I walked up to the teacher and nudged his shoulder. He rocked slightly but otherwise didn't move.

Outside, the streetlights winked out. Birds began twittering. As the room began to lighten, I noticed each boy seemed to have a kind of metal brace strapped to their backs. Each brace was fixed to a mechanism at the base of each chair.

Above me, there was a fast ticking sound. I straightened up as the fluorescent strip-lighting in the ceiling blinked and flickered on.

There were other noises then, from the teacher. Clicks and whirrs and more ticking sounds. When I turned to look at him, he was straightening up—remember, I said he'd been sort of tilted towards me.

It was like a machine. A clockwork toy, like Julie Andrews in *Chitty Chitty Bang Bang*. And then his head came up. His eyes were fixed and open. He blinked twice. His eyelids clicked each time.

There was another click and then a whirr as his head swivelled towards me. I recognised his face now. It was Mr. Spanton, the maths master. Slightly too-long hair and a beard. The boys had called him "Jesus" behind his back.

He looked at me, face blank. Then his eyelids clicked as he blinked again. I don't know how long he stared, but then his eyelids clicked once more and his head swivelled back to face the class. The boys still lay facedown on their desks. The surfaces of the desks looked different. Something on them, dried, crusted.

With a whirr, Mr. Spanton's hands came up, stopped. Then he clapped them together.

I woke up a second later. Just not quite fast enough.

The mechanisms on the chairs had all been triggered when he clapped. And the braces on the boys' backs snapped upright, sprang them all into a sitting position.

I woke up then, but I'd seen. I'd seen their faces.

Only, they didn't have any. Some of them had had their eyes taken out. Some hadn't.

What got to me, what really got to me was—

Were they still alive?

DR. PETRIE TAPPED HIS PEN ON THE DESKTOP. HIS SMILE LOOKED FORCED.

"Very . . . interesting," he said at last. "Now, if we could—"

"Doctor . . . look, all I want to know is does it—could it mean anything?"

"Mean?" Petrie managed to look impatient and mocking all at once. "What could it possibly *mean*?"

"The dream, Doctor. It's so like Grimshaw's drawings. . . ."

Petrie sighed. "Ah. I see. Frankly I'm surprised."

"Eh?"

"His problem's mental illness, not chickenpox." The families of patients seemed to find Petrie's smooth baritone reassuring; to Denholm it was just oily. "A shared delusion—*folie à deux*—can develop between two closely linked people, but that hardly sounds like you and Grimshaw. Does it?"

"No, Doctor."

"Grimshaw's psychotic. In the circumstances, I'd be surprised if you *hadn't* had the odd nightmare." Dr. Petrie leant back in his chair, making a steeple of his fingers. "But I'd've thought your new salary'd be ample compensation. Of course," the voice grew oilier still, "I can't compel you to work with Grimshaw. But I do think you should consider the patient's welfare *and* that of the home and its staff, with this particular patient."

Petrie raised an eyebrow. His list of achievements had grown: looking good, licking arse *and* making veiled threats. Denholm nodded.

"Splendid. Now," Petrie donned his reading glasses and made a show of studying some papers on his desk, "it's looking like a nice day out there. I think a turnabout the grounds'd do Grimshaw a power of good. What about you?"

"THINK YOU'RE THE DOG'S BOLLOCKS NOW, DON'T YOU?" SAID NOAKES.

"What?" Denholm turned from the drinks machine, looked at him.

Noakes leant forward. He was balding on top and stank of sweat. On top of that, Denholm'd known dogs with sweeter breath. "Too good for the rest of us, that it?"

Privately, Denholm had positioned Noakes several rungs below him on any evolutionary scale within five minutes of meeting him, but didn't say so. If he called him a *Homo erectus*, Noakes would probably assume Denholm was calling him a puff. "No," Denholm protested. "Look, it's not my fault, Geoff. I just went to school with the guy. *He* asked for *me*. Not like I could say no, really, is it?"

Noakes grunted. "Yeah, well. Just remember—it goes tits up with him, it's bad news for all of us. We lose out, cos way I hear it we're all looking at a good pay rise if we sort him out. All right? So just think on."

"No pressure or anything, then," Denholm muttered to the retreating back.

"What?"

Denholm held up placating hands. "Nothing."

ONE THING ABOUT THE PINES: YOU COULDN'T DENY THE GROUNDS OF THE place were nice. That was how they'd been designed. The building had been an old nineteenth century asylum, back in the days of "moral treatment." Closed down in the early eighties, bought up in the early nineties and put to a variant on the original purpose.

The stretch of path Denholm and Grimshaw were on led through woodland. A couple of large ponds were nearby. One was in sight as they rounded a bend; half a dozen mallards burst into the air, quacking loudly, wings beating.

Grimshaw leant on the safety railings. "Know what an oubliette is?" he said.

"No." Denholm did, but Grimshaw hadn't said a word since Denholm's suggesting the walk. If he wanted to talk, let him. *Think on.*

"It was like a little cell. More of a pit, actually. You'd stand in it. They'd put you in one when they wanted shut of you. Just drowning in your own shit as it filled up. Down in the dungeon . . . It's from the French. *Oublier,* to forget. Where you'd put someone you wanted to forget about."

He was silent after that, looking out across the pond. Finally Denholm decided to prod him a little. "And?"

Grimshaw stared at him, shook his head. "*Duh.* That's what this place is, isn't it? Haven't you clocked that?"

"Don't see anyone drowning in their own shit, Eddie."

Grimshaw sighed, shook his head, then turned away, shoulders hunched, arms wrapped round himself. "You're so *literal-minded,* Danny," he said, licking his cracked lips over and over. "*Up here.* That's where it's all going on. That's where they're drowning. Doped up like cattle. Battery hens."

"What?"

"Food supply. For Drakemire, Danny. Don't you get *anything*?"

Back on that again, groaned Denholm to himself. Out loud he said, "Right."

"Fucking patronise me." Grimshaw glared. Denholm looked away. Grimshaw stared into the pond again. "How much do you know," he said, "about what I did?"

Denholm shrugged. "You went back to Drakemire and tried to set it on fire."

"Tried? Burned the fucker to the ground."

"That's a bit of an exaggeration, Eddie."

"You reckon? Oh, I know, it's still standing, just about, but they're not rebuilding it. Cost more than it's worth. A hundred years in the brain-fucking business, and now Drakemire's gonna close down."

"Good for you."

"Is it fuck. Not for either of us."

"What you on about?"

"Do you still not get it?" Grimshaw's voice was rising. "Drakemire's *alive.* We were its food. Toys, too. Played with us. Remember all the little pecking orders there?" He began tearing at his nails with his teeth. "All the little hierarchies? The kids we picked on, picking on each other? Like a pyramid? A few at the top, a few more on each layer below, till you've got the mass at the bottom, crushed flat. That was *so clever.* Worked loads of different ways—like, one, a food chain. The small fry—you let the bigger ones eat them so they're nice and fat for you. Then when the kids come out, they're used to living like that. Preying on other kids, or being preyed on. That's what I mean, see? Training. The pyramid keeps itself in place, the structure. And of course, number three—we were all turning on each other instead of the structure, the school, the fucking teachers. Well, even the teachers were tools." Grimshaw broke off and sniggered. "Some of them were *right* tools, eh, Danny? Eh?" He laughed then snorted at Denholm's half-hearted grin. "Fuck off, then. But they were just tools, to make it all happen. Every boy ever went there had his head fucked with by that place. There's still a part of *it* in *them*. All I did was kill the body. The soul's still there. Ever see a hermit crab been got out of its shell? It's looking for a new home."

"What are you—" *on about*, Denholm was going to say, but stopped in time. "What do you mean?"

Grimshaw snorted, rolled his eyes. Two of his fingertips were bloody. "School. Prison. Nut-hatch. Places like this, for rich kids. How many of us do you think there are? Fucked in the head? It's bringing us back here. Feeding off us. It's going to make itself whole, get strong again. And then—"

"What?"

Grimshaw looked across the lake. "That'll do it for today," he said. "I fancy a walk. Be on my own."

He turned to go. "Oh," he said, and took a folded piece of paper from his pocket. "Present," he said, and walked off.

Denholm watched him go. In a moment he'd go after him. Keep an eye. He unfolded the paper.

It was a classroom. The teacher looked out of the picture at Denholm. He had longish hair for a teacher, and a beard. The boys sat at their desks. Some of them had eyes; some didn't. But all their faces were red blurs. And they were grinning.

"I REALLY DON'T SEE WHAT RELEVANCE—"

"Look at the *picture*, Doctor." Denholm spread it out on the desk. "*Look at it.*"

With a sigh, Petrie spared it a glance, grimaced and shrugged. "So?"

"Doctor, the dream I had last night—"

"Oh . . ." Petrie snorted, waved a dismissive hand. "That again?"

"*Look* at it. The drawing. That image . . . it's exactly what I dreamt last night. And no, I didn't say anything about it to Grimshaw. He bothers me enough without telling him stuff like that."

Dr. Petrie sighed. "Coincidence."

"Coincidence? Look at it. Even the teacher in the picture—it's Mr. Spanton."

"Oh, for goodness sake. It hardly looks like anyone."

"Long hair, a beard. There was only one teacher at Drakemire like that."

Petrie looked at him. "What are you trying to say, Mr. Denholm?"

"I . . ." He tailed off.

Petrie spoke slowly and gently. "Do you believe Grimshaw's claims that the school is alive?"

"Of course not."

"Is Mr. Grimshaw telepathic? Does he read minds, share dreams?"

"No."

"Very well, then. And so what *are* you trying to imply?"

"I . . ." The wind went out of Denholm. He had nothing to say, but that doesn't take away either anger or humiliation. "I don't know, Doctor," he finally said through his teeth. "I'm just concerned here. And I'd like to be taken seriously."

"I do, Mr. Denholm. You're doing important work. I recognise it's not easy. And I know some of your colleagues are putting you under pressure." Petrie put on an earnest expression that made Denholm want to throw up. "But we have to try and help Grimshaw, Mr. Denholm."

"Yes."

"Good. Don't worry. Have a little faith. It's not as if I haven't done this before. . . ." He broke off.

"Sorry?"

"Nothing relevant, Mr. Denholm. Before you joined us. I'd just like to clear up a few details."

"Which ones?"

"Your conversation with Grimshaw yesterday. A couple of names: Coneeny and Thwaites?"

Denholm nodded. "Joe Coneeny was one of the top athletes in the school. Won a lot of prizes. Not a very nice guy off the sports field—or on it, come to that," he added, remembering a couple of Coneeny's tackles on the football pitch. "Very photogenic, though. Last I heard, he joined the army. Officer training."

"I see." Petrie made a note. "And Grimshaw?"

"Hated his guts. Coneeny used to knock him about all the time. Wasn't just him; I mean, he picked on loads of kids. Teachers tended to look the other way because he was one of the star players. Credit to the school and all of that."

"Mm. And the other one?"

"Mark Thwaites was the Head Boy in our year. Studying Law. He's with a big-city firm now, I think."

"Another one Grimshaw didn't like?"

"Yeah." How did you explain it? There was the elite, the ones who stood out from the herd. And then there was everyone else. Like Martin Berry. There'd been rumours about Martin Berry. That there'd been more to it than bullying. Worse. But what?

"Mr. Denholm?"

He blinked. Petrie was looking at him. "Is there anything else you'd like to discuss?"

"No. Thanks, Doctor."

THE FIRST THING I REMEMBER FROM THE DREAM IS A NOISE. THERE'S ONLY blackness but there's a sound.

The sound is some kind of machinery or a boiler. Yes, a boiler—a slow, rhythmic rumbling noise. But there's something else. Another sound, woven into it. *Two* sounds, in fact. A sort of low noise, grunting, like someone running hard, or doing push-ups. And then there's the other sound. High pitched. Whimpering. A squeak. I think—it sounded like pain. But it reminded of the noise someone makes when they're being fucked, too. You can't always tell.

That's what it sounded like, but it sounded so like a part of the rhythm of the boiler, of the machine, I couldn't be sure.

Then I was looking out through the inside of one of the common rooms at the Pines. It was an overcast day and it was going to rain, I could feel it coming on. Standing outside on the lawn was a man in some kind of military uniform. RAF? Navy? Army? I don't know. I can't tell. I'm no expert. He had his back to me but I knew it was Coneeny.

I ran across the lawn. "Joe. Joe!"

I don't know why I shouted his first name. We'd never been on those terms. The age gap, for one thing, and that of status. And the issue of hatred on my side, contempt on his. But I shouted it as I ran up to him.

He wheeled round and slapped me across the face. His left eye was missing. In its place was a hole that went through to the back of his head. Through it I could see a train rushing and rushing and rushing past without end, behind a chain-link fence. He had a pencil moustache now, and blood was running from his eye socket down his face into his mouth, filling it up, bubbling on his lips. He kept having to spit it out.

"Don't fucking give me orders." His voice was shriller, younger. Bubbles of bloody spittle popped on his lips.

"Yeah, you little shit." I was shoved from the side. "What do you think you're doing ordering him around?"

"Yeah, he's better than you," said another voice.

"Dr. Petrie said to—"

"Shut up!" Someone else slapped my face now. Thwaites. It was Mark Thwaites. He was in his school uniform. So was Coneeny, now, and so was I. The top of Thwaites's head was missing, and it looked like bits had been taken out of his brain. A metal rim surrounded the wound.

Others were moving in. All kids from school.

"Danny?" I heard a voice from behind me. I knew whose it was. Martin Berry's. High and soft. "Danny, aren't you going to tell them? Danny?"

"Shut up, you queer bastard," said Coneeny, looking over my shoulder. "Fuck off out of it."

"But—"

"Fuck off!" they shouted in chorus, and Martin let out a thin scared cry and I heard his bare feet running away. I was actually afraid. I didn't want to have to see his face.

We were in the playground. We were in the school playground. Coneeny and Thwaites and their half-dozen or so mates were all grown-ups again now, dressed in their grown-up clothes, and closing in. Retreating, I had to move between row on row of boys standing motionless, staring out towards the train tracks. I didn't look at their faces. I would not look at their faces.

"Where are you going?" Coneeny bubbled through his bloody lips.

"Yeah, little shit. Where you going?" Thwaites.

"Where you think you're going?" Another man, laughing. He was very fat, and his mouth was split from its corners to his ears. A frame clamped to his head held his slit cheeks back from the bones, gums and teeth with an arrangement of steel hooks. He shouldn't have been able to talk clearly, but he did.

All the others were similarly mutilated or modified. They were spreading out, moving towards me.

I broke into a stumbling backwards run. A burst of metallic laughter rang out of them. Something in it made me stop. Their eyes gleamed. Their teeth were sharp. I thought of beaters on a hunt, herding the prey towards the guns, and turned around.

The school house had gone charcoal black. The windows glowed red; they were eyes. The big double entrance doors swung open. A stench like Noakes's breath gusted out. The doors were lined with teeth.

A bell shrilled.

"Dinner time!" shouted Coneeny and I heard them run towards me from behind.

I broke into a run, weaving between the boys in the playground—

lacuna

—weaving through tree trunks in the woodland beside the school; the scene shifted, changed, in an eyeblink. Behind me was a crashing through the woods, a shout of "Tally-ho!" A horn blared.

I ran on. The sounds receded. I fell against a tree trunk, gasped for breath. Heard murmured conversation and went still. It stopped.

I moved forward, reached a clearing. The clearing was bare except for a single tree in its centre. Martin Berry hung from it. He was naked from the waist down. His back was to me. There was blood and excrement on his legs. He began to rotate, slowly, on the rope, towards me.

Standing all around him, in a circle, were Coneeny and Thwaites and three or four others. They were staring up at him. They were boys, in their school uniforms. I blinked, and they were men, in city suits and army uniforms. They just stood and stared up at Martin's body. Coneeny was smiling slightly, as you might at a blue sky in May when the weather is fine and your mood is good. The sky overhead was grey and overcast. With a hiss, rain began to spot the ground. They didn't react, just looked up at Martin. I remained still, tried not to breathe.

Martin's body rotated on the rope, swivelling round to face me. His hairless prick was erect; Coneeny held his hips and sucked it. Martin's face was swollen and blue-black: his tongue, thick and swollen, bulged out through his teeth. His eyes were open and half out of their sockets. With a click, the eyelids blinked. Martin's arm rose and his finger pointed at me.

They all spun round and looked my way. Coneeny wiped blood and sperm from his mouth and smiled.

I turned and ran down the school corridor. Behind me feet thundered on the floor. A voice shouted, deep, male—a master. You mustn't run in the corridors. But I had Coneeny and the rest after me. I ran all the quicker.

Through a doorway, up a stair. Into a cupboard. Out the other side (Narnia). A room. A ceiling panel. Loft space. The roof.

Onto it, picking my way across—

"Den-holm!"

"Yoo-hoo!"

The shouts came from the playground below me.

I looked down. They were all stood there. Coneeny, Thwaites and the rest, in their adult guises. Mutilated. The rows of boys in the playground faced outwards towards the fence and the endlessly rushing train. I could see farther from here than ever before, but still saw neither end nor beginning to train or track, but as I watched they all swivelled round as one to face the school with a slithering sound of shoe leather on asphalt. I thought of moving parts in a machine.

Moving parts. Cogs. Mechanisms. Cycles. Circuits. The second hand completes the minute, the minute hand completes the hour, the hour hand tells off the day. And what then?

With a metallic *clash-clack*, like the bolt of a rifle snapping back, the boys in the playground looked up as if some steel brace had guided their heads, turning flayed faces up towards me.

I felt gears shifting, cogs turning, pistons moving, beneath the roof, under my feet. In the walls and attic space, basement and boiler room—

"Danny?"

Martin Berry stood next to me, naked. He opened his arms and puckered up for a kiss.

Laughter and jeers from behind. A chant: "Gayboy, gayboy."

Martin's eyes fell out and his jawbone dropped away.

"Gayboy, gayboy."

Gears and clockwork turned in the holes in his face. He fell apart, rained in cogs and laughter on the playground.

The roof shifted underfoot. Teachers stood around me, black gowns flapping from their shoulders. Spanton. Harkley, the English master, Liverton, the music master. The geography teacher, Burnslow, and Wildermoor, the history master.

I turned and saw the headmaster. Mr. Martinson. His eyelids clicked as he blinked. All their eyelids clicked as they blinked.

The roof tilted, dropping away and folding flat. The playground rushed up, the ground opening to reveal a pit lined with blades—

Or were they teeth?

I WOKE UP SCREAMING. NO SURPRISES THERE.

I felt sick. But I thought I'd be okay. Until I realised.

Realised I'd forgotten something, a lot of somethings. Realised just how much I'd forgotten about one person in particular, for a start.

It'd been shifting and stirring in me, ever since I'd encountered you. You mentioned him on the first day—the second, rather. Our first conversation, in the canteen. That was the first little bit of loose scree that goes sliding, dislodging more, which dislodges more, till the whole mountainside falls, crashing down.

You did it deliberately, Grimshaw, you bastard. You did it deliberately. Didn't you?

(Yes.)

Just so I'd remember.

(Remember what?)

Remember him.

(Remember whom?)

You won't leave it alone, will you, you bastard? All right. All right. I'll speak his name, although you already know. Martin.

I WAS NEVER ONE OF THE GOLDEN BOYS. WHEN I FIRST CAME TO DRAKEMIRE, back when I was eleven, fresh out of primary school, I thought I might be. It was a fresh start. A new beginning.

Primary school hadn't been much fun. But here was a chance to be something else. *Someone* else.

That's what I thought at the time. But I was only a kid. I know, I know. How naïve can you get?

When do they pick you? When's your destiny set in stone? Mediocrity or excellence? Favoured or fucked? I have no idea. Was there ever a choice? Could I ever have done anything differently, that would've changed the course and direction? And would I if I could?

No answer, and they're all irrelevant now in any case.

I remember that first day. All the new boys. Out there in the playground, waiting for the teachers to come and show us in. First day. Nervous.

I thought, I'll make a good impression. I stepped forward and started talking.

"Hi. I'm Daniel. . . ."

I tried to introduce myself to the others. Set myself up as a spokesman. A leader. Ridiculous in retrospect. Life story. Chapter and verse. They all just stared. Their faces said it all: YOU TWAT.

Signed, sealed and delivered.

Maybe it wouldn't've made any difference. Maybe I'd've been marked anyway.

They don't mark you, though. That's the thing about a place like Drakemire. It's not a comprehensive, where it's free. And it's not a boarding school where no one ever sees your face back home. It's fee-paying. It's like a factory, only instead of being paid to march in through those gates, your folks pay for you to be degraded. Beat that for sheer irony.

You wake up in the morning. You lie in bed, listening to the house coming to life around you. Distant traffic on the main road. Plates and dishes rattling in the kitchen. The radio on. Waiting till the last moment when you have to get up. A stone dread taking shape already in your stomach, growing in your belly like a pearl in an oyster. A speck of gravel, a pebble, a rock, a boulder. You can barely choke your breakfast down.

"What's wrong, Daniel?"

"Nothing, Mum."

"Are you sure?"

"Yes!"

"God! All right. You're like a bear with a sore head."

Leave me alone, you think, *leave me alone*.

You can't tell her anything, you see. One, because you'll never make it sound as bad as it is. Two, even if you could, what'll happen? She'll ring the school up. And the worst offenders will get pulled in, get a bollocking. And they'll lay off for a bit. For about five minutes. And then it'll come back worse than ever, with a new taunt added to the rest: *Mummy's boy*.

No. Not that. Never again. You will not. You can't tell your parents, because at best you'll get lectures on "controlling yourself," or not reacting. Ignore them and they'll go away. But they won't. They won't. Not unless the whole school's empty. They cluster round and they keep up until you crack. Their speciality is the kind of grief you won't be marked by. It's like one of the documentaries you see on *Wildlife on One*. Only when the leopard gets the gazelle or whatever, it's over, done, finished. Kaput. A bit of pain as the claws rip through the flesh, but that's over soon enough. Here they catch you, they maul you, rip you apart. Shove you around. Dead legs, dead arms, a knee in the groin. Punches tipped with a single, extended knuckle that numb you with the agony they bring. And the names. The whisper in your ear, the shouted insult. Hauled by handfuls of your hair. You can't take any more. You can't. You can't. But you have to. There is no choice.

This is your day:

Out the front door. Walk into town. Through the town centre and out again, to the edge of the leafy suburbs, where the school house is.

Off the main road, a driveway. A sign: DRAKEMIRE BOYS' GRAMMAR SCHOOL. EST. 1907.

Up the driveway. Trees shed leaves in autumn. Approaching from behind. The rattle of passing trains gets louder as you near the playground.

And now you've got to wait till they open the doors to the school. In the corridors, in the classrooms, you're easy prey, but out here in the playground, it's worse. You're anybody's mark. At least in the classroom you can pinpoint the position of the enemy fast enough. In the playground, it's shifting. You need insect eyes, with 360-degree vision, to keep track of the predators. Insect eyes, like the school.

What'll it be? Volleyed insults? Hair pulling by the big Irish kid doesn't call his day started 'less he's got your hair out at all angles? Or nick your schoolbag and sling it around, maybe go through it to see what they can find? Or shove you bully to bullyboy like a human fucking pinball?

There's more, but you get the idea.

Before and between lessons, there's the whispered insults, the snapped rubber bands, the dead-arms when you're not looking—eyes out for another danger, or talking to a friend. If you can be said to have any. This is the worst. Friends don't always stand by you. In a pinch, there are so many, almost all, who'll turn away, or worse, take the piss out of you, join in. When you need a rock, it's subsided treacherously back into the deep, and you find only the sea. To defend you is to be lumbered with you as a burden, as your protector, if they're lucky, if they're big and if they're strong. If not, they're meat for the beast, too.

During the lesson, you're afraid of getting a question. Afraid of getting one right, for all the cries and hisses of "teacher's pet" and allegations of sexual slavery on your part to the teachers.

The breaks and the lunch hour—turfed back out into the playground, the killing ground, the killing fields. The plain and the veldt, the rainforest and the tundra, the desert and the bush. The predator's ground.

If you're lucky, you can find your way to the library at lunchtime. If no one follows you in, to hound you even then. They can get you even in that place—sit at the table you've found and whisper more obscenities, insults, kicking you under the table, probing the shell for weak spots till you can bear no more.

Is it any wonder you fantasise some days about walking into school with a gun? That you daydream of the smirks becoming wide-eyed moans of terror, just before bullets smash faces that tormented you into pulp and gaping holes?

When, years later, you read of high-school massacres, like Columbine, you will be horrified and you will be disgusted.

But you will understand.

And then the afternoon. The final mercy of the exodus from school. The journey home, walking down side streets. Looking over your shoulder, waiting for the pack to fall on you. Sometimes they do; sometimes they don't. But they always *can*.

The other hard bit is that the list of enemies is never quite the same. Someone who made your life a living hell yesterday or last week is nice to you today. Why? You can't even begin to tell. It's like trying to divine the weather from chicken entrails. What's agony and the death of the soul to you, a passionate hatred, is just a way of passing the time for them. A pastime, a lark. They go home and forget about it, come in some days and can't be arsed, or think *leave it a bit, let the damaged parts grow back* (except they never will). It's hard to sustain an undying hatred when some days they do nothing to earn it. The list is never quite the same.

You go home and you do your homework. Watch a little telly. Maybe go out, or probably not because you never know which enemy's out there. Stay home; home is your refuge. Home is sanctuary. You do your best to hide from Mum and Dad any sign of what you went through today. Present a reasonably happy, normal face to the world, all the while screaming inside.

And so to bed.

And tomorrow you will do it again.

THAT WAS HOW IT WENT. I CAN SAY, WITHOUT EXAGGERATION, THAT I probably had it worse than almost anyone on my year. There were others got it bad to some degree—like Grimshaw—but I probably had it the worst.

All except for one.

Martin Berry, like I said, had the worst branding any pupil at a private all-boys school could have.

Big, pale-blue, long-lashed eyes. Wavy hair, a girlish mouth, a soft, high-pitched voice. He was effeminate.

In a place like that, no tag is more feared than that of homosexuality.

Puff, gaylord, gayboy, shitstabber, arse-bandit, shirtlifter, bender, queer, faggot, uphill gardener, bumhole engineer . . . etc. The list goes on. I was fat, but I could do something about it. (Although not easily, because comfort-eating was how I dealt with things.) What was Martin gonna do? Plastic surgery? Unlikely.

For all that, we didn't move in the same circles, didn't become friends till quite late in the game—fourth or fifth year. Martin was adamant he was going on to sixth-form college; my parents wanted me to take A levels at Drakemire. In the end, they lost. For the first time, at the end of the fifth year, I made a decision, an adult decision, and saw it through. I did my A levels at the South Trafford College, among a very different mix of kids. Some of them were even girls, a species unknown on the planet Drakemire. One of them was called Dawn Finnegan, who I had my first proper snog with and went out with for a while.

But that was to come. What did I know about girls? There weren't any at Drakemire. It was all boys. And I didn't get out enough to meet any others at evenings or weekends. It's another story, and a happier one. Or as much of happiness as I was ever likely to know after what'd happened.

There's a received wisdom in our society that you can rise above anything; conquer your past, cut loose. That it doesn't have to shape you if you don't want it to, if you don't let it. That it's all your choice.

It isn't true.

In fact, it's a lie, and a cruel one at that. Some events are a cicatrice, a branding: permanent scars. Like you were saying, Grimshaw; like a mutilation. You were right. Pieces of us are still back in Drakemire. In the School House. We look unmarked, normal, whole, but if people could see our souls they'd run screaming from the sight.

If you're Jewish or Muslim and they circumcise you, does your foreskin grow back? Does it fuck. Your cock's shaped like that for good. No really bad side-effects from that. But female circumcision, on the other hand . . . I saw the results of that once, as a hospital orderly, and I'll never bloody forget it. Not your fault, something you had no control over. But you're still marked by it for life. Not fair, but it's true.

You try to avoid self-pity. You do whatever you must in order to survive. You erect your defences. You carry on with a life, however circumscribed by previous damage. You forget stuff, if you have to; you pack it up and seal it away. Never doubt that it can happen. Haven't you ever thought of something and recalled an event that happened years ago but you just haven't thought of in all that time? *Good Lord, I'd completely forgotten about that.* That's all it is. Your memory's like a room of shelves, full of floppy disks. Some of them are dusty and you haven't looked what's on them for years. As you go on, some get damaged by fire or flood or just old age and you can't read any or much of what's on there.

And some, if you're sensible, you drop down the back of the shelving or kick under them, so they can't be found, the files retrieved, even by accident.

But you, Grimshaw—you turned the lights on in that dusty room, didn't you? You got me thinking, looking, probing. Where's that disk, the Drakemire disk, the Martin Berry one? I know it was round here somewhere—never knowing there was a damn good reason I hadn't been able to find it, couldn't remember what was there.

You let yourself, *make* yourself forget, if you have to. Till you're old and strong and distant enough to replay the old files. And deal with them.

Or not.

AND SO.

It was a lunchtime. A rainy April lunchtime. Not so rainy that we were all in the classrooms. A spattery sort of day. Odd, isolated showers. Light. Not enough to keep us in, but enough to make the library overcrowded. That would've scared me once. But not now, not anymore. I had another place to go.

Out in the corridors. No home and no roots, no shelter and no refuge. Prey. I would've been, right up till the middle of last year, my fourth at Drakemire. But not now.

Because by then I knew Martin Berry. I knew where he went.

I'd always been brought up to be a man's man. You didn't run away; you went back and fought the good fight. And, obviously, got your arse kicked. When I was at sixth-form college, I started working out and dieting, shifting the spare tyre cos I'd heard Dawn Finnegan say I'd be all right looking if I lost that weight. She was talking to Sara Woods and Nell Laine at the time, and she didn't know I'd heard, but I did. You could see the results within a fortnight. A couple of weeks after that, we were going out, Dawn and I. Didn't last that long, just two or three months, but it was a start. Gave me that boost. And I kept working out, not just for the girls but for the confidence, the power. I'd realised I could be strong. Swore I'd never be a victim again. Hard to believe, when I'm restraining a violent patient, that I used to be that fat kid everyone gets.

But you're never far from your roots. And right then, in any case, I was a long way from a leaner physique and Dawn Finnegan.

Martin, never brought up that way, had had more sense. He'd known he couldn't fight it. So he ran. And hid. If he hadn't, he'd have made his appointment with a tree and a rope a lot earlier.

So he found places to hide. And as we became friends, he trusted me enough to share them.

We got called the usual names, of course, for hanging around together. Bummer, bender, queerboy . . . see the earlier list. But there were two of us now. Martin was used to hearing it; I'd heard it myself already, because it's the ultimate insult in a place like that.

I ducked through corridors, down the stairs. Now it got tricky.

Martin'd showed me the way. I broke across a narrow courtyard to the annexe by the school caretaker's quarters; he was a sour, vicious man, who'd once hit me across the face for no good reason except simple dislike of my "squeaky little voice." So there was an added pleasure in sticking it to him. As it were.

There was a door, to the part of the building with the head's office in it. Near it, just below ground level, was a recessed window. With a last look round, I slipped down into the gap, cracked the window open—it was always ajar, the frame long warped—and clambered through.

The corridor I landed in was next to the boiler room. I moved away from it, although the low chugging hum of the boiler followed me, filling the air. There was extra space in that basement area, you see. Mostly used for storage, though it was rarely used now even for that. No one, not even the caretaker, usually went there.

The perfect place for me and Martin to hide. He'd found it by accident; on the run from the bullypack (Coneeny, Thwaites), he'd rushed into the courtyard and found it deserted. Seconds before they'd arrived, he'd spotted the grimy, barely visible window and slipped down against it. Nearly killed himself when it gave and swung wide. Thinking fast, he'd dropped down into the corridor—and found his little sanctuary.

Which now he shared with me.

I slipped down the corridor. There were three storage rooms, the third of which was all but empty. A few tailor's dummies (God knew why they'd had them), a couple of wooden crates and cardboard boxes, a small, chunky old wooden table. Nothing else.

Martin and I would hide down there, talk in whispers, swap books and comics, packed lunches and cans of pop. A den, a hideaway, a secret location. What all boys dream of . . .

First off, all I could hear, as I approached, was the thrum of the boiler.

As I reached the door, I heard something else. Two other sounds, woven into it like a backbeat round a melody. Or vice versa. The boiler was the backbeat. The low, repetitive grunting, the bassline. The thin, high whimpering, the rhythm guitar or the synth.

I pushed the door slightly open, knowing something was wrong but not what, or how much.

The door opened and I saw . . . I saw but I didn't understand, couldn't comprehend it, couldn't believe I was seeing Martin Berry, stripped naked, gagged with his underpants, wrists bound with his tie, his and someone else's belt securing each ankle to a leg of the small, stumpy wooden table. Whimpering through the gag while Joe Coneeny, trousers round his ankles (beltless, I noted, as it sank in; that'd be what was securing Martin's other leg), grunted, clutching his hips with hooked fingers that seemed to be trying to rip away handfuls of flesh, his own hips pumping away with a brutal rhythm.

I saw it, but I didn't believe it till Mark Thwaites grabbed my collar and pulled me through the doorway, kicking at my ankles as I went so I hit the floor.

I let out a cry and Thwaites landed on me, pinning me on my back. "Fucking shut it you queer bastard."

He held a Swiss Army knife to my eye, the blade almost touching it. Totally banned in school of course, but hey, Mark Thwaites was the kind of boy who'd become a Head Boy one day. He grinned down at me; all the while I heard Coneeny's grunts, Martin's cries, the boiler's thrum.

Coneeny finished with a snarled cry that sounded more pain than pleasure, or maybe it was triumph. Thwaites climbed off me, handed the knife to him.

Thwaites moved towards Martin, unfastening his trousers. Martin's bare back, sweatily gleaming, heaved with desperate breath. His ribs showed. There was blood on his legs. I smelt shit. The whiff of that, rectal mucus and spunk, particularly strong off Coneeny's undone flies.

He was looking at me with a sort of smile on his face, his hand in my hair. Not pulling, almost caressing. That was more frightening, in fact. Partly because the possibility of the pain was almost worse than the thing itself, but also because it made me think he might want to fuck me, too.

Thankfully he didn't. Of course, he'd spent himself already. But partly it was because I wasn't Martin. That was why they really hated him, of course. He was the nearest thing they had there to a woman, and embodied all they couldn't stand. Or acknowledge in themselves.

Anything in a school like that—if it's not *male*, if it's not rage and domination or braying pack lust, or at least dressed up as it—isn't allowed. Porno mags are okay, cos it's just bodies and holes. Tits, cunts, arses. *Phwooar. I'd shag that, fuck it to death. Fuck her brains out.* Sex and violence. Raw lust is fine. But anything else, any of the emotions that go with it—oh no.

Perhaps that was why they so hated Martin, went after him with a viciousness that eclipsed anything I'd been through. Nothing but sex misspelled. It'd never occurred to me there might be more complicated emotions than mere rage or cruelty involved in their treatment of Martin. That there might be other things dressed up as rage as well. A desire they couldn't acknowledge or admit to, building to a peak and vented as rage, making this scene not impossible, but inevitable.

Coneeny sat me back against the wall, knife to my throat and hand in my hair, my choice of views his face and Thwaites pounding into Martin until he, too, spent his loads. He let out the same grunted roar Coneeny had, then slumped over Martin's back, panting, hoarsely.

"Oi," called Coneeny. "Stop cuddling the queer boy. Come on."

Thwaites stood, pulling his trousers up, doing up his belt. Sauntering back, he thwacked Martin's arse. "Liked that, didn't you, puffter?"

They looked down at me. "What're we gonna do with fat boy, there?"

Coneeny laughed. "*I* know."

"GO ON, FAT BOY, GIVE YOUR GIRLFRIEND A CUDDLE."

"Stop covering yourself up. Go on, kissy, kissy."

The Polaroid flashed.

Got the picture?

I was naked. So was Martin. They made us pretend to fuck. And they took pictures. Blackmail, to shut us up. And then they went, leaving me and Martin naked and alone, still in the last embrace they'd made us pose for. For a moment it was real, for a moment I was hard. But then I pulled away, scrabbled for my clothes, dressed frantically, whimpering. Afraid someone else might come in.

"Danny?"

I didn't listen, didn't look.

"Danny?" Martin's voice cracked.

I knotted my tie, laced my shoes, beat as much dust as I could off my blazer and put it back on.

"Danny?"

I turned around. He lay on his stomach—the only position that didn't hurt him, most likely. His skin was girl-smooth, girl-soft. I'd got a hard-on, pretending to fuck him. Coneeny and Thwaites hadn't seen, thank God. There was still blood on him. He looked—

—beautiful.

"Danny?" His face, streaked with tears and fright.

"Put your clothes on for fuck sake," I said.

I went straight out. Didn't wait for him, couldn't look.

"Danny?"

WE SAID NOTHING. THWAITES AND CONEENY HAD THE PICTURES; THE only evidence of any queerness depicted us, not them. If I'd thought clearly, I'd've seen maybe they had more to lose. What'd they been doing taking them, after all? But then again, maybe not. My dad was relentlessly homophobic; pictures like that would've sent him mad. He'd've thought, *Some nasty little peeping Tom snapped that*, but the sight of his son and heir doing . . . that . . . no. It'd've been too much.

I said nothing, to my family or anyone else. After all, I'd only been humiliated. Again. A new and horrible kind, yes, and a new and horrible threat, but still, in essence, nothing I wasn't used to.

As for Martin? Well, how often does sexual violence go unreported out of shame? He was a teenaged boy, probably uncertain of his sexuality and made to feel, no doubt, responsible, by dint of his girly looks, his lack of *manliness*. Whatever *that* is. If it's being a Joe Coneeny or a Mark Thwaites, sign me up for a Pride march here and now.

But that wasn't what killed Martin. Oh, it put the rope around his neck and him up the tree in the first place, but it wasn't what pushed him off the branch to choke and strangle slowly. (Maybe he'd hoped a quick leap'd break his neck. It didn't.)

No. It wasn't Joseph Coneeny or Mark Thwaites that finally killed Martin Berry. That was me.

In the weeks that followed the rape, I cut him dead. We didn't hang out at lunchtimes anymore. We never went back, it goes without saying, to the basement room.

Martin would try to talk to me; I'd answer in clipped monosyllables that made conversation impossible. He'd try to walk down the drive with me after school. I'd walk away, fast. He'd try sitting next to me, on the bus or at dinner; I'd switch seats, or even get off the bus and walk home.

And then he did the unforgivable. He touched me.

We were walking down the drive, no one else in sight; I'd made sure I was first out, ahead of the rest, and he'd done the same. We walked together, me trying to outpace him, Martin trying to keep up.

At last, determined I wasn't going to avoid the issue, he caught my arm to turn me to face him. "Danny, we've got to—"

"Get away from me, you fucking queer." I didn't shout. It was worse than that. Even to me my own voice sounded strangled and inhuman. Unnatural and distorted. What Martin must have made of it, how it'd sounded to him, I can't imagine. Or what must've seen in my face.

Hatred, I expect. At the very least. All the rage and hate and venom and humiliation and shame, not just for the basement room but for five fucking years in Drakemire, boiled up and found a focus. A scapegoat. Coneeny, Thwaites: out of bounds, invulnerable, protected by popularity, power and status as well as simple blackmail. So I'd focussed on the powerless one. All the stuff I couldn't deal with, processed into something simple, like rage. Dressed up like it, like a queen in drag. Just like them.

Just like them.

He stumbled back, almost fell. I knew what I'd said was wrong. Soon as I said it, I knew. But it was too late to take it back, and I couldn't say anything that might salvage the friendship. I had to throw it off. Reject him utterly. *I can't deal with this.*

"Leave me alone," I heard myself say in a flat, dead voice sounding years older than mine. "Just leave me alone."

I turned away from his white, stricken face and walked down the drive. May was just beginning. Spring in the air. Sunlight. This time he didn't call after me.

Two days later, he was dead.

I WENT TO THE FUNERAL. A FEW BOYS FROM DRAKEMIRE ATTENDED. Thwaites and Coneeny among them. I didn't see either of them come near me, but when I got home I found a Polaroid in my blazer pocket. It showed me and Martin, embracing, sat with our legs entwined, eyes closed, mouths brushing together in a kiss. It wasn't the worst one, not by a long chalk.

I tore it into shreds, kept the shreds well, *well* hidden till one evening when my parents were out and I could burn them to ashes. I opened all the windows to let out the smell. Mum asked if I'd taken up smoking.

Somehow, I passed my GCSEs. Shit grades but I passed. Teachers couldn't understand. I'd always been a good student. They were enough for sixth-form college, though, and there I applied myself. Buried myself in work, and in girls, like Dawn Finnegan. Blanked out what'd happened. Martin Berry? Lad I was at school with. Got picked on a lot. Killed himself. Didn't know him well.

And I forgot. Until now.

THE HAPPIEST DAYS OF YOUR LIFE. THAT'S WHAT THEY SAY ABOUT SCHOOL, isn't it? I think of that phrase every time I read about some school kid topping him or herself because of some gang of halfwits making their lives a living hell at school. I wonder how much that stupid lie contributed to the decisions to end it all.

I wonder if it went through Martin's mind as he awkwardly straddled the tree branch, making one end of the rope fast to it, shaping the other into a noose. If all he saw, looping the noose around his neck, was an endless vista of life of more the same: predation and cruelty, intolerance, scapegoating and betrayal. Always betrayal.

And I wonder, as he let himself fall sideways, if he smiled to think he was cheating such a fate of its prey.

And how long it took him to realise he was wrong.

CROSSING THE LAWN. UP THE GRAVEL DRIVEWAY. GET OUT. A DAY OFF. GO into town. Coffee. A pub. Just away from here for five fucking minutes. Martin's face everywhere. Go. Get out. Out of Drakemire. No. Out of the Pines.

"Oi."

The iron gates, up ahead, closed. Walking faster.

"Oi!"

Coming from the gates, to intercept: Noakes. He blocks off the exit. "Think you're going?"

"Out."

"Oh, you think so, do you?"

"Clear off, Noakes. It's a free country."

Try sidestepping him; Noakes moves to block. "You're not going anywh . . ." He stops. Stares down. "What. The. Fuck?"

Flies undone? No. Zipped. Look up. Noakes's face wide-eyed, ashen.

Look back down. Hands. Hands are red, drying brown. Tacky. Darkness clotted under the nails. Trousers, shirt, stained, too. Noakes didn't notice at first?

Look back up at Noakes. Noakes takes a step back.

A shout. Turn and look. Petrie's running across the lawn. The look on his face—he's never looked like that before. Agitated? No. Terrified.

Dr. Feelgood's running, black bag of goodies in his hand. And he's not alone. Two, three other orderlies with him. The big ones.

Suddenly the need for a pint is physical, beyond tobacco cravings or hunger pangs. Time to go. Turn and run, skirt Noakes, get out the gate.

Turning back to run, but it's too late. Noakes's fist drives forward; behind it, his face, equal parts rage and fright.

(Noakes? Afraid?)

Explosion: BLAM. White light. Back, flying back. Sky: blue. Sun: flash white. Ground: hard impact. Grass: green. Grass: crushed, smell of.

Dizzy. Try to rise. Fall back. Noakes's face above, joined by the other orderlies'. Petrie's face joining them. Dr. Feelgood's mouth moving slow and slurred, underwater sounds.

Hands grabbing arms and legs, one orderly to each limb. Petrie holds up a needle. An arc of squirted liquid glitters on the tip. Petrie leaning forward.

A sting.

Thickness, rushing. Darkening skies. Fast falls the eventide—

And black.

The basement of the Pines contains a dozen soundproofed rooms with padded walls for patients who've become violent or otherwise out of hand. It's in one of those that Denholm wakes up.

He's lying on a cot. He tries to sit up. Can't. There are leather straps across his chest. Wrists. Ankles. He can't move. He strains. No. Helpless. What he always vowed not to be. Never to be, again.

He shouts. He screams. He makes threats. He makes demands.

No answer.

What the fuck. *What. The. Fuck?* That's what Noakes said before decking him. What *is* this? He's an employee. Not a fucking patient. All he tried to do was leave, got out, and they acted like he'd—

Denholm looks down. His hands are still stained. It's a brownish colour now it's dried.

His clothes, but his clothes aren't stained.

But—

That's because these aren't his clothes. He's wearing a white smock. His feet are bare. A white smock. A *patient's* smock.

The fuck?

What's that on my hands? What is . . . what happened?

Lacuna. There is a lacuna. A hole, a gap. He can remember the nightmare. The nauseating rush as what happened to Martin Berry came back. He ran to the bathroom. Vomited. Copiously. And then—

Then what?

Shower. Warmth. Heat. Dressing. Lacing shoes.

(Like in the basement room, afterwards. Martin's poor, pathetic voice bleating, pleading, behind him.)

And, and, and . . . what then?

Grimshaw.

What about him?

Something about Grimshaw. Looking for him. But . . . what had he . . . ?

There's a panel in the door. It opens. Framed in it: Noakes's piggy eyes.

"You sick fuck."

"What?" Denholm heaves at the straps. "The fuck are you calling *me* that for? You're the—"

"I've never seen anything like that, you cunt. I thought I'd . . . God, you twisted bastard."

"Mr. Noakes."

Noakes flinches.

"Let's try to keep this professional, shall we?"

Noakes moves away, mumbling. Denholm hears: ". . . should never have let him out . . ."

Petrie's face framed in the gap. "Daniel. How are we feeling now?"

Daniel, all of a sudden?

"Don't know about you, but I'm feeling fine." Denholm tries himself to sound casual about it all. Like it's all a joke. "Let me up and I'll show you how good I feel." He sees Petrie flinch, curses himself. "I mean, do a couple of laps around the lawn or something."

"I don't think that would be appropriate," says Petrie.

"Come on, Doctor. All I did was try and go into town. Get a pint. Haven't been off this place for . . ."

For how long? He suddenly realises he can't remember. His quarters are in the building—well, that's a bargain, isn't it? Accommodation included with the job?

Only, does any other orderly actually live at the Pines? Noakes or the others? He . . . he doesn't think so.

Why just me?

When did I last leave the building?

"I'm afraid you did rather more than that, Daniel," Petrie says. "Don't you remember anything?"

"No. Not since this morning. Since . . ."

"Yes?"

"Nothing. Nightmare."

"Nightmare. About what?"

"Nothing."

"Must have been about *something*, Daniel. Don't you recall *any* details?"

Noakes: *Grimshaw . . . never seen anything like that . . .*

The one thought on his mind on waking:

Grimshaw.

"What happened, Doctor?"

Petrie looks at him, into him, and says: "Grimshaw's dead, Daniel. You . . ." He can't say more about it. "Some sort of frenzy. A fugue state. That's why you can't remember."

"But . . . why? That can't be. I've never . . . nothing like this."

Petrie is refusing to meet his eyes.

"What?"

No answer.

"This is a set-up, isn't it?" Denholm begins to buck and thrash against the straps. "Fucking set-up!"

"Daniel, calm down! This isn't help—"

"One of your fucking inbred hooray-henry inmates did it, didn't they? You've shot me up—"

"You'll injure yourself—"

"—so I can't remember and now you're gonna fit me up for it!"

Denholm roars. In this moment, Drakemire and the Pines blur together, really *are* one in his head. The rage: all-encompassing. Petrie is Noakes is Thwaites is Coneeny is Martin is Grimshaw is . . .

The strap securing his right arm breaks. Petrie's face is white, mouth agape.

An ankle strap breaks; Denholm reaches for the strap on his left arm. Petrie snaps out of the spell, wheels away from the door.

"Mr. Noakes—"

Denholm's left arm snaps free. Bloodied, frenzied, his hands fly to the strap on his chest.

"Mr. Noakes!"

A thunder of feet, and the door bursts open.

TRAINS RATTLING. PATTERNS OF LIGHT FLICKERING ON THE WALL—FROM the train windows at night? Like a projector film, only there's no picture, just flickers and scrawls dancing in the milky light. There was a film called *Mothlight*: a director dusted the film with powdered fragments of mothwing. Looked a little like this.

Suddenly order leaps out of the chaos: the scrawled patterns form jagged, spiky letters on the wall:

DELAPSUS RESURGAM.

Quivering as in a high wind, and then, as in a high wind, torn away and gone. The light flickers. Goes black.

Whimpering. The light flares on again. The room, no longer empty.

Coneeny, blood running from the hole that was his eye. Thwaites, his opened and segmented brain. Martin Berry naked at the bedside, reaching out. His fingers, gently stroking, are cold.

Grimshaw there, too. His eyes are gone. His lips, too. Bitten off by the look. He tries to speak, but it's not easy. A hole where his throat used to be.

"Almost done." Who speaks? Doesn't sound like Grimshaw. Doesn't sound like any of them. "Almost done."

Flickering sounds. More figures standing in the room. Teachers. Heads bowed.

Clockwork turning. Heads rise. Eyelids click. Spanton, Harkley, Barnslow, Wilderman . . . Martinson.

Creaking and groaning as of huge gears. Moving parts. Mechanisms. Cogs. Cycles. Circuits. Second hand, minutes, hours—beyond that?

All looking, expectant. Martin smiling, unfastening the chest strap. The smile knowing, tender. Whimper with fright—if others see . . .

And the room is empty but for Martin. He leans forward. A kiss. Then the leather strap breaks and—

The thunder of the train, deafening. The strobe of its passage, and Martin's face rises from the kiss black and bloated, as he was found.

A scream and—

DENHOLM SITS UP, GULPING AIR. WHAT TIME IS IT?

Birds are twittering. Must be morning, then.

But—

But the confinement room is below ground and soundproofed. You can't hear birdsong down there.

But—

But this wasn't the confinement room. He looked around. These were his quarters. The windows open. Curtains shifting in the breeze.

Nightmare. Must have been.

So why is there still dried blood on your hands?

Is there? He looks. Nothing. He breathes out in relief. Sits up in bed. Naked. The sheets stink. What time is it?

He looks at his bedside clock. Blinks. Stares. 10:17 A.M. Way, way past his start time. Someone should've been banging on the door by now.

Clock must be wrong. What time . . . ?

He pulls back the bedside curtains, gazes out. The sun is high. The lawn deserted.

Except for a body, spreadeagled there. A patient, he thinks, but can't be sure. The clothes are dark with blood. The grass around the body, too.

This isn't right. Shouldn't someone be called? The police or whoever?

Denholm looks down. From the bottom of his field of vision, protruding into view past the edge of the sill, he sees an outflung arm.

He scrambles out of bed, dresses. Scrambles into the bathroom.

What. The. Fuck?

There is blood in the sink, blood on the floor, blood in the bath, blood handprints on the tiled walls. A bundle of blood-sodden cloth. He refuses to look to see if it used to be a smock.

Breath coming fast. Hitching. Denholm heads back into the bedroom. Pulls on his socks.

Shoes, where're my—

And he sees them, lying by the door, one on its side. The soles, still glistening, clotted black. A fly weaves a lazy dance above it.

In through the door, staining the carpet—dark footprints, dried brown on the pinkish, faded carpet.

Oh fuck. Oh fuck.

Breath hitching. What happened? Holes. Gaps. *Lacunae.* What happened? All this, so much, gone down the fucking hole, gone. What happened? Happened to Grimshaw? Was he in the confinement room? The nightmare with Martin, Coneeny, the rest—Was that just a nightmare? What about walking across the lawn, what about Noakes decking him?

He touches his jaw. It hurts. Feels bruised.

No. I didn't kill Grimshaw. I didn't kill anybody.

(Then why is there blood in the bathroom? On the shoes? Those hand and fingerprints in blood on the bathroom walls. If they were tested, whose would they be?)

They've doped me up. Made blanks in my memory. Told me I did it. This whole thing with Grimshaw was fucked from the word go. Stank. It's a fit-up. Set me up to take the blame for something someone else did—it has to be that—has to be. Have to get out. Find somebody. Get clear. Get clean.

He pulls on the shoes, bloody though they are. His fingers are dirtied by the bloodied laces but he doesn't care.

Have to get out have to get out—

He pushes open the bedroom door and—

THE SOUND OF A DISTANT PARTY. NIGHT. THE LIGHTS OFF.

I followed the sounds, alone, abandoned. The corridors seemed longer, more winding, than ever they'd been when I first was there.

A distant rattling: I looked out of the window (I was on the covered walkway) and saw the train still hurtling endlessly past the School House. Light flickering from the windows. Shadowy half-shapes, from the behind the glass, pressing hands to it, pawing at it.

The boys still standing in the playground, watching, their long shadows flying back, splaying out from them towards the building.

The sounds carry from up ahead. The teacher's block.

I pushed the door open to it. Down the spiral staircase to the ground floor. Which way? The door to the Assembly Hall again; flayed-faced boys stood in serried ranks. Braces on their necks. A *clack*, and the heads snapped towards me. I turned away.

Right up ahead. The head's office. The sounds coming through the orange-painted door. A deep breath, then forward and—

Instead of the head's office, a large drawing room. An extended table. Bottles of wine; half-emptied glasses. Cleared plates. Bones on a platter. No head or limbs but the ribcage huge. Human?

Coneeny has a thighbone. Breaks it with his teeth and sucks out the marrow. Blood from his missing eye runs down the splintered femur.

Music. There's music. Echoing tinnily. Elgar's Pomp and Circumstance. Other boys. The table extends into infinity, row on unending row of Old Boys, going back down the decades. Every few places along the table stands a teacher.

"Hello, Denholm." Thwaites. He raises a glass. "A toast, one and all! To Denholm! Arse-bandit extraordinaire!"

Laughter.

The tabletop's strewn with Polaroids of me and Martin. They're clapping slowly, mockingly.

"The man who tried to end Drakemire," says Coneeny.

"But in our end is our beginning," says Thwaites.

Laughter. Gaping mouths, teeth. The laughter so loud, the reverberating Pomp and Circumstance march growing ever louder with it, I clasp my hands over my ears, screwing my eyes shut and—

Silence.

I open my eyes.

The dining room's empty. The table covered in dust. A rat scuttles through the cobwebbed ribcage of the main course, its own ribs showing through thinning pelt, in vain search of some remaining morsel.

Square shapes, just visible beneath the dust. I pick one up; dust sifts away from it. Another photograph. Martin and me. Faded. I let it fall.

On the bare, peeling wall, two words daubed in long-dried blood or shit: DELAPSUS RESURGAM.

I blink.

The words are still there, but the room's changed. The headmaster's office, at Drakemire. But dusty like the dining room was. Photographs on the desk, beneath the dust. Except one faded picture, picked up and dropped again.

I look down. I'm wearing my school uniform. My hands are the small pudgy hands of my child-self. How long have I been standing here, waiting for the headmaster's judgement?

We're all still there, Grimshaw says.

A sofa, a leather sofa, is also in the office, slashed and ripped apart. The carpet pulled up, the floorboards bare. Tangles of bare wiring hanging from the ceiling and the walls. Wallpaper hanging down like dead skin.

The window is grimy and cracked but I go to it anyway. It overlooks the lawn of the Pines. Two bodies. The ones I glimpsed from my bedroom window before. A bird sings.

I hear the thwack of willow on leather, the gentle patter of applause. Cricket. The English game.

I go back to the headmaster's desk. I leaf through the pictures of Martin and me, and pick the one I like the best. I feel like I should cry but no tears will seem to come.

"Can I go now, sir?" I ask.

THE CANTEEN IS SILENT AS DENHOLM GOES IN.

Half the windows are broken. All of the striplights are gone; several of the ceiling panels have collapsed. The floor is filthy, crusted with rotten leaves, twigs, discarded beer cans. There are the remains of a crude fire in a corner. The remains of a small bird or animal skitter from his feet as his foot catches them.

No one has been in here for a long, long time.

He looks out of the window and sees two skeletons on the lawn.

He goes back to the counter. Behind it lies another skeletal shape. A few pieces of remaining skin, dried to parchment. Jawbone yawning in a scream. Skull split, by the cleaver lying on the countertop. Blood dried brown on walls and floor.

Denholm looks down and sees blood on his hands again.

The menu board is the kind where dishes and prices are spelled out in individual plastic letters. All these lie scattered on the floor with the dead, except those spelling out the two words:

DELAPSUS RESURGAM.

Denholm turns and leaves by the main canteen door.

I STAND IN THE TREES AT THE EDGE OF THE CRICKET FIELD.

Twenty-seven years old, tired and close to weeping.

Unshaven and grimy, in soiled corduroy trousers, t-shirt, sweater and long coat. Matted hair and a beard.

Not a man whose life has gone well.

I am Daniel Denholm; two weeks ago I was thrown out of my last digs. In arrears with the rent, and into the bargain kept screaming in the night and waking up the neighbours. Landlord gave me my marching orders. Nothing much to take with me except medication. And the gun in the right-hand pocket of my coat.

I bought it in more affluent times—as opposed to effluent ones, like these, ha-ha. It's always travelled with me.

Why did I buy a gun? For no reason I could easily explain. Just a vast, unruly dread. The sense of living in a constant state of threat. As I lived day after day at Drakemire.

I never left. God help me, in all important respects, I realise, I never left. I tried to put it behind me, to forget—no. Never. I'm still there. Still the prey.

I know that now.

That is why I bought the gun. For defence. I thought at the time.

But, of course, a good offence is the best defence.

In my coat's other pocket is a half-bottle of the cheapest whisky I could find. I uncap it and take a long swallow. Gulp it. Let it burn down.

Let it all burn down.

Applause. The sun is going down. Beyond the games fields, Drakemire rises. The distant rattle of a train.

The drugs. Legal and otherwise. All useless. None of it screened out the secrets I couldn't tell. Martin. The basement room. Coneeny. Thwaites.

All the dreams, of Martin—

No exit.

Lived rough. Begged and borrowed and stole, half-starved. But made it back to Cheshire, to Drakemire. Love and hate—their pull's obsessive force makes them almost identical. Found out what I needed to know.

Thwaites is up to bat, waiting. Coneeny is walking away. The devil's home on leave.

Are you going to do this? I know it's only me asking this, but it still sounds like Martin Berry.

"Yes," I say. "Fuck it."

I take the Browning automatic, ex-army issue, from my coat pocket, and pull back the slide. Take off the safety. Pocket it again. Inspect the whisky bottle. Only a couple of mouthfuls left.

Fuck it.

I drain the bottle, throw it aside. Step out of the trees and walk towards the cricket pitch, the Old Boys XI versus the Upper Sixth.

Coneeny sees me. *Scruffy oik, looks like a tramp, storming purposefully on. Probably on drugs.* I doubt he recognises me. He moves to intercept.

"What do—"

He gets no farther. I take out the Browning and point it in his face.

Army officer or not, he goes white. Well, you don't expect it here. Northern Ireland or the Balkans or Iraq, maybe, but not here, off duty, at your old school. Not here, to die like this.

His mouth opens. I think of Martin and me and shove the Browning in there and pull the trigger.

The shot changes everything. We are—I am—noticed. Hazed blood haloes out from Coneeny's head as he pitches backwards. Wet and copper-tasting, it kisses my face. There are screams. I walk towards the pitch.

Some scatter. Some are rooted. One of the latter is Thwaites, who stands frozen by the stumps, mouth agape. A wet stain spreads down his trouser leg. He turns to run.

I shoot him in the back three times. He falls flat. I walk to him. I fire one in the air to scatter more people. I stand over Thwaites.

"Danny Denholm," I say. He can't move—a bullet must have hit his spine—but his head is turned to the side, one eye visible. It weaves around, focuses on me. "Remember me?" I ask. "Or Martin Berry? I'm sure you remember Martin Berry."

I screw the barrel of the Browning into his temple. His eye screws shut. A high, whining scream escapes his mouth.

I pull the trigger.

As I straighten up, wiping blood off my face, one of the Upper Sixth Formers becomes a hero. Snatching up a fallen cricket bat, he leaps in close and cracks me soundly in the head with it.

Lights out

Lights out

Lights out.

DR. PETRIE IS AT HIS DESK, BUT FOR ONCE AND INDEED NOW FOR ALL TIME the good doctor has nothing to say.

He lolls back in his chair, mouth agape, shocked that death should spoil his careful plans for—well, everything. Not to mention his expensive shirt. A long cut runs down him sternum to groin, opening him up. Blood drips from the chair onto the floor. Flies buzz, even with the curtains drawn and windows shut.

Denholm hears none of this. He has the *D* drawer of the filing cabinet open, pulling patient records out, letting them drop.

Have a little faith, Petrie said. *It's not as if I haven't done this before.*

DENHOLM, DANIEL.

Denholm goes still. At last he takes out the file and opens it.

A ROOM IN THE INFIRMARY AT THE PINES. STRAPPED INTO A CHAIR. PETRIE. Nervous. Face beaded with sweat. Shining a penlight.

"Watch the light, Daniel. Just follow it with your eyes."

The penlight moving back and forth, back and forth.

"You're feeling sleepy, Daniel."

Side to side. Side to side.

"By the count of three you will be asleep, but you will still be able to hear me. One . . ."

Coneeny and Thwaites standing behind the doctor, bleeding from their wounds.

"Two . . ."

Thwaites and Coneeny, gone.

"Three."

Unable to move, staring straight ahead. Petrie looking off to the side. "He's under."

Grimshaw coming into view. Suited, hair short. "Carry on."

Petrie licking his lips.

"You know what you need to do, Doctor. You've been told."

"Yes, yes. Just nervous. With what he did . . ."

"He'll be perfectly safe. A model employee. Won't you, Daniel? Now carry on."

Petrie licking his lips. "Daniel? Nod if you can hear me."

Nodding as commanded, unable to do otherwise.

"Daniel, you've been remembering things that didn't happen. You need to forget about them, for your own good. And you need to remember other things. The things that really *did* happen. Firstly . . ."

Grimshaw, hands folded, smiling. Lips moving in a whisper: "Delapsus resurgam."

"'This sore combat lasted for above half a day, even till *Christian* was almost quite spent; for you must know that *Christian*, by reason of his wounds, must needs grow weaker and weaker. . . .'"

I put my file back in the cabinet. Will I get into trouble? I close the drawer and leave the headmaster's office.

"'Then *Apollyon*, espying his opportunity, began to gather up close to *Christian*, and wrestling with him, gave him a dreadful fall; and with that *Christian*'s sword flew out of his hand. . . .'"

It's coming from the Assembly Hall. I go in.

Thwaites is standing at the headmaster's lectern, reading.

"'Then said *Apollyon*, I am sure of thee now. And with that he had almost pressed him to death, so that *Christian* began to despair of life; . . .'"

Above him is a huge representation of the school crest. Below that, the school motto:

delapsus resurgam.

"'. . . but as God would have it, while *Apollyon* was fetching of his last blow, thereby to make a full end of this good man, *Christian* nimbly stretched out his hand for his sword, and caught it, saying, *Rejoice not against me, O mine enemy; when I fall I shall arise.*'"

Thwaites snaps the book shut and smiles at me. "*Delapsus resurgam*: when I fall, I shall rise again."

Striding towards Grimshaw. Grimshaw sat at one of the tables on the lawn at the Pines, reading. Grimshaw looking up, seeing. Rising, smiling. Says: "In my end is my beginning."

Lacuna.

Eyeless, no lips, no throat: Grimshaw lying in the blood-rusted grass. The head turning. Bloody lips moving:

"*Delapsus resurgam.*"

Denholm goes to the infirmary.

Grimshaw is laid out on a table there. Denholm pulls back the sheet. It's as he was told. No eyes. No lips either.

"Was this part of the plan for you, too?" Denholm asks. "Bastard."

He empties the last of the petrol into the torn, gaping face and throws the can aside.

Noakes is lying in the hallway outside Grimshaw's room. He's been struck with an axe, repeatedly. *Did I do that?* I wonder detachedly. *Where did I get the axe from?* Then I shrug. It doesn't matter, really. Nothing matters anymore.

I push open the door of Grimshaw's room and sit on the bed. In the distance, the roaring of the flames grows louder.

The door opens again but I don't look round.

"It's nearly over," says Coneeny.

I ignore him and look at the walls. Grimshaw stuck press clippings on it.

BLOODBATH AT SCHOOL CRICKET MATCH, 3 DEAD: HERO SCHOOLBOY PREVENTS WORSE TRAGEDY.

EX-PUPIL TELLS OF SEXUAL ABUSE. A blurred, bad photo of me.

"CRICKET KILLER" COMMITTED. I look down, stop reading when I see *Dr. Stephen Petrie.*

I look at the next two clippings: THE DEATH OF DRAKEMIRE: SCANDAL-HIT SCHOOL TO CLOSE.

FIRE AT HORROR SCHOOL.

I feel, hear, the turning of cogs, the grinding of mechanisms, circuits almost completed. The flames have reached the corridor outside. It's starting to get hot in here. "How have I helped you?"

"See for yourself."

I turn. Coneeny is gone.

I look back at the wall, and so are the clippings. But two new ones are there:

MYSTERY CARE HOME FIRE: DOZENS FEARED DEAD.

I stop when I see *The Pines.*

SCHOOL CELEBRATES CENTENARY.

I stop when I see *Drakemire*.

The roaring of the flames is deafening. The room smells of smoke. I open the curtains. Below, in the playground, the boys stand, flayed faces turned towards the passing train.

"Danny?"

I turn. Martin stands naked in the doorway.

"Come with me. Quickly."

I hesitate.

"Danny."

Smoke is creeping up through the floorboards. Martin takes my hand and leads me through the door.

The corridors of Drakemire are dark and endless, but cool after the heat of the room. Martin draws me out into the courtyard, leads me to the basement.

We slip past the thundering boiler. I assume we're going to the basement room, but the corridor goes on, becomes a tunnel of sorts.

As we go, I see more tunnels, half-filled with discarded tailor's dummies, just like the basement room had. Some of the dummies are naked and sexless, others wholly or partially clothed. Some are partly dismantled—missing an arm, broken in half at the waist. Wherever there's such a break, the limb or torso ends in a surface of smooth, pinkish plastic, from which a thick metal rod, threaded like a screw, protrudes. One of the dummies has Mr. Spanton's face. Their eyes move; I can hear the clicking of the lids, like the rustling of undergrowth in the panic flight of small creatures, as I pass.

"Jesus!"

I almost fall over it. It creeps on the stumps where its hands and knees should be. No hair; no face. The mouth and eyelids sewn up; nose and ears gone, the skin sutured. The featureless head angles towards me, seeing me somehow despite the lack of means.

"What is it?" I whisper.

Martin tugs my hand. "Come on."

The tunnel extends. Some kind of firelight illuminates it; I can't tell where from. The other tunnels are dark. Things move in them. I glimpse a couple. They used to be human. I think.

"Here."

We've reached a room. A stained floor. A table with straps. On a stand beside it, rusty scalpels.

Scuttling sounds.

"Come on."

The room is long. The walls are lined with shelves. Each labelled. A boy's name. They contain organs, limbs, parts of faces.

I see half a face in one jar. As I lean close, the eye opens. The lips move.

"Here." Martin points. An eyeball and some organs in a jar marked J. CONEENY. "Here." A skullcap of scalp and bone, fragments of pulsating brain: M. THWAITES. "Here." A face, Martin's face, in a jar: M. BERRY.

You don't want to look at him, but you can't stop yourself. His eye sockets are empty, but he sees you. Takes your arm. Points.

As you turn your head to look, you see Martin's eyes open in the jar and follow you.

In the jar beside Martin's, you see various things, but can't put a name to them, because all you really see is the label: D. DENHOLM.

You turn, but you are alone. Martin is gone. You stare at the jar. You stumble away. Blundering between the shelves, looking for a way out. . . .

You find a side tunnel.

Whimpering with relief, you stagger down it.

You stop and look back. Behind you is a dead end.

You turn away. Move down the tunnel. Vision is flawed; what's wrong? You try to whisper reassurance to yourself but something is wrong with your speech.

Round the corner and something faces you. It is naked. There are holes in its body where organs have been taken out. It has no lips. Below its top row of teeth is only a hole tapering into the throat and neck, rimmed with gristle or bone, edged with teeth. One eye remains; the other is gone, the socket fused, skin stitched crudely shut. The nose is a hole. Most of the skin is gone from the other side of the face; the surviving eye stands immobile and lidless.

You look at it a long time; at last you understand. But you do not believe, until you reach out and touch the mirror's grimy glass.

The mirror breaks and falls, becomes dust and less than dust. The firelight is going. With a groan of turning cogs, the tunnel roof lowers. You drop to all fours, and as the light dies, you run. And all you hear is the scuttling of those like you, and from far above, the endless rumbling of a train.

LEFT BEHIND

There was nothing else to do in the park that evening, so I was tossing coins at a chalk circle with Johnny when it began.

He looked up, over my shoulder, and his eyes widened. "Shit," he said. "Jez?"

I turned and followed his gaze. A man was walking. Towards us. He was wearing a suit.

You didn't see many like that, not in the park. Usually he wouldn't get ten steps inside the gate before one of the kids lurking in the undergrowth brought him down for his fat wallet, the wadded cash, the plastic cards inside like rare thin shells. That he'd got this far told me a lot. And he was walking fast, but not nervously, looking straight ahead. Straight at us. Straight at me.

I felt Johnny move away from me, farther down the bench. The man came up to us and halted, looking down. His eyes were like glass, his face unmoving. A mask.

"You Jez?" he asked.

I swallowed.

He didn't say anything, just looked at me.

He wouldn't have asked, I decided, if he hadn't already known. "Yeah," I said.

He nodded, once. "This way."

Never crossed my mind to argue with him. I got up, glanced back at Johnny. "See you." He nodded, not answering aloud. The man was already walking away, not looking back. He knew I'd follow. And I did. I didn't look back either.

That was the last I ever saw of Johnny.

THERE WAS A CAR OUTSIDE THE GATES; THE MAN BEHIND THE WHEEL MIGHT have been the first guy's twin except for the moustache. The first man got into the passenger seat. I got in the back. We drove.

The car was new, and flash. I could smell the fresh leather of the upholstery. Through the tinted windows I saw Blackfield, the grim terraced streets where every fifth window was boarded up and the looming tower blocks like glass-speckled gravestones, give way first to the motorway, then to the leafy suburbs, and then to the even leafier ones. My palms sweated; I clenched my hands into fists.

The car gritted its way up a gravel drive and into the forecourt of a big mock-Tudor house. The man from the park got out, held the door open for me, and walked me to the front door. He rang the bell once. An old man in a suit and cummerbund opened the door, smiled, then held it for us as we filed through.

IT WAS A STUDY. I'D SEEN THEM IN FILMS BUT NEVER WITH MY OWN EYES close to. A study. A big desk of polished wood. Shelves of books. A stereo in the corner. Even French windows and a fricking balcony.

I shifted from foot to foot, feeling the give of the thick pile carpet. My hands hung loose at my sides. They felt awkward. I clasped them behind my back. They still felt awkward. I let them hang loose again and decided to get used to feeling awkward.

The door opened. He came in. Walked to the desk and sat down at it. Didn't look at me until he'd poured himself a drink from the decanter and lit a fat cigar. Then he motioned me to sit down.

"You know who I am," he said at last. "Don't you?"

I nodded.

"And I obviously know who you are. That's why we're here. So we'll skip the introductions and take them as read. Okay?"

He wasn't asking.

"Yes, Mr. Sewell."

"Good," he said, looking down. "And I think you know what this is about."

I licked dry lips. "Think so."

"Good again. But let me spell it out." The cigar smoked in his hand; the rich scent filled the room. "I've had my eye on you. And I've been impressed by what I've seen."

There was a clock on the wall, somewhere in the room, the old-fashioned kind that ticked. It ticked and ticked away in the silence.

"Impressed enough to give you a chance to go further."

I felt weak; a bastard child of fear and excitement owned my body and made it limp, tremoring to the thud of my heart.

"I've got a job for you, Jez. Call it an initiation. Call it a final exam. Call it whatever you want, only don't fuck it up. Okay?"

Once again, he wasn't asking. "Yes, Mr. Sewell."

"Good." There were some papers on his desk; he pulled some of them over and started looking at them. "We'll talk some more when you get back."

If you haven't fucked it up. He didn't need to say that. It was there between us.

He didn't look up again either. "You can go now."

BEFORE I WENT ANYWHERE ELSE, I HAD TO GO TO THE TOILET. AFTERWARDS I splashed cold water on my face and looked in the mirror. I saw spiky orange hair and a thin pale frightened face spattered with teenage pockmarks and trickling water.

Outside, on the landing, the man from the park was waiting. "Let's go," he said.

HE DROVE ME BACK TO BLACKFIELD AND DROPPED ME OUTSIDE THE TRAIN station, then handed me some change. "Get off in the city centre at Greenhills," he told me. "There's a pub called The Judas Frost. Buy a drink. A glass of red wine. Sit by the window, or as near as you can. And then wait."

"What for?"

He looked at me coldly. Those eyes, like glass. "Just wait."

IT WAS A LONG WAIT ON THE PLATFORM. WEEDS POKED OUT THROUGH THE concrete floor, mired in a web of cracks. There was a wind and it keened through the gaps in the long-abandoned station building. My hands were still clammy with sweat; I put my ticket in my jacket pocket, afraid the sweat would spoil it somehow.

The train pulled in. I boarded it. There was hardly anybody aboard. I sat by one of the windows. It was grimy and a crack ran across it. I watched the scenery go by, what there was of it. A vacant lot. An abandoned factory. A stretch of disused canal, along which floated something that looked very like a body.

I wished Johnny and the boys could see me now. It was the only way out of Blackfield for the likes of us. For the likes of almost anyone. Get work for Sewell, or someone like him. Prove yourself to them and there was no more sleeping in poky bedrooms at your mum's house, watching rain trickle through the crack in the ceiling and huddling under old tattered blankets for their scant protection against the knifelike winds. No more living in cheap filthy bedsits. It was all silk sheets and roses and champagne from here on in. As long as you didn't fuck up.

Across the aisle from me, a seat creaked. My palms wouldn't stop sweating. It was a dangerous business, riding the train into the city centre. No one went there unless they had to. Or unless they were hoping to try it on with one of the passengers.

I looked across at the man opposite me. He was about mid-twenties. Thin. Almost everybody's thin round here, unless they work for someone like Sewell. He was staring at me with cold insolence.

"Fuck're you lookin' at, dickhead?" I asked him, staring right back.

Swish. Click. The flick-knife in his hand shot out bright steel. He stared at me. I stared right back. You can't show fear. It's like blood in the water for a shark. I had no knife. I had no protection. I wasn't Sewell's till I'd done what he wanted. Until then I was still a nobody. Waiting to be somebody.

The train rattled bumpily over the tracks. Shit suspension. I kept staring at him, like I had a knife, too, and knew I was better at it than him. Or a gun.

Bumpity, bumpity, bump.

He got up. I kept my face blank, kept staring.

Click. He folded up the knife and walked off down the aisle without looking back. When I was sure he was gone I looked out of the window again.

Nobody goes into the city centre anymore. There's nothing there. Or next to nothing. Nothing straight anyway. There's only people who have business there, and people with nowhere else to go. It's a toss-up, which is more dangerous. The city centre's dead. The city died a long time ago, but the bits around it keep on going. Sort of.

It was almost dark and all clouded up above when I got off at Greenhills and took the steps down to street level. I don't know why they called it "Greenhills." There's fuck-all green there.

Getting dark and none of the lights on. I walked down a street. Broken glass crunching underfoot. Empty buildings that no one had even bothered to board up the windows on. They looked like skulls. Boards on windows are like pennies on dead men's eyes.

I passed a doorway and a second later there was an arm round my throat. From the corner of my eye I saw something sharp rising. I swung an elbow, kicked back with my heel till it hit shin and drove it down, scraping bone. A scream of pain. I turned and kicked high, smashing jaw. My attacker went down; a bundle of rags that looked something like a man and stank of old piss. His weapon was an old bottle, broken jagged; it smashed on the floor. I kicked him in the face and stomach as he tried to get up, then jumped on him, stomping his ribs with both feet. Bone cracked. He rolled about whimpering.

I stepped in the middle of the road, fists balled, turning this way and that. Shadows moved and shifted, retreating into the caverns behind the lightless windows or the hollows of abandoned doors. When nothing else moved, I turned and started walking again.

THE JUDAS FROST IS ALMOST THE ONLY PUB IN THE CITY CENTRE. THERE'S a couple of others, but I don't know their names. Maybe they haven't got any.

I used to wonder how it got its name, but there's no sign outside to give a clue, so I doubt the mystery'll ever be solved.

There's an old pinball machine, even a jukebox. My granddad used to tell me all pubs were like that once. The carpet's threadbare and the seats are leatherette, gashed and unpicked in places to let hunks of kapok stuffing out.

That's how it was when I went there, anyway. I've never been back since, so it could've changed, but I doubt it.

The barman was greasy and half-bald, with a smell of sweat and most of his teeth missing even though he was years short of forty. Leaning on the counter with his elbows, he bared the ones he had in a mossy-yellow grin. "All right, my mate. What'll it be?"

"Red wine."

Everyone else in the bar was hunched over a pint at some table. A few heads turned. The barman took his elbows off the bar and stood up straight as though a man ordering red wine was the sign of a killer disease he might catch. "Right then, my mate," he said, grinning sickly, and poured wine into a dirty glass. "There you go."

He put it down quickly. I put the money on the bar. He picked it up and tilled it. There was a table by the window. I went to it and sat down.

There was an old clock on the wall. Like the one in Sewell's study, but with cracked, chipped glass and a generally fucked look. But, like Sewell's, it ticked and it ticked and it ticked.

HOURS PASSED. ONE. THEN TWO. PEOPLE STARED AT ME; I KNEW IT EVEN though I wasn't looking at them but out of the window at the gathering night outside. The first spots of rain began to peck and tick against the glass.

"You Jez?"

I turned and looked. He was old, with an axelike face and stringy white hair. He wore an old duffel coat and stank.

"Yeah," I said.

He sat across from me. "Name's Reeve."

"Good for you."

"Don't get smart-arsed. Go to the toilet. Second cubicle on the right. There's a package in the cistern. It's for you. Go to Stanhope Road. There's an alley leading into a cobbled square. Wait in one of the doorways near the alley. A car'll come. Red BMW. Guy'll get out and go through the alley. Follow him into the square."

"Then what?"

Reeve grinned evilly. His teeth were crooked, stuck in his mouth all anyhow. "You'll know when you see the package." He looked at the wine and licked his thin lips; they were cracked and scabby. "You drinking that?"

I shrugged. "Be my guest."

Reeve picked up the glass and gulped it greedily down, Adam's apple bobbing in his wattled throat. "Ta, mate," he said. "See ya round." And then he was gone.

I went into the toilet.

THE PACKAGE WAS WRAPPED IN PLASTIC, AND UNDER THAT IN AN OILY RAG. I unravelled it. Inside was a dull-grey revolver and six bullets.

I pushed out the cylinder and thumbed the slugs in one by one. *Slugs*. It seemed the right word. They were stubby, thick and fat. When the gun was loaded I clicked the cylinder into place, shoved the gun into one of the deep pockets of my jacket and walked out again.

THE STORM WAS A THICK, SEETHING DOWNPOUR BY THE TIME I REACHED Stanhope Road, falling so hard and fast that a thin mizzling fog of shattered rain hovered six inches above the ground.

The doorways of the abandoned offices were recessed deep into the wall, but none of the street people had so far claimed them. I stood in one and waited. I wanted a smoke, but didn't dare. Not yet. There couldn't be any warnings. No second chances. So I stood and waited cold and alone in the rain.

The hours passed. The chill damp seeped through my clothes, through skin and bones till it was soul-deep.

At last I heard an engine and saw the headlights round the corner, the beams of light cones of trapped rain. I pressed myself back into the doorway till I could see nothing but the lights. Then they cut out and the engine stopped; I heard a car door open and slam. Footsteps. The alley. Going.

I stepped out of the doorway and peeped round the edge. He was still walking. He wore a raincoat and a brimmed hat. I went down the alley after him.

He was halfway across the cobbled square when he stopped and turned. Flat, blind-eyed buildings loomed on every side, staring mutely down with the blank dead gaze of skulls. The rain fell and drummed on the ground. We looked at each other and the only sound was its spatter and hiss. I couldn't see his face properly beneath his hat-brim.

Then his hand came out from under his coat. Metal gleamed. A gun. I ducked, swinging mine up, and we both fired. We both missed.

I fired again and hit him in the chest. He staggered back. My third shot hit him in the stomach and he doubled over from the pain. When he tried to straighten up, I fired a fourth time and hit him under the collarbone. He crashed to the cobbles and screamed, body bent like a bow, bent and twisted all out of shape. Then he rolled towards me onto his side and tried to point his gun. I stood up straight, aimed down with both hands, and shot him one more time, through the chest, almost right on top of the first wound.

His body snapped out arrow-straight from the impact, and shuddered violently. The pistol slipped out of his grip and glittered on the cobbles like a fat drop of rain. Then he rolled onto his back and his hat came off. Wind blew rain into my face and bowled the hat across the square.

I crossed over to him. One bullet left. Make sure. I crouched down, grabbed his head, and turned his face towards me.

I saw spiky orange hair and a thin pale frightened face spattered with teenage pockmarks and trickling water.

Then I shoved the gun in his mouth and pulled the trigger for the last time.

The rain hissed and spat and fell on the square. I stood up and looked down at . . . him. And then I ran.

Outside the alley mouth, I slowed to a walk again. I threw the gun into the river, from a bridge I crossed on my way back to Greenhills.

THE CAR WAS WAITING FOR ME AT THE BLACKFIELD STATION. THE MAN from the park was smiling as I came up, even patted my shoulder. "Congrats. You passed."

I looked at him, and knew my eyes would look like glass. And my face, it wouldn't move. I had all I wanted now.

"This way," said the man from the park.

This time he took the back seat, and I was the passenger. I leant back and stared up at the raining night sky as they drove us, me, away from the city centre, and the Blackfield, and all else, good and bad, that I'd left behind.

HUSHABYE

arch started late that year, as if waiting for a cue it had missed. The conversion back to BST was scheduled for late in the month; the days stayed short, the nights dark, long and cold. When snow fell it lay for days in a brittle crust, and every other morning all stone was patterned with frost.

I was looking unsuccessfully for paying work that didn't drive me crazy after a fortnight, and still living out of cardboard boxes in my friend Alan's spare room. Although he'd said I could stay as long as I needed when I moved in, it'd been six months now and his patience had started to fray, all our little habits scraping at one another's nerves.

So I took to going for long walks around the area. I like walking, even in the cold night on treacherous pavements.

I went down Bolton Road to the roundabout where it met Langworthy Road, where I'd lived for a few weeks the previous year and was still trying to forget about. Unsuccessfully, as a friend of mine called Terry Browning was living there now, drinking himself slowly to death. I knew I wasn't responsible for that, but I still felt it.

I walked down Langworthy till I was opposite the abandoned shell of the Mecca bingo hall, and looked left; I was on the corner of Brindleheath Road, which ran under a bridge, past the edge of the industrial estate and a couple of vacant lots and up onto the A6 next to Pendleton Church and near a Chinese takeaway. I went down it to get some chow mein before heading back home.

As I came out from under the bridge, I heard a child call out, "No."

That was followed by a noise somewhere between a gasp and a cry, then silence. My skin prickled; I ran up the road.

I saw them vanishing into the bushes at the edge of one of the vacant lots: a small girl, tiny in a red coat, and a figure that looked like a shadow walking at first, till I realised it was dressed in black, only the white of its face visible. Then they were gone into the dark. They hadn't seen me.

I pelted up the road and crashed through the bushes, shouting. They were white in the gloom, or at least the girl's body and the man's face were. Something silver, brighter than breath, glimmering like motes of powdered glass, was pouring from the girl's opened mouth and into his. The man looked up. His face was long, pale; a thin blade of nose, one thick eyebrow a line across the top. The eyes looked black, too.

I kicked out at him, but he was already rolling away. He scrambled up and ran, vanishing into the shadows. I stood there, gasping for air; I couldn't see him and on the uneven ground all I'd do was break an ankle. And there was the girl to think about.

He'd worked fast; she lay with her clothes scattered about her, staring up at the night stars. For a moment I thought she was dead, but then I saw her breathe. I took off my jacket and covered her; she flinched from my touch as if stung, whimpering like a hurt animal and curling up on her side. I couldn't tell if it was the cold or the hate that made my fingers so clumsy as I dug out my mobile and dialled 1-1-2.

THE FIRST ASSAULT ON A LOCAL CHILD HAD HAPPENED IN HIGHER Broughton just before Christmas, in Albert Park. A six-year-old boy almost dead with hypothermia, his torn clothes scattered around him. There'd been more over the following months, the same pattern, police offering nothing but pleas for vigilance and information, the victims unwilling or unable to provide any leads.

They took the girl to Hope Hospital and me down to the police station on the Crescent. I was interviewed for two hours by a pair of detectives. Poole, the DS, was the hardest to handle, spending the first hour treating me as a suspect. In the end, the DC, Hardiman, put a hand on his arm and led him outside. They left me with a paused tape and a stony-faced policewoman; I heard raised voices through the breeze-block wall.

Hardiman took it from there. He was young, earnest and sympathetic. Poole stayed silent, looking at the scarred desktop, light gleaming on his bald crown. He had a drinker's lined, ruddy face. Hardiman's was smooth and pale as fibreglass. I told him everything I'd seen, except whatever it was I'd seen passing from the girl's mouth to her attacker's. I didn't want dismissing as a nutter.

"You'll have to excuse DS Poole," Hardiman said later, as we watched the identikit picture take shape. "He's got a kid of his own that age. Takes it personally."

"It's okay," I told him, meaning it. Normally I'm pretty scathing about heavy-handed policing, but having seen what had been done to the girl I'd've quite happily held Poole's coat for him while he threw the offender down the stairs several times. As long as it was the right man.

"It's not," said Hardiman. "My missus wants one, but"—he gestured at the picture to indicate all it represented—"you shouldn't have to think of this when you're thinking of a family."

"I know."

"You're sure this is him?"

I looked at the finished picture and nodded slowly. Hardiman rubbed his eyes and pushed his fingers through his sandy hair. "Okay," he said. "Come on. I'll drive you home. And I want to thank you. This is the first clue we've had of any kind." He must've been tired, to let that one slip out.

They had my details, of course, but I didn't hear any more from them for over a fortnight. In that time, Terry Browning died.

He'd choked on his own puke, sat in his armchair by the window with an empty bottle of Lone Piper beside him on the floor. The funeral was at St. John's Church, in the Height, about a week later.

He'd been a priest, but had left the church with a deep loss of faith the previous year; maybe they thought it was catching, as the only dog collar in sight was the one who read the service, which didn't mean anything to me or Terry's brother, the only other mourner, and probably wouldn't've to Terry any longer. I wasn't even sure if it meant much to the priest, but it was hard to tell. The bitter wind tore his graveside oration to shreds, like grey confetti.

Rob Browning and I went for a pint down at the Crescent afterwards, more to chase out the chill than anything else. We hardly said a dozen words to each other. He was smart and suited and had a southern accent; I knew he and Terry hadn't been close. He stayed for one drink and then left; I ordered a double Jameson's and raised the glass to the memory of a friend whose death I still felt a certain guilt for.

"Mind if I join you?"

I looked up to see DC Hardiman standing over me with a Britvic orange in his hand.

"How'd you know I was here?"

"Didn't make CID on my good looks."

I laughed. "Didn't think so."

He flipped me the bird and sat. "Sorry about your mate."

"Thanks. Looks like we're the only ones who are."

We sat in silence; I waited for him to probe about Terry but he didn't. In the end it was me who started fishing. "How's the investigation going?"

He shook his head.

"Nothing?"

"Oh no. Something. But . . . there are complications."

"How d'you mean?"

He didn't answer at first. "I looked you up on HOLMES. Quite the colourful character."

"Is that a compliment?"

"You say what you think and kick up a stink when you reckon you have to."

"Fair assessment," I had to admit.

"And you don't believe in keeping your trap shut or leaving things alone when not doing so would piss off certain people."

"People in high places, sort of thing?"

He nodded.

"Guilty, I suppose." I took a swallow of whisky. "Are you trying to tell me something?"

He studied his glass, turning it this way and that like a faceted gem. "The evidence I've got . . . it's taking me somewhere where shutting my trap and leaving things alone is pretty much what the doctor ordered."

Everything seemed to go very still. "I'm feeling on my own on this one in a big way," he said, almost to himself, then looked up. "Even Poole's not sure, and I thought he wanted that bastard more than anyone."

"Close to his pension."

"Yeah. I just thought . . . you'd understand where I'm at right now."

"I do." I studied my own drink for a minute, then looked up. "What are you going to do?"

Hardiman put his glass down on the table. "The little girl you found. Ellie Chatham, her name is. I visited her yesterday. To see if she remembered anything, or . . . I don't know. She's like an old woman. Five years old and she's like an old woman. Shuffles from place to place and just sits there. Breathing, staring. Waiting. I don't know what for. Death, maybe. Like something's just gone out of her."

I thought of the silver glittering I'd seen passing from her mouth to the attacker's. "Yeah."

"And the psychiatrist reports on the others . . . Christ, I don't think one of those kids'll ever be the same again. It's different for all of them, but . . . night terrors, rages . . . There's one, the boy they found in Albert Park, he flies into a rage every time he sees anybody black or Asian. Don't know why. There's no indication anyone non-white was involved. The opposite is how it looks, thanks to you. It's like he's full of hate and rage, but it's not going where it should, it's going at someone else, a scapegoat. Fuck knows why."

"I'll lend you one of my books on capitalism sometime," I said. "Might give you a few pointers."

He snorted a laugh. "That'll raise a few eyebrows in the canteen. All these kids, Paul, and he's taken something from them they'll never get back, that'll fuck them up forever. And my wife, she still wants us to try for a kid. I just . . . just want to know any child of mine is gonna be as safe as I can make it, from something like this. But I'm supposed to keep my trap shut and look the other way. Well, fuck that." He lifted his glass. "Here's to colourful characters."

I clinked my glass against it. "Amen."

TWENTY-FOUR HOURS AFTER HE SPOKE TO ME, DETECTIVE CONSTABLE Alec Hardiman's Ford Mondeo went off the motorway between Manchester and Bradford, on Saddleworth Moor. It was two in the morning, and no one ever knew what he'd been doing out there. His neck was broken in the crash. He left behind a wife, Sheila, but no children, actual or in the womb.

I would've gone to the funeral, but had a strong sense I wouldn't be welcome if I did. I watched it from a distance, saw a thin pale woman in black that I assumed to be Sheila Hardiman, leaning on two other women—mother and sister, at a guess. Other mourners included a grey-faced DS Poole and a lone man in his sixties, bald on top with a salt-and-pepper goatee.

It was this last mourner who turned up on my doorstep the following evening, with a brown paper parcel under his arm. My first thought on seeing him was, *Jesus, people still wear tweed?*

"Mr. Paul Hearn?" he asked.

"Yes."

"Don Hardiman." He offered his hand. "Alec's father."

"Please come in."

THE PARCEL SAT ON THE TABLE, BETWEEN US AND OUR COFFEE CUPS. DON Hardiman's voice was quiet and modulated, very clear; he was a university lecturer. There was a black armband round one sleeve of his jacket.

"Alec came to me the day before he died, and put the package into my keeping, along with your name and address and a request to bring it here. We weren't particularly close, and I wasn't the first person anyone would think of coming to for any little . . . legacies of this kind. Which is why I expect Alec chose me."

My hand kept twitching towards the package, but I kept stopping it.

"My son wasn't a paranoid man, Mr. Hearn—"

"Paul."

He inclined his head. "But he was definitely afraid of something and believed he could no longer trust his colleagues. I believe I have some idea of what's in there, and I'd presume you do as well."

I nodded. "I think so."

"I suspect as well that I wasn't intended to know anything about this. Alec did love me, in his way, and would want to protect me. But I loved him in my way, too. He was my son, and now he's dead. I'd like to help."

"Don—"

"Please."

"All right." I nodded. "Let's see what we've got."

TIMOTHY WAS THE SON OF ARTHUR WADHAM, A HIGHLY SUCCESSFUL BUSI-nessman known for his generous donations to New Labour's party funds. He'd inherited his father's charm and ruthlessness, by all accounts, but neither his looks nor his business acumen. Nearly thirty, he'd launched about half a dozen business ventures since returning from the all-expenses-paid-by-Daddy backpacking tour following his graduation from Cambridge.

All expenses paid by Daddy, in fact, seemed to be pretty much a—even *the*—recurrent theme in Timothy Wadham's life. All half a dozen business ventures had ended in financial disaster, but Wadham senior was always on hand with a blank cheque for the next one. Hard-nosed and void of sentiment he might be, but he clearly—like most parents—had a blind spot where his offspring was concerned. Under any other circumstances, a man who could cock up running a lap-dancing club in Romford would have been filed in the do-not-touch-this-fuckwit-with-a-bargepole category and left there.

Just another rich kid bombing happily through life secure in the knowledge that pater would always be there to bail him out. What money didn't solve directly, the connections it bought most assuredly would.

I picked up the photograph of Timothy Wadham; the long face and thin sharp nose, the black eyes and the unbroken line of the eyebrow. I showed it to Don Hardiman. Wadham's address was written on the back.

"Still want to help?" I asked after he'd finished reading. He looked up with a wintry smile.

"I'm not my son's father for nothing," he said. "What do you need?"

"WHAT IN THE BLOODY HELL DO YOU THINK YOU'RE DOING, PAUL?"

When my reflection didn't reply I opened the sock drawer and rummaged around in the back. I found what I was looking for and unwrapped the old t-shirt it was folded in.

I'd taken the Browning automatic off the body of a man called Frankie Hagen in Ordsall the month before. I hadn't killed him, any more than I'd had any idea what I thought I wanted a gun for. I began to wonder if I now knew.

I unloaded the pistol—there were eight rounds left in the magazine—and looked at myself in the bedroom mirror. I was wearing black, including a wool skully and Thinsulate gloves. I dry-fired the pistol with the gloves on. They didn't get in the way of the trigger pull; that was all I needed to know.

I took a few more deep breaths, looking at myself in the mirror, and asked myself a new question. Not, *What are you doing?* but, *Why are you doing it?*

For Ellie Chatham, old woman of five, and all the others naked and shivering in the cold, all leeched of parts of themselves whose absence they would never overcome. For Terry Browning, who had seen reality and refused to turn away even knowing it would destroy him, and for Alec Hardiman who had done the same. In some way perhaps it would atone for Terry, who could and should have received more from me, even if it had only been sitting up with him for a few nights. Could that have helped? It was too late to ask now.

And perhaps most of all it was for me, in my thirty-something dread of failure and the dark, so that at the withered arse-end of my life I could look back and say *this at least. Even if no one knows but me, I achieved this. Even if I started nothing, at least I ended something that needed ending; this, at least.*

Whether they were good enough or not, they were the only reasons I had, and so they'd have to do.

I pulled the curtains back and looked out of the window. Don Hardiman's Vauxhall Astra was parked outside. Fifteen minutes later he pulled up in a Volkswagen Polo. That one was for me. I reloaded the Browning and went out to meet him.

"Do you think Wadham did it?" he asked.

"Did what?"

"Alec."

I shrugged. "I suppose he could've. But more than likely it was someone looking out for him. Working for his dad, or one of his dad's connections. Don't suppose we'll ever know, will we?"

"No." He shook his head. "And it doesn't really matter, does it? The effect's the same."

"Yeah."

"Good luck, Paul." We shook hands.

"You too."

Don picked Wadham up first, coming out of his gravel drive in Sale in a BMW. We stayed in touch with mobiles, and I followed at a distance, picking up when I had to. We alternated pursuit like that for nearly an hour, until he reached Lower Broughton.

"He's parked up," said Don. "Shit, Paul, he's getting out of the car. Heading up Broughton Road, on foot. What now?"

"Leave it with me," I said. I was surprised how calm I felt.

Wadham was heading up from the Irwell Valley campus. Broughton Road led ultimately to the Broad Street roundabout, a stone's throw from the vacant lots off Brindleheath Road. The arrogance of the bastard; so close to where he'd attacked Ellie Chatham. Of course, there were a lot of roads branching off along the way. I pulled in near the roundabout where Broughton crossed Seaford Road. He walked past, head down; I ducked so he wouldn't see me, in case he remembered, too.

When he was gone, I got out of the Polo and followed at a distance, hands thrust into my pockets. He kept going up, over Lower Broughton Road, till he reached the low-rise blocks and estate terraces on the left hand side of the road. Then he vanished down one of the walkways and was lost in the shadows.

I hung back, waiting by a small birch sapling someone had optimistically planted on the green apron outside the terrace. It occurred to me that, dressed in black and loitering in the shadows as I was, I might easily be mistaken for my prey, and I had to smile bitterly at the thought. Should I follow him? In the dark, the walkways were a maze, and what if Wadham knew I was trailing him? Before I could make a move, he came back out again, leading a small boy by the hand.

The boy was maybe eight, wearing tracksuit bottoms, a t-shirt and a baseball cap, his hair almost shaved clean it was cut so close to the skull. The estate kids in Broughton are tough, they have to be, but the boy followed Wadham meekly as a lamb. Why he was out that late, or how Wadham charmed him so easily, I never knew.

Wadham and the boy crossed the road; they were heading for Broughton Park, a small zone of green surrounded by a multicoloured fence. Wadham climbed the gate; the boy waited patiently to be lifted over.

I ran across the road, scaled the gate, landed in a crouch. I couldn't see them. Then there was a whimpered cry from the child, and a sound of ripping cloth. I pulled the Browning from my belt, pulled back the slide and ran.

I floundered through the bushes; the boy lay on the open grass. He was naked except for his underpants; they came away in Wadham's hand with a final rip as I ran up. Wadham's lips were skinned back from his teeth; I couldn't tell if it was a smile or the snarl of a predator about to strike. His head turned as I reached him; our eyes met for the second time. Then I swung up the Browning and shot him in the face.

The bang was sudden and deafening; there was a flash and a brass cartridge spat out of the gun. Something warm and wet splashed my cheek. Wadham's face was black with it as he fell backwards, arms flailing, then jerked once and was still.

I turned to the boy; he was sitting up, hugging his knees. "Are you all right?" I asked. He nodded. Wadham hadn't had time to do whatever it was he'd done to Ellie Chatham and the rest.

I turned and Wadham's snarling face lunged up into mine, teeth bared. One eye was gone, the socket streaming blackness down a bone white cheek. He grabbed my throat; his hand was bitter cold. I shoved the Browning into his chest and fired twice, blowing darkness out of his back; he reeled away and fell to one knee, arms windmilling, then launched himself up and came at me again.

I aimed two-handed and shot him in the forehead, then again in the temple as he fell to his knees. He rolled onto his back and I stood over him; blood-covered, his glistening face was a blackness like the rest of him. There was a noise in his throat that was either a rattle or a laugh as he began to sit up.

I shot him in the face again and again, shell casings bucking clear of the gun, the sulphur smell of cordite in the crisp night air, and felt sprays of blood and bone hitting me. He reached out a hand to me as the gun emptied, the trigger clicking helplessly as I pulled it, then toppled back and lay still. But I could still hear him breathing, and after a while he began moving feebly. Then the breathing stopped and his limbs went slack.

I turned back to the boy. He began fumbling in the grass for his clothes. "Come on," I said, "let's get you home."

I STILL HAVE NIGHTMARES ABOUT TIMOTHY WADHAM'S ONE-EYED CORPSE slithering into my bedroom by night, smashed face grinning.

About a week into April, spring was finally underway. Crocuses and daffodils were in bloom. The sky was clean and blue and the air was getting warm. I opened the windows and cleaned the house; a late spring was better than none. Then the doorbell rang. When I answered it, it was DS Poole. "I think you know why I'm here," he said.

INSTEAD OF THE STATION, HE TOOK ME DOWN THE PUB; MULLIGAN'S IN town, to be precise. I've always been a sucker for Irish whiskey. Over a shot each of Black Bush, we talked.

"Worst part is," he said, "that Alec went to you, not me. He didn't trust me."

"He didn't know who he could trust," I said quietly. "It wasn't just you."

He glowered at me. "You think that helps? I was his partner. I wouldn't have let him down."

I wasn't sure which of us he was trying to convince, but I didn't press the point.

"I didn't see anything about Wadham in the papers," I said at last.

Poole grunted. "That's how it'll stay. The boy's mum called us in. No chance that one could just go away. His old man's not chasing up revenge—not through us anyway. The boy gave us a description of his rescuer. Or rather, me. No one else knows and no one else will. From that I put two and two together."

"And Wadham?"

"Up in smoke, Paul. Saw to it myself." He toyed with his drink, then looked up at me. "You know, when I saw how many times you'd shot him, I thought you must've hated him even more than I did. But when we burned the fucker, I understood why."

I waited, but I knew what was coming next.

"He was banging on his coffin lid," said Poole. "And then he was banging on the oven door. All the way through, till all he was was ash. And the ashes went in the river. Saw to that myself, an' all. With all the shit that's gone in the Irwell over the years, who'll notice a bit more?"

"They've just had it cleaned," I pointed out.

"Well, they'll just have to clean it all over again." We finished our whiskies; Poole looked towards the bar. "What's that bottle?"

I looked. "More whiskey. Midleton."

"Any good?"

"Supposed to be, but at a tenner a shot I wouldn't know."

Poole came back with two doubles. "To Alec," he said.

"Alec," I nodded, and touched my glass to his.

A SMALL COLD HAND

If you could go back. If you could go back and change one thing that happened, what would it be?

Not a question most of us like thinking about, is it? Most folk, you asked them, wouldn't know where to start. Apart from anything else, it's the kind of thing that unstitches everything for you, isn't it? All the might-have-beens and what-ifs. I don't think anyone's ever asked me that question: in fact, I know they haven't. I'd remember. But if they ever had, I know my answer. The one I'd've given then, and the one I'd give now. They'd still be the same; it never changes.

I'd go back to a rainy night in November when I was eighteen years old and behind the wheel of my first—my only—car, and I'd hit the brakes harder, or faster, or I'd swerve the wheel. Even if I'd smashed into the railings of the railway embankment, even if I'd gone straight through, electrocuted myself on the track or been smashed to buggery by an oncoming train, it'd be better than this.

On that rainy night in November, you see—I wasn't drunk, I should make that clear. Or stoned, or anything else. I'd had part of a spliff at a friend's house, but that was all, and it'd long worn off. I was sure of that. No way I'd've got behind the wheel otherwise. I wasn't like some, insisting I was safe to drive whatever that pink elephant in the corner was saying. I was safe as houses to drive. Or should've been. As safe as you can make an eighteen-year-old lad with his first car, anyway. Which really, isn't much.

It was past midnight on a weeknight, and it was in the school holidays. Streets were quiet as anything, silent and still. So I pushed the accelerator down.

It was a long road with no turn-offs. I didn't mean any harm, just—it was my first car. I wanted to hear the engine roar.

I looked down for a second, only a second, to watch the speedometer needle climbing. I was doing seventy miles an hour when I hit her.

I only looked down for a second. When I looked up, she was right in front of me.

I hit the brakes, but it was too late.

I will never, not as long as I live, forget that sound.

Or the white blur of her, flying across the bonnet to hit the windscreen, smashing it as white as her nightgown no longer was.

She was a little girl called Sarah, and she was six years old. She always will be, now.

SHE'S BURIED IN A LITTLE CEMETERY IN MY HOME TOWN. EVERY MONTH I go there and I lay a pot of flowers there. Fresh yellow orchids.

They're her favourites.

She told me so.

I SPENT THE FIRST MONTH OR SO PRETTY MUCH OUT OF IT—THE DOCTOR prescribed tranquillisers for me, cos of the nightmares I kept having.

When I stopped taking them—I didn't want to spend my life like that—Sarah was waiting for me.

Even though I'd only glimpsed her once, the second before I hit her, there was no mistaking that face. Even if I hadn't already seen it elsewhere, in a newspaper one thoughtless or vengeful bastard had left lying around.

She never said anything. Not for a long time.

But she never left me either. Every time I thought it was over, I'd glimpse her—across a crowded room, as they say. In the pub. About to light up a joint.

Or anywhere near the wheel of a car.

I still don't drive.

Or smoke dope.

But I do drink. A man has to have some solace.

I went away for a while. Not voluntarily. They pumped me full of drugs. They were going to give me electric shocks, too, but I lied first. I lied and said I couldn't see her anymore. That it'd just been guilt, like they said.

But guilt can't touch you, physically. Not the way she did.

Listen—

One night—it was after I'd got out of the hospital, and I was in a flat now, they'd rehoused me—I was there, smashed out of my head on very cheap whisky, and crying my eyes out, wishing, wishing like anything at all, that life had a rewind button. Sarah was sitting across the room from me, on a chair, her little bare feet swinging just off the floor, little plump hands in her lap, looking at me gravely.

She was a pretty kid. Blonde hair, big blue eyes. Would've grown up to a be a heartbreaker, you just knew it. If she was—if I hadn't—she'd be married now. A husband, kids, all of that. But I'd taken that from her.

And so I cried, wanting to be dead, wondering if there were enough pills in the bathroom to do the job, and all that stopped me going looking was the thought that maybe even if I did she'd still be there, with me, haunting me, reminding me. Suicides go to hell, don't they? That's what I was always taught, anyway. And someone once told me that hell is a personal place, tailored to your own personal specifications.

Mine would be this room I was in, with Sarah there, watching me.

I dropped the whisky bottle, drunk as I was, and the last of it glugged away on the carpet and I cried some more for its loss. Maudlin and pathetic, I know.

And that was when I heard the creak, as she got out of the chair and began to cross the room.

Coming towards me.

I was too drunk to stand. I just tried to scramble away, into the lining of the chair, as she approached, all the while watching me with those huge, sad eyes.

I shut my eyes, hunched up in the chair sobbing.

And she took my hand. In both of hers. They were solid as real flesh, not insubstantial as a ghost's should be. And they were cold.

"Don't cry," she said to me. "Don't be sad."

And I don't remember much more.

OVER THE YEARS THAT FOLLOWED I GOT USED TO HER PRESENCE. I KNOW that sounds strange, but I just did. I'd resigned myself to a minimal existence. No friends, no wife, no kids. I had people I saw and knew, but all I really wanted was to be alone. With Sarah and my guilt.

That night was the first time she spoke to me. It was also the last for three years.

I'd talk to her, of course, when there was no one around. She came with me when I moved house, away from parents and other folk whose well-meant concern was only an annoyance.

And most of the time there was an equilibrium. I accepted my lot. A penance, for what I'd done.

Except one night, I remember, when I was drunk and bitter at all I could've been and wasn't. Never would be, now.

"Why me?" I shouted at her. "Why are you always with me? Haven't you got a family?" I knew she did, of course. A mummy and daddy, tear-stained on the news. "Why don't you go and haunt them? Why bloody me?"

And she turned away from me, her head bowed. In the years since her death, she'd never done that. Never spoken, except that once, never looked away. Sometimes smiling, sometimes sad—once or twice she'd laughed when I said or did something funny—but she'd never once looked away.

I was sorry, wretched, the moment I said it. And I was going to say something, do something—even dare to give her a hug, which I'd never done before—when she spoke.

"They lied," she said.

I blinked, stunned. She'd spoken again. The last time I couldn't be sure it was real, I'd been that drunk. But although I was drunk this time, it wasn't so much. Not so bad. I couldn't put it down to anything else. This time I knew.

"Who lied?" I asked at last, bewildered.

I didn't think she'd reply, but she did.

"Mummy and Daddy," she said. "They lied. In the paper. They said I was naughty. I wasn't." She started crying. "I was never naughty, but . . ."

"But what?"

She didn't answer me. It would be a long time before she spoke again, as it turned out. She only cried.

After a long time, I went and held her.

She was as cold as a stone.

After that, I went back home. Just a quick visit—down by train, of course. I almost bought two tickets, one for her.

Normally I went down once a month, quickly, there and back. To lay my flowers, my guilt, in some small measure, to rest. But I went down early, made a day of it.

I visited my parents. We talked without saying anything, them hiding their sadness and disappointment for me as best they could, and me—hiding Sarah, really.

But I was really back to check the local library. Microfiche; they had the back issues of the local rag there. I scrolled back through the 'fiche, till I found what I was looking for: GIRL, 6, KILLED ON ROAD.

She was always sneaking out, her dad was quoted as saying, to play at night. They kept trying to stop her, told her it was dangerous, but she never listened.

"They were lying about that?" I whispered to Sarah, who stood silently beside me.

And then I asked the question I'd never even thought to ask before, because the one thing I'd never done was look to place responsibility anywhere but only and solely on my own shoulders, where it belonged.

"Then why were you out there that night?"

But she only shook her head. And began crying again.

And I held her best I could without attracting attention, but she wouldn't, couldn't tell me.

And then I started, perhaps, to guess.

But it wasn't till I woke up the next morning that I knew for sure.

SARAH'S MOTHER HAD DIED TWO YEARS AFTER THE ACCIDENT. A HEART attack. A broken heart, some said. But her dad was still alive.

He'd moved away, but I found him. I surprised myself, with how easy it was. I was able to *do* something at last. Achieve.

He lived in a semi-detached house, in a nice neighbourhood. I knocked on his door.

He was a big man in his forties. Beefy, big muscles under a layer of fat. "Yes?"

So I told him who I was, and for a second I thought he was going to hit me. Then the air seemed to go out of him and he opened the door wide to let me in.

"Do you want a drink? Whisky or anything?"

"No. No thanks."

We sat. We faced each other in silence.

"So . . ." he said. "Sorry—what can I do for you?" I didn't answer. "I mean—I want to say we never blamed you. Not me or Deirdre. We knew it was an accident. And I know you must've been through hell. But it wasn't your fault. Really. Sarah was always bunking off at odd hours like that—we said at the time. We told her and we told her, but . . ."

And then he stopped.

While he'd been talking, you see, I'd unfolded the little piece of paper from my pocket and spread it open in front of him, on the coffee table.

He looked down at it. It was a pretty crude drawing, and it took him a moment or two to work it out, although the arrows pointing to the figures in it, with *Sarah* above one and *Daddy* above the other, must've helped.

First of all the blood drained out of his face, and then it rushed back, gorging it scarlet. His big fists clenched, and this time I *knew* I was going to get punched.

"What—what the fuck are you—you bloody pervert—"

"I've brought someone to see you," I said, quietly, and behind me the living room door opened.

"Hello, Daddy," said Sarah, but I didn't turn around.

The blood drained back out of his face and he sagged, shrinking in his chair.

I stood up. I didn't look at Sarah, because I knew she wouldn't look the way she always had to me. She'd look the way she did—after.

"She couldn't tell me," I said, and pointed to the coffee table. "So she drew me a picture."

I felt her brush past me, and heard her lever herself, with a child's comical effort, into the armchair I'd just vacated.

I went to the door, and looked back once. He was still in his chair, white and staring at her, seeming to dwindle visibly as I watched. All I saw of Sarah was her head and her shoulder—the stained nightdress, the matted golden hair. He didn't even seem to notice as I let myself out.

HE DIED THREE MONTHS LATER; THREW HIMSELF UNDER A TRAIN. TOO quick, of course, in all senses, but maybe—I like to think it was just the start.

I have a job now, a good one; it's early days yet but I think I'm doing well. Perhaps I have a future after all. But I'll always have a past.

I still go to the cemetery, every month, and put fresh flowers on Sarah's grave. I went yesterday, in fact. I brushed a little dirt from the stone and I stood up.

"You okay?" I asked.

Sarah nodded.

"Okay."

She came back the day after his funeral; well, where else has she to go?

She took my hand and we walked together to the cemetery gates, cold fingers laced through mine.

THE PROVING GROUND

I could say the day began like any other, but it wouldn't be true: a lie *and* a cliché all at once. It was like any other at first, I suppose, but only on the surface. The usual rituals; Radio One in the background, Mike Reid babbling away between songs—including "Relax" by Frankie Goes to Hollywood, whose lyrics he hadn't then comprehended— toast and marmalade. Once there'd've been cereal, too, but not anymore. Dad had been made redundant two months earlier.

They drank tea; I drank orange juice. It was carefully rationed; if ever I'd tried to sneak more than that one glass at breakfast, there'd've been shouting, tears, maybe even a slap. At the time I didn't understand. Now, I look back and see how it was: the long struggle up from the bottom of the heap, the fear of sliding back down, watching meagre savings slip away like sand, job applications, being turned down for interviews, interviews that came to nothing, self-worth draining away like the money.

On the surface, a day like any other. Only, I wasn't going to school that day, though it was a Wednesday and I wasn't sick. There was a taint, something that wasn't talked about, seeping into the silence, poisoning the air.

Dad finished his toast, drained his tea. "Come on," he told me. "Get your coat."

Mum forced a smile and looked away, gathering dishes from the table.

All these years later and still I ask, What did she know? It's academic now. I thought I'd get to ask her one day. I packed that morning's events away where they couldn't be seen, only distantly aware of their ever happening. I'll talk to her about them another time. When I'm older. When I can. There's all the time in the world.

Only there isn't. She was killed crossing a road when I was twenty-two. Some dickhead overtaking on a bend; she was looking the other way, down the lane the traffic should've been coming along. Never saw him. *Thud. Crunch.*

When I think of my mother's death, I don't see her in the Chapel of Rest, or the coffin sliding through the screen at the committal, but as I last saw her that morning; waving farewell in our living room window.

A cold morning. February. Still winter. Clear but wet, cold water clinging almost as ice to the pavements and the ground, walls and tree branches, out here in the suburbs. Wellington boots, a duffel coat, bobble hat and mittens. Ten years old.

Dad's hand, ungloved, folds around mine. Big, calloused, work-roughened and hairy-backed. Veins like rubber tubes beneath the skin, ridges. I wonder if my hands, small and pale, smooth and soft and featureless, will ever resemble his.

(They did. And I came to wish the change undone. Memory has a Doppler effect; you look forward to what you'll become, and having become it look back to what you were.)

Turning onto the main road, then off that onto Monk Street, a thin, bare road along the edge of the industrial estate. Cuboid buildings on the left side; brownfield giving way to wilderness, sturdy saplings and barbed wire brambles on the right.

At the end, where the road petered out, Starkey's Wood.

It hadn't always been a wood. There'd been buildings of some kind there once. Some said a factory. Matt Taylor, in the playground, said a school; bombed in the war, everyone inside killed: all the kids, all the teachers. And all the dead were blinded and deafened by it; if you went into Starkey's Wood at night, you'd hear them—teachers shouting the dead kids, kids shouting their dead teachers, crawling round in search of their missing body parts, and never able to hear or find one another, except briefly by blind chance. That was what Matt Taylor said. On the other hand, he also reckoned the moon landings were faked in a film studio.

At the end of Monk Street stood a pair of concrete gateposts. There was no gate, or even a wall or fence, but we went through the gateway just the same. A cinder path gritted underfoot, then turned to dirt as we went in among the trees. I looked back once; through a mesh of bare twigs I saw the squared-off buildings of the estate, wire-topped walls and burglar alarms, the yellow greasy grass of the brownfield, and Monk Street tapering towards the world I knew like a thinning umbilical cord; then Dad called my name and pulled me on, and when next I dared look back there was only the wood.

On either side of the path rose trees of varying age, mostly silver birches, trees that made me think of white bones pitted with dirt and rot. Chunks of rotting wood lay among the grass, loose bricks and lumps of concrete. Now and then, a section of brickwork rose from the ground, part of a wall still mired in the earth, or fallen pieces of structure embedded there.

"Dad?" I asked. "What's going on?"

He didn't answer, just dragged me along.

It wasn't my first time in Starkey's Wood. We all played there. Dared each other to do so. Because there were monsters in the wood. Just as our parents told us not to. Because there were monsters in the wood.

"Dad—"

"Come *on*!"

"Dad!" I tried not to cry but couldn't help it. My hand hurt where he'd gripped it; my arm where he'd pulled. "You're hurting."

For a moment he glared and I didn't know him. I rarely saw him angry—though more of late, since he'd lost his job. Was that because of the lost job, or just because I saw him more now? I didn't know, and in later years, I didn't want to. Something seemed soured in him ever since then, that's for certain, but I've never been able to ask if it was always that way.

Then it was his old face again, and he knelt. Big branch arms around me, stubbled cheek to soft, a gentle kiss. "It's all right." It was a whisper. "I'm sorry. It's all right."

I sobbed, couldn't help it. Shoulders hitching. Couldn't stop the crying.

"Sh. Sh. Stop— don't cry. *Don't cry.*" An edge in his voice; I gathered breath to wail again. "Sh. Sh. Don't cry."

He rocked me and I grew quiet. Then he stood. "Come on then," he said.

"Where are we going, Dad?" I almost said "Daddy," something I'd ceased to do after I was seven and decided I was grown up now.

Even at ten, I could see his smile was forced. "Play a game," he said.

"A game?"

"Yes. A game."

And I didn't believe him. How could I? All through the last week, there'd been a sense of something coming, something my parents wouldn't talk about. A surprise, but not a good one, I could tell.

A couple of nights before:

". . . choice have we got?" My dad, shouting at my mum. He never did that. It'd shocked me out of near sleep. The voices'd subsided to a dull murmur thereafter, returning the argument to its previous low pitch.

But I knew we weren't here to play a game. And he knew I knew. But we each kept up the pretence, all the same.

We kept walking. The trees grew thicker. There'd been birds singing as we'd entered Starkey's Wood; now there was only silence.

The trees opened out into a clearing.

It must've been some central part of the factory or school. The basement, most likely. The ground sloped down to a sunken area the size of a swimming pool. Under a scrub layer of dirt, tiling showed like an old mosaic half-excavated. I'd never been here before, never ventured this far in.

We'd stopped at the edge of the embankment, looking down. I looked up at dad. He gave my shoulder a gentle push. "Go on, son. Climb down."

"Down there?"

"Yeah. That's right. Go on."

It was a gentle slope, only about three feet. At the bottom, I turned and looked up at him again, but he stood and made shooing motions at me.

"Go stand in the middle," he said, backing away.

"Dad!" I knew he was going; I could tell.

"It's okay," he said.

"What about—what about the game?"

"This is where you play it," he said. "This is the proving ground, see?" He tried to sound authoritative, as he did explaining magnets and miracles, frogspawn and insect pupae. And succeeded. That's the worst of it.

"Dad!" I heard and hated the crack in my voice. "Where are you going?"

"I've played it already. I'll come back when it's done."

"But how do I play?"

"You'll know," he said, and he wasn't looking at me, he'd turned his face away. That was appalling, like he was rejecting me. I called out to him once more, and then he was disappearing into the trees.

I called out again, but there was no answer. Something moved and fluttered in the undergrowth, and made me jump.

My legs were beginning to shake. I wanted to go home. I wanted to run after dad, but I didn't know if I could find him. I was afraid of being lost in Starkey's Wood. It scared me, more than the proving ground, or the game, whatever it was, did.

At first.

I was still staring into the trees where I'd last seen dad, when I heard rustling from behind me again. This time longer and louder and more sustained; too much so to be a bird or a rat or—

I turned around.

It stood at the top of the embankment behind me. It wore a sort of boiler suit, baggy and sort of blue-green beneath layers of paint spatters, mud, leaves and twigs, dirt. Tattered and worn. Gardening gloves on its hands, heavy boots on its feet. Its face was hidden by an old World War Two gasmask, two glass discs for eyes. Its hair was black, tangled and stiff, matted with mud and leaves. It was breathing, hoarsely, through its mouth by the sound. A loud rasping noise. Its gloved hands were by its sides. The fingers curled and uncurled. In the cold morning air, steam puffed out of the sides of its face.

I stepped back and it moved forward. Then it leapt from the top of the embankment, landed on the tiling in a crouch. Straightened up. Giving out a sort of low, grunting laugh.

It wasn't much of a game. I broke left—it broke to my left. I broke right—it broke right. Whichever way I went, it blocked me. If there was a game, it was just for it to amuse itself until it got bored and decided to finish things off.

Its laugh became a roar and it ran at me.

I screamed, I screamed for my dad, and he didn't come. If the game was meant as a rite of passage, that was the only part of it that worked on me: like the story of the father who tells his son to jump off a wall, Daddy'll catch him. The boy jumps; Daddy lets him fall to the ground. *Let that be a lesson, son*, he says, weeping; *you can't trust anybody*. I learned it; in all the years since, no one has come close.

I scrambled up the embankment wall; I suppose I did well to get so far. It was upon me, of course, long before I reached the top.

I can't really remember anything much after that. It was sometime in the afternoon when I recovered consciousness. My head ached. I felt numb. I was naked. My clothes lay beside me, neatly folded. My t-shirt was torn, but that was the only damage. My thighs and shoulders were scratched; crusted blood dried on my white, goosepimpled skin like brown snail's trails. I was sore, couldn't stand or walk properly.

Shivering and weeping, I pulled my clothes back on. I gave a yelp as more undergrowth rustled, but then my dad's voice called my name. "Are you okay?"

"Daddy?"

He scrambled over the embankment and hugged me, very tightly. When I saw his face properly, his eyes were reddened. "Are you all right?"

No, Dad, I'm not. I never have been since. Any more than you and Mum were all right, after that day. Any more than you and me have been. Any more than we've ever really talked.

But all I said then was "Yes, Daddy." And cried.

He picked me up and started to carry me home.

"I didn't know how to play the game, Daddy."

"Sh."

"I'm sorry."

"Don't be. You did fine."

"Daddy?" Not understanding the rules, I had to ask. "Did I win?"

He held me tight as he carried me towards Monk Street and the gateposts, Mum, hot chocolate, fish and chips. "No, son. You didn't. But nobody ever does."

Angels of the Silences

We're on the bus, up from Manchester through Salford to Bolton, on our way to go camping in Kearsley. We piled on at Victoria Station—we'd all been in the square between it and Chetham's Music School. It's where all the kids like us'll go—the moshers, the punks, the greasers and the goths.

All the ones like me and Biff.

I'm Emily. That's me there, stood on the luggage rack and waving all in black: fingerless fishnet gloves, black eyeliner, black hair with gold streaks. Bit merry on blue WKD. I think I look pretty cool.

There's Biff. About half my size—she looks fourteen or maybe twelve, depending, but she's seventeen, same as I am—peaked cap and a Misfits t-shirt, parked on some lucky lad's knee who looks like he thinks Christmas's come early.

Biff's being rude again. She likes doing that.

"God," she says, "I'm sweating like a girl in a spit-roast." She bites a lip. Porcelain face, baby-doll looks. No wonder they all fall for her. "Sweating like Michael Jackson in a nursery!" That gets a few laughs, so she tries again.

"Sweating like Gary Glitter on a school bus!"

Big laughs. Even a couple of old dears smile.

Biff, see, she's rude without being rude, you know what I mean. She's never *nasty* to people. Just high spirits, I s'pose you'd say. Both of us.

Biff. She's my best mate. I love her.

"I love cock!" she shouts. She catches my eye and grins.

I grin back.

We've been dead for nine months.

When it happened, after he'd gone, we stood in the cold and quiet dark looking at our bodies. Biff was shaking. I wasn't much better off myself. Well, there's nothing to match it, really, is there? Can you think of anything that'd come close?

Biff . . . I couldn't look at her, at what he'd done. But she couldn't look away. She bit her lip and shook her head and hugged herself.

I just looked down at what he'd done to me.

"Ems."

The state of my face. The wound in my throat.

"*Emily*."

I turned and looked at her.

"What we gonna do?"

SO WE MAKE CAMP FOR THE NIGHT IN A FIELD UP ROUND KEARSLEY MOUNT. Orange lights gleam like crushed-up glass on the hills. Pylons looming up against the sky like giants as darkness comes.

Midsummer and grey, hazed over and spitting rain.

Johnny's got his ghetto blaster. Makes a change. Everyone else's got an iPod or at least a Discman. Huddled up alone with their music and no one else's. But this way we get together round the fire and have a laugh, sharing it.

Johnny fancies Biff, sits next to her chatting her up. So she goes with him, a snog and a cuddle. I dunno how she can. Not cos of Johnny, Johnny's all right, he's sound. Just . . . just cos he's alive and she's . . . I mean, it's just not *right*, somehow.

Least he doesn't have to worry about her getting pregnant, though. Not that he knows that, or can.

Petey makes a play for me, later. He's all right, in his way. Long greasy hair, spots, but I've had that, too, so I can't call him, can I? 'Sides, if I was all hung up on *looks*, I wouldn't be like this. I'd be listening to Galaxy 102 and Britney Spears—Shitney Smears, Biff calls her. And it'd be all halter-tops and dyed blonde hair and giggling over the celebs in the *Sun*. Petey wears a Dead Kennedys shirt and these big baggy kecks, with a dog-chain hanging off the belt. He smokes weed and stutters a lot and you normally can't get a word out of him with anything short of a chain and winch. But he's okay, just shy. Sooner or later, he'll meet a nice girl and she'll help him out of his shell. And all that.

It's just not gonna be me.

Maybe I should just tell him I'm a lesbian. Half of them believe it anyway, 'specially since that time I snogged Biff. It was just some creepy guy hitting on me in Jilly's, so we did that to put him off. I'd been on the orange Bacardi Breezers; she tasted of the watermelon ones.

In the end I fall back on the old one (they're supposed to be the best, aren't they?) and tell him he's a nice bloke but I just don't fancy him. He goes all mopey after that, so I get up and go for a shufti round the fields.

Stretch my legs, head for the woods at the edge. I reckon if there's any real grief going tonight, that's where it'll be kicking off from.

And I'm right. Wouldn't you know it? I always am about these things. I can always spot it, a mile off. Biff can't, but she's better than me at handling it.

'Cept that one time, when we both got killed, of course. But I don't blame her for that. She did her best. And she *is* my best mate.

I hear it at the wood's edge:

"Fuck *off*—" It's one of the girls, Caz; she went there for a pee, and—

"Don't be fuckin' makin' a racket, or—" A young voice, but harsh, like broken glass.

I'm into the trees before I know it. White blurs in the black. Caz and a couple of older kids. Not like us. In *their* uniform, the colours of *their* tribe: Rockports and trackies and baseball caps. Doing a spliff or two in the woods; fair enough. But they hate kids like us. Had enough grief off them while I was living. Still get it now I'm dead. Weird bitch, fucking mosher, all that crap. But they don't scare me anymore.

They wouldn't scare Caz that much either, not normally, but they caught her with her pants down, literally. And she's still trying to pull them up, but the other kids keep snagging at them, pulling them back down, baring her, and she looks so *scared*. Little *shits*. One grabs the dog-chain hanging off her belt-loops—most of us've got them—yanks her off-balance. And the only reason she isn't already screaming her head off for us is cos of what they might do if she tried. A girl learns it quick. How easy it is for things to go dangerous and bad, especially with lads like these. I used to think me and Biff knew all about that. Course, now we do.

Just nasty teasing, so far, but a hair away from worse.

"You all right, Caz?" I ask.

The boys stop, look at me. It's changed now; I'm out of easy reach. "Emily?" she says.

"Yeah." I come forward. "Go on, Caz, leg it."

"Don't you fuckin'—" one of the boys says, yanks the dog-chain. She falls over, lies there groaning, her face in the grass.

And I'm glad he did that, really I am, cos now I can scare him like he scared her, I've got my excuse, and Caz is out of it, Caz won't see.

"Leave her," I tell them, and I make the red light glow in my eyes, and do the thing with my face, let them see it as it really is now, as it really will be in the basement of the old farmhouse.

"Fucking hell!" screams the first, lets go of the chain and runs. The other just stands and stares at me as I come closing in, hands raised and hooked into claws, my fingertips bone.

"Leave her while you can," I tell him in my best Linda Blair in *The Exorcist* voice, and he breaks and runs. Think he might have soiled his trackies into the bargain. Good. Least he deserves.

They won't be back. No mobs with torches to burn out the devil's children. What they gonna tell their mates? One mosher girl scared 'em off? Demons? Vampires? That's a laugh. They'd be told they're mad. Or done too much weed. By the time they've got away they'll've convinced themselves it was all joke-shop stuff, makeup and that, and they'll call us every filthy name they can think of. But even so they'll keep away, and that's what matters.

"Ems?"

It's Biff. She always knows when I need her. 'Cept she's a bit late.

"You okay?" Silly question. How can it not be?

"Yeah. Just give us a hand with Caz."

We help Caz up. She looks a bit dazed; she's banged her head. But she's just shaken up, winded, really. She saw nothing, heard nothing. She'll be fine. Thanks to us.

We guide her back to the campfire and tell the others about gobshite scrotes in the woods; scallies, chavs. Bastards, say the boys and girls. True enough.

Spitting rain drives us into the tents. When it ends and we come out again, the sky's clearer, and stars are scattered out across the deep-blue velvet like fairy dust.

• 2 •

THE NIGHT YOU DIE STARTS OUT LIKE ANY OTHER.

We were out with the posse; Breezers and WKD at the Salisbury under Oxford Road Station, where all the rockers and goths and the like go for a few before they hit Jilly's.

Jilly's. The old-timers call it Rockworld, but it's Jilly's now. Same thing though. Only club in town plays our kinds of music.

Now normally we don't have any trouble getting in, but that night me and Biff were in the Ladies' a bit too long. Caught short. The others left and we were late. Funny how little things like that make you dead.

So we got to Jilly's late, and they wouldn't let us in. Asked us for ID. That'd never happened before. Biff reckoned it was cos she might've copped with the girl in the ticket window's boyfriend the week before last. Anyway, the rest of the posse were in there and we weren't.

We tried ringing them on their mobiles, but no one was answering. Well, gets a bit loud in a place like that. So we headed back to the Salisbury for a few more.

Pissed off and mopey, and there wasn't much of a crowd in there—most people'd gone on to Jilly's cos that's their kind of place.

So it was one of them. Too early to go home, but fuck-all to do.

And then Adam turned up. Christ.

He seemed nice enough. A bit older than us, but only by a couple of years. Looked all right. Long hair, couple of piercings. Yeah, in a film we'd know he was the bad guy, but that's films, and they're bollocks. We knew lots of bloke with long hair and piercings, and they were all right. For the other kids who were like us, Adam would've been like one of those nice clean-cut boys whose mums and dads live in a semi in the suburbs and he helps wash his dad's car on a Sunday. That kind. And they can be monsters, too. Just read the papers if you don't believe me.

But, looking back, how thick were we? All I can say is we were fed up and a bit pissed. Like I said, I'm the one usually smells trouble, Biff's the one gets us out of it. Got us out of it. That night, though—my spider-senses didn't tingle.

He seemed nice enough. Bought us a couple of drinks. Had a laugh, talked about music, films. Then he said there was a party he was going to later—that was why he hadn't gone on to Jilly's. And did we fancy coming?

"Yeah!" said Biff. "Come on, Ems. It'll be a laugh."

Thing was, it ought to have been. We'd done stuff like that before, and we'd been all right. Made a few new friends that way, too. Got a boyfriend or two and all, but that's another tale. So I said: "Yeah, all right, why not?"

Cos I was going to my fucking death, of course. That's why not.

So we got in his car and he drove. I got the passenger seat, and Biff vegged out in the back. I greyed out a bit, too. Too many Breezers in the Salisbury. Or maybe it was more than that. Maybe he spiked 'em. If he did, they didn't work properly.

Maybe that's why—I do remember—just before he killed us, I saw a bit of sweat running down the side of his neck.

Then I came out of the grey and saw where we were, or weren't.

Middle of nowhere. A dark lane. Farmland. Hills. An old farmhouse, the windows empty; gutted. No party there.

"Hang on," I said, "where are we?"

Adam didn't answer.

I looked at the dashboard clock. *Way* past midnight. "Where's this party exactly?"

I saw his knuckles were white on the steering wheel.

"Ems?" Biff's voice from the back, all the drunken fuzziness from before gone.

The empty road, the no houses, the gutted farmhouse.

"Stop the car," I said. I could hear my voice getting louder. "Stop the—"

Adam took his hand off the wheel and punched me square in the face.

My nose broke. I heard and felt it pop. Blood filled my mouth up and my eyes were—just—it was all blurred. I heard Biff screaming—rage, not anything else. She told me later she was on Adam like a wildcat. I couldn't see much with my eyes streaming but what I saw fits. I've heard of fighting tooth and nail, but Biff bloody meant it.

The car swerved off the road and ploughed into a ditch. Biff hit the windscreen headfirst, starred it white. With a bit of red.

Adam gave a sort of roar and grabbed her, threw her into the backseat like a doll. Well, she was only little. Then he scrambled after her, and I heard him punch her, too.

I should've fought. If I had—and I should've helped Biff. But I—I just couldn't.

Instead I got the door open, staggered out. Was I just running away, or going for help? I don't know. I want to think I was going for help, but—

I didn't get far anyway. Maybe five yards, something like that. Then he got me and hit me in the stomach, and then the face again.

Next thing I knew, we were indoors somewhere. Cold, wet stone floor under me. I couldn't hear properly; there was a thin shrilling noise in my ears. Blackened walls, wooden ceiling beams, dripping water.

Someone was beside me. I looked. Biff. On her back, her baby-doll face half-pulp. Blood coming out of her ears. Was she dead then?

I almost hope so, cos—

Someone above me. I looked up. Adam.

I tried to scream, but nothing came out. And besides, there was nobody to hear.

And then he bent down and—

No. I'm not going to tell you what he did. You can fill in the blanks yourselves. And if you can't, tough.

I thought it would never end. But it did.

All through it, what kept me going was this thought: *One day I'll kill you.*

When he was done, he cut our throats. It happened too fast to stop. One minute he was doing up his trousers and the next—

I saw a silver flash, and then I felt the skin of my throat gape open. It didn't hurt. But then I started choking on my own blood.

I wanted to jump up and get at him, but I couldn't, of course. So weak. And then I felt my body flapping and jerking like a fish pulled out of water and I couldn't stop it or control it. All I could do was watch as he bent down over Biff and did the same to her.

And then he straightened up, folding the knife shut after cleaning it, and he smiled.

The smile was the last thing I saw: gleaming white, Cheshire Cat job.

As everything faded to black, it gleamed, like a little piece of silver in the darkness, in a coal cellar, like the one my granny used to have before she went into the old folks' home and died.

Black.

THERE WAS A PASSAGE OF TIME. I DON'T KNOW HOW LONG. BUT IT couldn't've been too much. And—suddenly I was standing at the back of the cellar, looking at Adam's back.

He was standing there looking down at two dark, raggy bundles, with shoes at the end pointing towards me. A small pair of trainers like Biff's. And a pair of black boots. Like mine. Just like mine: one even had a little yellow smiley face like the one I'd painted on its sole.

The last few minutes were blurred, a jumble. I could remember what'd happened but it was all broken up, like a jigsaw. And I didn't want to put it together, but I knew I would. Had to, really.

I knew there was someone standing beside me, but I couldn't tell who, and I couldn't look. Couldn't move or speak or anything. Couldn't be seen then, either, cos Adam turned round and looked straight at me; through me, I suppose it must've been. He stared, blinked once, then shook his head and turned away.

He kept looking down at the raggy bundles with our shoes on for a bit. And then he turned and went out.

But still I couldn't move.

After a bit, I heard a car start and drive away. I often wonder what he told people about the busted windscreen.

But still I couldn't move.

And then—I don't know how long it took—finally the jigsaw all clicked together in my head. I mean, if I *had* a head right then. And I knew. I suppose deep down I always had—if there is a deep-down when you're dead like me. I just hadn't wanted to admit it. Couldn't accept it. But in the end, I had to.

And I knew, *knew*, what those raggy bundles were. But I had to see for myself.

And that was when I got my body back.

Or *a* body. I don't know what it was, is. But it looked—and looks—as real and solid as the one that was lying on the cellar floor.

And I had a head and arms and legs, hands and feet and clothes. I looked down and saw the same boots that were on the bigger raggy bundle on the floor. And I felt the cold damp air and I saw my own pale hands and bitten nails painted black.

I had to know, had to be sure, had to see. So I started forward, slowly because though I *had* to I didn't *want* to. And as I went, I knew that I wasn't on my own, but I wasn't afraid. I knew who it was; who it had to be.

But I didn't turn and look at her. I could only focus on the route ahead, my vision tracking over that cold stone floor towards what lay at journey's end.

And finally I was there and I was looking down at myself and at what he'd done to me, but I couldn't look at Biff, and I knew it was the same to her. She could only stare at herself and what that bastard had done to her.

"Ems. Emily. What we gonna do?"

WHAT WE DID, AT FIRST, WAS HANG AROUND THE FARMHOUSE.

After a bit, we got sick of the sight of our bodies. Or we would've if we could still puke. We went upstairs, explored the empty house.

We looked just like we had before. We even had reflections and shadows. We stared at ourselves, at our new bodies, in a cracked and grimy mirror in the farmer's old bedroom, and thought of what the old ones looked like.

Biff found an old apple tree out the back, grabbed a branch and lifted herself clear of the ground. Up and down, up and down, up, down. Then it snapped and she landed on her arse with a yelp.

I laughed. The first time I'd laughed since we died. Biff glared at me, then she laughed, too.

Then we stopped, because it didn't seem right, laughing like that now.

"WE CAN'T STAY HERE," SHE SAID.

"Why not?" I asked. Dawn was breaking, and I could hear birds cheeping in the distant trees. I wondered if we'd dissolve in the sunlight, melt away like shadows and dust. We didn't.

"Cos—cos—well, why should we?"

It was a good question. Thing was, what if we *couldn't* leave? I assumed we must be ghosts. We were dead, after all. Only, I'd never thought ghosts were solid, with reflections. We looked and seemed and felt alive. We could touch and feel. Would we bleed if we were cut? And could we die twice? And if we did, would that be it, or would we come back *again*?

If we were ghosts, weren't ghosts supposed to stay where they'd died? Could we leave the farmhouse?

"Maybe we can't. But we won't know 'less we try, will we?"

It was a good point. Like I said, Biff was always good at getting out of a mess. Mind you, this one was a bit of a tall order, even for her.

She was always dead practical, though. Or practical, even dead. We seemed solid enough, and other people might be able to see us.

We had our clothes and that, but nothing else. Keys, wallets and purses, mobiles and iPods—we had to search through the bodies' clothes for them. That was foul. But we did it. Adam hadn't robbed us. He wasn't into that, at least. We even still had our bus passes.

"That'll come in handy," said Biff. "Come on."

We walked from the farmhouse to the lane. Nothing stopped us.

"Which way?" I asked.

Biff pointed. "Right. That's the way his car was coming from. So town's gotta be that way."

We started walking. The lane seemed to go on forever without end. I thought for a while it never might. Or it'd lead us back to the farmhouse. Maybe we were in the land of the dead now and could never find the living.

A car rushed past us, blared its horn. The driver shouted something. The noise made me jump. Then the car sped on and was out of sight.

"Dickhead," muttered Biff.

But at least we knew we could be seen, and we were still—in that sense, if no other—in the land of the living.

No one'd come to get us. No angels and no devils. I wondered if we'd go to hell. I hadn't believed in anything like that for years, never even thought of it, but now I knew it didn't finish when you died, I didn't know *what* was coming next. But I was scared.

Later on, Biff told me she'd felt the same.

Eventually, the lane opened out onto a bigger road. A few more cars swished past. And then we saw a bus stop. We went to it and saw the buses were heading into Manchester.

We waited. A bus came. We got on. Showed our passes. The driver nodded, didn't give us a second look. No one did. They saw us, but they saw nothing different, nothing special. They didn't know we were dead or anything. There was no sign, no giveaway. We looked just like them.

That was a scary thought. What if this was a bus for the dead? But no. It couldn't be, could it? There was a teenage mum with her pushchair—but what was she doing up so early? An old wino, mumbling and sipping from his bottle. Two scallies on the backseat. A middle-aged woman looking tired and hungover. No, this couldn't be a bus for the dead. Could it?

But if it wasn't, if it was just a *bus* bus, in a way that was even scarier. Cos—how many other people could be walking around dead like us?

I didn't let myself think about it. I just wanted to get back to the city. Crowds, people. Maybe all of this would seem like a nightmare. Could we sleep? I wondered. Could we dream? If we nodded off, would we wake up? And if we did, where?

The bus rattled on. After a bit, Biff's mobile went off. She took it out, looked at it; the caller ID said *Mum*. Calling to see where she was, if she was okay.

Biff didn't answer the phone. She just stared at it. After a bit, it stopped ringing. And after a bit longer, Biff started to cry.

Oh yeah. The dead weep real tears. I've touched and tasted them, and cried my own. I put my arm around her and hugged her close. A couple of passengers stared at us, but paid no mind. Probably thought she was just crying cos of a boy. And I suppose she was, but not the way they thought.

• 3 •

WE GOT OFF AT VICTORIA. IT WAS A SATURDAY MORNING, BUT STILL TOO early for the other kids like us to show up. Only a few pigeons, pecking last night's sick up off the paving stones. Ugh. That minged on an industrial scale.

"Where do we go now?" asked Biff.

"I dunno," I said.

We sat by one of the fountains and watched the birds for a bit. Then Biff spoke again.

"Ems?"

"What?"

"I'm hungry."

I realised I was, too. Biff grinned; things were a bit simpler, for now. "Let's go find a caff," she said. "Sausage butties and a mug of tea. Yeah?"

"Yeah." I grinned back at her.

She stuck an arm through mine and off we went.

We passed a couple of places, but we didn't go in. I didn't understand why at the time, but hungry or not, we just went past. They weren't what we were looking for.

Finally Biff stopped. "This'll do it," she said. She'd stopped outside a little brightly painted place called the Moon Café.

We went in. It was a proper, lovely little greasy spoon. Six tables, each with a plastic cloth and a bowl of sugar, a salt-and-pepper shaker and a bottle of Sarson's. A couple of newspapers, red-tops. One bloke sat in the far corner reading the *Guardian*, a cig smoking away in the ashtray. There was one of those on each table, too. Ugh. We didn't do that. Except for the odd spliff. But we didn't have to worry about it anymore.

There was a big, friendly-looking Greek lady behind the counter. Biff went up and ordered two mugs of tea and two sausage barms, and then we got a table by the window and watched the cars and trucks swish by up the road.

The sausage barms and the tea came, and we bolted them down. I wasn't just hungry; I was *starving*.

After we'd eaten Biff got in two more mugs of tea. And then her mobile rang again.

It was her mum, still. She stared at it, trying not to cry again. I hadn't sniffled once; I couldn't. Couldn't even think of, picture, my mum and dad. It was like a big blank. Cos I knew once I started with that I'd never stop.

Biff sniffled, tears dripping on the plastic tablecloth as the ringtone cut out. "Aw, fucking hell, Ems. What we gonna *do*?"

"You *can* go back home if you want to, you know," said a voice, and we both jumped. The bloke who'd been sat in the corner was standing over us.

"What's it to you?" snapped Biff. You could tell she was upset; she was never *rude* rude like that without a good reason.

The man spread his hands. He was a big bloke, muscly, with grey hair in a little ponytail, and a spade-shaped beard. He looked like he might've been a kid like us, once. Listened to the same kind of angry music, been on the outside looking in. But that doesn't mean much. Look at Adam.

"My name's Jake," he said.

"So?" Biff's head darted forward as she spoke, shoulders hunched. Like a cornered cat, back arched and spitting. Out of the corner of my eye, I saw the Greek lady looking at us. She smiled sadly and went back into the kitchen.

Jake took out his wallet and opened it. He took out a newspaper clipping and spread it on the tablecloth.

"What—" began Biff, and then stopped.

The clipping was an old one, yellowed. The date read 1974. It was about a bloke getting killed in a motorbike crash in Rochdale. There was a photo of him. We looked from it to Jake and back again.

"That's right," said the man who according to the article, was called Jacob Goulding. He gestured towards a chair. "Can I sit down?"

"Death," said Jake, "it's different for everyone. No one goes through quite the same thing. Some people don't come back at all. They go straight on."

"Straight on where?" asked Biff. "I mean, heaven? Hell? What?"

Jake spread his hands again. "Don't know. Nobody does. Once you go on, you don't come back."

The ones who hang around—some of them are just a whisper and a voice; some of them are just a shadow and a smell—a rustle of old velvet, a flicker in the light, a scent of oranges or violets. Some look solid and real till you try to touch them and your hand goes straight through. And some—

"Now and again," said Jake, "you get people who stick around, and they look just the same. They're solid. They can eat, drink—they can do pretty much everything they did when they were alive. They can punch a grown man unconscious, even break his neck if they're the type. No one knows why it happens that way. Why some people go and some stay. Why some people are like us and some aren't. It just happens."

"Some people," he said, "stay because they've got something to do. Something that keeps them going. They have to stay till it gets done; they don't have a choice. Once whatever it is gets done, they vanish. *Poof*. Like that."

I thought about Adam: *One day I'll kill you*. Was that it? Had Biff been thinking the same thing?

I said this. I told Jake quietly, haltingly, what'd happened to us. Biff gave my hand a squeeze.

"Three teas," the Greek lady called out, and Jake went and brought them over. "On me," he said.

"Thanks," said Biff.

Jake shrugged. "It could be why you came back. But like I said, there's not really any rhyme or reason to this. I don't *think* you're like that. The ones that are—well, you can just *tell*."

"How do you mean?"

"There's just something about them. Anger. A lot of it. And—*direction*. Like you know to get out of their way, cos they know just where they're going and what they're after. I don't get that from you."

"We've only been dead five minutes," said Biff. She gave my hand another squeeze. "We're still a bit scattered, you know?"

I had to smile, though I suppose it was a bit of a weak one.

Jake scratched his beard. "I could be wrong. Like I said . . . anyway. What I was telling you before . . . No one'll be able to tell the difference." He looked directly at Biff. "So you can go home, see your mum and dad and all that."

"I live with me mum," said Biff, tightly. "Me dad fucked off when I was a kid."

It's a sore spot with her.

"Sorry," said Jake. He ground out one of his smokes. "What I mean is, for now anyway, you can both go on as if you're still alive. Your families and friends, they don't have to know you're dead."

We stared at him. That, of course, changed everything.

Before we said bye to Jake, he walked us back into the city centre. Near Victoria, again, on Deansgate, a narrow, sweaty old building was squashed between two shiny new ones. Blink, you'd miss it. I knew I must have, cos I'd been past a dozen times and not seen it. But then, of course, I'd been alive.

"What's that?" said Biff.

Jake looked from her to me. "If you go in there, there's a cage lift. You know, one of those old ones, like you see in films?"

"Right. And?"

"If you get in it, you'll be able to go on."

"On?"

"To wherever you're to supposed to when you're dead."

"Wherever that is."

"Wherever that is. Anyway, it's there if you need it."

"Proper stairway to Heaven, then?" I asked. Jake laughed. "Yeah. Stairlift, anyway. There's a few like it, dotted round. See, some of us get to choose when we go. I think you two might be like that."

Jake spread his big arms, arched his head back and stretched. "I've got the key to it, so if you decide you want to use it, leave a message for me at the caff. They know me there. Okay?"

"Okay," I said, hugging myself a little.

"Thanks," said Biff after a moment, still playing little tough kid.

Jake grinned at her. "You know, you don't half remind me of a lass I went out with."

"Thanks a lot." Biff pulled a horrified face at the thought of going out with an ancient like Jake. He laughed out loud.

"Never said it was a compliment. I've still got the knife scars. . . ." He winked, rolled off down early morning Deansgate.

"Ponce," muttered Biff. I knew that meant she liked him really. So did I. He vanished into the crowd quickly enough; if he hadn't been so tall it'd've been quicker still. There was nothing to mark him out from anyone else. Any more than us.

Biff's mum Angie runs her own modelling agency. Nothing tacky; arty stuff, that kind of thing. She'd earned extra money from that herself, when Biff's dad left. There was a painting of her over the fireplace in Biff's house, a nude one; used to embarrass Biff something rotten. I hadn't known where to look either, but I'd always keep drifting back to it and clocking how pretty Angie'd been. Felt really weird, thinking that about my best mate's mum.

Anyway, Angie'd earned a lot like that, got a lot of work—she'd told me all about it one time when I'd been s'posed to meet Biff at hers but she was running late—and she'd had more people wanting her to model for them than she could oblige. So she started putting clients in touch with other models she knew. That and place ads for new ones. It was a good deal; she took a cut and the models didn't end up with sleazebags.

Yeah, I liked Biff's mum. She was a bit *seventies*; you know, all feminism and flower-power, but she talked to me like a grown-up. And she was a *sight* less boring than my folks. My mum never seemed to do anything except clean and tidy the house or put makeup on and Dad was a *dentist*. You don't get much duller than that, or if you can, I don't want to know about it.

But right then, I really could not wait to see them.

"Give us a bell later, yeah?" Biff said at Piccadilly, as we went to get our different buses home. She had her hands in her jacket pockets and was chewing gum, trying to look like Little Miss Don't Care, and she didn't fool me for a second and she knew it.

"Yeah. Yeah. I will." I hesitated. "Posse'll be out tonight. Saturday and all."

"Yeah, I know."

"We—are we gonna go out?"

"Jesus, Ems, I dunno. Dunno what we're gonna do." A tremor got into her voice.

"C'mere." I gave her a hug.

"Cheers, mate." She was trying to put the front back up soon as I let her go, wiping her nose on her sleeve. "Take care, yeah?"

"Yeah."

So I went home my way and she went home hers. I hugged Mum and Dad long and hard, which surprised them. But I was used to not giving anything away. I had the original parents who didn't understand, or rather wouldn't if they knew. They'd've popped gaskets if they'd known even half the stuff me and Biff and the posse got up to. So in a way, it wasn't so hard for me. I was used to keeping everything out of sight and boxed away. Biff, though, her and her mum were used to having big heart to hearts, telling each other everything, all of that. It was a tough job for her.

When she'd said "later," I'd been thinking about eight or nine-ish. Half past seven, *she* called *me*.

"Ems?" She was crying.

I was in my bedroom at the time and Mum and Dad were watching *Corrie* downstairs, so I wasn't worried about anyone hearing. "Biff, what's up?"

"I'm okay, I'm okay. Just gone for a walk. Get away from Mum."

"Oh, shit, Biff, you've not had a barney, have you?"

"Na. Na. Nothing like that. Thought I'd have to though. Been doing my best not to let on owt's wrong, but—you know what she's like. She can tell."

Downstairs, the *Coronation Street* theme and my dad's voice asking Mum if she wanted a coffee. "Yeah," I said. It was the first time I'd been glad of my parents in that way. I mean, I still loved them. Sort of. Under it all. But even so . . . I mean, I really was *dead* and they hadn't noticed. Not that I'd wanted them to, but still.

Biff's mum notices when she's *dead*, I imagined myself throwing at them in the middle of a foot-stamping family argument, and had to clap a hand to my mouth so's I didn't laugh.

"D'you wanna go out, meet up in town?" I said.

"Yeah," said Biff. "Please."

SO WE DID. AND BY THE TIME SHE HOPPED OFF THE METRO IN ST. PETER'S Square, she was the same old Biff I knew and loved. Washed-out denim jacket, peaked white cap, evil baby-doll looks and chewing gum—well, at least till she flicked it in the bin as she came towards me.

I was gonna hug her, but she swung her body so her hip and shoulder bumped against mine. "Y'okay, mate?"

"Yeah." I wanted to ruffle her hair, but I knew she'd hate that. She was back in tough-girl mode. A moment later, I realised why.

"We gonna meet up with the posse?" she asked.

"Can do. I mean if you wan—" Then I realised. "Oh shit. The Salisbury."

"Yeah." Biff's face was tight and hard; she took a deep breath in and out, and tried to make the set of it more like toughness than fright. I bumped my shoulder off hers. "We don't have to."

"No."

We'd started walking though, and we were heading down Oxford Road, to where the Salisbury was.

"You think he'll be in?" I asked at last.

"Adam?" It was the first time we'd said his name since dying. Even when I'd told the story to Jake, he'd just been "this bloke," "him," "that bastard," all that kind of thing. "Might be. Fuck, I hope so." She grinned tightly. "Imagine his *face* if he saw us walk in there?"

I laughed out loud. "Fuck, he'd shit himself."

"Be sweating like Gary Glitter on a school bus."

"What if he *is* though, Biff?"

She stopped, turned, looked at me, hands deep in her jacket pockets. "I fucking hope so," she said. "Cos I can't die twice."

It wasn't a pose. Biff, see, she'll lay on the tough-girl act even though she's not all hard-shell, but the hard bit's real, too. Angie brought her up to have pride in herself and stand up to people and when you're little like she is, you'll get picked on. She was pretty, too, which made some of the other girls at school jealous.

But Sue Harper at school found out the hard way you didn't mess. She was a big girl, two–three years older'n us. And she made Biff's life a misery for about a fortnight before Biff snapped. It took two teachers to pull Biff off Sue, and she was a mess when she'd finished. No—Biff knew how to fight. And in her defence, or mine, or anyone she gave a monkey's about, she'd be lethal. Some people talk big, say they'll kill such and such or belt them. When Biff did, when you knew it wasn't for a joke, you got a bit of a chill, cos she always meant it.

I remembered her jumping on Adam, punching and clawing and scratching. If the car hadn't ditched and thrown her into the windscreen, it might've all gone differently.

But though it hadn't, Biff was right. She couldn't die again.

Then I thought of something else.

"Biff!"

She'd started walking again. "What?"

I caught her up. "Biff, if he *is* there . . ."

"Yeah, I know, we'll get him."

"No, Biff. I mean . . . what about the posse?"

She stopped, looked at me. "They'll stick together," she said, but she wasn't so sure. We were all kids after all. Easy enough for someone to get left behind. Shit attention span and all. And Adam, waiting in the shadows . . .

My dad used to go fishing. I remembered him talking about them, the different kinds. The biggest and the deadliest was the pike. The thing about a pike is it doesn't go chasing its prey all up and down the river or round and round the pond. No. A pike—a pike *waits*.

It lies quiet in the waterweeds, dead still and silent, waiting for something to come close. And then, then it'd leap. Lunge. They were deadly fast, Dad said. They'd bend their bodies and *SNAP* forward and grab whatever it was that'd got too close in their jaws, *crunch*. From which there was no escape. That was Adam. He hadn't chased me and Biff. We'd just swum in.

And even if Adam wasn't there, there were other predators like him, big or small.

"Come on," said Biff, and we hurried on down Oxford Road.

Adam wasn't in the Salisbury. We made sure all the posse left together. While we were there, I mentioned his name to a couple of folk I knew, ones who'd been in there the night before. None of them really remembered him; they'd all been pissed. The barmaid thought she knew who I was talking about, but she couldn't be certain, and if it was him she'd never seen him before. Big help.

Maybe last night'd been his first time in there; maybe he wasn't local. Just passing through and after a bit of a laugh. What he'd call one anyway.

We went on to Jilly's and this time me and Biff got in, no trouble.

It was just another night like old times. We had a laugh. But me and Biff were always watching; always, now we knew there were real monsters out there.

Later, we watched the others get off, as we hung around the bus station, waiting.

"So what we gonna do?" she asked me, but the way she said it I knew she'd got an idea now.

"I dunno. But *you* do, don't you?"

"Yeah. Yeah. Think I might, Ems." She bit her lip. She only does that when she's thinking.

We went to a bench and sat down near the Gardens. Biff hugged her knees.

"I'm not ready to go and get in that lift thing yet, Ems."

"Me neither. Just doesn't feel right, does it?" The night sky was painted orange. Pissed-up blokes in chinos and lime or orange shirts went past, bellowing and singing. One of them shouted something at us. What did we look like to him? Just a couple of miserable weirdoes. Normal as anything, though, in their way. But here we were, in the middle of the big bad city, and we were dead. Dead and trying to make sense of it.

"I don't think Adam's coming back," she said. "Not to the Salisbury, and I dunno where else to look for him."

"That what you think we should be doing?"

"No. I dunno, Ems. But we oughta be doing *something*. Do you think Jake was right? I mean, it just happens, people coming back like we have, and there's no reason?"

"I dunno, Biff, do I? Mean, Jake should know if anyone does."

"Huh." She bit her lip again. "But—he's still out there. Adam. And he could do it again. What he did to us—"

"Easy, Biff."

"Gerroff!"

"Soz."

"No. I'm sorry. You all right?"

"Yeah."

"You're my best mate, Ems. I'm—na."

"What?"

"I was gonna say, 'I'm glad you're like me, too.' But that's wrong."

"I'm glad I've still got you, too, Biff."

"Yeah. That's what I meant. I s'pose—I just—think we should be doing *something*. You know?"

"Yeah. I do."

"So I'm thinking we keep on like nothing's happened. And we stick with the posse and we look after them. We make sure if Adam comes back they're safe. And—aw, even if he doesn't."

I laughed.

"What?"

"No, just—you and me, guardian angels?"

And Biff laughed, too. But it was signed and sealed from then on. That was what we were gonna do. Protect our friends. So they didn't end up like us.

A GREY SUMMER MORNING SUN, KEARSLEY MOUNT. TENTS GETTING PACKED and the posse heading back to the main road and the bus stop.

Caz comes up to me. "Thanks, Em," she says.

"It's okay."

"No. *Thanks*."

She gives me a hug, then goes red and trots on. She's younger than the rest. Fifteen.

Biff pokes me in the ribs. "Think you've got a fan there."

"Oh, shurrup."

"No, you have though."

"*Shurrup.*"

"Is it a bird? Is it a plane? No! It's Super Ems!"

"Oh, piss off."

We link arms and follow the others to the bus stop, laughing.

So yeah. What happened with Caz wasn't the first and it wasn't the worst. Most of it's been like what happened with her—vicious little scrotes who want to pick on kids like us. Because we're different. It's just like tribes, that's all. We're the different ones, so . . .

But it's not always been like that. There was this one time in Jilly's, and we saw Debs in a corner, weaving around drunk, and this guy, his arm around her, trying to steer her out. It might've just been a shag he was after, a randy bastard taking advantage, or . . . it might not. Either way, me and Biff got in there and got Debs away from him in time. Didn't need anything special from us, that; all we had to do was run in, distract him, steer her away to the rest of us. He glared after us, trying to look mean and hard. Biff smiled sweetly and flipped him the bird. Compared to Adam, he was a fluffy toy.

That didn't take anything special from us, just being awake and alert. We don't get pissed anymore, or not like we used to anyway. I still like me Breezers and WKD, but I can neck two dozen of the buggers now and not feel anything more than a slight buzz. Biff has to smoke enough weed to lift an airship before anything really happens there, either. And we don't get tired. We never need to sleep. That's weird, I can tell you. But anyway, it's just watching; that's the big thing.

In between, we'd go to the Moon Café and see Jake, and he'd tell us things he knew. Tricks. Like what I did in the woods—my eyes and my face, and my voice.

"It's like smiling or frowning," he told us. "You can control how you look with them, right? This is the same, except it's *deeper*, and you can change way more than your expression. See?"

I didn't at first. It's getting your head around it that's the tough bit. Biff, she clicked like *that*. Scared the shit out of me first time she did it. I had to practice for weeks and the first time I tried it in public my eyes went pink. Not quite the same thing.

The worst that'd happened was a bunch of scallies going after Johnny. He'd cut through a rough estate, Poet's Corner in Swinton, and half a dozen of them'd started knocking him around. We got there. Don't know what they told their mates; Biff picked one of them up and threw him down a flight of stone steps. She was always sweet on Johnny. That was why . . . that was why it hit her so hard when . . .

I'd been feeling for a bit that it couldn't go on as it had been and that sooner or later something was gonna break. There was nothing spooky about that, no signs or portents or anything like that. You couldn't get much more down to earth and straightforward. It was A levels, and letters from UCAS. All of that.

Most of us were at sixth-form college, where we'd all palled up. Me and Biff were already mates from school. That was what made us the posse. We were in the same place and we liked the same things. That makes friendships and the like easy. But when that breaks up . . .

We were still kids, me and Biff. Living in the moment and all of that. It'd been great, the college time, and we couldn't even see the end. But it was coming now.

And what'd we do then? Go on to uni? We hadn't thought past going back to our families, or the posse. What now? How much of a life could we have? Or *should* we? We wouldn't get old. And how could we protect the posse, like we'd said?

And then, a month after I'd saved Caz, ten months after we'd died, we realised we couldn't.

• 4 •

IT WAS NO ONE'S FAULT. THAT WAS WHAT THE POLICE SAID.

It was just off Poet's Corner again in Swinton. Johnny came barrelling up Stevenson Road on his bike, that long steep road that cuts down sharp off Chorley Road, the big bus route of the A6, pedalling hell for leather, and he scooted straight out into the main road and he couldn't stop in time and neither could the number thirty-six bus. It was a double decker and all. Slammed and smashed straight into him and he was under the wheels before the driver could even brake. Least he wouldn't've known what'd hit him. That was one good thing. The only good thing.

They couldn't even have an open casket at the funeral. No visits to the Chapel of Rest before they closed the lid. His mum didn't even get a last look at him when she ID'd him; the dibbles brought her what they'd found in his pockets. *Are these your son's?* And how she must've wanted to say, *No, they aren't.* But she couldn't.

When I saw her at the funeral, any doubts I might've still had about coming back went out the window. Cos I barely recognised her. I thought at first she must be his older aunty, maybe even his granny. Johnny's mum'd always been such a big, jolly woman, red-faced with laughter. Now she was white and shrunken and silent. Except when she cried.

Biff stood next to her. Johnny's mum'd asked her to. What with Biff being Johnny's girlfriend. He'd been mad about her. In love. And Biff . . .

Oh God, my heart broke for her. Cos it's like I told you; the hard bit of Biff's real as anything, but it's not the whole story. Never is about anyone 'cept maybe the like of Adam, "Gitface" as we called him—when we talked about him—taking the piss so's he couldn't scare us anymore. Biff's heart's as big as anything.

I told you before, dead people cry. They cry and cry, just like the living. Can't even sleep to escape it. Just have to deal with it. Non-stop, without a break.

Biff liked to crack on like she was a proper man-devourer, but she wasn't. I mean, she didn't die a virgin, but she wasn't a slag or anything. And afterwards—oh, she might've snogged a few lads, but she only ever did it with Johnny.

Dead people cry. I did. And so did she.

Cos dead people can love, too.

I'd never seen her look so tiny, so like a kid. She really did look about twelve. Tiny and all lost in the black she was wearing. Her eyes were vampire red and if she'd worn makeup it'd've been streaked all down her face.

I was sat a few rows back; Biff was with her mum and Johnny's on the front row. And the priest talked about what a good kid Johnny'd been and all the rest, and how we'd meet him in the afterlife, and I really wanted to believe him. But no one knows where the lift goes.

Biff's head hunched down and her shoulders gathered up and she shook with crying. I stood between my mum and dad and I cried, too, for Johnny and for her, wanting more than anything else to be able to take it all away from her, to make it stop. But knowing I couldn't.

Mum put an arm around me, and so did Dad. I hoped they didn't feel the absence of a heartbeat. Not like they'd be looking for it. Felt so glad to have them now. Realising I loved them, and so glad again that they thought I was still alive cos it meant not putting them through what Johnny's mum was suffering. And Biff.

Biff and her mum were outside the church door as we filed past. I gave Johnny's mum a hug, but what I needed and wanted now was Biff, and there she was with Angie, who hugged me, too. Felt like I was running a hug gauntlet, all to get to where I had to be.

And finally I was.

She'd put herself back together, best she could. Those lovely big eyes, all reddened, and her little face all white. "Ems," she said, in such a tiny, tiny little voice.

"Oh, Biff," I said, feeling the love I had for her and knowing it was enough for whatever she needed.

Her face crumpled up, twisted, the mask broken. "Ems—"

She sobbed into my shoulder and I rocked her to and fro. Funeral guests filed past.

In the end I led her out among the graves and we just stood there crying. Angie caught my eye, gave me a little smile, went over to comfort Johnny's mum. That was fine. That was fine. Biff needed *me*, and I was there.

I CALLED ROUND TO SEE HER THE DAY AFTER THE FUNERAL. WE'D GONE through the wake, and all the rest. Me and Biff were approaching eighteen by then, so no one minded. And neither of us ended up being sick. Although neither of us'd ended up that drunk either. All we'd really done was skrike.

"Hi, Emily." Angie smiled and gathered me up in a motherly hug. "Are you okay?"

"Yeah. Yeah."

"Louisa's not in."

"Not—" It took me a second to realise she meant Biff. It always did. "Do, do you know where she is?"

"I— she said she was going up to"—Angie nodded, twirled a finger in the air—"where it happened."

"The Poets?"

"Yes."

Another time, I'd've been pissed off at Biff for not being round when I called. Even though I hadn't phoned ahead or anything. Not that that'd've stopped me grumping normally, cos her and me went everywhere together. Today, though, anything she did was okay. "I'll go see if I can find her," I said.

This time I rang her mobile. She was there. And yes, she'd wait. She said thanks in that little voice again.

I FOUND HER EASILY ENOUGH. THERE WAS A BUS STOP, JUST A FEW YARDS up from Stevenson Road, near the railway flyover. A bit down from it, near the corner, was a lamppost. There were two or three bunches of flowers tied to it. Biff was sat next to it, head resting against the post, hugging her knees.

She was dressed in her usual gear—the white jacket and the jeans, the punky t-shirt, the white peaked cap. It was like she was trying to be the old Biff, the don't-give-a-shit one, by wearing the clothes again. But it wasn't working. They looked huge on her, and they never had before.

"Biff?"

"Hiya."

I stood over her a bit, but she didn't want to get up so I sat down next to her, our shoulders touching. "You all right?"

"Don't be stupid."

"Soz."

She shook her head. There was something old about it, somehow. Do you know what I mean? It seemed like something she'd do ten years from now when she was twenty-eight, not eighteen. Except she'd never really be twenty-eight, of course. Kept coming up against that.

"S'all right," she said. Between her feet I saw flowers—dandelions and daisies, mostly, a couple of roses she must've pinched from someone's front garden. She sniffed. Saw me looking.

"Got these for Johnny," she said, and nodded up at the lamppost. "For that, yeah?" There was a nice bunch. I guessed one of the posse had more money to throw around than us. "Pretty wank, aren't they?" she said, looking down at her pickings.

"They're all right. It's not what they cost."

"They're wank," she said, and looked miserably down at her scraggy little bunch of flowers, thinking of how crap they looked next to all the others when she was the one who'd loved him best and all that.

"Well, your mum'd've given you some money to get a bunch, Biff, if you'd asked her."

"Na." She shook her head. "Wanted to do it meself. You know? Just from me. On my own. Stupid. Thought. Thought maybe if I did—" She screwed her face up tight, lips curled in and bitten down on.

"What? Biff, what?"

When she spoke, her voice wasn't a voice. It was this horrible sort of squeak cos she was crying too much to breathe or talk properly. "I just thought I might see him, Ems. Just once . . ."

I put my arm round her but she crunched up into herself making these horrible racking noises, pure fucking pain that no one, not her, not me, not even Johnny if he'd been there, could've dug out. All I could do was say, "Sh," and stuff like that. Cars swished by. Behind us, feet slapped on the pavement, and I tensed up waiting for some sneery remark, but thank fuck it didn't come.

She tried to talk a couple of times, but couldn't get the words out. After a bit, the horrible noises died down into ordinary crying, which was a bit better, if not much. Finally, she relaxed a bit. She didn't uncurl and sit up straight, but she wasn't hunched and locked in as she had been.

"It's just . . ." Her voice hitched, and she gulped. "It's just, I keep thinking, What's happened to him? What if he came back, like us?"

"We'd've seen him."

"Maybe not. Maybe he didn't know what to do. Maybe he's not been to the Moon Café and doesn't know—or—maybe he's just like a *ghost* ghost. You know? A shadow. Or a voice, like Jake said. I mean, what if he's not gone on, but he's stuck here all on his own?"

Her face screwed up again, then got sort of angry before it cleared up. "I just—aw, shit, Ems, thinking of Johnny like that—it's horrible, it feels—" Her voice hitched and she gulped again.

I hadn't thought about that. I hadn't thought of Johnny as being like us now. But he was, of course he was. Or maybe not *just* like us. That was the thing.

"So I came here and I hoped I'd see him. Cos—maybe he'll know now I'm dead, too, and I could help him. . . ." She hiccuped. "Oh fuck." She hiccuped again, twice in quick succession.

I started to giggle. I mean, a hiccuping ghost? I couldn't stop myself. "Don't—*hic!*—fucking laugh at—*hic!*—me, you bi—*hic!*—tch!"

That set me off even more. "I'm not," I got out between the fits of giggling. "I'm not, it's just the—" I got the giggles again big-time and couldn't go on speaking.

"What? *Hic!*"

That set me off again.

"Stop it!"

I tried.

"Stop—*hic!*—it!"

I tried again, but this snort like a motorbike starting up burst out through my clamped lips when I did.

"Ems, you bitch—*hic! Hic! Hic!*"

And that just did it. She went into this massive hiccuping attack. The angrier she got and the more she tried to talk, the more she hiccuped, and the more I giggled, so the angrier she got. So she started trying to slap me, which I managed to fend off, and I giggled and she hiccuped till finally she stopped trying to slap me and started flapping her hands around as she tried to hold her breath but kept hiccuping. She looked furious and frustrated and close to crying again.

"Biff!" I grabbed her hands. "Take a deep breath and hold it. Go on."

She did, and hiccuped straight away.

"Try again. I'll count to ten. See how long you can hold it for. Come on."

We got as far as two the first time.

Three the second.

Five the third. I was just starting the *s* in *six* when she went off.

Anyway, finally, she got them under control. We looked at each other and both giggled. It was the first smile I'd seen off her since Johnny's death.

"Thanks, Ems," she said, and gave my hands a squeeze.

"S'all right."

The streetlights'd started coming on by then, and the pavement was getting cold under my bum. "Can we get up now?" I asked. "We'll get piles."

"Can you when you're a ghost?"

"You can get hiccups," I pointed out, and that sent her off again, swatting my shoulder.

"God, imagine being a ghost with piles. Anyway, what you worried about? Petey wanna do you up the ricker or what?"

"*Biff!*"

She laughed her old wicked laugh, and Biff was Biff again, the one I knew before. "Does he, though?"

"No! I'm not going wi' Petey anyway!"

"You not going with anyone, though, are you, Ems?"

I shifted about, uncomfortable, and not just off the pavement. "Na."

"Why not?"

"Cos—cos—" I looked round, lowered my voice just in case "Cos I'm fucking dead, Biff."

"Yeah, so am I. Didn't stop me, did it?"

"I know, but . . . it just . . . it feels *sick*, thinking about it."

"Oh, thanks a lot!"

"No, I didn't mean that. I'm just—I mean, we're dead."

"Yeah, I *do* remember."

"But going with someone who's still alive—"

"Can't tell the difference. Come on, Ems. We do everything else, pretty much, we did when we were alive. Why not that?"

"Well, I—I didn't, did I? When I was alive?"

"You, you mean, never?"

"Na."

"But—what about Danny Laine? I thought you and him—"

I shrugged.

"You lying bitch!"

"Yeah. Well. You'd just—with Timmy. Wanted to keep up with you."

She shuffled. I stared. "You mean—"

"Yeah."

"Call *me* a lying bitch!"

"Yeah, well."

"So—Biff?"

"Yeah?"

"I mean—did you? Ever? You know, before you—"

"Died."

"Yeah."

"Yeah, course I did. Loads of times."

I looked at her. She shrugged. "Well, all right. Just once."

"Who with?"

"Petey," she mumbled.

"You *what*?"

"Petey, all right?" she hissed. Ghosts can blush, too, and by now you could've fried an egg on her cheeks.

"You went with *Petey*? But—"

"He's had a few actually. That little-boy-lost thing? It's all an act."

"The little . . ." We both broke up giggling again. "Well, I'm *double* not going out with him now!"

"Should hope not. He's crap anyway." She watched the traffic a bit more. "You should give it a go with somebody, though, Ems. Before we do—go on."

I looked at her. "You thinking of doing that, Biff?"

She shrugged again. "I dunno, do I? I mean, all that stuff, looking after the posse and everything—seems so *stupid* now, doesn't it?"

"What?" I hesitated. "Cos of—Johnny?"

I braced myself for her to start crying again, but she just nodded. "Cos of Johnny, yeah. And—well, not just Johnny. Cos of everything, you know? I mean, everyone's going off to uni and that. Posse's gonna break up. We won't see half of them again."

"Come on, Biff—"

"We won't, Ems. How many kids we were mates with at school we still see? Eh?"

A train rattled by under the bridge.

"I mean, you and me hadn't both gone on to college at Pendleton, think we'd still see each other?"

"Biff, don't say that! We're best mates."

She just looked at me, and for the second time she seemed to be an older Biff, a sadder wiser one, the one she'd never grow up to be.

"They'll make new friends," she said, "and we'll just be people they see sometimes. And they'll change. Everyone. Everyone but us. We're not gonna get any older. And how we gonna explain that? To our folks and everyone else?"

I swallowed hard. I'd been avoiding that one, but she was right.

"And what if someone finds—what's left of us?"

"Oh, shit."

"Yeah."

"What we gonna do?"

"Might be better to just—go on."

"But our folks—"

"Ems, we're dead. They're gonna have to go through what Johnny's mum's going through sooner or later anyway. It's just when and how."

I shifted away from her a bit. I wasn't angry with Biff, but I didn't want to think about it for now. Worst bit was that sooner or later I'd *have* to.

"Yeah," she said. "I know, Ems."

After a minute, she spoke again. "But you should get off with somebody before you go." She grinned. "Just not Petey."

"What's the big deal with it?" I said.

"Cos you should, just once in your—life." She looked at her nails. "You know what really made me decide to do it with Johnny?"

"No. What?"

She looked up at me. "I didn't want Gitface to be the last one I—"

I put my hand over my mouth because I thought I was gonna throw up. It all came back. Too, too much of it—lying on that cold stone floor with his weight squashing me into it, face grinning into mine, his stinking breath.

"Shit—Ems, I'm sorry."

"S'okay. S'okay. Just—just—leave us a sec, yeah?"

"Yeah."

I stared at the cracks in the pavement till I felt all right again. Till all the bad memories were safely locked away once more. "Yeah, I'm okay now. Jesus, though."

"But you know what I mean, yeah?"

"Yeah. Yeah, Biff, I do. Thanks."

"S'okay."

Funny. I'd come so I could comfort her, not the other way round.

"C'mon, then," said Biff. "S'pose we'd better get up. Just in case we *do* get piles."

"Why? You been taking it up the ricker and all?"

"Emily Harper! You dirty bitch!"

We got up laughing. "Hang on," I said, "Your flowers."

"They're shit."

"Let's put 'em up anyway."

"What with?"

In the end, I peeled off one of my fishnet gloves. It was pretty stretchy. I tied the flowers to the lamppost with it, above all the others, and knotted it fast.

"Thanks, Ems."

"S'okay. Come on."

And we started walked back. At the top of Stevenson Road, Biff stopped again to look down it. At first I thought she was just—saying goodbye, or something. But then I saw how still she'd got, and the set of her face, and—

"Biff? Biff, what's up?"

"Look how steep it is," she said softly.

I looked. It was steep, plunging down into the Poet's. You could see green hills in the distance, from the top of the road. "Yeah," I said.

"How fast'd Johnny have to be pedalling to come pelting out into the road like they said? On that slope?"

"I dunno, Biff. Pretty fast, yeah."

She turned to look at me. She was crying a bit, again, but that wasn't what was mostly living in her face right that second. It was anger. "Johnny wasn't a mad-head, Ems. He wouldn't come onto a main road like that."

And I knew she was right. Johnny got about *everywhere* on his bike, near enough, 'cept when we were all going into town, when he got the bus or the Metro. So he knew how to take care and he always did. It was so obvious

I'd missed it. Maybe someone'd tried telling the dibbles, but they hadn't listened. Kids, after all. Specially on bikes. Never listen, never take care, do they?

"Why was he going so fast, Ems?" Biff was almost whispering now. Her hands were fists as she looked down the slope. "What was making him go so fast?"

I knew the answer, but I didn't say. All of a sudden, I was scared of Biff. Scared of what she might do.

"Someone was chasing him," she said. "Some of those scrotey little gob-shites down there. They went after my Johnny again. Picked on him. Chased him. Must've been that. Only way he'd've been going that fast."

She turned and looked out onto the main road. They'd cleaned up the tarmac pretty well. There was no sign of what'd happened, except for the flowers on the lamppost.

Biff's breathing quickened till it sounded like a snarl. I wanted to say something, but I didn't know what.

She looked back down the slope.

"They killed him," she said. "They killed my Johnny."

"Biff—"

But she was already walking, striding down the slope.

"Biff!"

But she kept going as if she hadn't heard me. Maybe she hadn't. All I could do was go after her, so that's what I did.

"Biff—"

"Come on," she was muttering. "Come one, you little shits, come and have a fucking go if you think you're hard enough. *Come on!*"

That came out loud.

"Biff, don't. Come on, come back, let's—"

"Fuck off. I wanna word with those little bastards. *Come on!*" she shouted again, striding down.

Oh fuck, oh fuck. What could I do? What else? I stuck with her. I mean, I knew Biff wouldn't, couldn't, get herself hurt. But who else had a chance of stopping her hurting anyone else? Cos that'd be all kinds of trouble. What'd happen if she got nicked? Or if they *tried*? We couldn't die, but we could get caught. And if that happened . . .

"What you fucking on about, shortarse?"

Oh shit.

Slouching out of a sideroad, about half a dozen kids. Four boys, two girls. Thought they'd found something to play with.

Biff stopped, turned, and smiled.

They were spreading out round us. They hadn't clocked the look on Biff's face, hadn't seen she wasn't scared.

The biggest kid came up. "What you fucking weirdoes doing here?"

"Fucking druggies," one of the girls said, though if she hadn't had a spliff or two I'm Chinese.

Biff folded her arms and looked straight at the big kid. "You remember that kid got killed round here last week?"

"What you fucking on about?" He pushed her in the chest. Biff smiled. Oh shit.

"She means that one got knocked off his bike up on the main road, Dean," said a fat kid with a shaved head and glinting little eyes. The only one of the other boys I took note of, cos after that it all started happening.

"Oh yeah, him," Dean grinned. It wasn't a pretty sight. "One less fucking mosher. So what?"

"Were you chasing him?" asked Biff. "That why he ran out in front of a bus?"

Dean didn't know real trouble when he saw it; too used to being it maybe. That or used to it looking like something else, something taller and more male. "What you papping on about, you stupid bitch?"

"Fucking druggies," said the same girl again.

Biff stepped forward. "I asked you a question," she said.

"Ooooooo!" Dean pulled a mocking face. "'I asked you a question!' So fucking what?"

"Come on, Dean," the girl said, taking the piss once more. "She did ask you a fucking question, you know."

She swayed up, a nearly-empty Breezer bottle in her hand. "Now why don't you fuck off, you slag, or—"

I don't know what she was gonna say next, cos she shoved Biff in the chest as she spoke, and that was when it all kicked off big-style.

Biff moved so fast even I didn't see it. All I know is, next thing I knew, little miss "fucking druggies" was on her arse, Breezer bottle gone flying and a gobful of blood.

Dean moved fast enough after that. He knew what to do when fists started flying. He punched Biff smack in the face.

Biff rocked back on her heels but didn't go down. She just smiled at him. "That the best you can do, cunt face?" she asked.

Dean stared at her, but only a second before he swung at her again. If something annoyed him—well, *when in doubt, twat it* seemed to be his motto.

Biff rocked again, but kept smiling. "That it?"

He hit her again; this time she laughed, unfolded her arms, and took a step towards him.

"Fuck," said the fat kid. The other girl got the first on her feet and they ran away. Good move. Fatboy and the other two were standing there trying to work out what came next.

Dean swung at Biff again, but this time she didn't let him land the blow. She swatted his hand aside before it could land. Hard. I heard the bone crack. Dean screamed.

"My turn now, is it?" Biff asked.

"Biff, no—" I lunged as she punched him, grabbed her. I took the worst out of it; bone crunched and cracked again, but all that happened was that Dean went flying and lost some teeth. Okay, and he broke his nose, too. And all right, I think she might've done something to his jaw, too, it was hard to tell from the noises he was making. But it was better than a broken neck, or decapitation, which were the alternatives on offer.

Fatboy and the other two tried rushing us, but Fatboy got there well ahead of the others. Trying to tackle Biff, he knocked me over. Big mistake, cos there was no one stopping her now.

He tried to pin her arms to her sides. She kneed him in the goolies. Hard. He squealed. Then she got her arms free and threw him away. He hit a lamppost and fell in the gutter crying.

The other two boys saw Biff's face and me getting up to stand next to her, then turned tail and legged it, too, without another word.

Fatboy was wailing and yowling; Dean was sitting in the middle of the side-road trying to get up, holding his bashed face, blood dropping through his fingers like he was clasping a sponge soaked in it to his face.

Biff started walking towards him, fists closing and opening.

"Don't like it when it's you, do you?" she said.

"Biff, no!" I got in front of her, between her and Dean.

"Get out of the way, Emily," she said. Her voice was all choked.

"Biff, *no.*"

She swept me aside with an arm. I jumped back in front of her. She raised a hand to hit me. "Biff!" I said.

If she had hit me—I don't know where that might've gone. I don't like to think about it. But she didn't. I suppose it was the same with her—through all the red in her brain, she realised what she was about to do and stopped herself. She blinked. "Ems?"

She stumbled back.

I looked at Dean. He fell to the ground, crying in fright. All you could hear was crying. Dean snivelling and whimpering and Fatboy yowling in real, broken-bone pain.

God, those are ugly noises. Nothing uglier. And when I looked back at Biff, they'd brought her the rest of the way back. Her eyes were big and wet.

"Ems?" she said, dazed, lost.

"Come on."

I got hold of her and hurried back up Stevenson Road.

"YOU KNOW HOW THEY ALWAYS USED TO TALK ABOUT SIN IN SCHOOL?" SHE said later. We were back at Angie's, curled up in Biff's bedroom with mugs of cocoa and a plate of Jaffa Cakes. Dead or alive, never underestimate the healing properties of chocolate.

Funny really. Except for that one time, right after we'd died, we hardly ever got hungry anymore. I sometimes think we only got hungry that time so's we could go looking for a caff and end up at the Moon. Now we ate more from habit than anything else. And cos we still liked chocolate. Oh, and to keep our folks happy. Bit of an effort sometimes. But—you know. Teenage girls who don't wanna eat—that's the kind of thing gets parents really worried. Would've worried Angie, anyway. Still wonder about mine sometimes.

"Yeah," I said.

Biff nodded. Green Day played on her stereo, sound down low so we could talk. "American Idiot"—loud simple chords, over and over again.

"Always thought that was bollocks," she said. "I mean most of it. I mean—you know, I'll have a drink, smoke a spliff—shag a bit—but I never felt like a *sinner*. You know what I mean?"

"I think so, yeah." It doesn't matter what other people think is wrong, as long as you don't think it is. Well, up to a point, anyway.

"Yeah," said Biff. "Not till tonight."

I passed her the Jaffa Cakes. She took two. "I mean, I'd've killed those two. I really would've."

"I know, babes. I was there, remember."

She gave a little smile. "Yeah. Thanks for—you know, stopping me."

She put her mug down and hugged herself. It was another *old* thing she did, another of those funny little moments.

"If I'd killed them . . ." she said. "God, that'd've been *bad*. Don't think I'd've ever . . ."

I nodded and gave her a hug. She squirmed free. "Gerroff. I'm all right."

"Okay."

"But I wouldn't've been. I mean, they were little shits, but they didn't deserve . . . I just wanted to get someone for Johnny. You know?"

"Yeah. Biff, I know. It was fucking horrible what happened to him. I mean"— I knew that'd sound patronising—"I know you and him were . . . but he was a mate, too, and—"

"It's all right. Know what you mean. But—Johnny'll be all right now."

"Yeah?" I remembered what she'd been saying before, the thought of Johnny wandering round lost.

"Yeah. I mean, sooner or later—if he's not gone on, he will, won't he? It's just—time. And you've got forever when you're dead. So—it doesn't matter."

"Still not right, though," I said before I could stop myself. I could've kicked myself into the middle of next week, but Biff shrugged.

"No. S'not. Now—you nailing those Jaffa Cakes or what?"

"Greedy bitch."

"Yup."

• 5 •

THE NIGHT YOU LAST SEE ALL OF THOSE YOU LOVE, SAVE ONE, STARTS OUT just like any other.

We were out with the posse again. Who else? The first night out since Johnny died. It was sort of for him, as well, I suppose. And our first step towards life goes on. Well, death goes on, or afterlife goes on, in mine and Biff's case, but you know what I mean.

I hadn't told my mum and dad I loved them. Didn't do it the night I died either. Didn't realise that night was gonna be the one. Who does? And I didn't realise what this night had in store either, so . . .

Anyway, it was the usual round. On to the Salisbury, then Jilly's. It was the same old same old. Everyone getting pissed save us, although we were drinking the same as everyone else.

Everything went the same as it always did. And then the next we knew it was out of the Salisbury and on towards Jilly's and only then—

"Hang on," I said. "Where's Caz?"

Petey turned and stared at me. "Y'what?"

"Caz, where's she gone? Can't see her."

"Prob'ly in the bogs. Or she copped."

"What?"

"She was talking to that bloke."

No. Couldn't be. But . . . I looked at Biff. She bit her lip. "What bloke, Petey?"

"Older one. Beard and the piercings and that."

"Right back!" yelled Biff, and whirled, running back the way we'd come. I went after her.

We got back to the Salisbury and—no Caz. In to check the ladies' and—no Caz. I went up to the barmaid—same one I'd asked about Gitface the night after we died, and—

"Oh yeah, little Caz?" she grinned. She knew Caz; they all did. "Yeah, she pulled. Left with—yeah, long hair, beard, piercings." She didn't seem to think of the conversation we'd had that time. But it was a while back, and she was never the sharpest tool in the box.

"When?"

"'Bout a minute before you came back in. Looked like she'd had a few. She was weaving a bit."

Had he got the drink-spiking thing right at last?

"Any idea which way they went?"

"Sorry, love, I do—"

My mobile rang. Biff. I looked round. She wasn't in the bar. "Biff?"

"Get out here now!"

I RAN OUT OF THE PUB. BIFF WAS WAVING AT ME ACROSS THE ROAD, ON THE corner where the HSBC bank was, and pointing down the side street. I ran across, dodging the blare of traffic horns, and joined her.

"Down there. I saw them. It's him."

Christ, you stop looking for a reason to carry on, and . . . and we were supposed to *protect* them. And now we'd taken our eyes off the ball for a minute, and now Adam had Caz.

An engine roared, and he didn't see us but we saw him—the same old Ford roaring past as the one he'd taken us in, and Adam behind the wheel, a cool smirk on his face and Caz lolling in her seatbelt in the passenger seat.

"Shit!" screamed Biff, and the car turned up Oxford Road.

"Oh fuck," I said, "oh fuck. Biff, what do we do now?"

"Call someone. Call someone."

"The police?"

"You can try—ring 'em! I got an idea!" She pelted off round the corner. Shit. Thanks, Biff. Leave me in the lurch. I got out my mobile and dialled.

"Yeah. Police, please. Yeah. Yeah. Hello? Yeah. Yeah. It's my mate. She got in the car with this guy and I think—yeah, yeah, she's underage. Licence plate? It was . . . it was . . ." Oh *shit*. "I dunno. It's a Ford, though. Red. I think." Sodium lights make it a bit tough to narrow down the colour. "But—listen, he's a nutter, he is, he's a serial killer or something. What?" How did I know? Er, well, cos he killed me, officer. . . .

I trailed off, hung up in despair. What now—

My mobile went again. "Biff?"

"Yeah. Any joy?"

"No," I said miserably.

"Okay. Just stay put, okay? We're coming to get you."

"We?"

I got my answer a couple of minutes later, when a banged-about Reliant Scimitar swerved into the side street and Biff stuck her head out the passenger window. "Get in!"

I did. "What—"

Jake turned round and grinned at me. "Hold onto your hat. It's gonna be a bumpy ride."

I bet he'd always wanted to say that.

He wasn't kidding, either. Fumbled my seatbelt on. "How'd you—"

"I got his mobile number off Maria at the Moon," Biff said, grinning. "Just in case we ever needed him in a hurry."

"Bloody lucky I was having a drink in town," grumbled Jake. "In I come like bloody Batman."

BIFF'D RUN UP PRINCESS STREET GOING HELL FOR LEATHER FOLLOWING the car—down Brook Street next, to the motorway junction. She'd managed to clock which lane as well.

"Still, how we gonna find him?" I asked.

"He was heading out Oldham way," she said.

"So? *Oh*." Cos then it kicked in. Cos that was where the old farmhouse was, out Oldham way. "Oh God."

Biff reached into the back and gripped my hand. "He can't hurt us now, Ems." Red light gleamed in her eyes. "But we can fucking hurt *him*."

FROM THE MOTORWAY TO THE A-ROADS, THEN THE B-ROADS, AND THEN, AT last, the little dark winding lane I remembered so well.

Memory lane. But no good ones here. I was breathing faster. Even dead, this place put the frighteners on me.

Dead, twisted-looking trees swished by us. And then—

Like little red devil-eyes, glinting in the dark. Taillights.

"There. Is that him?"

"I think so. *Yes.*"

Over a rise, and then, spread out below us, the gutted shell of the old farmhouse.

"Oh, shit, Biff."

"Ems. Ems. It's all right."

The Ford pulled to the side of the road, and the lights went out. The door opened. Adam dragging a limp Caz out of the car.

"Oh, shit, Biff, is she—?"

"Don't think so. Think he's just mickey-finned her. Rohypnol or something. Drive past, Jake. Like we haven't seen."

He did. Biff twisted round to stare past me. I looked, too. Adam crouched, staring after us. Then we rounded a bend.

"Keep going a bit. Then pull in. Yeah. Now."

The car stopped. We got out. Scrambled through a hedge and the three of us, picking our way across an overgrown field towards the farmhouse.

"I'll deal with the bastard," Jake growled.

Biff stopped, turned on him. "No, you won't, Jake. This fucker's ours." She started walking again. "You just get Caz out of there, okay? And make sure she doesn't"— Biff sucked in a breath—"*see* anything. You know?"

I remembered what was in the cellar.

"All right," said Jake.

Biff looked at me as we went. "You up for this, Ems?"

I remembered the promise I'd made. "Oh yes," I said.

THE FARMHOUSE. GAUNT AND BLACK AND UGLY AND EMPTY-LOOKING. But not.

As we got closer, I saw thin, faint lights gleaming through the glassless windows. I found Biff's hand and took it.

We went to the front door. Moved to a window. Squinted through.

A kitchen table. A hurricane lamp glowing on it. At a chair at the end, Caz tied up, a crude gag in her mouth. Crouched over her, Adam, slapping her face to wake her up. She stared, eyes opening. She struggled, tried to scream. Adam clasped her jaw in a grip that hurt me just to look at and snarled something into her ear.

I'd seen enough. "Get us in there."

"With pleasure." We went with Jake to the front door. Two good kicks booted it in and off its hinges.

I heard Adam yelp, "What—?"

I hared past Jake and Biff, thinking Adam, you bastard, thinking Caz, who trusted me. And I was through into the kitchen.

Fuck, it stank. Shit and piss and god knew what. He must have been living here, at least some of the time. With us down in the cellar. Sick fucker. He whirled and saw me. And gave out a scream.

Caz's eyes, wide above the gag. "Mm-lee!"

"It's all right, darlin'," I began. "It's—" And Adam's fist swung at me. I reeled back from the blow, teeth clicking together. And then grinned. "Fucker," I said, and punched him back, so he flew and slammed into the wall.

"Jake!" Biff was yelling, and blundered through, swept the table aside so it slammed into Adam. He yelled out in new pain.

Jake ripped Caz free of the chair. "Get her out of here!" I yelled.

Jake swept past, and was gone.

And it was just Adam, and us.

He scrambled to his feet. Stared at me. A dark stain grew at his crotch.

The back door was a yard behind where Caz'd been sitting. He darted towards it—

—but Biff was already there. And she made her eyes glow red.

"Where do you think you're going?" she demanded, turning her face to a rotted skull.

"Yeah, Adam," I said, and I did the same to mine. "Where's the party you promised us?"

He backed away as we advanced, till he was up against—no—it wasn't the wall. It was another door. With a whimper, he yanked it open and bolted through it. And *down*.

A stench of decaying things boiled out to meet us. To escape us, he'd fled to where we were.

We followed. He kept backing away from us. Good.

A few candles were burning—down, low. When must he have lit them? They were scented. To cover some small part of the stink. There were about half a dozen Calor-Gaz cylinders stacked against the wall as we walked down. All mod cons.

What was left of us still lay on the floor. We weren't quite bone, but it was close. I stared, couldn't look away. Adam stopped.

"Emily?"

"Yeah," I said. "That's me."

"Oh, Adam?" said Biff sweetly, and wandering up to join me. "Don't you remember me, either?"

He blinked, sweat running down. "Yeah. Yeah. Biff, yeah? Biff?"

"Oh, Adam?" she said. "Wake up. Smell the coffee. Or rather the camping gaz."

I smelt it then myself. Thick and cloying in the air.

Adam went white. "Fuck!" He ran to the nearest couple of candles and beat them out. "Fuck! Fuck. Put them out. Or—"

"Or what?" Biff picked up one of the candles. "Or what, Adam?"

He stared at her. "No," he moaned.

"Or what?" she said. "Or—this?"

And she lifted the candle, and the air caught fire.

A WAVE OF FIRE. THE PERCUSSIVE THUD. A SHOCKWAVE. METAL ERUPTING, stone shattering and tearing. And then—the fire. The fire, everywhere.

The cellar was full of it. But through it I could see the night sky, where the farmhouse had been.

And Adam was still alive. Torn by flying metal, seared with burns, shaking and half-mad with terror and shock, but he was still alive.

Wailing, he ran through the flame for the cellar steps.

"Oh no," said Biff, and seized him. He struggled. He rained blows down on her, but this time, the advantage, the strength, was ours.

She wrestled him back and pinned him down.

"Biff, no," I said. She looked up, shocked.

"He's mine," I said.

She smiled, understanding, and let him go. He scrambled up and ran, beating at the flames with outstretched arms. I opened mine wide to receive him.

And I caught him and crushed breath from his lungs in my embrace, and then I carried him to where the flames were fiercest and we knelt down together.

One day, I'd promised, *I'll kill you.*

This was one day.

He screamed for a long time, till his lungs melted.

When he was little more than bones, I let him go.

• 6 •

Saturday afternoon in the Moon Café, and cars and trucks swished up and down Great Clowes Street.

"D'you want another brew?" I asked Biff.

She shook her head.

I reached a hand across the table to touch hers. She withdrew it.

At the counter, from the corner of my eye, I saw Maria shake her head and smile, the way adults will at the petty squabbles of the young.

And usually they are. I was old enough to see that now. Kids'll fall out over nothing. Over a band, over a boy, over anything. And it always seems so big, so important. And it isn't really.

But this was.

Dawn, and the farmhouse ruins still smoking, turning the air rank with fumes.

Yellow incident tape flickering in the wind.

The police, the fire crews, the circus—all been and gone. The men in the white space suits, all around the site. The three body-bagged bundles carried away.

A bird sang in the trees.

Huddled in the roots of a dead tree on a hillock, me and Biff climbed out and looked down at the ruins. We knew, somehow, without being told; the time was now.

Down we went. Bits of the farmhouse were scattered all over the field. Most of where it'd been was just a big, smoking hole. We went and stood over it. And waited.

After a moment, at last, there were faint sounds in the dark. Scrambling, scrabbling noises. Rats you might think. At first. But soon you knew it was too big.

At last, through the thin, reeking mists of smoke and early morning rain, Adam scrambled out into the light.

He looked the same as he always had. Only a bit more lost and scared.

He crouched, looking this way and that. We stood looking down at him. "Adam," said Biff at last.

He whirled round and saw us with a faint squeal of fright. Slowly we came down towards him.

He backed away at first, then stopped. A cunning grin spread across his face, and he crouched, hands balled into fists.

As we reached him, he swung a punch at me.

It went through my face and out the back of my head, as if I were smoke.

But no. *He* was.

Less even than that. A shadow. A shadow, and a voice. He stared from one of us to the other. He lashed out at Biff, too. Same result.

Biff took another step towards him.

With a faint, terrified cry, Adam turned and ran. A mist was descending. We watched it swallow him up.

There's no rhyme or reason the way folks come back, if and when they do. We'd just stayed to make sure of him. Now we were.

Roam the earth, Adam, and be afraid to go on. Walk the earth in limbo, just a shadow and a voice, till the span of every life you ever cut short is lived out, past and gone.

And after that, do what you like. Cos I don't care, and nor does Biff. Or maybe she does, eh? Pray you never see her again, you big brave killer, you.

And the trucks and cars swish by up Great Clowes Street, and Biff doodles circles on the plastic tablecloth with a tea spillage.

I look at the corner where Jake used to sit, and I miss him.

Jake found us not long after Adam'd gone away. We were still sat by the hole where the farmhouse was, the mist pressed in close around, when we heard a tramp of heavy boots, and a shadow loomed in the mist, and it was Jake.

"Need a lift, girls?"

"Cheers," said Biff, rising. "Come on, Ems. Get piles, sitting on this ground."

IT'D BEEN A BAD FIRE, SO I GUESS WHAT WAS LEFT OF US WAS TOO BADLY burned for anyone to guess we'd been dead so long. Dental records and the like'd've checked out. And no one'd be looking for any clues to the truth. Or if they did get the right result . . . well, they'd know they must've got it wrong, wouldn't they? File it away and forget about it. The case was closed.

Jake'd driven Caz to the nearest police station, raised the alarm and driven off. Within a couple of days, it was all over the papers.

Me and Biff were two little have-a-go heroes, who'd died saving their friend and stopping the mad killer, who still hadn't been identified. Maybe no one'll ever know who Adam really was. Hope so. He doesn't deserve the paltry immortality he'd get from it. And he'll never have the mystique of a Jack the Ripper, the killer who was never caught. Suits me fine.

At least our folks'll remember us well. I don't know how much difference it'll make to them. I'm guessing they'd rather just have us back. But we were a long time dead, so I suppose we made the best of it.

"BIFF?" I SAY.

"What?" She says. She doesn't look up.

"Biff, I'm gonna have to go soon."

"Huh."

"Will you come?"

"Where?"

"Come with me?"

"No."

"No, I don't mean—we've been through that. I mean, just as far as—"

Biff blows out through her nose.

"*Please*, Biff." I sound dead whiny and I hate that—like I always hated the way Biff seemed able to do without me when I couldn't do without her—but I can't let it end like this.

At last, she rolls her eyes. "All right."

"Thanks."

MY PARENTS HAD ME CREMATED. CHRIST. AS IF I HADN'T BEEN BURNT enough. Ashes in the Garden of Rest. A little plaque. EMILY HARPER. BELOVED DAUGHTER. AT PEACE.

Better than making a big fuss, I suppose. Says more that way, sometimes.

Angie had Biff buried properly, though. Headstone, lots of flowers. We went there—not the funeral, obviously. But to the graveyard, at night, once the stone was up.

LOUISA RAWLINSON

1988–2006

And a Bible quote, not that Angie was ever religious. Okay, slightly modified:

> *GREATER LOVE HATH NO WOMAN THAN THAT SHE LAY DOWN HER LIFE FOR HER SISTER.*

Biff cried.

So did I.

"I WOULD'VE SAVED YOU," SHE SAYS AS WE WALK DOWN DEANSGATE.

"What?"

"From Adam. If I could. You know I would, don't you?"

"Biff—"

"I mean—it's not—you don't blame me, do you?"

"What?"

"Forget it." Biff walks ahead. She goes fast despite the little legs.

"Biff, what you—you don't think I ever thought it was *your* fault, do you?"

"No! Come on. Don't be thick."

She's back in her shell. I can't blame her, cos I've hurt her, you see. But I so have to get her out of it, before I leave.

JAKE LEFT TOWN AFTER THE FIRE. COUPLE OF DAYS. THERE WAS AN ARTIST'S impression in the paper, a bit too close to the truth. And they had his car details—not the licence, but everything else.

Not that he was in trouble. The police and papers were calling him a conscientious citizen, even a hero. Jake laughed about that. "Never called us owt like that when I were alive."

So he went away. He'll be back again, one day, I suppose. Biff might see him again, in the Moon Café. But I won't.

I'm leaving, you see. That's why Biff's angry at me. I'm going on.

It's just time, I think. I can't see any reason to stay. Except Biff, maybe. But she doesn't need me. She'll get along without.

Maybe it's just having a best mate who's always looking up to her. I don't know. You can get used to it.

End of the day, I'm going and it hurts her. And Biff doesn't like that. You let someone get close and they can hurt you, which is why nobody ever gets really close to Biff. 'Cept Johnny, and me. He hadn't got any say in how he hurt her, didn't make a choice. But me, I did.

So now I'm going. So now she tries to act all half past give a shit.

"Don't know why you have to go now," she grumbles.

"Cos it's got to be sometime. Otherwise it'll go on forever, all the saying goodbye and that."

"Huh."

"You could come, too, Biff."

"Yeah, and you could stay."

No answers there, from either of us.

"I'll be fine," she says. "Go out, see the world. There's a lot of bastards out there. And I don't have to worry about getting hurt."

I start to laugh as we walk.

"What?" Biff demands.

"Is it a bird? Is it a plane?"

"Oh, fuck off."

"No, it's . . . Super Biff!"

"Piss off, Harper."

We get to the little narrow building Jake showed us. Maria at the Moon gave me the key. I open the door, turn back to Biff.

"Go on, then."

"Yeah. Biff, I—"

"Yeah. Yeah, I know. Go on. I'll say goodbye here, yeah? If that's okay."

"All right," I say, and give her the key. "Take that back to Maria, yeah?"

"Yeah. Seeya then, Ems."

"Seeya, Biff. I—"

But she turns and she's going. My eyes prickle. I turn back to the door.

Running feet, and, "Ems?"

I turn, and Biff reaches up and kisses me. Tongues and everything. Not pissed this time. She doesn't taste of watermelon Breezers. She just tastes of Biff.

Finally she pushes me away. "Go on then," she says.

I nod. "Yeah."

We don't say anything else. I walk down the hall, get in the lift, pull the cage door shut, and push the button. Biff stands in the doorway watching me go, and the door swings shut.

And the next I know, I'm over Deansgate, going up, up, up. And down below I see the busy street, and even with all the people on the pavement, I can see Biff, my Biff, my little Biff, walking, head down, hands in pockets, up the street and into the wind in search of battles to fight and monsters to kill, and then the clouds flicker shut all around me in white, and she's gone.

Wonder if they do wings up there in black?

. . . And Dream of Avalon

When all you thought would hold you up gave way, where else was there to go but back? Matthew had been able to think of nowhere, but all the same, at the slip road, he stopped the car.

There's a time you're attached to as though by elastic; sooner or later, it pulls you back again. Perhaps it's when you're a child; perhaps later. When you're, say, nineteen—friendless childhood and unhappy schooling behind you—and at college, yet to collide head-on with realities like mortgages, bills, salaries and jobs that become a ball and chain instead of a means to an end.

He couldn't see the house from here, only the lake, sparkling in the summer sun. He rubbed his face. It hadn't been a short journey; he felt equal parts tired and foolish. Someone else would be living there now, or staying there at least. Students, maybe. And what would he say to them? What could he?

I was here once. So what? they'd say. *I was like you once.* They'd surely turn their faces from him then, rejecting the inevitability of what lay ahead, its narrowing down of choices, so sure there was a way out, to escape the leaden monotony that seemed to grab everyone else. Like death, you believe, in that one and golden time, that it can never happen to you. As he'd believed, that summer.

As much as he still wanted to believe that some achieved that escape velocity, he doubted it.

What do you want?

To touch base once more, perhaps. Be reminded of how it had been, and felt. Let the old magic rub off on his fingers again, as though it could heal him, or at least point him towards some private Avalon.

Stupid, a self-made superstition, but it was all he had, a measure of how low he'd sunk. There might be no magic left. Only bricks and mortar, dull and prosaic as all else now. But he could hardly leave emptier than he was.

So, in the end, he drove down.

THERE WERE STILL TREES LINING THE SIDES OF THE SLIP ROAD, LONG WHITE silver birches, as the gravel spat and crackled under his wheels. Back then, he'd thought of white columns, marble in the moonlight as he'd driven down with the rest, all smashed on fat, leafy joints. Today, he saw the dark spots on their bark, pittings of lichen or moss, and could only think of bones driven into the soil.

Rounding the road's last bend, he felt something break achingly and drop away from him; a last rag of hope, perhaps. The forecourt had come into view. It had been a clean asphalt apron, back then. Now he could already see the shrubs bulging and cracking the surface, casting long spidery shadows in the evening light.

He almost stopped then, almost turned back. But somewhere on the gravel road he'd passed a point of no return, and could only let the car cruise to a halt almost of its own accord, as if the sight that met his eyes had drained the battery as it had him.

There was the house, all right, the big old house called Avalon. Or what remained of it. Most of the roof had fallen in, and the east wall. The windows were empty, and around those not thickened with ivy into green-edged holes, the smoke of some ancient burning still lingered in smudges of black. The door was gone, too; the sunlight, breaking in through the roof, showed him glimpses of the desuetude beyond.

It had been a beautiful place; that, even he, religiously left-wing as only the young and middle-class can be, had had to admit. The wide lawns were a snarl of weeds now, the flowering bushes long choked and gone. The ornamental fountain, with its Manneken-Pis style figurine they'd laughed over and, one drunken night, sought to emulate, had been smashed, two hollow legs, green with verdigris and a slimy moss, all that remained. Beside the lawn, more ivy rose in a wide low hump, like a barrow for his hopes. Wind flicked loose creepers up from the bodywork of a long-abandoned car. It looked like a Jag, an old E-Type, like the one Ben used to drive. Ben had been car crazy; he'd bought the Jag from his dad's scrapyard and spent years lovingly restoring it. Matthew remembered it on the road to Avalon that first night as they'd all come down, red paint glinting darkly in the moonlight, and Ben with one arm hung out the window and the wind blowing sandy hair back from his chiselled face. Some part of himself, Matthew thought, might have been in love with Ben. But only a little. Not like with Emily.

Even a ruin can be beautiful, in its way, but not this one, not one so fresh and rich in personal significance. For perhaps the first time in his adult life, Matthew wept. Only briefly, and mostly dry sobs, but a couple of tears seeped out. That in itself might be something; he'd never been a man who easily cried.

In a sense, perhaps, it was better this way. There were no residents, no one to disturb his reverie, no one to chase him off or break the spell. He would not be made to feel a sad, lonely failure with so little to show he could only come back to moon over his lost youth. He knew all that already. He had not come here to be reminded of it, but to forget. And to remember. That summer. The boys of summer.

"The Boys of Summer." That had been their song. Don Henley. Middle-aged eighties pop-rock he'd ordinarily have turned his oh-so-serious nose up at. But it had fitted them. Cheap sentiment, perhaps, but at the time it had seemed so right, to all of them—young and fit, clean and happy, full of wild joy. Immortal. For a moment, the memory of it was so fresh, so clear, he thought he could hear it again, faintly, as if playing on the stereo of a passing car, or inside the shell of its former home, but when he stopped humming it, there was only silence.

Eight weeks it had lasted, eight golden, glorious weeks. It had been Holly's idea. Against all expectations they'd been bosom friends—well, maybe it hadn't been so unlikely. Holly had been higher up the class scale than him or practically anyone else on their year. And like him, in rebellion against her parents, her upbringing, against everything. It was before you realised the leaden strength of monotony, mediocrity and apathy, their slow grinding force, when the feeling you had, the passion you knew, the fire you held, seemed great enough to blow them all away.

Avalon had belonged to a friend or relative of her family; Matthew forgot which. Had never been able to remember, even then. It hadn't mattered, wasn't important. Whoever he was—it had been a *he*, Matthew knew that at least—he'd been willing to rent it out for the summer. Cellar stocked, wine, beer and food. A bargain rate, seeing as it was Holly. One lump sum, if she and her friends could drum it up between them.

And of course they had. A dozen of them, twenty? He'd racked up an overdraft at the bank for spending money, dealt a little grass and speed on the side for the rest. Driving down crammed into half a dozen beaten-up old cars, through a hot summer night. Looking up to see the trees' spread branches whip and cut and slice the moon to ribbons that healed effortlessly back again. Stoned to glory on the back seat, he'd mused on the image and thought it fit them all—their light, their brightness, would never die, could never be broken. He'd even—God help him—written a poem that was probably still in his flat somewhere, or his ex-wife's loft, hopefully never to see daylight again.

That said, the others had whooped and applauded when he'd read it out that summer—the second night? The second week? The second month? Hands had thumped at his back; cans of lager had been thrust towards him and he'd glowed. Such pride. Such pride.

Which goeth before a fall.

The air in the car felt suddenly stale, unbreathable. He threw the door open, climbed out, stretched aching limbs. There was a wind off the lake, light and not too cold, and this at least still smelt fresh and clean. On the far side of the water, there was the hill, still thick with trees—that, at least, hadn't changed, hadn't fallen and decayed—that curved round on his left to bracket the lake's far end. To his right, a face of stone rose sheer to cup the road. At the foot of the hill, willows trailed in the water, giving way to birches and oaks farther up and finally pines at the top. These last twitched in a sudden gust of wind; he smelt their sap.

There was no traffic on the road. He'd lived too long in the city, or long enough; the great hush that descended, broken only by the soughing of trees and the soft slap of wave on stone, was alien to him. But not unpleasant. He felt no sense of threat. Instead, he felt cushioned and comforted, and not alone.

He walked across the forecourt till it gave way to the concrete landing stage. Weeds prised up through the gaps; the old mooring rings were thick hoops of rust. Yes, there'd been boats here; they'd taken them out on the lake time after time, right across to the hill. He went to the edge and looked down. The guardrail on the stone steps was rusted, too; the wind might crack it if it rose a notch. The shore it led down to was gravel, grey contrast to the gold at the hill's foot, sand soft as icing sugar. And there was still a boat. It slouched in the shallows with its stern full of stagnant water. Matthew felt his brightening mood dim a little, but then looked back across the lake, at what remained the same. He sat down at the edge of the landing stage, feet dangling into space, and watched the sun begin to sink.

There was a noise behind him, thin and faint, a dry scratching. It was sudden and he jumped, but when he looked there was nothing to see, except a flicker of motion in one of Avalon's empty windows. A frond of ivy, caught by a gust. He relaxed again, gazing back towards the hill.

He'd gone boating out there with Holly a couple of times. Strange, really. He'd chased—well, yearned or lusted after—most of the girls on his course at one time or another, but never her. She wasn't unattractive, with a squarish, strong-boned face and thick honey-coloured hair, but there had never been anything between them of that kind, a circuit with some vital connection absent.

Now Emily, on the other hand . . . he couldn't help but smile. Emily had that effect on everyone. Always smiling, whether in mischief or simple joy it was impossible to tell. It had been puppy love, maybe, but love, still. And then there had been Camilla, Claire and Chloe, the three Cs as they were called, and Danielle—and Holly, and Sam, and Brian, and Pete, and Adam, and Ben, and Foxy, and Karl . . .

All the boys of summer. Even the girls.

Nothing lasts. He sighed. That was the sorrow of it. Everything ends.

The sun sank a little lower. The green began to fade from the hillside, though the dusk was still warm. Silhouetted, its lines grew jagged, less comforting than before. It occurred to him that at nineteen he might have found some meaning there, but he doubted it. At nineteen he might have flattered himself he could make a poem of it that wouldn't be excruciatingly painful to read in maturity, but the metaphor intrinsic to the image he'd have rejected as too bleak.

He'd gone up the hillside once with Emily. They'd packed some food and borrowed the boat. He remembered the heady pine scent, the dappled cool of the tree cover, the bright jags of sun through the mesh of leaves and branches that cut the moon by night. That and the excited banging of his heart throughout, the silent prayer she'd agreed to this jaunt for the same reason he'd suggested it, and the soaring, unbelieving joy when he knew she had.

The wind wrinkled the lake surface; the hilltop's jagged lines wavered and crumpled. Something skittered behind him. He turned in time to see it skip from the cracked asphalt before it spun down like a sycamore seed.

It landed facedown, some glossy image on its fallen side. A photograph; taken, discarded, caught by the wind. He turned it over.

That night, one of the nights—they'd all blurred seamlessly into one another, impossible to separate or pin down—they'd all got together in the front garden, and Holly had set up her camera on a timer before running back to them, dropping down beside him where he was on one knee, an arm flung casually round Emily's shoulders, the other slipping round hers, their warmth drawn close and treasured, lover and friend. . . .

And then they'd all gone home. The summer had ended, as everything does. The first breath of autumn had ghosted through the birches, sycamores and oaks; the willow trees had wept their leaves away. The three Cs had left first, inseparable as always; all three had sought and found jobs with a firm in London. Later that day, it had been Adam and Ben; Danielle, too, bickering with Adam, their raised voices fading with the engine's growl. A note of discord, even then; a harbinger.

Over the next few days, the crowds had dispersed. Emily had gone the day before he was due to leave with Holly and Sam. They'd hugged and kissed to such an extent that the others had made retching noises and stuck their fingers down their throats. The intensity of the parting, remembered now, seemed to come almost from a foreknowledge of what was coming to an end. They'd exchanged phone numbers, promised to call. She'd waved from the car. He'd cried a little. Others had teased him, more or less gently, but only Holly had understood, bringing him a joint as he sat in the garden, hugging him round the shoulders, talking softly, seeking to reassure.

It would have been kinder to be brutally honest, perhaps, but had even Holly known?

In the end you could sum it up in two short words: *Summer's gone.*

She and Emily were the only ones he'd stayed in touch with afterwards, but even their signals had faded. Less and less to hold them together; finally, nothing at all.

Just before they'd lost contact, Holly had told him about Sam.

Years later, there'd been one final encounter: he'd run into Karl in a Manchester bar, tired, run down and a good two stone heavier than Matt remembered him; he'd just lost his job, and Matt had been all at a loss for a single word that could help.

The photograph in his hands was a little worse for wear, but considering the time elapsed it was virtually pristine. There they all were. All the boys of summer.

The wind gathered and blew again; the picture leapt from his hand before he could grip it tight. The wind caught it once more; it spun and flew over the dulling lake like a dazzled moth.

The wind's hiss died and left only the lapping of the lake, into which another sound intruded. Music; sweet music.

He turned, slowly, towards Avalon. Don Henley's voice grew louder; the guitars built, the music rising. And inside the house, light rose in the empty windows, like the glow inside a lantern in the waxing of a candle flame.

In the windows, shadows moved. One raised a hand and waved.

And another flickered in the doorway, growing; what cast it moved forward into the dying light.

"Matt?"

Her figure was more rounded now, less lithe, than in the old days, and her hair cut shorter, but he would always know her voice. On the third try, he managed to speak. "Holly?"

"Yeah! What you doing here?"

"I . . ." The music was booming out now. "Just dropped by."

"Yeah? Brill! Come on in!"

"What's going on?"

Holly came down the path towards him. "We get together every now and then. Roughing it a little, but you know. It's all right inside. We've done it up. Come and see. The gang's all here."

The music and the wind. "Emily's here," she added. "She'd love to see you again."

"Emily?" said Matt.

And suddenly there were tears in his eyes. Holly grinned. "Same old Matt. Always were a soft sod, weren't you?"

"Holly . . ."

"C'mere."

They hugged tightly. She was solid, real in his grasp.

"Holly . . ."

She sniffed. "Change the record, you big girl's blouse, or you'll have me at it, too. Now come on."

He laughed and wiped his eyes with the back of his sleeve. "Okay."

She led him up the path. He didn't think, and he didn't care. Holly was here, and that was all that mattered. And Emily. Emily, too.

They went in through the oak front door. The hallway was just as he remembered it: white skirting and sky-blue woodchip walls. A big pendulum clock ticked above a display case of bone china, and a stuffed owl under glass glowered from the foot of the stairs. Foxy, if he recalled aright, had christened it "Toby." Music and voices pressed against the closed front room door.

"Hey!" called Holly as she went opened it. "Look what the cat dragged in."

Heads turned, and he saw faces he hadn't seen in a decade or more, heard the kind of full-hearted laughter, and felt the sense of belonging he hadn't known in as long a time.

"Hey, mate." Ben gripped his hand tight. "How you doing?"

"I'm good," Matt said, meaning it for the first time in years. "You?"

"Never better."

"Yeah." Matt stared round the room; it, too, seemed unchanged. The gilt-framed oil of Victorian London by night above the marble fireplace; the same sky-blue walls as in the hallway; the smooth but comfortable leather sofas, the big onyx coffee table, the thick white shagpile carpet. He remembered the car he'd found under the ivy outside. "You still got that old Jag?"

Ben nodded and laughed. "You know me. Fancy a spin later?"

"That'd be good." Ben's sandy mop was untouched by grey, hardly thinned at all, the boyish features barely softened with age; the weight of Matt's years felt painfully heavy on him. "You're looking well," he said.

Ben grinned. "Don't worry, mate," he said, "we'll have you back to your old self in no time."

"I'll drink to that," said Matt, and as if by magic a beer was in his hand. Foxy rolled up, good old Foxy, fat now where he'd been skin and bone, but his blue eyes still crazy, laughter still manic, offering a fat, smouldering joint. "How 'bout smokin' to it, too?"

"Why not?" said Matt, and took a grateful hit.

They all came up; Adam and Danielle—still joined at the hip after all these years—the three Cs, Pete, Brian; Karl, full of the ease and confidence he'd lost . . . he was hugged, kissed, pounded on the back, and whichever hand wasn't at that moment clutching a drink or spliff was pumped till he thought his arms would detach at the shoulder.

Then the crowd parted and . . .

She stood there and smiled at him.

"Matt."

"Emily." He couldn't think of another word to say. He didn't have to. When he held her, it was as though summer had never gone.

AND ON THROUGH THE NIGHT THE PARTY WENT, TIME BLURRING, SLIPPING by and finally ceasing to exist. Beers and joints were passed round, and the house rang with laughter and the stereo's thunder. And again and again their song was played: "The Boys of Summer," a great hymn to all that once had been, and now had come again.

Matt talked with Holly, with Ben, with all the rest, but in the end, who else would he want most of all to talk to, this and every night to come, but Emily? They ended up on the front room sofa, holding hands like moonstruck teenagers, and finally kissing, breaking out of it with sheepish grins as the congregation broke into whistles and applause. And nothing could have seemed more apt, more right, than when Emily took his hand to lead him from the room and upstairs, to one of the bedrooms.

They undressed feverishly, Matt aware of how his body had changed, sagging where it had once been at least comparatively taut, threads and touches of grey showing already in his once-black hair, the youthful smoothness of his skin beginning to fade. He braced himself for those same signs in Emily, but couldn't see them. When he looked at her, perhaps it was a trick of the light, but her face and body seemed unaltered. The dim, softening light, perhaps; he hoped it was as kind to him.

All these years they'd kept the faith, coming back, and he'd never known. Why hadn't they told him, sought him out? He felt his eyes sting again and his chest tighten at the thought of all the times when he could have been where he belonged.

"Hey." Emily's hands slid down his body. "What's wrong?"

He opened his mouth to speak, and she kissed it. "Come to bed."

Meekly, he followed.

"I've wanted this so long," one of them said. He was never sure which.

AFTERWARDS, HE CRADLED HER IN THE CROOK OF HIS ARM AND WATCHED her, smiling up at him, eyes heavy-lidded.

"Why did no one tell me?"

She shook her head. "Don't ask that, Matt. You're here now."

Her lips' soft touch silenced him before he could reply, and then her eyes closed in sleep.

He'd have lain here happily all the night and longer, but the body has its own demands and after a while he rose, touching his lips gently to her forehead. Still a little self-conscious, he dressed, then tiptoed onto the landing. He used the bathroom, came out, and walked into Sam.

"All right, mate."

"Sam." They shook hands. "Good to see you again. All of you."

"Don't start gettin' all mushy on me." Sam grinned cockily at him. Same as ever. "Talk to you in a bit, yeah? Nature calls."

Sam moved past him towards the bathroom. *He doesn't look any different at all*, thought Matt. *Same as back in that summer, before . . .*

Sam.

Just before they'd lost contact, Holly had told him about . . .

"Sam?"

Sam turned. "Yeah, mate?"

"I thought . . . I mean, I heard . . ."

"What?"

Sam looked at him unsmiling. "Daft, really . . ." mumbled Matt.

"What?"

"That you . . ."

Sam just looked at him. No smile on his face. No nothing.

The silence gathered between them, and in it the summer warmth of Avalon died. Then Sam turned and went into the bathroom, the door closing behind him.

Matt stood on the landing for a moment, then turned back to the bedroom door, but his hand froze halfway to the knob, then fell back to his side.

Downstairs, the party went on. And once again, "The Boys of Summer" played.

Matt went down. Halfway there, he stopped before a silver-framed mirror on the wall. He stood and stared while the big clock ticked away in the hall, then finally reached out and touched his shivering fingers to the reflection of the boy he'd been a dozen faded summers gone.

THEY WERE ALL STILL THERE IN THE FRONT ROOM; ALL BUT EMILY AND SAM.

"Hey, mate!" Holly waved a bottle in the air. "How you doin?"

"Good," he said. he felt as if he was on autopilot, acting normally in a place where reality had ceased to apply. "Holly, I just ran into Sam."

Was it just him, or did her smile seem to twitch? "Yeah?"

"Yeah. But I thought . . . I'm sure it was you who told me . . ."

"Matt . . ." Was there a warning note in her voice?

"You told me he was dead. That he topped himself."

The music died. Then and there. So did every whisper of conversation in the room.

Matt turned and looked around. They all stood there, looking at him as if he'd just cracked the wrong kind of joke.

"Oh, Matt," said Holly. "Matt, why did you have to?"

"Had to happen sooner or later," said Ben. He wasn't looking at Matt as he spoke, but down into the depths of his glass, swirling the contents round and round. "Always were a bright lad."

"Too bright for your own good," said Foxy, sighing. "Always made yourself unhappy that way."

"Houses remember," said Holly softly.

"What?"

Her hair was dry and lacklustre, where before it had been glossy and bright. "Houses remember, Matt. Not just the bad times. The good ones, too. Even when they're not much more than ashes and dust. Avalon remembers. It remembers us."

"And we remember Avalon," said Adam, drawing Danielle to his side.

"We knew you'd come back in the end," said Holly. "Just wondered what took you so long."

"Back down memory lane," said Ben, knocking his whisky back. "Sam was just the first. We all come home." He flung the glass at the fireplace, where it shattered.

"Ben!" said Holly.

"What?" said Ben. "It's true, isn't it? How we all came back here? One by one? And realised there's more for us here than there'll ever be out there?" He gestured out of the front window. He was white, bloodless now. As Matt looked around, he saw that they all were, their eyes black hollows scooped in their faces. And the window was smashed into spines of jagged glass, the floorboards bare, and the walls charred black, water dripping down from a leak above; the fireplace was a stripped, gaping hole in the wall, below an empty, lopsided picture frame from which limp dead melancholy flags of rotten canvas hung.

"Didn't realise it at first," Foxy said, almost to himself. He pushed a hand through his wild hair, and Matt saw the black, bloodless gash along the inside of his forearm. Foxy looked up, his eyes red. His other hand rose, flapped limply at the air, fell back to his side. There was a gash along the inside of that arm, too. "Ran away. Tried to forget it. But I knew, even then, I never would."

"Too bloody right," Ben said bitterly. "None of us ever can." His face was ruddy but unmarked. There was no sign of violence on him at all. Carbon monoxide poisoning, maybe? That would fit Ben. Lead a hosepipe from the exhaust of his beloved car in through the window, run the engine, drift painlessly away. And the others . . . Danielle's and Adam's tongues pushed blackly from their mouths, eyes swelling, faces darkening. Round their throats the flesh sank in in livid collars, showing the bite of the rope. And the others, too. Karl, Camilla . . . all of them.

Holly's hand tugged at his arm. His head turned before he could stop it, and he saw the bluish marbling of her waxy flesh, the way her filmed eyes were crumpling hollowly in at the pupils, as if deflating.

"Matt . . ." she said.

He pulled his arm free and stumbled towards the door. They closed in on him, but they were weak and slow in their death and decay, and had no power to hurt. He shook them off and stumbled down the hall.

"Matt?"

He froze at the front door.

"You going without saying goodbye?" Emily asked, behind him.

He couldn't answer. He made his hand reach out and grasp the knob.

"Matt . . ." Sorrow, and an aching loneliness. "Matt, don't."

The knob turned in his hand. The door opened in an agonising slow motion as her footsteps creaked the bare boards and her voice drew closer.

"Matt," she said, "I love you."

The door swung wide, but he couldn't seem to go through it.

Her voice rose in bitter fury. "Won't you even look at me before you go?"

And it was that, more than anything else, that drove him forward, out into the night.

Matt ran past his car, didn't even think of trying to start it, and on back up the slip road. He looked back once, and saw Avalon, its frontage pristine once more, the roof restored, lawns trimmed neat again, bushes spattered bright with colour and the figurine pissing merrily in the fountain's pool, rich and lush as a flower on a grave, ripe and lusty with stolen life, and then tore his eyes away to run again. Behind him, he could hear Holly calling his name, and the others. He refused to listen, in case he heard Emily among them, blundering on, outstretched hands batting branches away, all the way to the main road, till he couldn't hear them anymore.

DAWN FOUND HIM PICKING HIS WAY BACK THROUGH ANKLE-HIGH MIST TO the forecourt. The car stood alone; its wing mirror showed him his old familiar face of the day before. Avalon was empty and still again, its restored glories fallen back into ruin.

There was a photograph, crumpled and stained, beside the front wheel. An old picture of the lawn, a lone figure kneeling on it, arms outspread, hands hung down as if draped over the shoulders of people who'd been beside him, but were no more.

In the end, we all come home.

For now, he drove away.

WINTER'S END

Spring and summer of 2005 weren't such great times for the world at large, but my personal life, for once, was on the up. I'd cut back on the drinking, got a decent job—even been promoted—and graduated from a friend's spare room to a flat in Salford Quays. I wasn't quite sure how, but I was glad.

And I was in love; on March 28th, I'd gone to a gig at the Night and Day in Manchester, to see, among others, a singer called Helen Damnation—a small, wiry woman, face a white pointed oval; hair a spray of crow feathers, mouth a red berry, wide eyes green, voice low and throaty or high and clear depending on the song's requirements.

She was too good for the four sullen moshers she was fronting; the set's high point was two acoustic numbers she played while they sloped off for a sly joint out back. I went up to her after the gig, expecting a few minutes' conversation and a signed CD. When the bassist demanded her help clearing the equipment, I took it as my cue, but she touched my sleeve and asked if I was hanging around. Between then and the bar closing at 2:00 A.M. we downed shots, set the world to rights regarding music, politics and anything else that came to mind, and arranged to meet again.

The Night and Day gig was her last but one with the band. She was done with them by mid-April; by the end of May she'd played a solo gig at the Centro Bar on Tib Street, and had moved in with me. We had three perfect months; then the shadows began to fall.

HELEN GOT HOME FIRST THE DAY IT BEGAN; I'D PICKED UP A TAKEAWAY en route to save either of us cooking. I parked next to her bright blue Corsa and went in.

I knew something was wrong when I opened the flat door; the lights were off. It was one thing we'd bicker about; Helen insisted on having all the lights on all the time, even when, as now, it was nowhere near dark. I called her name; she didn't answer. Only when I pulled the door shut with a loud *click* was there a sharp gasp.

"Helen?"

She was in the living room, huddled in a corner crying, knees hugged to her chest. The phone lay on its side on the carpet. My first thought was, *Oh God, rape*, but I went to her, and she was unharmed. She clung onto me like a gin trap snapping shut and cried nonstop for several minutes. The shock was how *reduced* she seemed; strength of personality'd always made her seem far taller.

After a few minutes, she pushed me away. "I'm okay. Just— something got to me. I'm okay. I'll have a quick shower and we'll eat. Okay?"

She wouldn't say anything more about it. It was only while she was in the shower that I thought to check the answerphone.

"Did you listen to them?" she asked, quite sharply, over dinner.

"No."

She looked suspicious, but nodded at last. I'd lied to her, but she'd been evasive at the very least.

The only message on the phone had been wordless. All I'd heard was someone breathing, wetly, in and out.

Unpleasant, more in fact than I'd've thought something like that could be. Something about the noise'd made me feel queasy and unsettled. It felt— *intimate*, somehow, as if that slack, wet mouth was slobbering all over me. But still, it was unlike Helen to be so deeply affected. Or was it? It was the old realisation that comes to everybody—madly in love or not, you never really know anyone else. Everyone always keeps big stretches off limits.

I put it out of my mind, but the first wrong note'd been sounded, and I'd always be listening out for it from now on.

THAT WEEKEND, WE DROVE UP TO GREENFIELD NEAR OLDHAM, AND VISITED Dovestone Reservoir, cradled in the craggy Lancashire countryside at the edge of the Peak District and gleaming beneath an unclouded sky and brilliant sun. We ate a packed lunch at one end of the reservoir, gazing longingly at the water—at one end, kids and a few adults splashed about in the water in open defiance of the signs forbidding swimming—and then strolled along the path over the hills overlooking the waters. From up here I could see the car park on the opposite side, the hills we'd traversed to reach here, and in the distance the town of Oldham. The first two fingers of Helen's left hand were hooked through the first two fingers of my left; linked, they swung a gentle pendulum beat, back and forth.

"It's been good, this," she said at last.

I agreed. "We should come here more often."

She shook her head. "Not just mean today," she said. "I mean, all of this. The last few months. Us."

"Yeah," I said. I swung her arm a little harder than before, wanting to affirm the linkage. What she'd just said had hit another wrong note; she was talking as if something was about to end.

"It's been good, Paul," she said, stopping to squint Oldhamwards. "I've never been happier."

I felt touched and apprehensive, I tugged gently at her fingers till she turned to face me. "Same here," I said softly, taking the fingers of her other hand. "I haven't either."

It hadn't been true until I said it. My last girlfriend, Sonia—I'd been crazy enough about her, but it'd been something different. We'd met at a political rally the SWP'd organised; I used to joke we were comrades first and lovers second, only by the time we split it hadn't been a joke, least of all to her. Helen was different. I'd had odd stabs at musicianship in my youth, never coming to anything much, but if anyone'd ever said I'd be happy carrying someone else's guitar case I'd've laughed. Now, though, I could believe it quite readily.

She smiled at me, then looked away.

"No reason that has to change," I said, "is there?"

I said the last two words lightly, but the question was there and she didn't answer it, and still she wouldn't look at me.

"Helen?"

"If I had to die, it'd be here," she said.

That pulled me up short. "What?"

"Just hold me," she whispered, and so I did.

"What is it?" I whispered, but I only felt her shake her head. "What?"

She squeezed my arm. "It's okay," she said.

"It's not. What's *wrong*?" I sounded whiny even to myself.

"Nothing. Nothing." She waited. I stroked her hair, brushed it with my lips. Helpless, so fucking helpless. Banging on the door, shouting, *Let me in*. Looking a fool to the whole damn world. Me and everyone else who ever felt that way.

"I've just got a feeling," she said, "something bad's going to happen. I can feel it."

"Helen—?"

"Just hold me."

I knew she was lying; she knew more, but it was all she'd say. So I held her. When I wasn't murmuring reassurances or brushing that crow-feather hair with my lips, I was mouthing curses over gritted teeth at her for shutting me out. Each was as real as the other.

Sun sank; air cooled. We walked back to the car in silence, Helen wrapped up in her own dread. So was I, but there was no mystery in my case; what gnawed into me, deadly as cancer, was the conviction I was about to lose her.

WE DROVE HOME IN SILENCE, BUT I COULD FEEL THE ANGER, THE ARGUMENT brewing between us, like the heaviness in the air before a storm, knew it was coming and had no idea how to stop it. I was angry because she wasn't talking to me; that, in turn, was starting to piss her off.

By the time we got home, we'd managed, without saying a word, to annoy each other to the point that she got out of the car the second it stopped, slamming the door behind her. I sighed, slammed my own door, too, and followed.

I only got into the lift by dint of running—the doors were already closing by the time I reached the foyer. Helen looked away from me, folding her arms. I made myself look away from her, too. We both knew we were one wrong look, word or gesture away from the storm breaking.

Fourth floor. The lift pinged, the doors opened. Helen swept past me and into the corridor.

Fuck this, I thought, and went after her, ready to finally vent all the anger in a few well-chosen—or more likely ill-chosen—words. I strode towards her, then stopped, because everything had changed.

Helen was stood stock-still about three feet from our front door. It was ajar. She turned and looked at me. And her face was that of a frightened little girl.

I went and put my arms around her. After a moment, I disengaged myself and went for the door.

"Paul . . ." she said.

I raised a hand. Pushed the door open.

"Jesus. What's the fucking *smell*?"

"Paul, be careful."

"It's okay," I said, then ventured into the flat. The bedroom door was ajar. I pushed it open; then it was my turn to grow still. "Helen?"

"Yeah?"

"Call the police."

AT LAST A FAMILIAR FACE, AND A HALFWAY WELCOME ONE. DS DOUGIE Poole was an old associate, and the two of us had crossed paths on more than one occasion with the kind of things that never found their way into official police reports. On the downside, he'd come to regard me as an expert on what he called "weird bollocks." On the plus side, I could call him in and knew he'd keep an open mind.

The evening was still warm and light; Helen and I sat in the car park while the SOCO team went it. After a bit, Poole came out to see us.

"Christ, Paul, who the hell did you piss off?"

Helen looked quickly away. I hoped that'd escaped Poole's notice, but of course it hadn't.

"I don't know," I said truthfully.

"Okay," he said finally. "I'll need statements from you both. D'you mind going with this lady, love?" He motioned Helen towards a maternal-looking WPC in her mid-thirties, then beckoned to me and offered a cigarette.

We smoked a while in silence. "So?" he asked.

"I don't know."

"It's connected to her, Paul. It's got to be."

We could both have guessed that. The . . . *stuff* smeared around the bedroom had been smeared on *her* side of the bed, *her* bedside table, *her* makeup things on the dressing table. It'd been *her* clothes torn from their hangars, smeared and ripped to shreds and trampled into the carpet. It could've been a random pervert, but we knew it wasn't. There was something too *personal* about it; it, and Helen's reaction.

I hesitated for a moment—was this disloyalty, or concern for her?—but in the end I told him all I knew.

"I can't see her folding up like that over one heavy-breathing call on the answerphone. She seems tougher than that. What's she hiding?"

"You think this is linked to the phone call?"

He looked at me almost pityingly. "You don't?"

He had me there.

"SOCO're gonna want the place a bit longer," he said. "My advice is, you and her book into a hotel tonight. Speak to you in the morning."

WE ATE IN THE HOTEL DINING ROOM IN NEAR SILENCE, DRANK TOO MUCH wine, went upstairs, climbed into bed. Failed to sleep. Lay in silence, staring at the ceiling.

After a while, I reached over and touched her shoulder. She squirmed away. "No, Paul. I'm not in the mood."

"Helen."

"What?"

"Why won't you tell me what's going on?"

She could've fenced around with me some more, but what would've been the point? She seemed to deflate. "Because I can't."

"Why not?"

"You wouldn't believe me."

"Why don't you try me?"

She looked up into my eyes for what felt like hours, but could only have been seconds. "In the morning," she said, and kissed me.

"Helen—"

"In the morning." And before I could protest any further, she trailed her hand down my chest, over my belly to my groin, cupping and squeezing lightly.

I knew I was being played, that this was to shut me up and stop the questions, but all the same I let her, because I had a terrible fear this would be the last time.

I WOKE IN THE GREY SPACE JUST BEFORE DAWN AND SHE WAS GONE. ON THE pillow beside me, where she'd lain—a strand of her hair clinging to it—was a note:

Paul—

I'm sorry. I have to go. I can't tell you and I can't run anymore. I'm sorry. I love you.

Goodbye.

Helen.

As I stared at that, my mobile rang. I snatched it up. "Helen?"

"Paul?"

I breathed out. "Poole?"

"Well, it's not the fucking tooth fairy." When Poole was burning the midnight oil he saw no reason not to spoil others' beauty sleep. "Where is she? Done a runner?"

I resisted the urge to tell him to fuck off. "What you got?"

He hesitated. "Is she there?"

"*No.* Okay? Fucking happy now—?"

"Oi, oi, oi. What's up?"

"She's—look, never mind that now. What is it?"

"You sitting down, mate?" Poole's voice had gone quiet.

"Yes." I had trouble getting the words out.

"Okay."

WHEN HE'D FINISHED, I CUT POOLE OFF AND IGNORED THE PHONE AS HE tried to ring again.

It still wasn't dawn. It would still've been dark when she left. I stood looking out of the window for a moment, watching the sky's edge lighten. Then I realised where she'd've gone and why. I pulled on my clothes and ran outside.

We'd driven to the hotel in our separate cars. I revved the engine into life and cut through Manchester to the motorway, heading for Oldham.

THE DAWN WAS COMING SLOWLY UP OVER THE HILLS AROUND GREENFIELD I was drove. My eyes were gritty. Birdsong seeped through the shell of the car.

Helen Winter had been found squatting by the body of her father, Michael, when she was thirteen years old, naked but for a pair of half-torn knickers and covered in bruises and scratches. Some fresh, some not. He'd been stabbed repeatedly in his face, chest and throat with a pair of scissors. She was still holding them.

Her mother had left home when she was eight. The abuse most likely began shortly after. Helen spent three fairly shitty years in care, then moved into a housing-association flat in her home town, Wakefield, and got a day job. She'd always had a good singing voice, and once she had her own place and knew anything she valued wouldn't automatically be taken away, she bought a guitar from a charity shop. That was how she'd learned to play.

She'd moved from city to city over the years; London Ipswich Glasgow Liverpool Aberdeen Sheffield Birmingham Leeds York Newcastle Sunderland Gateshead Swansea Cardiff Truro Penzance Plymouth Southampton. Always on the run. I gripped the wheel, and thought of the songs I'd heard her play, her own ones, the ones that voice of hers sang the truest. Songs about cruel lovers and trust betrayed; about being on the run without a place called home.

Poole on the phone, after filling me in on her past, one she'd never shared with me, leaving it to a DS in the GMP: "That stuff smeared on your bed and the walls and that, Paul, it was . . . well, it was rotten flesh. What was left of it. 'Putrefied organic matter,' the pathologist said." He'd paused uncomfortably. "Almost certainly human."

I thought of a formless mouth, breathing wetly into the telephone mouthpiece.

I turned down the slip road leading to the car park. The woods on my right blurred into a thick indistinguishable mass that could be hiding anything. Gravel spat out from under the Mondeo. The car park was deserted, except for a bright blue Corsa. I braked to a halt and scrambled out.

I ran across the car park to the reservoir wall. I looked across the water, to where a small figure sat huddled at its far edge.

I shouted her name; my voice bounced off the hills and she looked up. Even at that distance, I saw her face was a smudge of misery.

"Paul, just go away." Her voice floated forlornly across the water. "Just go, *please*, love."

I was going to argue, I think—though I hadn't had a clue what I'd say at any point, and my only argument was, *Don't go, I love you*—but there wasn't any point any more. All I could do was shout and point; from the bushes halfway down the hillside above her something had emerged that looked vaguely like a man and might once have been one, but wasn't any more, spider-like on its long, long limbs.

She turned and looked up at it, and she didn't move. By then I was already running. She must have thought she didn't care anymore, had just come here to be found so the wearying endless game might end, but at the last, as it leapt for her, she flung herself sideways with a strangled cry. She went sprawling and it crashed headlong into the water. As she scrambled to her feet it reared up, floundering back out onto the bank and lunging towards her, arms outstretched.

She screamed, and the worst part was that I heard that sound as my run had taken me to the bend in the footpath where I couldn't see her. I went off the path into the sucking mud where the summer heat had partly dried the reservoir out, stumbling and tripping over stones and bricks, and reached her.

Helen was huddled on the bank; the thing was crouched over her, hands at her throat. That was when I started screaming. I tore a rock free of the mud. Swung it. It connected with the thing's head. The head rose. I hit it again. It lashed out, sent me flying back winded. It scuttled towards me on all fours, shovel-sized hands and bayonet fingers ploughing trenches in the mud as it came. I noticed, queasily, that something thick and cylindrical jutted out from between its insectile legs.

Its shape was shifting. The head seemed one minute to rise directly from the shoulders, neckless, a "face" made of three gaping holes—two staring eyes and a mouth that seemed to be an agonised scream, a bellow of rage and a ravening gape all at once—and the next I seemed to see a face in it, a real face, one that looked a lot like Helen's own.

The stench of it rolled out to meet me as I tried to stand and almost knocked me back flat down without any physical assistance. Its tall, spindly frame seemed to be made of glistening, greenish-black mud. Except of course it wasn't mud. It grabbed my throat and pushed me over, bearing me down. I saw that face, so like Helen's but not hers, snarling and giggling; I saw that other face, three gaping holes. The mouth hole opened wide into a roar. My face felt like a balloon pumped full of air, ready to burst.

Helen appeared behind it, and began pounding on its back with something in her hands. An iron rod, salvaged from the mud. It grunted. Roared. She hit it again and again. It let me go, reared and stood. Roared, staggered toward her. But slowly, as if it were fighting a high wind.

She hit it again and again, screaming things at it, and it tottered. When the iron bar was torn out of her hands, it was by the force of a blow she'd delivered. She punched and hammered it with her fists after that, and it fell to one knee in the plain of mud. Warding her feebly off, it stumbled back towards dry land. Helen followed, not only punching but tearing at it now, ripping away handfuls of that greenish-black muck, pounding it as if her fists were mallets. Tearing substance away, beating it out of shape. She was screaming things at it. I couldn't make all of it out through the blood that roared and thundered in my ears, but I heard one word over and over again: *Die. Die. Die.*

It fell to its knees as if pleading and she brought her doubled fists down. The neckless dome of its head collapsed like an upturned bowl of wet clay, and it fell.

By the time I reached her, it was fast losing what form it had left. Helen was on her knees, hugging herself, shaking, sobbing and occasionally screaming. I didn't want to touch her at first—the muck splattered and smeared her body and face and gloved her hands almost up to the elbows, clotted under the nails—but finally I did.

SHE LEFT A FEW DAYS LATER.

"You ever coming back?" I asked her, at the station.

"If I can," she said. She brushed her lips briefly across mine and got on the coach. I watched her go, then started walking in the direction of the nearest bar.

People never forgive themselves. Not her, for what she'd done; not me, for what I had, or hadn't. Like a cancer that comes back, regrowing every time it's cut away, till it kills you or you're so weakened you just give up.

When the barman came to take my order, I asked for a Diet Coke instead. I could leave the whisky in its bottle. Perhaps, this time, she could leave her father in his grave.

THEY WAIT

Ican see them from my window now, standing in the shadows of the old bus shelter, a bus shelter with the naked, signless pole of the stop beside it. The bus doesn't run down here anymore, but they never got around to taking the shelter apart. More's the pity. But would it have made any difference? If not there, they would have found another place to congregate.

The air feels so stuffy in here, tastes so stale. The walls seem to close in, to the width and height and breadth of a coffin. I can't breathe. Claustrophobia. I must get out. I have to go out.

No. I mustn't. Mustn't.

But sooner or later, I know I will.

Before I do, I have to set it down. Concentrate, Christopher. Concentrate on the task at hand. It'll help, for a little while at least.

When did it start? That's the tough bit. It has to start somewhere, but there must be so much that's led up to it. I don't think I can honestly tell you where it started. But I can tell you where it began for me.

I DIDN'T SEE THEM GET RUTH HAMILTON. I SAW THE AFTERMATH, GLIMPSED the huddled shape on the kerb, but the light that stands directly above the shelter is busted, has been for a long time, months. I expect they did that. Preparing the ground.

It was a while before I plucked up the courage to go out. It used to be a nice neighbourhood, but in the eighties it got run down. The council dumped all the tenants it didn't want here. Now I don't like to go out after dark. But it looked like a body fallen by the shelter. I couldn't see any of them there.

The kids. The children who gather there at dusk. They smoke cigarettes and they drink cans of lager and bottles of cheap wine. They're all about thirteen, fourteen, fifteen years of age. I think. I've never been very good at guessing. By night, all you can see is the odd little gleaming coal of a cigarette, being passed back and forth. Or maybe it isn't just cigarettes. You hear about all sorts.

Anyway, eventually, I nerved myself to go out. I wrapped up warm—at my age, you start to feel the cold more than you did before—and walked up to the bus stop. My palms were clammy with sweat every step of the way. They always are, outside after dark. The old aren't safe outside, not around here, not anymore.

At last I reached the shelter. Something glistened on the pavement, wending its way over the kerb and into the gutter. I thought it was blood at first, but then smelt its acridity and realised that it wasn't. It was urine.

She lay there, limbs out flung, headscarf disarrayed over her grey hair and wide-eyed, agonised face. Her mouth yawned, too, in death, and her false teeth had slipped out.

Why do our bodies betray us so? All through life it happens, more and more as the time goes away from you, but so often at that last moment, bowels and bladder failing, a final humiliation. A last sneer. Death must be a young man, I often think, a "scally," as they call them round here, the children at the bus shelter. Unfeeling and unthinking, jeering and cruel. But perhaps there's not much room for finer feelings, growing up in a place like this. A vicious circle; a place dark and empty, nothing to do and nowhere to go, and no money to do it with either, unless you steal it. Parents who have nothing—except, all too many times, drinking problems and drug problems and all the rest of it. I try to understand, really, I do but sometimes it's just beyond me. Ben never tried to. He clung to all his own certainties, the same ones his parents issued him with as a child. Sometimes, I envied him that.

In the distance, a few streets away, a siren started wailing.

I crouched painfully beside her, old joints creaking, and felt with stiffening, arthritic fingers for the pulse in her neck and throat. There was nothing. Her skin was already going cold. I felt a coldness, too, starting from the inside and spreading out, an oppressive weight inside my chest and stomach like a ball of tightly packed ice stitched in there. Her glasses were askew, one lens cracked. Gently I slipped them off and closed her eyes.

AFTER THE FUNERAL, I WENT DOWN THE LEGION WITH BEN CRABSHAW. WE loosened our ties and unfastened our collars and nursed pints of bitter at a small, chip-topped table in the corner, for all the world, I suspect, like two old crows in our funeral black.

I'd known Ruth Hamilton for a long time. We'd both been born and bred in this area, lived in the same houses we'd been born in. Ben was a newer arrival, coming in the years after the war. He was a bitter, sour-faced man, right-wing even by the standards of the times. A Londoner by birth, it was rumoured he'd marched once with Mosley's blackshirts. At times I could believe it. All through the eighties, he managed to contrive to blame the one Pakistani family in the neighbourhood—they'd taken over the old newsagents—for its decline. And they say today's children are bad. If we'd met in our respective youths, we'd have battered one another to a pulp.

Still, for all that, I suppose you could say we were friends. Politics and unsavoury suspicions aside, Ben wasn't all bad. He had a sense of humour, sometimes cruel but always laugh-out-loud funny, and he was full of those small generosities that are appreciated and make a difference. And it was hard to tell if he believed any of it anymore, or was just going through the old motions to convince himself he still knew who he was.

Besides, when you reach a certain age, it gets harder to pick and choose your companions; he was the only one my own age left around here, now that Ruth was gone.

She was a beauty in her time, was Ruth. For a little while, once, when we were younger, we'd walked out together. But then she married someone else. We stayed friends. Stan, Ruth's husband, didn't come back from the war. He was taken prisoner at Dunkirk, but died in a German POW camp. I was never sure what of. By then, Ruth and I were too used to being friends to be anything else; and friends we stayed, and I wouldn't have changed that for anything, but I regretted it all the same, what we had, or could have had, and lost. Isn't that always the way?

Ben was quiet in the Legion, gazing down into the dwindling cap of froth on his pint of ale, hands cupped around it like a child's round a mug of cocoa, in from the snow on a winter's day, as if it would warm instead of chill. He'd always carried a torch for Ruth. They'd seen each other for a few months in the fifties, but soon enough Ruth decided she'd rather just be friends, same as with me. I think that really she was a one-man woman, just as there are one-woman men. Ben, I think, felt the same sadness as I did over that—well, perhaps not quite the same. As I said, there was a bitterness to him as well, an anger, an old wound that never quite healed. I'm not sure what; we were friends, but there were some depths to one other we never quite plumbed.

He was angry then, about Ruth. I could hardly blame him, but who could you blame? She'd collapsed in the road from a heart attack; it was as simple and brutal as that. There was nobody to blame.

So I thought. But Ben didn't agree. And much as it pains me to admit it, he was right.

"THOSE BLOODY KIDS," HE GROWLED, KNUCKLES WHITENING AROUND THE glass. "Little bastards. Bloody vicious little shits."

"Come on, Ben," I said. "You can't blame them. They were nowhere near."

"Bollocks," he spat. "That's all you know."

"Oh? And what do you know that's so different?"

It was an old argument, and I was sorry as soon as I spoke for what I'd said. We'd bickered about the kids on the estate many a time; to me, they were just a symptom, the result of all else that had gone wrong, but to Ben, they were proof positive of how the younger generation didn't have the strength or the steel of those who'd gone before. An old argument it was, and tired. The same as me. I hadn't the energy for it again, not now, not with Ruth just bade farewell to. But I'd get it anyway, I knew.

Except I didn't, not in the way I'd expected at any rate. Ben wasn't angry, not in the same way; the brief flame of it guttered and blew out, left only the smoke of his bitterness, the ashes of a torch carried long and burned away at last to nothing.

"I told the police what I saw," Ben said quietly. "But none of them believed me. No one believes me."

"What do you mean?" I frowned, not understanding. "What was it you saw?"

"Those bloody kids. They were at the shelter when Ruth walked up past them. God!" The fires flared up again; Ben clenched his fist and slammed it down flat on the table. Heads turned. Ben glared at them. They looked away. He turned back and looked at me. His eyes were wet and tinged with redness. "What the bloody hell was she doing out there, Chris? Out there on her own, that time of night?"

"She wasn't the type to be intimidated," I said softly. "If she wanted to go out, she wouldn't let a few snotty-nosed little kids stop her. You know what Ruth was like, Ben."

He managed a smile. "Aye. Don't I just." He was quiet for a few moments, and we both mused, together but apart, on the woman we'd both, at our separate times and places, loved and lost. "But what they did, Chris . . ."

"Who? The kids?" He nodded. "What did they do?"

"They spread out as she came up. Right around her. I saw them from my window. They were talking to her. I don't know what about. Then—" His breath caught and he took a gulp of beer, then wiped his eyes on his sleeve. I took out a crumpled tissue from my pocket and handed it to him. "One of them took a knife out, Chris. One of the girls. She stabbed Ruth. I saw it."

I spoke as gently as I knew how. "Ben, Ruth died of a heart attack. She wasn't stabbed. There were no injuries. They—"

"I bloody know!" He shouted. More heads turned, and Ben rose angrily, glaring about him. "What're you bloody looking at?"

"Ben—" I caught his sleeve and he knocked my hand away. "Ben, calm down—"

"Oh, bugger off," he spat contemptuously. "You're just like all the bloody rest."

He turned and stalked off, his pint all but untouched.

I was tempted to follow him, but didn't; I knew from long past experience that wouldn't work. When Ben was angry, the only thing to do was let that anger run its course.

So I stayed and finished my own pint, debated draining Ben's for him as well, and then decided not to. Wouldn't be right, somehow. Besides, in less than an hour it'd be dark. And I wanted to be safely indoors by then.

I WALKED HOME SLOWLY. THE KIDS HAD ALREADY STARTED GATHERING by the bus stop; a couple of them, a boy and a girl, were there. The girl had found something to perch herself on, and all I could see was one foot, in a training shoe and the leg of a pair of tracksuit bottoms, swinging to and fro. The boy wore tracksuit bottoms, too, and a jacket of some kind. Kappa, I think it said. He wore a baseball cap, too, his face pale with a couple of small tight clusters of red spots. His eyes were like little black olives, set in sleepless panda-rings of darkened skin. He was sucking, hollow-cheeked, on a cigarette, and those olive-black eyes seemed to follow me as I walked.

I looked away and walked a little faster, fast as my old bones dared. Home felt a long way away.

When I was indoors, I took off my coat and made a pot of tea. I took it with lots of milk and sugar, and then went upstairs to my room. From the window, which looked down the street, I could see the bus shelter.

They were gathering there now, in the dusk. There were seven of them. There always were. I recognised them now. I'd never noticed before how it was always the same group, always there, always turning up with clockwork regularity. Four boys, three girls. I could hear their laughter, raucous and sharp, through the thin pane of glass.

Looking more closely though, I could see that one of the girls was different. I remembered now. One of them had always had blonde hair. Really blonde, catching the dying sunlight like gold. The other two were mousy brunettes, one straight-haired, one curly. I could see them, but the third girl had long hair that was very dark, almost black. Glossy. Not blonde at all.

Perhaps she'd dyed it. I shrugged. It was none of my business anyway. And I was about to turn away, and perhaps would have made no more of the whole thing, when I saw a car pulling up by the stop.

What caught my eye was the make. It was a BMW, new and gleaming and silver. You don't see many of them around here. They wouldn't last long.

A door opened and the woman got out of it. She was quite tall, and very elegant, beautiful and groomed, with long, expensively styled blonde hair. Expensively dressed, too. I put her in her early twenties, though as I said I'm not great with guessing people's ages.

The blonde-haired woman leaned against the side of the bus shelter, slouching just the way the kids did, and started talking to them. She got out a packet of fags and offered them around. She laughed. The children laughed. And then another odd thing happened.

She got chatting with one of the boys. He moved up close to her. He put his arm around her waist. She put hers around his shoulders. Then they started kissing.

I don't mean gentle pecks either. This was full-on mouth-on-mouth stuff, just like the clumsy grapplings I'd seen the kids doing with each other. He put his hands on her chest, pawing her breasts through the cotton blouse. She stuck her hand down between his legs and started rubbing.

Finally they pulled apart, flushed. Then she led him by the hand to her car. They waved to the others as they got in. The other kids waved back, or called out to them. Then the BMW pulled out and was gone, and there were only six kids left. One of them looked up at my eyes and seemed to see me. It was the boy I'd seen before at the bus stop; even at that distance, I could make out the cold little blacknesses that were his eyes. I stepped away from the window and went back downstairs. There was a tin of beans in the cupboard and I heated them up for tea. I've never been a great lover of beans, but you make use of what you've got. Don't you? We all do.

Later I went to bed, but sleep was a long time coming. I kept thinking of Ruth, her laughter and her ways, her smile and her bright eyes, and her hair when she'd been young, glossy and black as a raven's wing.

BEN CAME ROUND LATER THE FOLLOWING DAY. HE LOOKED TIRED, AS IF HE hadn't slept.

"Afternoon," he grunted from the porch as I opened the door.

"Afternoon, Ben."

We looked at each other for a couple more silent seconds, and then he snapped, "Well, for God's sake, can I come in, then?"

I held the door open for him. "Be my guest."

I made coffee for us both.

"I'm sorry about yesterday," he said finally.

I shrugged. "You were upset. It's only natural."

"Be nice if something round here were," he said darkly. "Seen that new girl who's taken to hanging round the bus stop?"

I thought back to last night. "Her in the Beamer?"

Ben looked at me as if I'd gone mad. "No, you prat. Her with the dark hair."

"Oh, aye." I nodded. "Thought she was dyeing it or something."

"Or something," Ben muttered. "Did you see her face?"

"No. Just the back of her head. Why?"

Ben hesitated and chewed his lip, then shook his head. "I'm saying nothing. Next time you see her, have a look at her face."

"Why?"

He shook his head, pensively. "Just do it. Then we'll talk about it." He sighed. "Just the two of us left now, isn't it?"

I nodded.

"Funny, really. House starts getting you down after a bit. Too bloody small and too bloody big, all at once. You know what I mean?"

"Aye," I said. "I know."

"It's been getting worse lately. Can hardly stand to stick in there. Funny that. If I'd lived with Ruth I could have understood it, maybe, but I didn't. Should be nervy about out there, not in here. But no. It's been getting worse. You find that?"

I didn't, in fact; for me it had been no different from the usual run of things. Ruth's death hadn't engendered any fear, only a slow, sullen ache of loss. But I shrugged and half-nodded, so he wouldn't feel as though it was just him.

The conversation petered out, but Ben still hung around. We sat up, watched the television and took in the late film. *White Heat* with Jimmy Cagney: I can remember seeing that when it came out at the pictures. They made a fuss then about how violent it was. God knows what they'd make of films now.

I watched Ben walk home, to his house a few doors down. Across the road, at the bus shelter, the coal of a cigarette gleamed in the shadows, like a tiny blind red eye.

IT RAINED THE NEXT DAY, HISSING DOWN FROM A DULL GREY SKY, BLOTCHED and grimy-looking like stained and dirty cloth. The road and pavements glistened; droplets of water ran down my bedroom window, puddled on the sill, leaked through a crack and dripped onto the carpet. I sighed and wiped up best as I could, pushed a dishcloth up against the crack.

I drank cups of tea and later one of cocoa, when the lightning started flashing and the thunder rolled down the street. I used to love thunderstorms when I was a boy, long as I was safely inside and out of their way. Still do.

The storm passed off and sunlight cracked the shell of the clouds, just in time for old Sol to go down again. And as dusk gathered, the children began coming to the shelter once more.

The boy with the olive-black eyes, and there was the other boy, the one who'd gone off with the lady in the BMW. The other two lads. The girl with the curly hair. And then the last two. The straight-haired brunette girl; and the new one, the one with the glossy black hair. She started chatting with the other two girls, and finally half-turned so I saw her face for the first time.

I'd made another cup of tea, and was holding it in my hands when that happened. I dropped it with a cry, and it scalded my thigh before splashing all over the carpet.

Because, remember, I'd known Ruth Hamilton since she was a little girl. Since she was the same age as the kids out there, and younger.

The face of the girl at the bus stop was the face of Ruth Hamilton, as a child. Identical in every line and curve.

Ruth had never had a child. No brothers or sisters. What I was seeing couldn't be real. Perhaps I was senile. Perhaps . . .

But I saw her there, smiling and gossiping, a fag leaking smoke through her fingers, and then I had the bedside drawer open and pulled out an old picture, from before the war. Me and Ruth, back when we were about fifteen, sixteen. I held it up as I went to the window, and looked from face to face; the old dead one in black and white, and the living, breathing one, fresh and pink in living colour at the bus shelter. And they might have been twins.

And I lowered the photo, and I stood and stared. As the sun went down.

THE WOMAN IN THE BMW PULLED UP AGAIN, GOT OUT AND TALKED TO them. She stroked the face of the boy she'd taken off with her the other night, and kissed his cheek tenderly, then kissed him again softly on the lips.

When she smiled, she looked very like the blonde girl who'd vanished from among the shelter kids, but older, of course. And luckier. After a decade or two of breaks that would have passed the shelter girl by and condemned her to teenage motherhood, alone, chain-smoking and buying the cheapest food, eyes puffy and tired from long, low-paid hours, skin grown bad and rough and prematurely old, always on the edge of legality in the unequal running fight to support her tiny family, fighting the despair that drags you down to smother your child or slit your wrists.

She got in the car and drove off. The sun slipped on down and it started getting dark. The streetlamps that worked began to glow a dull cherry red.

And the children turned and stared.

Stared across the street at one of the houses.

It was as I followed their gaze that I realised whose house it was.

Run for the phone, I thought. *Ring him. Warn him? Say something. Invite him over if you have to.* But I didn't. Couldn't. I couldn't seem to move or speak. Only watch.

As, one by one in the gathering dusk, lights blinked on behind Ben Crabshaw's windows. Later, I saw his shadow moving about. And still the children stood there, staring, passing round their cigarettes, taking swallows of beer and cheap wine, watching, waiting.

Ben's shadow, moving to and fro. Pacing furiously. Restless, uncomfortable. In a house at once too small and too large.

I knew then. I knew, and I couldn't move.

A kind of ritual; a cheap, rough magic, homemade out of desperation and the yearning to escape. New lives rich in possibility. In exchange for a sacrifice. A soul to trap and mire in the same despair from which they flee; someone to take their place.

I stood there for more than an hour.

Until Ben's front door flew open and he stormed down the drive, across the road and towards the children.

Why not the old? Who'll remember us as we once were, when we were young? And who's most to blame for their ruined, blighted lives, stunted and hopeless? Who's spent longest as architects of their kingdom?

While they go on from hopeless childhood to instant, promise-filled maturity, to build that world anew. Probably exactly the same way as it is now. Only worse.

They spread out as he reached them, encircling him. Two of them caught his arms, one of them the girl who looked so much like Ruth Hamilton. And then the boy who'd been kissing with the blonde lady came forward. I saw the metal gleaming in his hand. Saw it flash out. Heard Ben's muted, throttled cry.

Saw them scatter as I saw him fall, dispersing and vanishing like shadows before the light, as Ben rolled and twisted painfully along the kerb before he finally slumped half in and half out of the gutter. And, at last, was still, the lights from his own house reflecting in his blank, open eyes.

AND SO NOW I'M HERE, READY TO CLIMB THE WALLS. I WENT TO THE WINDOW before, and all seven pairs of their eyes gleamed as they stared towards my house.

After the funeral, the few mourners all went back to Ben's place. He'd no family either. We each took a thing or two of his. Mine was his old photo album. It's right beside me now as I write. I still haven't opened it and looked. Can't.

They never found a mark on him of course. Another heart attack. They don't believe me when I tell them what I saw, any more than they did Ben.

New faces at the bus stop this evening. The girl in the BMW was back, and she brought a feller with her. Tall dark and handsome. The boy she was kissing isn't there any longer, but the new man has the same dark hair, the same cheeky smile.

And there's a new boy, too. He seems to be talking a lot with the girl who looks like Ruth Hamilton once did. Very friendly. Too friendly for my liking. And there's something very, very familiar about him. That's why I don't dare look in the photo album. There'll be pictures of him as a lad in there.

They're all staring at my house. Even away from the window I can feel it. Feel it in the coffin-like oppression of these four, sturdy, once-sheltering walls, in their echoing, lonely emptiness. Too big and too small, all at once, at the same time.

Been here before, haven't we?

Perhaps it won't be so bad. I wonder how much I'll remember? To be young again, even if it's life lived at a dead end. With Ruth. If I can cut in ahead of Ben bloody Crabshaw, who looks like he's already getting stuck in. Maybe it can be good. A swap rather than a theft. A second chance.

Or so I tell myself.

I have to, you see.

Because I really can't hold out anymore.

In a minute or so, I'm going to put this pen down and go to the front door. And then I'll open it, and walk out into the night.

Down the road, to the bus shelter.

THE CHILDREN OF MOLOCH

A *dark and stormy night . . .*

Was then, is now. Dusk on a bleak windswept moorland in the north of England, a town's lights gleaming dully into far-off life. Grey and black clouds thicken in the distance. A promise of rain.

The Cortina's engine clanks and knocks. Doesn't matter now, however this goes. Just get me that bit farther. Then maybe idle for a little while. Not long.

And a road, long overgrown and cracked by sprouting weeds, that leads through thickets of silver birch which in the twilight look like bones, to a clearing where a gutted house looms, the dark, pale walls blacked by fire.

Hillview.

I stop the car; the engine ticks and cools. I get out, walk towards it. The years haven't been kind; they've almost finished what the fire began. Standing in the front doorway, I see most of the first and second floors have fallen in. Above, the roof's a cage of charred and rotted ribs.

Lightning flashes in the distance. Thunder cracks as I go inside. Motion flickers at the edges of my sight. Shadows, rats, birds. No. They're more. I *need* them to be more. Outside, the woods lose definition in the failing light. *Without form, and void. And darkness was upon the face of the deep.*

High on the moors, clean air, green for miles around; this should have been a haven for the children in its care. Should've echoed with their laughter. Instead it was a cavern for their weeping. Some of it mine.

I can hear it now; can hear it still.

It's never stopped.

"Get up. And for fuck sake cover yourself, you filthy little shit."

Brownlow pulls his zip up. I hear it, don't see. My face is in the pillow, my teeth still biting down.

"I said, 'Move.'"

I'm afraid to. Feels like he's torn me open down there; if I sit up my guts'll fall out my arse. Always feels that way, but each time I'm afraid it'll be for real. Brownlow whacks my arse. I squeal, can't stop myself. "Get fucking *up*," he says.

I do as he says. "Get dressed." I do that, too. My pyjamas and dressing-gown are on the floor. Something wet runs out of my bum, down my leg. I whimper with fright; I was right, I'm going to die.

"You filthy little trog. You've shat the bed." Brownlow cuffs the side of the head. My eyes sting again. I won't cry anymore. "I ought to make you lick that up." He did, once. But not tonight. Tonight, he's spent. Can't be bothered now. "Go on, fuck off."

I keep my head down, but glance up once. Brownlow lights a cigarette, adding smoke to the room's stale reek of sweat and come. He's tall and thin, pale and barefoot in his jeans. Bare-chested, too. Thin face, blue eyes, a fringe of blonde hair like a broken wing falling across his eyes. He smokes in silence, eyes lidded and dreamy; already he's somewhere else. I inch towards the door. Then he notices me again. "Why are you still here? 'Fuck *off*,' I said."

"Yes, Mr. Brownlow." I cinch the dressing-gown cord and go out fast, before he changes his mind.

HILLVIEW'S CORRIDORS ARE LONG AND DARK. WIND HOWLS, MOANS; OUT-side the trees heave and thrash like a black and spiky sea. They don't look like trees anymore.

Lots of shadows in the corridors. Corners, alcoves, bends. Places for things to hide. Here and there light peeps out under doors. *Staff.* I tiptoe past. One opens. A big shape stands in it. It's Ronnie. A giant from where I'm stood. Hairy forearms. Black hair gone wild. Jowled, hairy face. A permanent reek of stale sweat. He grins, lick his lips and blows me a kiss.

I want to run, but I don't. No running in the corridors. I walk. Fast. His eyes on my back. I can feel them.

"Brownlow's little bumboy," I hear him call. "You're mine after him."

I look back at him. Everyone knows Ronnie. He's the worst of the lot. Even worse than Brownlow.

"He's promised me," he says. "Once he's got bored of you."

THE COLD DARK. THEY SWITCH THE HEATING OFF MOST NIGHTS, EVEN IN November. Even up here on the moor. Scabs says they skim money off the heating budget. Wrapping thin scratchy sheets tight around like a mummy. The sick warm trickle from my arse. Sure it must be soaking through the seat of my pyjamas. Shit, blood and spunk. Oh God.

Tried sneaking in, on tiptoes. Hoped no one'd hear, no one'd know.

But of course they did

"Martin Carr, Martin Carr, sell you his arse for a Marathon bar."

Tommy Chapman in the bed next to mine. He's got one joke and won't shut up with it. Keeps going, on and on. Chinese water torture. Won't fucking shut up.

"Martin Carr, Martin Carr, sell you his arse for a Marathon bar."

Like he thought I had a choice. Like any of us do.

"Mar-tin is a bum-mer." Low, hateful crooning. A whispered chant. The kind kids do. That's from the other side of me, from Kieron Harvest's bed. "Mar-tin is a bum-mer. Martin sucks Brownlow's di-ick."

"Sell you his arse for a Marathon bar. . . ."

Sniggers and whispers in the dark. No one else is joining in tonight, but no one here's gonna stop it either. Half-glad of something to laugh at, a bit of blood sport, and half-glad it's not them.

"You suck Brownlow's shit, don't you, Carr. You suck it right out his arse-hole. Don't you?" Kieron's face is a thin, white blur. He talks about this stuff a lot. Too much. Scabs says he's queer but won't admit it. Kieron's not that big, but he's wiry and cruel and his hard, knobbly fists punch at the pain spots with a sniper's aim—balls, solar plexus, the big muscles of the arms and legs. But he's even better with words. "Eh? Eh? I'm talking to you, Carr. Said you suck Brownlow's shit."

"Martin Carr, Martin Carr—"

"You suck his shit. You're licking his dick. Does Scabby Charlotte know, Carr? Does she? Does Charlotte know?"

The thin hissing whispers, wet and gloating like snakes, probing and violating. Just like Brownlow. Just like Ronnie and the rest. I'd kill these fuckers if I could. Kieron Harvest most of all.

"Does Scabby Charlotte know you suck Brownlow's co—" And then Kieron's cut off, squealing in pain but muffled like a pillow's shoved over his face while about a dozen hard meaty smacks sound. The sniggers and whispers all about have cut off. Even Chapman's shut up. Stillness. Then:

"Call us that again you little fucking cunt and you'll die screaming." It's a girl's voice but no one laughs. Much less makes a move to help Kieron Harvest. The hitting's stopped but Kieron's still making noises even through the pillow jammed to his face. I can't see what she's doing but I can tell it hurts and I think, *Good*. She doesn't stop till Kieron's crying, and then she pulls the pillow off his face and lets him breathe. "Now shut up, Harvest, you fucking scum." Her low voice is soft and coarse at once: hard and gentle, tender and cruel. There's sex and passion in it and I don't even really know what they are yet. "You okay, Tinny?"

Only Scabs calls me that. "Yeah," I say, to sound hard. Scabs's eyes gleam black in the darkness; I see her coiled like a cat on Kieron Harvest's bed. "No," I say, because I can't lie to her.

The eyes gleam and smoulder. "All right. Come with me." She kneels up on the bed; lean and thirteen, damaged and magnificent. "And none of you saw me. I wasn't here." She jabs at whimpering Kieron. "Specially not you, cunt. Right?"

There's a sob from Kieron that she takes as assent. "Come on, then."

"All right."

I pull my dressing gown on. Scabs slides off Kieron's bed and walks like a cat for the dormitory door, and I follow.

RAIN-SPOTS FALL THROUGH HILLVIEW'S SKELETAL ROOF. THE GROUND'S uneven and doubly treacherous in the failing light. The rubble's clogged with rain-washed earth and overgrown with brambles and grass.

One wing's almost intact. Almost. There are holes in the floors and the walls are still black with soot. Rotted flights of stairs lead up to higher levels and I crave to go up them but know I won't. Too dangerous. Not risking it.

Maybe I should. Playing safe's not got me anywhere so far.

A noise, behind me. Dull echoes in the corridor. I turn. Nothing there. a flicker of shadow. Trick of the light. Or movement, perhaps. Sudden, impossibly swift. Nothing moves as fast as that, but if it did, I might just have caught the briefest glimpse of it.

There's a pocket torch in one of my pockets. Among other things. I put my hand in the pocket, grip it tight.

"Tinny."

I spin about but there's no one there. It's getting dim. I take out the torch and switch it on, shine it about.

Lightning flashes, almost directly overhead. I must be mad, coming here. But I had nowhere else to go. The thundercrack shakes the building. Flakes of rot and wood whisper down.

A hole in the wall, gaping out over the rubble sprawl that fills the building's floor. When I flash the torch over the wreckage, for a moment I see a row of long, thin black bodies and thin white faces, eyes aglitter and cold. And then there's only the quickening rain, glittering in stray light, and the coiling play of shadow and twilight in the dust.

"Tinny."

I spin and shine the torch. Up a staircase, and for a second I think I see her.

"Scabs?"

The torchlight marks a patch of white on a dark, stained wall. Scabs's face. No. She was there. I'd know her face from a bit of unmarked plasterboard for Christ's sake. But would I, now?

A sign, though; it's a sign. Or so I choose to think. And if it's madness to think that, then madness let it be. Sanity, or what I've seen of it, seems overrated now.

Slowly and carefully, I climb the stairs. The risers bend and soften underfoot. And yet they hold.

"That nice?"

"Yeah." My voice is a thin breath; my breathing ragged and fast.

"Keep doing it, yeah?"

"Yeah."

"Yeah." Scabs kisses my forehead, strokes my hair, brings my face to her breasts. They're surprisingly big for a girl her age. She's not much older than me, not even by a year, but in another way she is. I had a family who kept me safe, till they died. I say a family. I mean Mum and Dad. They died. And I fell into the trap. Got volleyed from foster parent to foster parent. All fuckers like Ronnie, Brownlow, the other bastards who run this place. Said I had a bad attitude. A problem child. So no one'd want me and I'd end up somewhere like here. Scabs was always different. Got her name because she used to scratch herself. Her cunt. So the skin bled and there were scabs there. And then no one wanted to fuck her. Called her Scabs as an insult. She wears it as a badge. Charlotte's her given name; she hates it. *Charlotte got fucked*, she told me once. *Scabs never does.*

Her hand goes up and down my dick. "Suck it," she tells me, and I take her nipple in my mouth. She breathes out through her nose, makes a noise in her throat.

We're naked under blankets, in the place Scabs calls the Nest. It's at the end of a corridor on the third floor, past the day rooms, the play rooms. It's a sort of little nook with a window, a dusty little place. For someone to sit in with a book and look out of the little round window over the moors. The door's long been sealed up. But Scabs knows her way around Hillview. Climb through a hatch in the ceiling, crawl across timbers in the narrow space between the ceiling and the floor above, and you'll find a gap, a gap in the ceiling of the Nest. Scabs has never told me how she found it, but she makes sure no one else can, fitting up a piece of board to cover the way in. It's our place. She keeps things here: blankets, toys, comics, books, a first-aid kit she stole from somewhere. Spare clothes. She looked me over, cleaned me up, and now we're doing other things.

Her free hand guides mine between her legs, to a thin thatch of coarse hair and what feels like a puckered wound. I rub at it and hope I'm doing right, although it's hard concentrating on anything other than what her other hand's doing.

Scabs comes fast; before me, even though she started me before. She grips me tight, breath quickening; pushes her face down into my shoulder and lets out a muffled, squeaking cry. We stay like that for a moment or two, her hand loosely squeezing my dick; then it starts to pump up and down again and she lifts her head, her chin touching my hair, pushing my face down into her breasts again.

A moment later, it all goes away for a few precious seconds. Hillview, Brownlow, Ronnie, the pain of my ripped arse, everything. Gone. There's just a warm delicious tingle that races through my body, down arms and legs and chest and head that rushes down to where Scabs's hand is before surging, spurting out. I gasp, squeeze my eyes shut; I see colours, bright, shifting. Then still. We fall against each other, sit up. My arms about her, hers about me.

I move my head on her breasts, letting their softness shift and pillow me. Her skin is soft and smooth and warm. Without Scabs I don't want to think about my life here. Without Scabs I couldn't survive. There are ways out, always. There have to be. Scabs is one. Without her it'd be a razor, something sharp up along the wrist, or a belt looped round a coat hook. Others have left that way. Left for good. I only leave now and again. For brief seconds, and then come back. And Scabs is how I leave.

She kisses my hair. "I love you, Tinny."

"Love you, too."

"No, you don't."

"Yeah, I do. I do."

"Okay."

I don't know why she sought me out. Scabs needs no one. Even Brownlow and the rest are careful with her. The other kids fear her, even the boys. But for some reason, she took to me. Maybe I remind her of someone. I don't really care. I just cling to her.

Rain rattles on the grimy window glass. Scabs's fingers smooth my ruffled hair. After a bit, she starts to sing softly. "All the Pretty Horses." Then she stops.

"Tell you a story?" she says.

"Okay."

"Kay." A pause. Thunder and wind. "You ever wondered what we'd be like, if we were wild?"

"Wild?" I tilt my head up, look at her. She kisses my mouth, absently, then strokes my head to make me lower it again.

"Wild," she says. "Like the wolf. Think about dogs, what they're like. They're tamed. They do what we say. We're tame, too. People. But wolves. Wolves are wild. Imagine if people went wild like that. Like if you turned dogs loose in the woods. Made 'em fend for themselves. Some'd die. Couldn't hack it. But the ones that lived. They'd go wild. They'd become like wolves. And they wouldn't let anyone tame them again. *Ever.*"

I close my eyes. Lightning flickers through them. Wind. Rain. Howling. Thunder.

"Did you ever hear," asks Scabs, "of the Krail?"

"No."

"No." She thinks, looks for the words. "They used to be like us, Tinny. Kids like us. *Just* like us. You know? They were in a place like this. With fuckers like Brownlow and Ronnie and the rest. They were just like us."

My eyes still closed. Outside the only sound's a soft hissing. The wind's died and the rain falls straight. *Hiss. Hiss.* A thought: the still calm centre.

"And it went on for years. Until. They turned. Turned round. Turned on the bastards."

Her hand smoothing. Stroking my hair. But her arms are round me now like iron.

"The house they were in—a place like this—it burned. Burned down. And all the bastards—the Brownlows, the Ronnies, the Kieron Harvests—they all died screaming. They burned to death. And the children. The other children. The good children, like you—"

"And you, Scabs."

She squeezes me, briefly. "Yeah. And me, sweetheart. The good children like you and me. They ran away. Out into the woods and onto the moors. Into the dark. Into the wild."

Hiss, hiss, hiss, goes the rain. The slow smoothing action of her hand on my hair. "And?" I ask.

"And, they never came back. They're still out there. Never came back to the grown-up's world." There's a crack in Scabs's voice, a hitch and a hoarseness, and I squeeze her hard. "Why would they? They've got their own life now. Their own life. It's beautiful and it's wild. They're nothing like us, not anymore. They're wild as the wolf. Have you ever seen a wolf, Tinny? I mean a real one?"

"Just pictures." In books of fairy tales when I was a kid, cos wolves were always evil. Big, bad wolves. But I've seen photos. Used to watch stuff like *Wildlife on One*. I've seen the real things. Briefly. "Telly."

"Yeah. Then you know. They're proud and they're beautiful and they know things dogs've forgot. Like how to hunt and kill."

"Kill?"

"Kill."

Hiss goes the rain, and then a far-off rumble.

"They're out there still, Tinny, and just like the wolf they've learnt things we don't know. How to live in the wild, in the trees and the water, in the earth, on the moors. They live in the night. Night people. They've learnt magic—tricks of hiding, seeking, catching. They're out there still, and even though they're nothing like us anymore, they remember they once were. And sometimes—just sometimes—if it's the right kind of night, the right time, the right place—if you're lucky—they might be listening. They might hear your call."

"And what if they do?" I'm not sure I like the sound of the Krail at all.

"They bear you away, Tinny." Her voice is a whisper choked by tears. Like she's drowning in the rain. "They take you with them, to where they live, to become like them. They bear you away."

GOD KNOWS HOW OR IF I'LL EVER GET DOWN FROM HERE. THE RISERS HAVE snapped under me twice and it's almost pitch black now. Maybe, maybe I won't have to.

Please let me not have to.

I've gathered things on the way as I climb. The things I need. They go in my pocket with the things I've brought. I've gathered broken feathers, torn the leg off a decaying bird carcass. A rusted nail, slid free of woodwork softened by decay to the crumbling consistency of a chocolate Flake. All of it goes in there. To build the shrine.

Nearly the only part of the third floor that's not gone is the Nest. I pick my way down the disintegrating floor towards it. It wasn't brick that sealed it off, only plasterboard, wallpapered over. All now rotten and mostly gone. I tear the last of it away and clamber through. The attic, above, is all gone now.

The Nest's floor is stone. The floor is safe. The window is unbroken, but even lighting the candles is hard—winds blow through the ruined corridors. The reality of it quivers me for a moment; here I am, perched in this brickwork blister on the building's flank. So easy for it to break loose, so close to falling to the ground to shatter. Is that how it'll end for me? At the last, a pratfall, the punchline of a bad joke?

I can't afford to think about that. I take my treasures from my pockets and lay them out on the floor. The thin heat of the candles, perched on the windowsill, briefly warms my face. Then I pick up the first pieces of wood and stone, and I begin to build the shrine.

"NEARLY THERE. COME ON. SH. COME ON."

Scabs brought a few little treasures from the Nest. One of them's the torch she shines up ahead of us, lighting up the attic space. Scabs knows Hillview and its cancered heart. She has the map. Dust swirls about us. Dry, catching at the back of my throat. I stifle a cough.

"Sh." Crouching low—more from instinct than from need, because the attic windows are narrow and dirty and who's going to be looking through them?—Scabs crosses the attic floor. Her feet are bare, the soles dark with dust, almost black. "Here. Sit. Watch."

The torchlight plays over it. There's a thing she's made from three short planks of wood. Stands about two-feet high all told. One plank lies flat, a heavy stone on each end to weight it and to prop the other two. They rest against each other so there's a triangle. Where the two planks rest together, a hole's been bored through them and a loop of rope passed through both to secure them into place. The hole's wide enough for a thick stick to have been pushed through as well. Three pieces of string hang from it. One's tied round a seashell. Another, a piece of bottle glass. The third, a mouse's skull. Found up here, maybe, or from an owl pellet in the woods. The woods round Hillview are full of owls.

"What is it?"

"Shrine," she says.

"Shrine?"

"To the Krail." There are other stones laid out on the bottom plank that serves as the floor of the shrine. A tin ashtray in its centre coated in layers of char. Scabs takes out two candles and a box of matches. She lights the candles one by one. She drips melted tallow on the shrine floor, on old rings of congealed wax, and fixes them in place.

Scabs takes paper, dried grass and twigs from a pocket. Shreds and breaks them into the ashtray. Pats them flat down. Gropes across the floor without looking at me—eyes on the ashtray—looking for my hand. I reach out and our fingers grip.

"Been in a few places like this," she says. "In and out. They say I'm trouble. Don't fit. And then some bastard like Brownlow. But I kept my eyes open. Ears, too. Learned how to get by. How I heard about them. The Krail. And I learnt how you call them. You take wood and stones like this, from the place you are. See how it's all done? The stone roots it to the ground. The wood"—she lets go of my hand, looks upwards as she thrusts steepled fingers towards the ceiling—"channels it up. And you need the rope to hang your offerings in the smoke. See? Something grown." The cockleshell. "Something made." The bottle-glass. "And something dead." The mouse skull. "Like a radio to send a message out to them. If they listen and if they want to help." She takes a folded scrap of paper from her pocket, puts that atop the tinder. "You put your message on first. Then your gift. Gift last of all." She takes something from her pocket. A glint of purple foil. A bar of Dairy Milk, or part of one. The stub-end of a big bar. She unwraps it. Four squares of chocolate. She breaks them up and puts them on top of the message. Then strikes a match. The flame glows and swells in the dark. "And then—then you just send your message." And she lights the tinder.

It flares up fast. The glow is fast and warming, but the chocolate burns and it's a harsh jagged smell and I flinch back. Scabs takes my hand and holds it tight.

"Same every night," she says. "Every night when I come up here. Send the same message. Get us out. You and me. And anyone else wants to come. Burn Brownlow and Ronnie and the other fuckers. Burn them to dust. Burn this place." Her voice is choked and ragged. To my horror I realise she's nearly crying. "Just get us out of here," she whispers. The glass and the cockle-shell, the mouse's skull, they bob and swing and dance in the hot smoke. "Bear us away."

I don't know what to say. Scabs is mad. Must be. The thought of the Krail is so scary I can't believe it. Don't want to maybe.

"Why?" I ask her. "Why'd you want them to do that?"

"Why?" Her face is ravaged, adrip with tears. "Why? Why would you not fucking want them to, Tinny? Why'd you want to stay like this? Get fucked up the arse off cunts like Brownlow or Ronnie, bastards like that. And just have to take it and take it, cos you're just a kid and they're grown-ups? Cos no fucker'll believe you? Bastards. And it'll be the same when we're older. Or we can be like the Krail. Don't get old, don't die."

"What, like vampires?"

"No, you div, not like that. Whatever. No bastard'll hurt us ever again if we're like that. If we're Krail. And we can make fuckers like Brownlow pay and pay and pay for what they've done to us."

She's pinned everything on this. But she's mad. She loves me and maybe I love her, too, but she's mad. Must be. But what if she's not? What if they're real? What if they come? I try to picture the creatures she talks about and fail. Try to imagine being one of them. I still believe in heaven, hope it's a place I can escape Brownlow and Ronnie and Kieron Harvest one day. Hell would be this place, Hillview, only without Scabs, and me their prey for all eternity.

I'm still wondering if I can ever put that into words and opening my mouth to try when the lights come on with a *click*—dull, naked yellow bulbs, a wide-spaced row of them hung from the ceiling—heavy footsteps creak on the floorboards and Ronnie's low, hot snigger fills the attic room.

A PLANK ACROSS THE WINDOWSILL. STONES TO WEIGHT IT. THEN THE OTHER two planks, bracketed by stones, the ends rested together. I loop the rope through, with thick, shaking fingers, and tie it tight. Then the stick. And then I tie on the three things. The trinity of this black and secular faith. Something grown—the flared, complicated cup of a beech nut, the string tied round its brittle stem. Something made—the nail, old and rusted. And something dead—the bird's leg, its claws splayed and reptilian.

A tin pub ashtray goes in the middle, between the flickering candles. In it go things I don't need anymore—my driver's licence, two years old, my national insurance card, snapped and broken, the last crumpled notes of paper money.

I see my face in the glass, white and pale and gaunt. Wasted. Looks slack on the skull, like the skin's ready to fall off the bone.

A gnawed, cracked ballpoint and a little pocket notepad. I scribble my prayer on one piece, fold it up tight. Shred the others to add to the rest. Anything else I can find that'll burn goes in the ashtray, too. My folded note goes atop.

My offering? What can offer them, what can I give? What do I have they'll value? A glassine baggie of reddish-brown dust. A few coins. What else can I give to back up my plea for another chance, not to let one mistake, one failure of nerve, to be always held against me? My blood? My tears? I nick myself and drip the blood onto the rest; a scrap of tissue soaks up and adds the tears.

At last it's time, the moment of truth; I strike the matches, thrust them one by one into the kindling; as the fire flares my empty harrowed face shows in the window glass. When it dies there are other faces, narrow pale blurs in the storm, hovering in the dark and regarding me with cold and slanting eyes. A scream locks in my throat, on the brink of escape even though I've called for them. And then they are gone.

Gone but not gone. Gone from the window but not from what remains of Hillview.

I hear, feel, movement behind me. Swift, sudden, skittish, ghostly. In the collapsing corridors. In the gaps between floors and ceilings. I don't turn round; I sit, fingers locked on my knees till the knuckles whiten, and I wait.

There's something in the air. A thrumming, a buzzing. Like sitting beneath a pylon, like being next to a generator or a live cable. An insect hive. I am not alone.

"Hello, Tinny," says Scabs.

RONNIE'S SNIGGERING. IT'S LIKE KIERON HARVEST'S SNIGGER ONLY OLDER, hoarser. Not much deeper, despite his size. He's just another Kieron Harvest, but with Brownlow's tendencies to boot.

"Been here listening to that," he says. "Fuck knows how I didn't piss meself laughing, listening to all that shite."

Scabs shifts position, so she's just slightly ahead of me, closer to him. I can feel her beside me, tight and taut and rigid. But at the same time, she doesn't seem so strong now. Her strength's in her brains. Outwitting the bastards. But this time they got ahead of her. Or Ronnie did. And now she's just a teenage girl. And he's Ronnie. An animal. A beast. She won't stand any more of a chance than I would.

"Krail," he laughs softly. "The fuck did you get that old shite from?" He puts his meaty hands together, cracks the knuckles. "And all this old bollocks?" He makes for the shrine. Scabs sees what he's about and pushes me aside, crouching and tensing ready to fight, but he just kicks her, hard in the stomach, and she doubles up and goes flying, landing on the boards retching and clutching her belly, knees pulled up to her chin.

I'm frozen as Ronnie goes past me. He's decked Scabs; kicked her to the ground like she was nothing. Her face is screwed up and she's crying with pain. Really crying. I can see the tears streaking down her face.

"It's all bollocks!" Ronnie's foot stamps down on the shrine. Rocks scatter away and the planks collapse. He kicks and stamps at it. I hear little things break with a brittle crunch under his boots—the bottle glass, the mouse skull. The ashtray scatters embers and ashes across the board and Ronnie stomps on them. "Krail. Krail my fucking arse. You belong to us you stupid little fucking slag." He grabs her by the hair and pulls her hair up. Scabs tries not to scream but a high snarling animal noise comes out through her clenched teeth, and her eyes spill tears like rivers, and Ronnie laughs. "We own you," he says. "Fucking always."

And I run in. I scream something—I can never remember what—and run at him in the one act of physical courage I will ever commit. I kick and punch at him, think go for the balls because that'll hurt, but then his other hand grabs my hair and he shakes me like a rat. I scream, can't help myself. The pain's too bad.

"Shut up." He throws me to the ground and kicks me in the ribs. Scabs makes a noise and I hear another blow. The attic rocks and spins. My face in the dusty boards.

"Right, you."

He's speaking to me, and I know what's coming. I roll onto my side, still wheezing my breath. Scabs has slumped onto her back, head lolled to one side, face turned away from me, legs tangled up and limp, arms outflung as if for crucifixion. Ronnie grins down at me and starts to unbuckle his belt.

"Fuck waiting for Brownlow to finish with you," he says, unzips his fly and starts to fondle himself. "I'm having a piece of that tonight myself."

There's a humming in my ears. But then it dies. Instead there's a low thrumming. A buzz. Like a power-line. There are little white specks of glittering, glassy light swimming in my sight. But then they aren't there any more, or rather they've migrated into the shadows around the circles of weak light painted on the floor by the bare bulbs. They're in pairs. Twinned. Like eyes. Like eyes.

They are eyes, I realise, just as they start moving, darting into the light to meet Ronnie.

They are—

They are—

I can't describe them. How can I try? They shiver and flicker and blur like the picture of a TV when the reception's bad. A flicker, a blur, a darting streak of snatched, smeared blackness, and then it all seems to snap to a halt, quiver into a shivering, unstable stasis, then blurring and flickering and vanishing again.

Ronnie lets out a faint, throttled moan. His face is slack and his eyes weave back and forth. His big, meaty fists clench and unclench. A dark stain widens at his crotch.

It's as if they've grown so far beyond the human form that any shape's a limitation, something that can only be held by effort and concentration. How else to describe them? Imagine thin black jagged shapes scribbled in shadows in the air. Impossibly long limbs, all of them black except for the faces, the narrow hawkish faces, beautiful and cold, cruel and watchful, deadly and pitiless. With slanted eyes. Eyes that glow with a cold, pale light.

Oh, I know them, of course I know them; what else could they be? The Krail have come. Theirs is a terrible beauty, but it is a beauty nonetheless.

Scabs is stirring, waking. Light gleams in her open eyes. She looks up as one of the shadow figures leans over her and she smiles like a child, and reaches up a hand to take the thin black claw that reaches down towards her like a bristling of blackened sticks. I watch, clambering upright, as she is drawn upright and stands before the Krail, reaching tentatively out to caress its raggedy black shape, while its face, inscrutable as a painted mask, knowing who knows what emotions that any human would understand, surveys her.

Two or three of the Krail circle Ronnie, darting, near-vanishing, reappearing. Their long black, shadowy hands feint swift, ripping blows at him, which he flinches from with panicked cries. Scabs turns to look over her shoulder at him; sees his terror; smiles.

Over near the window are little orange sparks and whiffs of smoke; there's a faint scent of burning in the dusty air. A Krail approaches it; extends a long black hand to caress the smoke. It writhes and coils around his, her, its fingers; it's like watching someone pay with a pet snake.

Its fingers circle over the embers, and then open. They squeeze gently at the air and as I watch the smoke streams upwards and the ember-glow brightens, brightens, then flickers into a tongue of flame.

Scabs has seen this, too, and is watching raptly.

The tongue becomes a rushing surge, dancing easily under the Krail's hand. A quick motion and the flame has left the ground, and instead it writhes and twines around the hand. The Krail's other hand cups and moulds the fire like so much clay.

Ronnie has turned slowly to face the Krail with the fire. Its hands now cup a ball of flickering incandescence. It holds it up, and the fire spurts out. A brief jet, licking Ronnie for only a second, but it's enough. He screams. Fire clings to his face, chest, hands, then becomes black smoke and pours upwards and is gone. He staggers and falls to his knees. And I see he has no face anymore—only white bone grins through the blackened charcoal that was his face. His hands are bone claws and his ribs show through at his chest.

"Yes, you bastard," says Scabs. "Yes. Yes."

Ronnie's trying to scream, but can only make thin muffled whining sounds. The Krail close in on him. And that's when I run.

As I do, I hear Scabs scream my name.

THE FIRE ALARM'S SHRILLING AS I RUN THROUGH THE CORRIDORS. I PASS A window—a first-floor window—and something sweeps past, carrying a ball of glowing, brilliant fire.

People are screaming now. I run for the stairs. Behind me are thundering feet.

I reach the hallway. As I run for the main door I hear a voice shouting. I turn as I pass the doorway to an office and see Brownlow, in his dressing

gown, clutching a phone and shouting into it. "Hello? Hello? For fuck sake—"
Then he turns and sees me. "You!" Does he know, somehow, the unwitting
role I've played? "You, you little sh—"

But the window behind him explodes and something thin and black
and ragged with a pale and beautiful face crouches in the frame, cupping fire in its hands. Flame shoots out and Brownlow is ablaze. He flails
screaming round the office; papers ignite. Another ray of fire catches him
and he falls. The Krail blurs into the room to stand above the thrashing,
screeching thing on the floor, blasting it with flames until its struggles
cease. It's still doing so as I back out and stumble away, as if hosing every
trace of Brownlow from the earth, with fire instead of water. Cleaning
it of filth.

I make it out of the door and something black and cackling swoops
by me, trailing fire in its wake, then flinging it against Hillview's walls.
Another flies to cling against a wall and blasts fire through a window,
holding it steady and remorseless despite the screams from within.

The whole building's already going up. There are screams—but are they
only of terror and pain? Are there other notes in there, ones of exultation
and transcendence? Can I hear Scabs's voice among them?

I can't be sure. The Krail bolt and weave around the destruction they're
causing. Someone runs screaming out of the front door, falls writhing at
my feet, rolling on his back to put out the flames: Kieron Harvest. In spite
of everything he's done I reach out to help him but he coughs, smoke and
blood spilling from his mouth, then falls back and lies still, eyes fixed
open, catching the light of Hillview's flames.

The screams are dying away. There's just the crackle of flames. And the
dark tattered figures flitting round the collapsing rooftops. Going still.
Gazing down at me. With their coldly bright, slanted, pale eyes.

I turn and run; through the woods and into the night, not even caring
that these are the Krail's true domain. I don't stop and I don't look back,
not even when I think I hear a lone, forlorn cry of *Tinny* far behind me,
fading on the cold night wind.

I CAN SEE HER FACE IN THE WINDOW GLASS. IT'S SCABS, OR WHAT WAS
her. In some ways she looks no different; in others the difference is vast.
Her narrow face is narrower, more angular still than it was, and the wild,
brambly black hair more so than ever, like a crown of painted thorns. Her

mouth is the red of berries and blood. Changed, but in a sense, simply made more of what it always was.

But the eyes—the eyes are utterly different. Slitted and aglow with the pale light of a winter moon.

Other shapes moved behind her. They whisper and they rustle. And beyond the window, clinging to the ruined walls or hovering in the night.

"Hello, Scabs," I say.

"I'm not Scabs anymore, Tinny." Her voice is a kind of cold music, bringing warmth and chills as one.

"I noticed."

"Ha." A brief laugh, a single note, showing teeth grown to points. She studies me in the glass. "But there's still enough of her to count, Tinny. At least as far as you're concerned."

A sob clenches my throat. My eyes sting. Something brittle and feathery caresses my head. I don't look at my reflection to see what it is. "It's horrible out there, Scabs."

"I know, darling. I tried to tell you."

"I know you did. You were right. I ended up in more places like this, afterwards. Would've been worse if I hadn't stopped trying to tell folk what really happened here."

"They'd never believe you."

"They never did. They let me out, in the end. But there's nowhere to go. I don't fit. Not anywhere."

The brittle, feathery thing strokes my head. "Sweetheart, I'm so sorry."

"Scabs, you were right. And I love you."

"Tinny—"

"Please. Please, Scabs. Take me. Take me like they took you. Please."

"I can't."

"Bear me away."

"Tinny, I can't."

"Don't leave me like this. Please. Scabs, I said you were right. Do you want me to beg? That it? I'm begging you, Scabs. I'm fucking begging you—"

She laughs. The brittle thing leaves my head. When I look in the glass I see it's covering her mouth. "I'm sorry," she says at last. "People just look so . . . funny to us now. Even you, Tinny."

"Please, Scabs. Please."

"I can't." There's a touch of impatience, of irritation in her voice. "Don't you understand, Tinny? Can't you? It's too late now. You're too old."

"Scabs . . ." It's a whisper and a breath and a prayer.

"It's not that I won't, Tinny. It's that I *can't*. It has to happen when you're young. It's the only way you can survive the change. That night . . . here at Hillview . . . it wouldn't have worked if I'd been older. Don't you see? You've lost your chance, Tinny. I'm sorry. But you can never be one of us now."

The noise that comes out of me doesn't have a name. A howl, a wail; it's none of these, more than any of them. When it's spent, I fall forward to my knees.

She gathers close to me, her thin brittle body but oh so terribly strong. Her long, terrible fingers stroke me. "Poor, poor little Tinny," she says at last. "I loved you. I really did."

I try to say I loved her, too, still do. But I'm crying too hard. And did I ever really love her? Or was it just need: comfort, sheltering, pubescent lust? It doesn't matter now. All that matters is that I had my chance and I blew it.

Her soft lips brush my cheek and draw blood. "I'm sorry, my love," she says, and then she's gone. I can tell. I'm alone again, and that strange thrumming in the air is gone.

I climb slowly to my feet and look around. I don't know how long I wait before I clamber back out of the Nest, and begin the long descent in the dark.

Perhaps she gives me that one last gift, guiding my steps safely down.

I WAIT IN THE CAR TILL THE DAWN COMES, HOPING AGAINST HOPE SHE'LL change her mind, come back, give me something, at least try. . . .

She does not.

Crows caw in the birch trees.

A thin line of weak grey light shows in the east.

I tape the hose to the exhaust pipe, feed the other end into the Cortina.

I turn on the engine and let it run.

I breathe deep. The engine sound becomes the thrum of the air around what Scabs has become; a little later it becomes Scabs's voice as I once knew it, murmuring to me of the Krail as she pillows my head on her breasts, singing "All the Pretty Horses" to me.

Her song fades away, back into the engine's growl.

Scabs, hear my prayer. Let my cry come unto thee. Spread thy dark wings.

Bear me away.

AND CANNOT COME AGAIN

Where do you start? Where do you say this began?

I could say it started last week, or I could say it started in the summer of 1993. I could say it started with a phone call last Wednesday, or the train pulling into Barmouth station; I could say it started with a glimpse of a sad, wild girl's face across the aisles of a converted chapel. I could say, in the finest clichéd tradition, that it started with a kiss, or I could say it started with a scream.

I could even say it started all the way back in 1985, when I first met Thomas Owen. Because without his friendship, this wouldn't have happened.

That's not to shift the blame from me. God knows, as I sit here, writing this, that I can't deny my responsibility. I wouldn't be writing this if I didn't. What I'm saying is when I look back I see so many chances, so many possibilities, so many things that could have gone one way or another. And yet they all added up this way, brought things to this pass. Brought me to where I am now. Is that proof that there's no such thing as chance, or that there's nothing but?

God knows, if he exists, and wiser men and women might, but I don't. I'm not here to give answers or make sense of what happened; I'm not here to try and find meaning or a moral. I'm just here to witness, and record. Because what happened needs to be recorded: the reason for what's already happened, and for what's about to happen to me. Viewed one way, the punishment is just; viewed another, it isn't at all.

But I've run all I can. Now I have to face what's coming. Because it's mine. Bought and paid for.

It started last Wednesday, with a phone call. Thomas Owen. For a blessed second or two, I didn't recognise the name.

"Who—" I said, or started to.

And then I remembered.

"Tom?" I said.

"Yeah." His voice was clipped; heavy breathing and static filled the silence on the line.

"Been a while," I said.

"Yeah."

Both of us, you could argue, were masters of understatement. It had, in fact, been twenty years since Thomas Owen and I had spoken. We'd seen each other a couple of times, on the mercifully rare occasions I'd had cause to visit Barmouth since the summer of 1993; the last had been three years earlier, on a blustery winter's day, at my gran's funeral. That had been good of him; I hadn't expected it. But still, we hadn't spoken. If Dewi Pritchard or Pete Griffiths had been there, I wouldn't have had anything to say to them either. Some things either bring people closer together or split them apart. The four of us were in the latter group.

"What do you want?" I asked. *Not how are you, mate,* or even *what can I do for you. What do you want.* A transaction; I'll give you this, and you'll go away.

"We need to talk," said Thomas.

My stomach clenched up, like someone's fist had smuggled itself in there and closed. At the same time, it rolled, as if I was spinning end over end. Fear can do that. No, not fear. Call it by its proper name. Dread.

"What about?" I asked. He didn't answer. "Thomas?" More silence. "You said we need to talk," I said, in case he'd forgotten. It didn't seem likely, though; last I heard he was a police officer, and they tend to expect you to have a decent attention span.

"Not like this," he said. "Face to face."

"What?"

"Face to face. You and me." His Welsh accent got thicker; it always had when he was stressed. "You need to come up here, to Barmouth. Now. Today."

"What? Whoah. Just a minute—"

"You need to come up here," he said flatly. "Now. Today."

The first time, he'd been asking. The second time, he wasn't.

I could hear the threat, feel it, beating behind the words. He didn't need to speak it out loud. But he did, anyway. "I'll make it official, if I have to."

I breathed out.

"You there?" he said.

"Yeah. I'm here."

"I wouldn't be talking to you if I didn't have to," he said.

"Thanks."

"You telling me it's any different for you?"

I breathed out again. "No."

"It's about . . ." He spoke two words. The names of letters. Not the name itself; even twenty years after the fact, he couldn't say the name. But the initials were enough.

"Well, then," he said. "So?"

I looked at the clock. It was nearly 6:00 P.M.; I live in Manchester, I don't drive, and Barmouth's at least four hours by train. "Can't make it tonight."

"Tomorrow, then. Come on—you still work from home, don't you?"

"Yeah." I didn't like admitting it; didn't like conceding him anything. Whatever he wanted, it couldn't be good.

"So, bring your bloody laptop—"

"iPad."

"Whatever you bloody call it. Bring it with you and you can work on the train, or in your hotel room. Should only be one night."

"Okay," I said, finally.

"Take my number." He reeled it off; I wrote it down. "Ring me tomorrow when you know what time you'll be in."

"Okay."

I DIDN'T GET MUCH WORK DONE ON THE TRAIN. PARTLY IT WAS THE countryside; the Cheshire landscape it had to cross to get to the border is pleasant enough, gently rolling and green, but the North Welsh countryside has a special beauty all of its own.

You soon know when you've entered Wales; there's not only a different flag but a different language, on road signs and people's lips. But the landscape alone tells you very quickly that you've crossed. It's craggier, more rugged; roads don't run straight because great blocks and spires of stone break constantly from the rich earth. Hills rise like waves on a green-grass sea, crested with spars of lichened slate; pine forests sprout on them, and between them run rivers and streams as tortuously winding as the roads.

The landscape caught my eye, and the glimpsed towns where the Welsh red dragon flag—*Y Ddraig Goch*—flew from flagpoles in place of England's Cross of St. George. It had been a running joke between Thomas and I, in better times—*"Your lot might be in charge, but our flag's miles cooler."*

I had to smile, remembering him say that. How old had I been, when I first met Thomas Owen? Five, six? Mum and Dad used to bring us up to Barmouth in the holidays—Easter, Whitsun, summer more often than not—to stay with my gran; Thomas's family had lived next door, so it was almost inevitable we'd become first playmates, and at length fast friends. I'd also become friendly with Pete and Dewi, two lads he palled around with, but Thomas and I had been "best buds," as they used to say. He'd even come up to Manchester to visit a few times. And it had lasted, too, until the summer of 1993.

When I remembered that, I looked away from the landscape and down at the iPad, in front of me on the train carriage's tabletop. I switched it on and tried to work. But I was still staring at the screen an hour later, when the train reached the iron bridge across the Mawddach Estuary.

The river Mawddach opens out, via the estuary, into Barmouth Bay, which opens out in its turn into the Cardigan Bay and thence into the Irish Sea. Going over the bridge, if you looked one way you saw the hills, each side of the river, rolling apparently endlessly inland; look the other and you saw the sea, glimmering blue and—it seemed—equally endless in the May sun.

I shut off the iPad, packed it away and slung on my backpack as the train took the viaduct over the quayside and sank down to ground level. Left of the railway was the beach, and beyond it the glittering bay. I went to the door and waited.

Thomas was standing on the platform; tall, square-shouldered, wavy black hair and blue eyes. He was wearing a Berghaus fleece and Reebok trainers; his jeans were probably another pricey brand. Someone was doing well for himself, anyway. *Crime pays.*

That thought wiped the smile off my face.

The doors hissed open and I stepped out onto the station platform.

"Thomas," I said.

He nodded.

We didn't shake hands, much less hug like the long-lost friends we'd once been. We just stood there looking at one another.

"So?" I said.

"Sling your bag in here first. Then we'll grab a coffee." He turned and walked to his car, a four-by-four BMW. *Chelsea tractors*, Dad had used to call them, but I supposed out here you had more justification to drive one.

I dumped my backpack in the Beamer's boot, then walked down the seafront with him to the harbour. Thomas didn't speak and neither did I; he'd clearly made up his mind that he'd choose when and where the conversation began. A power thing, maybe? Was he going to try blackmailing me? Good luck if he did; he earned a lot more than me, by the look.

Davy Jones's Locker was still there, a little cave-like café sited in a 14th century stone building. Looking out, there was a view of the harbour, the bridge, the mountains; inside, the white-painted walls were hung with sea-faring memorabilia—a sawfish's rostrum, glass buoys in rope netting, an old brass diver's helmet, even a huge stuffed fish above the door.

Thomas ordered two coffees, nodded me to a table in the corner.

"Okay," I said. "Come on. What's all this about?"

"It's about Pete and Dewi," he said, and took a sip.

"What—for fuck sake, what about them?" Heads turned toward us; I looked down, face burning, but my fists stayed clenched. I was sick of this, sick of him doling out whatever scraps suited him, jerking me about like a puppy on a leash.

I looked up. Thomas looked back at me, arms folded, eyebrows raised, leaning back in his chair. "Finished?" he asked.

"Fuck off." I took a deep breath and pushed the chair back. "Either you tell me what's going on or I'm grabbing my bag and getting the first train back."

"Okay. Okay." His hands were raised. For the first time, I saw a shadow of fear on him. He glanced around to make sure nobody was still looking at us, then motioned me to sit down. I didn't move; he motioned again, more urgently. I decided I'd made my point and sank back into my seat. Thomas leant forward. "They're dead," he said.

"What?"

"Dewi and Pete," he said. "And I think I'm next." He picked up his coffee and took another sip. "Of course, now you're here, it could be you."

THE SUMMER OF 1993—AS I REMEMBER IT, ANYWAY—WAS LONG AND bright and hot, making Barmouth the perfect place to be.

I spent all that summer with my gran. That was my parents' idea; although I didn't know it things hadn't been going well between them for some time; the last thing they needed, while their marriage imitated Yugoslavia and broke up (though far less amicably), was a moody fourteen-year-old shambling back and forth through the no man's land between the trenches.

So, my poor long-suffering gran—who, for reasons unknown, doted on me—was saddled with me for the duration of the summer. Not that she had to deal with much, beyond a few meals—I was out the door first thing most mornings, up on the hills, on the beach, walking inland down the estuary road, over the bridge to Morfa Mawddach and Fairbourne or up the coast towards Llanaber. Or a bus to Harlech, or farther inland to Bala—there were plenty of places to go.

And usually, I went there with three other lads my age—Thomas Owen, Dewi Pritchard and Pete Griffiths.

Thomas—well, you've seen Thomas. He was much the same at fourteen, only younger and smaller. He worked out, ran, played football, and it showed. Dewi was smaller and tubbier, a science-fiction junkie with a truly enviable collection of books and videos. He was a mine of information on almost any trivial topic you could name; the hard part was getting him to shut up about it. Pete was both the tallest of us, and the thinnest; Thomas and Dewi had a running joke that if he turned sideways at school he'd be marked absent. He was good-natured and soft-spoken, but—as they say in Manchester—daft as a brush.

And me? I was taller than Dewi, but not as wide, shorter and thicker than Pete and a bit brighter. I was in better shape than either of those two, but nowhere near as good as Thomas.

I found an old photograph of myself from that time, not so long ago; I stuck it quickly back in its box, pleading embarrassment to the girl I was with at the time. And I could have made a very good case for that being the cause. The picture showed a skinny lad with a thin, pimply face and an enormous dyed-blond fringe hanging down over his eyes like a broken wing, wearing jeans, floppy trainers and an open lumberjack shirt over a black Nirvana tee, trying to look moody and angsty and as if he knew the first thing about life. Naturally, I knew nothing about it. Not then. I didn't look for any photos of myself a month or two later. I sometimes wonder what I'd have seen in that.

No, it wasn't embarrassment that made me hide that picture away. It wasn't embarrassment at all.

Anyway, that day—

It was getting near the end of the summer, I remember that. I remember that because the "holiday spends" my parents had given me had almost run out. We were all in much the same boat, which cut our options down. We decided to go up to Harlech, wander round the castle. We'd just missed one bus and there was a good hour to go till the next one came, so the four of us were moping around Barmouth, killing time.

Finally, we wandered into The Price Is Right, which should give you an idea of how bored we were. It is, or was, a converted chapel—there must be four or five of those in the town now, plus the still-functional ones—selling the usual seaside stuff. Plastic buckets and spades, fishing nets on bamboo poles, crabbing lines, boxes of fudge, jars of rock, Welsh flags, cheap mugs and rude postcards. Not much, but it was something, so we mooched up and down the aisles trying to feign interest in what was on offer.

One thing half-caught my interest—a mug with a four-frame cartoon on the side. The first frame showed a man and a girl kissing outside a nightclub. In the next frame she was saying, "I suppose you'd like a w**k now?" "Well I wouldn't say no!" the man answered. "Fine, then, I'll see you when you're finished!"

I grinned a bit and took it off the shelf. Not that I thought I'd get away with buying it. My gran would have gone ballistic, and neither Mum nor Dad would've approved either. And there's not much point having something like that if you can't let anyone see it. But it made me grin anyway.

I turned to put it back, and looking through the gap it'd left on the shelf, I saw her for the first time.

What did she look like? Physically, I suppose—suppose because at twenty years' remove and no photograph to prompt me, memory's an unreliable guide—she wasn't that remarkable. She was about my height, thin, with shoulder-length black hair. Her eyes were grey; that's what I remember with stone-cold, icy clarity, even now. A pale grey, grey as the thin haze of smoke from a cigarette. I see them sometimes still, in dreams.

I'd seen girls around the town before, of course, and yes, I was at that age when you start to notice them, but she was different. Different how? Simple: she noticed me back.

She flinched away when our eyes met, but only briefly. A moment later she looked back at me—shyly, sidelong—and I realised she must have been looking at me for a while, without my realising.

Her eyes darted sideways, then back to mine; after a moment, she smiled. Not knowing what else to do, I smiled back. All of a sudden, I was both scared and excited. Something new was happening here, something unfamiliar.

"Hi," she said.

"Hiya," I said back.

We looked at each other. She glanced around again, then looked back to me and grinned again. It was bright, too bright. Needy. I know that now. But hindsight's 20/20, as they say. Back then I was fourteen years old, raging with hormones, and a pretty girl—well, a girl—had noticed me. Hadn't walked by with her nose in the air. I don't know many fourteen-year-olds who wouldn't be interested.

She was dressed quite formally, in a grey dress; she looked like she'd just got out of school. Also, no makeup. Her pale face was scrubbed clean, and of course that didn't do her any favours either. She was some way from the girls I fantasised about. But put all of that in one pan of the scales, and put one thing in the other. She was interested in me. And at that age, that weighs heavier, every time.

"Not seen you about before," she said.

"Been here all summer," I said.

"Oh?"

Oh. Almost formal. Most kids our age would say yeah. It wasn't a local thing because I knew how Thomas and the others talked. But I shrugged. "Yeah. My gran lives round here. Come up a lot."

She nodded. "What's your name?" she asked.

So I told her. I was about to ask her hers, when suddenly she glanced sideways and froze. Quickly she looked back at me. "Meet me here tomorrow?" she asked. "Please?"

I blinked. My mouth hung slack. Had she just—?

"Please?" she said.

"Yeah. Sure." Was this a date? I didn't know. And what time. "When?" I asked, but before she could answer, a voice barked out.

"Ceridwen!"

She jumped, a hand going to her throat.

"Ceridwen, come out of there immediately."

The whole shop had gone still. The girl—Ceridwen?—had gone red; at that age, there's little worse than humiliation.

The voice had come from the doorway to the street, and it was like thunder. I didn't want whoever owned that voice to notice me, but if I leaned sideways and peered between a couple of the other objects on the shelves, I could see him.

He was a tall, burly man. Thickset, big-shouldered, with big, knuckly, toil-reddened hands. Despite the heat, he wore black, as if going to a funeral. Iron-grey hair and a hard, square face, with black heavy brows bent V-shaped in a frown. He didn't have a beard, but I can't help but think he should have; looking back, he had that Moses on Mount Sinai look about him.

As I said, he wasn't short, but from where I was standing he looked like a giant. And there was a feeling in the air, like the closeness before a thunderstorm breaks.

The man's frown deepened. "Now, Ceridwen," he growled.

"Yes, father." She turned to replace whichever little knickknack she'd been inspecting, and used her arm to block her mouth from his view. "Two o'clock?" she whispered. She didn't say *please*, or at least her mouth didn't; her eyes were another matter.

I nodded.

She put the knickknack back on the shelf, then went out. In the doorway Ceridwen's father raised a hand as she passed. She flinched. He glanced around, at the watching eyes, then lowered his hand. "Get in the car," he said.

Ceridwen bolted out of the shop without a backward glance. Her father glared around the shop—I found myself actually stepping back to avoid his glower, even though as far as I could tell he didn't even know I was there—then turned and stalked out. Leaning forward again, I saw a battered old Land Rover parked across the street; Ceridwen stood beside it, head down. Her father pulled the door open, pointed. She'd barely got in before he slammed it shut again. Even through the glass, I saw her jolt with fright. Her father walked round to the driver's side, got in, started the engine and drove off. He never looked at her once, and her head stayed bowed.

"DEAD?" I SAID. "WHAT HAPPENED?"

"Well, I don't know that exactly," said Thomas.

"What do you mean?"

"Haven't found the bodies."

I stared at him. "Then how do you know they're dead?"

"Well, Dewi wasn't going to just bugger off, was he? He was like you—worked from home. Had a missus, two kids. And he just vanished. Nothing's missing—not even his car. The money in the bank's not been touched."

"Could he have had another account his wife didn't know about?" I felt stupid as soon as I said it, but Thomas shrugged.

"Could have, just barely, but it's not very likely. Only reason he'd have to do one would be if he was in some sort of trouble. And he knew he could come to me if he was."

"Course."

"I owed him." Thomas raised his mug in my direction. "We both did."

I couldn't answer that.

"Besides, he was drinking in town. Pretty regular thing he did—go down the Last Inn with a few of his mates, then potter home. He was seen in the pub, then the last anyone saw of him he was making his way back through the Old Town."

Barmouth's at the foot of a group of hills called *Dinas Oleu*, or the "Fortress of Light"; the Old Town is built up hard against the lower slopes, stacked up on several levels.

"And?" I asked.

"And, nothing," said Thomas. "Last anyone saw of him. He never got home. There's nothing—nothing to indicate he was planning any sort of flit. Nothing to indicate he was having an affair or anything. His wife certainly didn't have any suspicions. And before you say it, I know they often don't. But even if Dewi was playing away—and I've a bloody hard time believing that—why pull a disappearing act that's going to cause a sight more hassle than just filing for divorce? You know?" He swirled the coffee in his mug. "Besides, I found what might have been blood in an alleyway."

"What?"

"One of the little ones, you know. Go up to the steps that lead you up into the hills. Ah, I can't be sure. It'd rained like a bastard, that night; washed the traces away. There wasn't enough to analyse."

"But?"

"But, hell of a coincidence, the night someone disappears. That little alley-way—it's a good place to pop into if you're caught short on the way home." He half-smiled. "As we all are from time to time."

I half-smiled back. It was the friendliest thing either of us had done since I'd got there. Neither of us spoke for nearly a minute after that. Then I asked. "So, when was this?"

"'Bout a week, ten days ago."

"What about Pete? You said him, too?"

"Yeah."

"So?"

"I went round to his flat, Monday."

"You stayed in touch?"

"Not so's you'd notice. He'd lost his job again. He was living in a crappy little council flat down the north end and spending most of his benefit on Special Brew and wacky baccy. Most contact I'd have with him was trying to make sure he didn't end up getting sent down for some stupid bollocks he was doing."

"Because you owed him," I said.

"Because I owed him," Thomas said.

"So?"

"So, I went round his flat to warn him, and . . ." Thomas shook his head. "Place was trashed. Looked like there'd been a mother of a fight, but God knows who with or over what. But there was blood on the carpet. Definitely blood. No rain to wash it off inside. Matched Pete's blood type." Thomas drained his coffee and put the mug down, pushed it away. "There was a lot of it."

I'd hardly touched my coffee. I took a swallow, more for the sake of having something to do than any real need.

"Kitchen was a mess," said Thomas, looking up at the ceiling. "Maggots crawling in the sink, stuff like that. Flies all over the show. But no Pete. Of course, he was always a mucky bastard. Could have let the flat get into that state out of sheer laziness. But the blood on the carpet was old. Long-dried. Forensics reckoned whatever happened in there, happened a good fortnight ago."

"So, even before whatever happened to Dewi . . ."

"That's right. Pete was the first to go, then Dewi."

The coffee was lukewarm; I drained it at a gulp. "You said you went to warn Pete."

Thomas smiled without warmth. "So I did. You don't miss much. You always were bright, weren't you?"

"Not always, no."

"No."

"Come on, Thomas. Cough it up. What did you go to warn Pete about?"

The smile faded. He leant forward. "Someone's been following me."

I waited, still.

He shrugged. "Sometimes it's just a feeling. But other times? No, it's more than a feeling. Something was rattling at one of my windows last night. Before that—a couple of times, I've had something prowling round my property. Saw its eyes gleam in the dark. Went out looking, with my da's old shotgun. Know what I found? A fucking crow. Half-eaten."

"Fox?"

"Fox nothing. It was left for me to find." He clasped his hands on the table and for the first time I fully saw the fear he'd been hiding; when he breathed out, it rattled in his throat like he was emptying out his soul, and he seemed to sag and deflate. "Daytime's not so bad. It's night—*night*—when whatever it is starts following me. I've had it follow me when I was alone out on the coast road, on the beach—hell, even in the middle of town. Whatever it is, it's good at creeping around."

"It?"

"I don't know what the bloody hell it is. But I'll tell you this—it's not a human being. But what kind of beast it could be, I don't know."

"So why warn Pete?"

"Why warn—? Why do you bloody think? Someone followed Dewi and jumped him. Now someone's following me. Something. Christ alone knows what. This is Barmouth—it's a quiet bloody town, not Manchester or London where everyone's killing each other every five minutes. There couldn't be two separate things. So that meant a connection. So you tell me, What connects Dewi and me? Only one bloody thing. The same thing that connects both of us with Pete. You. You and—" He stopped, wouldn't say the name. "You and *her*, and her bloody maniac father."

"Have you checked on him?"

"Who?"

"Her dad."

Thomas snorted, then sighed and rubbed his eyes. "Forgot. I didn't tell you."

"Tell me what?"

"Isaiah Hughes died three weeks ago."

I breathed out. "About a week before whatever happened to Pete happened."

"Yes."

"I see." Outside, a gull cried. Green mountains, blue sky, blue river and sea asparkle with warm afternoon sun; the first holidaymakers of the season pottered along the quay, eating ice cream from the parlour a few doors down. It was a few steps away, and it was another world.

"So what happens now?" I said.

"It's you and me now," he said. "We need to finish this."

"Finish what?"

"Whatever this is. If it can be finished."

"You're a Detective Inspector, aren't you?"

"So?"

"Well, can't you—"

"No, I can't. Use your bloody loaf." He pointed a finger at me. "With what we all did back then? I have done enough for you already, Christ alone knows why. I am not giving up my freedom. You owe me—me, and Dewi, and Pete. You owe all of us. And now the debt's come due."

I rubbed my mouth. My hand shook. "So, what—what do you want me to—"

"It all started when old man Hughes died. So I think that's where we look."

"Where?"

"The house. Plas Merthyr. Where else?"

"Haven't you been up there?"

He shook his head impatiently. "There's this big tussle going on between Hughes's brother—hard to believe, I know, but he had one—and whatever loony church he ended up with in the end. It was the old family place, apparently, but his church is saying he left it to them and his brother's saying the old bastard willed it to him. So back and forth it bloody well goes. Place is sealed, and I could hardly get a warrant, could I? What can I tell them? Not the bloody truth. No. There's only one way to settle this—go up there and find whatever's there to be found. There'll be something, I'm sure of that."

"So where do I come in?"

"I'm not going up there on my own. My da had two shotguns. You take one, I'll take the other." I opened my mouth to protest and he leant forward again, jabbing that finger at me. "No bloody arguments. This isn't a discussion. You owe me—us. So just for a bloody change, you keep your end up and pull your damned weight."

He fell back in his chair, hands clasped across his belly. "Any questions?"

I shook my head. "Think you've summed it up pretty clearly."

"Right. Back to mine, then. We'll go when it's dark."

"Dark? I thought whatever you were scared of only came out at night."

"So far."

"Well, wouldn't it be better to go now?"

"You mean, now, when anyone could see us? It's not *that* isolated. I want to be free of this, for good and all. Not get whatever killed Pete and Dewi off my back just to go to prison afterwards."

"All right. All right."

"Ever used a gun?"

"No."

"You can have a few practice shots before we go."

"Okay. Okay."

"Come on then."

I followed him out, and we walked back to the station through the Old Town; the same way, I realised, Dewi had gone.

BACK TO THAT HOT SUMMER'S DAY IN 1993, WHERE I'M STILL STARING through that gap in the shelving, through the doorway, to where the Land Rover had been. Where Ceridwen and her father had been.

Meet me here tomorrow? Please?

"Bloody hell," said a voice. I turned; through the gap in the shelving I saw Thomas, Dewi and Pete at his side. "Were you just chatting up Crazy Ceri?"

I felt my face heat up, shrugged. "Wasn't chatting her up."

Thomas grinned, scenting blood. "Oooh. What do you reckon, lads?"

Dewi sniggered. Pete blinked, looking from one to the other of us, then sniggered, too.

"Piss off," I muttered, and headed out of the shop. Thomas and the others followed. "Someone's got a girlfriend, someone's got a *girl*friend—"

"Piss off," I snapped, and got a filthy look from a mother passing with her little girl. "Didn't say anything to her. She was talking to me. Who is she, anyway?"

"Crazy Ceri," said Dewi, smirking.

Ceridwen, I wanted to say; felt like smacking him one, too. "Yeah, I know that. So? Who is she? Why's she crazy?"

"It's her da who's bloody weird," said Thomas. "Scary bastard, isn't he?"

"Just a bit." The four of us wandered back towards the seafront. The tide was out. A couple walked down the beach; a dog ran ahead of them, then ran back.

"He's some sort of God-botherer," said Pete. We all looked at him; as I said, Pete didn't speak much. "It's just him and her, stuck up there." He nodded towards Dinas Oleu.

"They live up there?"

"Farmhouse," said Dewi. Thomas leant back against the sea wall, arms folded, amused. "I don't know what church he goes to. Not sure if he goes to any. He thinks they're all too soft. Everyone's gonna go to hell, he says. Your da had to have words with him 'bout that, didn't he, Thomas?"

Thomas nodded. "Mad old bugger tried to go preaching in the market once. Saturday, middle of summer, in front of the tourists and everything." He sniggered. "Right to-do, that was."

"Isn't there a mum?"

"Oh no," said Dewi, "she died popping out Crazy Ceri. So old Isaiah—that's his name, Isaiah Hughes—says that she's his punishment for sinning with his missus." He made an *O* with his thumb and forefinger and thrust the other forefinger repeatedly in and out. "Doesn't let her out much, except with him."

"Probably not a very good pick for a girlfriend, then," said Thomas.

"She's not my girlfriend, you spacker." But I kept thinking about those pleading eyes. *Meet me here tomorrow? Please?*

"Lads?" Pete was pointing. "Bus is here."

"Shit," said Thomas, and ran for it. We ran after him, but we were all too late.

The Harlech trip didn't happen that day; in the end the lads decided to go the next day, but I begged off. "Got something to do," I said.

"Yeah?" Thomas looked pissed off. "What's that?"

I didn't answer.

"Girlfriend," said Dewi. "Crazy Ceri, innit?"

"Piss off."

"That it?" said Thomas.

"None of your business."

"Fuck off, then," he said, and turned away.

Dewi blinked, then ran after him. Pete stared at me, then at their retreating figures, trying to work out what had happened. "Seeya," he muttered, then shambled after Dewi and Thomas. "Wait up, lads."

I perched on the stone jetty at the harbour mouth for a while. People came; fisherman, casting their lines into the deep, undertow-ridden waters. I wandered back along the beach and finally found myself on Church Street, outside The Price Is Right, at about five to two.

I sat on the low wall outside and waited, thinking that whatever this was, it had better be worthwhile.

"Hiya."

I looked up, squinting against the sun. Ceridwen smiled down at me. "Hi," I said, and stood up.

We stood there looking at each other. She looked exactly the same as she had the day before—no makeup, and wearing the grey dress. I was dressed pretty much the same, too. It was a statement, or so I told myself.

After a moment, she jerked her head to indicate I should follow her, and I did.

We didn't speak, not for some time. I followed her over the railway footbridge, past the memorial and up the steps to the coast road. Then she darted across the road, to the steps leading up onto Dinas Oleu itself.

Didn't she live up there? I thought of that scary bastard of a father she had, the one who'd practically dragged her out of the shop. I didn't fancy running into him. My imagination decided to go a little wild at this point, imagining a scenario where she lured me back to him as a human sacrifice to whatever bonkers religion he really followed. But I followed her over the road anyway, and up the steps, until we were actually on the well-worn footpath along the mountainside itself. Finally I said, "Where are we going?"

And Ceridwen turned and, taking a deep breath, drew herself up and said:
"Somewhere we can be alone."

And then she turned and carried on.

THE WASN'T MUCH I COULD SAY TO THAT, AND SO I FOLLOWED HER, mouth dry, stomach tight and heart thumping (and no, that wasn't due to the exhaustion—I was up Dinas Oleu, surefooted as a goat by now, every other day that summer).

The view from Dinas Oleu is as fine a sight as any you'll see in Britain—you can see out to sea as far as Anglesey on a good day, and for miles both up and down the coast and inland—but she wasn't stopping to admire it. I supposed, living up on the hill as she did, she saw enough of it. And I'd got familiar enough with it all not to be mesmerised. Besides, here was something new; another world, another country, of a very different kind.

She stopped at last though, on one high slope, looking sideways and down. By now I was getting out of breath, so I was glad of the stop. I halted behind her, taking deep breaths. My mouth and throat were parched from the heat and I was soaked in sweat.

I followed her gaze; below was a stone farmhouse. A couple of chickens were clucking, somewhere in its muddy yard.

"Where's that?" I asked.

"Plas Merthyr," she said. Her eyes didn't waver from it; they were moist and staring. Finally, she looked away and walked on without another word.

Farther up the hillside, she stopped by a thicket of thin, gnarled saplings, branches twisted askew by the constant wind. She lifted them; underneath was a slope and below that the remains of a stone wall. She slid down on her backside, then turned and looked up. "You coming?"

I slid down. Ceridwen was already sitting on the wall; she patted the space beside her.

The "wall" was about knee-high and traced the outline of what had been a small building—a cottage, maybe? A small one if it was—fifteen or twenty feet long and maybe ten wide. But it was cool and shady down here, under the trees, and when I sat down the stone was soft with moss.

"I'm Ceridwen," she said.

"I know," I told her. "I heard your dad—"

She looked away; I stopped. "Sorry," I said.

She shrugged. "Doesn't matter."

"So," I said, smiling and trying to sound breezy. Failed miserably, I expect. "Here we are."

She glanced at me and smiled. But she didn't speak. So, of course, I did, and being nervous, babbled like a fool. About where I was from, what I planned to do. She just kept glancing at me and smiling. Her little thin hands were knotted together in her lap, twisting and writhing over one another; she bit her lips, then licked them.

At last I ran out of things to say, but still she didn't speak. I wasn't yet at an age where I could leave a silence alone, so I searched for something to say. "So," I managed at last, "you live at Plas Merthyr, then?"

She stopped smiling and didn't look at me. *Way to go*, I thought. "Yes," she said. "Just father and I. And some chickens. And the sheep, of course. Couldn't have a farm in Wales without them."

I didn't know what to say to that, so—maybe purely out of luck—I left a silence for her to carry on talking in. "He's religious, my father," she said at last. "I expect your friends told you about that."

"Yeah."

"Yes. Doesn't belong to any church. None of them are *pure* enough for him." She spat the word out, hugged herself. "Nothing's pure enough. Nobody."

"Not even you?"

"Especially not me. I killed my mum. That's what he says. Did your stupid mates not tell you that as well?"

I blinked at the venom. *Crazy Ceri*, Dewi had said. I sneaked a look around the little dell where the cottage ruins nestled, looking for an easy way out. Towards the far end of it, sunlight broke through and I could see open ground. I looked back at Ceridwen. She was smiling at me.

"I'm not going to hurt you," she said. She shuffled closer to me. "I saw you in there and I liked you. I . . . I . . ."

I think, looking back, that if it hadn't been me it would've been someone else. That's the brutal truth; there was no special quality that drew Ceridwen to me. She was alone, she was a teenage girl and she wanted to be with someone.

"What?" I said.

She smiled, reached out an arm and slipped it round my neck, then leant in close and kissed me full on the lips, her tongue sliding deep into my mouth and touching mine.

Thomas lived in the bungalow that'd belonged to his parents, both now long gone. It was up on the coast road, with a good view. He was lucky to have inherited it; a place like that would have been hard to afford on a single copper's salary.

He motioned me into the front room, picking up the cordless phone. "I'm going to order a pizza. Okay with you?"

"Yeah, fine."

"Any preference?"

"No pineapple."

He smiled. Just for a second, it could almost have been old times. "No, I can't bloody stand that on a pizza either. Pepperoni and mushroom do you?"

"Some anchovies, maybe?"

"Yeah, why not?" He rang in the order and replaced the phone. "You want a beer?"

"That a good idea? We've got to go up there later." I nodded upwards, towards the hills.

"One beer won't hurt. More than that could be a problem. So?"

"Go on, then."

We popped the tabs on the cans. Mine foamed up; I cupped a hand on it to catch the drips, went through to the kitchen and cleaned up.

Thomas had emptied his can into a pint mug, and by the time I came back half of it was already gone. "Ask you something?" he said as I sat back down.

"Yeah," I said, and took a sip from my can. "Sure."

"You ever think about it?" he said. "I mean, what happened that day?"

"Yeah. Course I do."

"How often?"

"How—? How the hell should I know, mate? I don't keep count."

"'Mate,'" he said, and snorted, shaking his head. "I don't think you know the meaning of the word."

"That's not true."

"You don't even understand something as basic as taking responsibility for what you've done," he said.

There was a short silence; he was waiting for me to fill it, so at last I did, hoping it was what he wanted to hear; he looked angry all of a sudden. A mean drunk's mood can switch like that, but Thomas could hardly be drunk, not on half a pint of lager. Not unless I'd greatly misread him. No, he was wired on something else.

"How often do I think of her?" I asked. "As I said, I don't know. Days go by, weeks, sometimes even months, where I haven't even thought of her. And then"—I gestured—"it'll all come back. And I'll realise she's always there. What happened—it's always on me, touching me in a million different ways. Like a shadow."

"Or a ghost, maybe?" said Thomas.

"Or a ghost," I said.

Thomas swilled lager round the bottom of his mug. "You believe in them?"

"Ghosts?"

"Ghosts."

I shrugged. "I think when you die, that's it. Lights out."

"Simple as that?"

"Yeah. But"—I leant forward—"people can be haunted. Not places. People."

"By what?"

"Things they did, or things they didn't do. People they've lost."

"You're talking about guilt. Conscience. That's not what killed Dewi, or Pete. That's something else. Something solid."

"Yeah," I said. "And I've no idea what it is."

Thomas finished his beer, then crossed to the window. "Where's that bloody pizza?"

I looked past him, out across the bay where the sun was sinking. "What about you?" I said finally.

He turned back. "What? I've no more bloody idea what's after us than you have."

"I didn't mean that."

He snorted, peered out of the window again. "What did you mean then?"

"Ceridwen." At last I said the name, and the room was still. Thomas stood like stone, unmoving. "Do you ever think of her?" I said.

"Every day," he said. "Every day of every week of every month of every year of my bloody life since then." He glanced at me. "Okay?"

He looked out again. "There's the pizza now," he said, and went to the door.

AFTER WE'D EATEN, HE UNLOCKED THE STEEL CABINET IN HIS OFFICE upstairs and took out two shotguns. One was a bog-standard farmer's gun, double-barrelled, side-by-side; the other was pump-action and stainless steel, gleaming coldly under the lights.

Thomas slipped each one, along with an ammunition bandolier and a box of cartridges, into a zip-up bag, then took them out to the BMW and put them in the back. "Get in," he said.

We drove up the coast road, through Llanaber, till we came to a stretch of woodland. He pulled in, took the bags out and central-locked the four-by-four. Then we walked into the woods. They were pines and the air was heavy with their scent.

Finally we reached a clearing. Thomas entered and I followed; in the middle of it stood three gaunt figures with outspread arms. I started, then relaxed as I saw what they were: scarecrows, basically. A crude wooden cross made of broomsticks, each with two straw-stuffed sacks tied on—one for the head, another for the torso.

"They won't hurt you," Thomas said. He propped the bags against a tree trunk, unzipped one and peered inside, then passed the other to me. "That one's yours."

I unzipped the bag. Inside was the double-barrelled shotgun. "Break it," said Thomas, taking the pump-action from its bag and thumbing cartridges into the breech.

"It's not loaded," I said. I'd seen him check before we'd left the house.

"Break it," he said. I fumbled at it, found the lever that released it so that the barrels folded down. The chambers gaped, empty. Thomas looked back at me. "Now you're sure."

We put cartridges into the bandoliers and tied them on. Finally, on Thomas's orders, I loaded two loose cartridges into the shotgun and snapped the barrels shut.

Thomas stood straight, put one foot forward, pumped the weapon's slide and set it to his shoulder. "Like this," he said, "for balance. Sight down the barrels." We were about ten, fifteen yards from the scarecrows. "I expect we'll be no farther off from anything we meet than that."

He fired.

The shotgun's blast was deafening. Like thunder. No, those are clichés. It was that loud I felt as much as heard it, coming up through the ground and then me. At the same time smoke and fire flashed from the muzzle and the barrel jerked upwards. But straw and torn sacking scattered suddenly from the sack making the right-hand scarecrow's body. There were a dozen coin-sized holes in it, all smoking round the edges. A high thin *eeeeeeeeeeee* sounded in my ears; over it I heard the *clunk-clack* of Thomas working the shotgun's slide.

"Now you," he said. "You need to cock it first."

I pulled the hammers back with my thumb. *Click.* Shouldered the gun and aimed down it at the middle scarecrow's chest. I curled my finger round the triggers and—

A flash, reeking smoke; sound that jolted through me. At the same time it felt as if a horse kicked me in the shoulder, and I went staggering back, almost falling. I dropped the gun and teetered, arms windmilling for balance.

As the smoke cleared and the blast's echoes faded, I saw the middle scarecrow was practically headless. Scraps of charred sacking and bits of dried straw drifted slowly downwards through the warm, late-spring air.

Eeeeeeeeeeeeee, went my ears.

"You dick," said Thomas. I looked at him; he shook his head. "You fired both bloody barrels, didn't you? You've got two for a reason. To give you two shots." He picked up the gun and held it out to me. "Try it again. And get it bloody right this time."

IT WAS SUNSET BY THE TIME WE DROVE BACK TO THOMAS'S HOUSE. My shoulder ached where the shotgun's stock had recoiled into it again and again, from all the firing it had taken before Thomas declared himself satisfied. We got out of the car, carried the guns back inside the house, then went out the back door. At the end of the back garden was a gate. Beyond that there was a footpath leading up into the hills.

We walked in silence, Thomas leading and me following, and I remembered another silent journey, twenty years before, that had also led me to Plas Merthyr, or at least past it.

Near dark, with everything now grey dusk, the open hillside gave way to woodland and it grew darker still. We both had torches but Thomas had made it clear they weren't to be used till he said so; there were other farms nearby and they might see the light.

Thomas held a hand up. I stopped. "We're here," he said.

He knelt down, unzipped the carry-bag, took out the shotgun and tied on the bandolier. I did the same.

"Leave the bags," he said. "We'll get them later."

I followed him out of the woods; directly below us, dark and lightless, was Plas Merthyr.

There were little cracks and rustles in the undergrowth as we went. Small animals, night creatures, startled away. Or perhaps something larger—watching, waiting, ready to attack.

Thomas reached the door, took out a bunch of keys. "Got a mate at the estate agent's," he said. "Or rather, a chap who owed me a favour. He let me make some copies on the sly." He unlocked the door and pushed it open. An alarm began beeping; Thomas stepped quickly inside, pushed buttons and the beeping stopped. His face appeared, a pale blur in the gloom. "Gave me the alarm code, too," he said, and smiled.

Across the hillside, I saw a house's lights gleaming. I wished I were there, not here. But wishes get you nowhere. I went inside.

Thomas's torch snapped on, shone down the hallway. "You sure we can't just turn the lights on?" I asked. "It'll be easier. Quicker."

He considered. "Okay. Quicker we're in and out, the better."

He switched the light on. The hallway was bare—naked boards, no furniture, a cross on the wall.

"Thought you said nobody had touched the place," I said.

"Nobody has," said Thomas. "It was like this when he died."

"Jesus," I said.

"No phones. He didn't believe in them. No computers. No TV. Like the nineteenth century, or earlier. Surprised he even had electricity."

"Got to power the burglar alarm somehow."

"That's true."

It was the same story in every room downstairs; bare boards, bare white plastered walls, hard wooden furniture. All functional, no comfort. Only one ornament in each room; a plain wooden cross like the one in the hall, with a gaunt, tormented Christ, arms stretched high above his head while the walls' white emptiness seemed to scream.

The one exception was the living room; on the mantelpiece, above the fire, was a framed photograph. A wedding picture; I recognised the man as Isaiah Hughes. The woman with him didn't look exactly like an older version of Ceridwen, but it was close enough.

No pictures of Ceridwen anywhere, though. Not in that room, or any-where else in the house.

The kitchen was the most modern-looking part of the house. There was a dishwasher, a washing machine, a tumble dryer. I wondered if Isaiah had always had those, or if he'd only got those after Ceridwen wasn't there to skivvy for him. I hoped for the latter, somehow; part of me was glad of the petty hypocrisy it implied. It made Isaiah less monolithic, more human and vulnerable. Oh, yes: although I'd only ever met him once, and never exchanged a word with him, I feared the old bastard. I'd learned enough about him through Ceridwen; if the events of that summer had been a shadow on my life ever since, Isaiah had been a shadow within the shadow.

But even here, in the kitchen, hung above the sink, was that racked and tortured Christ.

What must it have been like for Ceridwen, to live in this house? But of course, I didn't need to ask. I knew. It was clearer to me still in retrospect. But even if it had been clearer at the time, what could I have done?

Nothing: I kept telling myself that as we went upstairs and searched the bare rooms. Nothing. But it didn't help.

There was another of those bloody crosses in each upstairs room as well—even the toilet. How anyone could do their business with *that* looking down was beyond me.

One room was bare—and I mean utterly bare. It was the smallest room upstairs, squinched into a corner of the top storey, the only view the slope of the hill behind the house. Little light would have got in here, even on the brightest day. Above the bricked-up fireplace, another of those crosses. But no furniture, no sign of the room being used in any way for anything.

"This was her room," I said.

Thomas looked at me.

"It was Ceridwen's," I said. "She would have lived here. It's the meanest, littlest room. All he'd have thought she was worth. And when she—when she wasn't there anymore—he . . ." I shook my head. "You know downstairs? The wedding picture on the mantelpiece? That's the closest thing Isaiah could come to building a shrine to his dead wife."

Thomas looked out onto the landing, then back at me.

"If that old bastard ever loved anyone, it was her," I said. "That's why he hated Ceridwen. She killed his wife. And it was his fault because he'd sinned with his wife to conceive her. This? This is like . . . an *anti*-shrine. He cleared out every trace of Ceridwen, any sign she'd ever been here or that he'd ever had a child. And then he . . . left the room empty. Never even used it again. It's like burning the city down and sowing the ground with salt so nothing will grow." I found myself looking at the cross on the wall. "But that thing had to be here. Had to be everywhere."

I didn't even know I was going to do it until I did it; I snatched the cross from the wall and stamped it under my heel till I felt it splinter and break. Thomas started towards me, then leant back against the wall, peering out onto the landing again. I stepped back and kicked the broken pieces of the cross, scattering them across the room.

"That make you feel better?" said Thomas.

"Not really."

We checked the rest of the upstairs rooms, found nothing. There was an attic, but it held nothing but an old Welsh dresser with empty drawers.

We went downstairs, turning all the lights off as we went. The darkness collapsed inwards, like a living thing the lights had pressed back.

I didn't—still don't—know what exactly Thomas had hoped or expected to find here. Signs of some weird ritual, maybe, proof that Isaiah's faith had been something darker and stranger than anyone knew—something for raising, perhaps, a vengeful demon. But there'd been nothing. There'd been few enough places to hide anything, and all of them had been empty.

"What now?" I asked him in the hallway.

Thomas opened his mouth, then closed it, then slapped his forehead. "Of course," he said. "I'm a bloody idiot." He turned and went back into the kitchen.

I found him standing by the fridge. "What?"

"Look at the wall," he said.

"What about it?"

"It's papered."

"So?"

"It's the only wall in the house that is."

"Right." I thought I followed. "Yeah. Everything else is bare. No fripperies. Nothing unnecessary. So why paper over this one—"

"—unless there's something in it he didn't want people to see?" Thomas felt his way along the wall. "What, though? Can't feel anything."

I looked at the fridge. It was a big bastard of a thing, taller than either of us; new, as well. Isaiah must have splashed out a fair bit on it, and recently. And then it clicked, and I moved to peer behind it. "Thomas?" I said.

"What?"

"Help me move this thing."

"Why? What have you—"

"I think there's a door behind it."

And, as we discovered after much huffing and puffing, grunting and heaving, there was. It was quite small and narrow, but it was there.

"Handle's gone," said Thomas, kneeling. "He took it off, papered over it, just left a hole for the key. Nice little secret entrance."

"Question is, where's the key?" I asked.

Thomas held up the bunch he'd got from the estate agent. The keyhole was for a mortise lock; there were three mortise keys on the ring and he tried them one by one. The first two wouldn't turn.

"If it was a secret, maybe he hid it somewhere?" I said.

"If needs be, we'll force it," said Thomas, fumbling with the third key. "Blast it off its hinges with the shotgun if I have to. Not coming this far just to—ah, there we go."

With a clunking and clicking, the lock's tumblers shifted. Thomas turned the key so it would stay fast in the lock, and pulled. The door gave, shifting outwards; Thomas pulled it all the way open.

The air that billowed out was cold and dank and musty. Thomas switched on his torch and shone it down a flight of steps, then turned to me and smiled.

"Think we just found what we were after," he said.

CERIDWEN AND I SPENT ABOUT AN HOUR KISSING PASSIONATELY, MY RIGHT hand cupping a small firm breast through her dress and bra, before she pushed me away, red-faced and panting. "Got to go now," she said. "Da'll expect me back on the farm."

"Oh." I was out of breath and had a truly non-negotiable erection straining the front of my jeans, to the point where I feared the material might actually give way. Ceridwen's face might be unremarkable, but her lean, taut body was another matter entirely; while I hadn't actually seen it, I'd touched it and felt it pressed against me for most of the last hour, which had driven me to a pitch of unrequited lust known only to teenage boys. "Okay," I managed at last.

"Tomorrow?" she said.

"Tomorrow?" I said, stupidly. "What about tomorrow?"

"Same time," she said. "Meet me here? You can find your way on your own now, can't you?"

"Yeah," I said at last. "Yeah, course."

"All right." She kissed me on the mouth. "Better go."

"Yeah." I got up and plodded towards the sunlit end of the glade.

"What are you—no, don't!"

Ceridwen caught my arm, pointing. "Don't. It's dangerous."

"What?" All I could see ahead of me was thick grass and snarled brambles.

"The old well," she said. She bent down, picked up a stone and went forward, then dropped it into the thick of the brambles. After many seconds' silence, there was a splash. "It's all overgrown. Fall through that and—"

I flinched. "Thanks."

She grinned. "Up here," she said, and pointed at the slope. "The way we came."

We climbed back up to the edge of the trees. "Best let me go first," she said. "Give me a couple of minutes, okay?"

"Okay."

She kissed me hard on the mouth again, tongue probing deep, then pushed herself clear. "Tomorrow," she said, grinning, then slipped back through the trees and vanished down the path.

I waited for a couple of minutes, giddy and dazed. I needed to pee now, but I had to wait for the erection still straining my trousers to subside before I could attempt it. Once I'd done that, I stepped out of the trees, and made my way back down the path.

"I'M TELLING YOU," SAID THOMAS, "SHE'S A BLOODY NUTTER. AND SHE'S A tramp. Picks up fag ends people have dropped to smoke 'em herself."

"No she doesn't," I said. Not that I'd seen.

"She does," said Thomas. "Doesn't she, Dewi?"

"Yeah," said Dewi. We were sat near the bus stop again, waiting in the sunshine.

I didn't believe him either—or didn't want to, maybe. Dewi would say anything Thomas told him to. "Look," I said, "I said I'd see her again today. You'll be all right without me."

"She fucks her dad," Thomas said.

"That's enough!" I was on my feet, fists clenched. Why was I doing this? Oh yes; she was my girlfriend. At least, I assumed she was. I hadn't actually called her that out loud, any more than she'd called me her boyfriend, but what else did I call her?

Thomas squared up to me, glaring; we stood like that for a few seconds. Dewi and Pete, still sitting, both gawped at us. God knows where it could have gone right then; at that age, it's a lot easier to back yourself into a confrontation like that than it is to work your way out of it. But finally Thomas shook his head and turned away. "Fuck off, then," he said. "Go on, then, go see her. I don't give a shit."

"Fine," I said. "I will."

I didn't look back as I strode up Church Street, face burning. All this shit because I wasn't going to Harlech with them again. What would any of them be like if it were them with a girlfriend? They were just jealous because I was there first.

As I went up Dinas Oleu, I tried to puzzle out my own feelings here. I was still young and naïve enough to believe that sex and love went together. I knew people got divorced, of course, but it had yet to touch me close to home: that would come when I came home at the end of that summer, to learn that my parents' marriage, after the failed, last-ditch attempt to retrieve it in my absence, was at an end.

As far as I understood—in all the pulpy novels I read back then—a man and woman met and fell in love and had sex, more or less in that order. I'd read enough porn mags to know there were married women who regularly had sex with other men while their husbands, like as not, fucked other women, each with the other's approval, but while I found the stories in those magazines arousing, the people in them might as well have been from another planet for all I understood their mentality.

Well, here was something else. Here was Ceridwen. And I'd seen her three times now, and each time we went a little farther. The last time she'd put her hand on me through the strained fabric of my jeans—I was beginning to suspect the denim of having almost supernatural properties—not for long, but long enough for a surge of pure sensation to sweep through me, so pleasurable it was almost pain.

Writing this now, I realise how jaded you get with age, and how easy it is to forget the sheer intensity of sexual passion when it first awakens in you. It takes over completely, leaves you helpless; it's as scary as it is exciting because it's so beyond your control. Like a wave, a tsunami, sweeping everything else aside.

All of that was from Ceridwen; but just as in that time and that place she just wanted a boy, any boy, to stop her feeling alone, so any girl would have affected me that way. I knew I should love Ceridwen; I should feel something for her, anyway. But I'd been in love—or at least, the burning, unrequited puppy love teenage boys know so well. And this wasn't it, wasn't even remotely kin. But it was mine—for the asking and for the taking.

Looking back, I can see all that very clearly. But for the boy I was back then, all that was too complex. I still saw—still *wanted* to see—the world in the simplest, most black-and-white terms. And so, climbing Dinas Oleu, I tried to convince myself I loved Ceridwen Hughes, all the while half-craving and half-fearing the effect her body had on me.

The fear deepened, of course, as Plas Merthyr came in sight. A dark shape moved in one of its windows and I ducked down. Was Isaiah on the prowl, did he suspect? Then I heard a bird caw; I looked up and saw all I'd seen was the reflection of a tree's branches, moving on the window glass as a crow flew from it. I breathed out, moved on.

Soon enough I reached the stand of trees. I glanced around, whispered her name. No answer. I slipped through the trees and clambered down the slope; below, Ceridwen got up from where she sat on the wall and moved to meet me.

We kissed long and hard, then sat back down on the wall. Our hands moved over one another, touching, stroking, caressing. I felt giddy; my cock was throbbing.

"I love you," she whispered. "I love you."

"I love you," I whispered back; even then, I think, I had sense and understanding enough to know that wasn't the case. I felt her hand fumbling at my belt—

And then a rustle of bushes, and a sniggering.

I went rigid, broke away from Ceridwen and twisted round; up at the top of the slope, bushes moved. A moment later and I heard the snigger again—high, breathy, stupid. Dewi.

"Twats!" I snarled and hared up the slope. They were there, all three of them, Dewi down on one knee and looking down. Pete was hanging back, farthest down the path; Thomas was slouching, hands in pockets, a couple of yards from Dewi.

It was Dewi I went for, though; he was closest, he was peeping, he was giggling and perhaps most of all, he wasn't Thomas. Thomas was supposed to be my best mate, after all. I didn't want to fight him. Dewi, though; yes, I could fight Dewi.

He gaped at me, too slow on the uptake to realise I'd been coming up. I kicked out and caught him in the thigh. He yelled and fell over on his side. I stood over him, fists clenched; I had the initiative now, but couldn't decide what to do next.

Something slammed into my chest, sending me staggering back. I almost fell. As Thomas stalked towards me, Dewi scrambled away, back towards Pete.

"Come on then," said Thomas, fists raised. "Pick on someone your own size." Which was a bit daft, really; I was only two or three inches taller than Dewi, while Thomas was a good head taller.

I wasn't much of a fighter; on the other hand, I had enough experience of the playground to be able to block a few blows. He swung a punch at me, and I blocked it, then another.

The only other combat technique I had in the playground was to kick my taller opponents in the balls and then run like hell. I carried out the first part of it, kicking out more in hope than anticipation but hitting the target dead on. Thomas cried out, staggered, then collapsed into a foetal position, curled up around the agonising pain.

Pete was helping Dewi to his feet. Both of them stared at me. What now? I had no inkling of what my next move should be; the initiative had passed from me, but there seemed little chance of Thomas starting anything else, and neither Pete nor Dewi looked like they had a clue either. Therefore, impasse.

Then Thomas let out a strangled groan of pain, rolled over, half-rose and crawled towards the other. Pete helped him up, too.

"We're going," I heard Thomas say. His voice was choked.

"Thomas—" I said, stepping forward. I'm not sure if either of us quite understood how things could have come to this point so quickly, over so little.

He rounded on me. His face was red; I could see that he'd been crying. "Fuck off."

The others turned their faces from me; the three of them shuffled off down the path. When they were out of sight and I felt sure they weren't coming back, I climbed back down the slope to Ceridwen.

She'd been crying, too; when she saw me she flung her arms around my neck and kissed my face over and over. "I thought—" she said, "I thought they'd . . ."

I didn't know what to say. At the start, I might have just been suitable, available, whatever—someone who was around a lot but wasn't local, wouldn't shun her because of her crazy father—but by now I was something else, God help me.

Ceridwen Hughes loved me; I know that much. What she thought I'd done to deserve it I have no idea. For so many peoples' sakes, it would have been better if she hadn't.

THOMAS SHONE HIS TORCH DOWN THE STONE STEPS. "YOU FIRST," HE SAID.

"Why me?"

"Because I bloody say so." He hefted the shotgun. "Besides, I think it's safe to say I'm the better bloody shot, eh? Anything turns up down there I can get it from the top of the stairs."

I wasn't a hundred percent convinced—it was a shotgun, after all, not a sniper rifle—but I went to the top of the stairs and took the first hesitant step down. Thomas switched his torch on and held it in his left hand, gripping it and the gun's slide together. I did my best to hold both my torch and my weapon's barrels, my right hand clutching the pistol grip and my finger near, but not actually on, the triggers. Christ, if I slipped and fired by accident . . .

"Get a bloody move on," Thomas hissed.

I went down. The torch's beam bobbed and wove about. The cellar was cold. The floor and walls were all tiled in white; bare, but grimy now from years of neglect.

At the bottom of the steps, I moved to the side, swept the beam around. No, there was no one there; no one and nothing. The cellar was empty. One wall had a light switch; from the ceiling hung a bare bulb. And against another wall, the stone steps. And that was it.

Halfway down the steps, Thomas lowered the shotgun. "That light switch," he said. "Try it."

I moved across the cellar and clicked it on, squinted as the light flared into life. Thomas clicked off his torch. I did the same as he climbed down into the cellar.

"There's nothing here," I said at last.

"Oh, there is," said Thomas. "You can bet your arse there is. That old bastard didn't go to all this trouble to hide this place for no good reason."

He paced the cellar. "What wouldn't I give to get the forensics boys in here, I'll tell you. Bet they'd find something."

"You sure we can't?"

"Yes, I'm bloody sure. D'you think we'd be here if there was any way of doing this officially? There is no way to involve anyone official without what happened coming out. And I'm not having that happen, not now. I'm not losing more than I already have on your bloody account. Okay?"

"All right," I said. "All right."

He looked around the cellar. "There's something here. There must be something. But he's hidden it. Question is what he's hidden, and where, and why?"

Thomas crouched, setting the shotgun down on the floor. "Something here," he muttered. "Might be dried blood. Or could just be dirt. But it looks like something's been dragged here. Dragged . . ." He looked up to stare at the wall opposite. He picked up the gun and went to it. "Something's been dragged to here," he said. "And then the trail just—stops. Now why would that be, unless . . ."

He raised the gun and rapped the butt against the wall. Then he did it again, at a spot three feet to the left. Even I could hear the difference. One sound was dull, heavy, the other light and hollow.

"A false wall?" I said.

"Yup." Thomas rapped at the wall in a number of other places with the gun butt. "About the size of a doorway." He knelt, probing at the tiles. "Ha!" Mortar ground and scraped, and he prised a tile free. Underneath was another keyhole, this time with a metal pull-ring above it. He dug out the bunch of keys and tried the mortise keys again. The same key that had unlocked the cellar door unlocked this, too; I heard the tumblers *clunk* and *click*—smoothly, as if well-oiled. Whatever all this was for, Isaiah must have been using and maintaining it until recently—must have been doing so pretty much right to the point the old bastard had dropped dead.

Thomas looked back at me. I nodded and hefted my shotgun, my torch held against the barrels. I switched it back on. Thomas's torch clicked back into life, too. He took the pull-ring and tugged, and with a grate and scrape a door-sized section of wall swung out; it was attached to an old, heavy wooden door, beyond which lay only blackness. The air that blew out to meet us was colder and danker still than that of the cellar, but carried other odours with it. There was the stench of excrement, the ammoniac reek of piss, and another smell that seemed to slide into my mouth like a pair of fingers and touch the back of my throat; it was the smell of something in decay.

Thomas stepped back, aiming torch and gun into the dark beyond. I aimed mine, too, and at last we saw.

"Jesus Christ," said Thomas.

Beyond the doorway was a cave, sloping down. Our lights shone along it, to where it opened out.

Thomas went to the entrance. "He was hiding something, all right."

"Yeah. What, though?"

"Only one way to find out." Thomas stepped over the threshold. "Come on."

"Thomas—"

He looked back at me. "Get your arse in here."

There wasn't much I could say to that; I followed him.

The tunnel from the cellar expanded into a wider cavern; three other tunnels branched off it. The cavern itself stank. The floor was dotted by the char and ash of extinct fires, and I could see what looked like the remains of birds and animals. Some lay among the remnants of the fires, while others had been shied into a corner of the cavern. The remains of chickens, rabbits, a lamb, a crow, a gull. Among the burned-out fires were scraps of scorched animal hide, blackened, dirtied feathers, pieces of bone. Including . . .

"Thomas?"

"What?"

"That." I nodded at something lying among the ashes. He moved to my side and muttered, "Fucking hell."

They were discoloured and cracked, and worse still, gnawed. But they were still clearly recognisable as the bones of a human hand.

"We need to get out of here," I said. I felt sick.

"No," said Thomas. "We carry on." He looked at me. "What are we going to tell people, eh? Why were we poking around up in Plas Merthyr in the first place? Why make such a detailed search? Besides, who knows what else we'll find down here?"

"Like what?"

"Like maybe something that links us with this? Hm? I told you before, I'm not taking that bloody risk."

I couldn't really answer that. I shone the torch around the cavern. "Jesus, look at this," I said. The light played over the blackened walls, and words crudely daubed on them: HIDE THY SHAME. I WILL REPAY, SAITH THE LORD. LORD, HOW LONG WILL THE WICKED TRIUMPH UPON THE EARTH?

I recognised two of those as biblical quotations, but then there were other phrases that weren't, at least not that I recognised. But the language was very much the same.

O SINFUL WOMAN, TAINTED IN THE FALL OF MAN, AUTHOR OF THAT LOSS, ALL INIQUITIES ARE DUE TO THEE.

BEHOLD, THOU HAST BROUGHT SHAME UPON THY HOUSE AND GRIEF UPON THY FATHER'S SOUL, AND BEHOLD HOW THE RETRIBUTION OF THE LORD HAS FALLEN ON THY LIFE.

THERE IS BUT ONE SURE TOKEN OF THY REPENTANCE, AND THAT IS BLOOD.

THERE IS BUT ONE PATH TO REDEMPTION IN THE EYES OF THE LORD, AND THAT PATH IS TO DO HIS BIDDING AND TO WORK HIS WILL UPON THE EARTH.

THOU ART THE INSTRUMENT OF THE LORD'S VENGEANCE.

"Isaiah," I said. "He wrote all this."

"Mad bastard. He was crazier than we thought. But—"

We looked at one another.

"It can't be her," he said. "She's dead. She's—"

Thomas moved away, put the gun to his shoulder and shone the torch down one of the tunnels. I could see it came to an end farther down, but a chamber of some kind opened off it to the side.

He started down it. "Thomas," I hissed. "Thomas!"

But he kept going. I eyed the other cave entrances, and then I went after him. As I went, I realised I could smell smoke; it was choking, but it was better than the other odours that permeated the place.

Thomas had stopped at the end, staring into the chamber. The gun hung slack in his hands; the torchlight played over the ground at his feet.

"Thomas?" I said. "Thomas, what is it?"

He didn't answer. I reached his side and looked.

Christ, I wish I hadn't.

There were hooks in the ceiling. I suppose Isaiah must have fixed them there, back when he made this place. In the corner lay a heap of torn, stained rags that had once been clothes. In the middle of the floor, a fire of sorts of was still smouldering.

Smoking. It was smoking the meat. The meat that hung from the ceiling hooks in chunks—legs, arms, torsos, heads, organs. The faces were discoloured and sooty, but I still recognised them, much as I wished I didn't.

"Pete," croaked Thomas. "Dewi."

ON THE GROUND, IN THE DELL, AMONG THE COTTAGE RUINS, WE LAY AND kissed and grappled.

My jeans were pulled halfway down my thighs; Ceridwen's hand was round my cock, rubbing faster and faster. I had a hand up her skirt and between her legs, inside her knickers; the other was inside her unbuttoned blouse, her bra pushed up, cupping a breast, pinching the hard little nipple between finger and thumb. And her tongue was in my mouth, mine in hers.

In that moment she could have asked me anything, anything, and I'd probably have said yes. But she didn't; all that existed right then was our passion for each other.

The last three weeks of the summer had passed all too quickly. Thomas and the others had kept away from me for several days after the fight on the hill path, but thankfully that hadn't lasted. Neither of us wanted to blow off our friendship over Ceridwen. Thomas knew what I lacked the honesty to admit out loud, that whatever lay between her and me was purely physical and would pass. On my side, at least.

So, it had become a commonplace that most afternoons, I'd slip away to meet Ceridwen; I still spent time with the boys, our lives all rearranged, just slightly, to accommodate the fact. The afternoons were filled with hot and heavy sessions like this, which Thomas and the others would then quiz me about. I said as little as I could get away with; while I mightn't be in love with Ceridwen, I knew that boasting about this sort of thing wasn't the kind of thing a gentleman did.

Her hand moved faster. I tensed up; in her knickers, my fingers probed where she was wet. We hadn't fucked; that never happened. Ceridwen wouldn't allow it. Whether it was fear of pregnancy—I had no idea how to lay hands on a condom—or some vestige of her father's religious teachings, she wasn't going there. Or perhaps it was just a line she wasn't prepared to cross, a personal *no*. I have no idea. All the same, though, she was happy to go as far as this. Or farther. She'd even taken me in her mouth once.

"Go on," she whispered. "Spunk up. Spunk up."

I could feel it sweeping through me; everything else was going away, vanishing, leaving just the rushing sensation that poured through me—through to where she held me in her hand.

"Ceridwen," I gasped.

"Spunk."

I let out a grunt and then the orgasm hit me, so intensely it was close to pain; I felt, as never before, the violent muscular contractions that expelled spurt after spurt of come from me. Ceridwen let out a gasping cry of her own—whether she'd come, too, or was feigning it, or just reacting to the climax she'd evoked in me, I was never sure; there was never chance to ask afterwards.

We lay like that for a while, face to face, hearts thumping, gasping for air; then she rolled away from me, dug out a tissue, and cleaned her hand.

"That was good," she said at last. She leant over me and kissed my mouth again. "I love you."

"I love you, too," I said, but knew it was by rote, said out of duty rather than feeling.

She twitched a smile and looked away, then tugged up her knickers, shifting her bottom to pull them back on, before smoothing her skirt down and readjusting first her bra, then her blouse. She gave me another tissue. "Best clean yourself up," she said.

"Thanks."

"So," she said when I'd finished, "what's the plan tomorrow? Train?"

"No," I said. "My dad's coming to pick me up."

She nodded. "Okay. What time should I show up?"

"What?" I had visions of my dad's face when Ceridwen told him what we'd been getting up to; the bloody hell was she playing at?

"I can't wait to meet your mum and dad," she said. "I've only the one suitcase—see?" She reached into a gap in the stone wall and pulled out a small case. "Not got much to bring, see. So, where'll I be staying? Is there a spare room?" She grinned, eyes gleaming. "Or do we get to sleep in the same bed?"

My stomach was tightening inexorably; I knew enough to feel dread now. But at the same time, I couldn't believe it; she had to be joking, couldn't really believe that—

And so I laughed. I laughed in her face, not in malice but in disbelief.

Even now, I don't quite understand how she could have convinced herself that it was going to happen that way; that she could just get in my dad's car and be driven back to the north of England, and that would be the end of it. Magical thinking, maybe: she must have wanted so badly to escape her father—and who could blame her for that?—that she believed in it because she had to, unable to bear another day of her life at Plas Merthyr. Perhaps Isaiah loathed her so much he'd have said nothing, but let her go, glad to be rid of her.

Or maybe she just decided all he'd told her were lies. We hadn't exactly had many deep philosophical conversations, but he'd drummed stuff into her head—to shame her, to control her. The wickedness of sex and the sinful flesh, that kind of thing. On top of that, he'd doubtless told her plenty of other things to keep her in line and in her place. If she'd decided he'd lied about one thing, mightn't that call everything into question? Mightn't it be that she could just walk away?

I don't know. This is all stuff that occurs to me now, two decades after the event. It didn't occur at the time; all I could see was her demanding something that could never be, that she'd have to be crazy—*Crazy Ceri*—to believe would ever happen.

Unless, of course, I'd truly loved her as she loved me. Then, perhaps— who knows? The two of us might have been standing there when my dad arrived at my gran's house, with a tale of woe to tell. Of course, it might have made no difference; he came with the knowledge that his and Mum's marriage was over, after all. But perhaps that might have moved him to pity at the sight of us; perhaps he'd have told someone—the police, social services—and perhaps, or perhaps not, something would have come of it. Whatever had happened between Ceridwen and I thereafter, if I'd loved her then perhaps, just perhaps, she'd have been freed of Isaiah, would at least have had a life.

If I'd only been able to love her, I could look back upon that summer with pride and say this much good, at least, I did.

If I had only loved her.

But I didn't, and so I laughed; and so doing, I doomed us both.

The light faded in her eyes; the grin shrank away. It was like seeing the sun go behind the cloud. "You've got to take me with you," she said, and there was an edge in her voice like none I'd heard before. It was jagged and discordant; it was fear and desperation. It was an ugly sound, and it frightened me, because I knew it was about to become something uglier still. "You can't leave me here with him. I hate him. I can't stand that place, not any more. He's getting suspicious, I know he is. Oh God—if he finds out—if he finds out—" She was shaking. "You said you loved me. You said—"

"I can't—" I was already on my feet, moving away. "I can't."

There was more, but you understand. We paced around each other and the ruins, her voice rising, my speech and body language growing evermore clipped and withdrawn. By the end of it I was shaking and she was in tears; I turned away, sidling towards the slope.

"I'll tell," she said.

"Tell what?"

"What you did to me here."

"What? That we're both underage—"

"It begins with an *R*," she said.

And do you know, even then I still didn't understand. "Roaming?" I said— she called it that, sometimes, when we let our hands explore each other, without barrier or pause.

"It's called rape," she said.

I stared at her and she stared back, weeping but implacable. "I'll tell him. I'll the police."

Tears were starting from my own eyes now. I didn't understand any of this, and I didn't deserve it. What was my crime? To desire without love? Was that so terrible? "Don't," I said. "Please—please—"

I'd heard how my dad and so many others talked about men accused of crimes like that. *Hang the bastard. Evil scum.* Never a thought that something like this could have occurred. And I know, I know—it doesn't, that often. Cases like this are the tiniest fraction of the whole. But still, very rarely, for good reasons and bad, they happen.

An accusation like that—I thought of how my parents would react. Would they disown me? What about school? What about—all the dreams and hopes I had would be dust before starting: this taint, this stigma, would be with me always.

I fell to my knees, crying. Yes. That quickly. Any strength or dignity or courage I'd possessed had been stripped from me in seconds. "Please," I said, "I'm begging you—"

And then it was Ceridwen Hughes's turn to laugh in my face; it was a short laugh, bitter and cruel. She folded her arms and turned away from me.

I got to my feet, the tears already stopped. Something else had been born in me now. As if at a button's push, the fear, the grief, even the hate and fury that'd flared at her laughter were gone; what remained was a terrible sense of necessity. The blurred whirl of emotions was shouldered aside by something much older and colder by far; some ancient, ruthless part of me, older than pity or morality, concerned only with survival at any cost. *You've got to kill her*, it said in me like a voice. *Kill her before she kills your whole life.*

I wish I could tell you that it was conscience or decency that stopped me acting on it; wish I could tell you I thrust aside temptation purely out of knowing it was wrong. But I can't.

Oh, I was revolted by the thought; I'll give myself that much of a break. I was shocked to find that in me—I was still young and naïve enough to see the world in black and white terms, to believe that good people did good things and evil was only done by evil men and women. There was no middle ground, no foul rag and bone shop of the human heart where all-too-comprehensible hopes and dreads bred atrocity. Or at least there hadn't, until just now, when I realised it was in me to kill in cold blood.

But the worst is that what stopped me was not so much that appalled recognition but the fear. Even if I could do it—and who was to say Ceridwen wouldn't fight me off?—I'd have a body to hide, and how would I do that? With Thomas and the like and God knew who else knowing she was my girlfriend? They'd find the corpse and what then? They'd trace it to me and I'd be a murderer. Who'd believe after that that I wasn't a rapist, too?

No, it was fear that stopped me; fear and pragmatism. To obey that cold and ancient killing voice would be an irrevocable step; there would be no going back, no escape. Whereas where I was now—somehow or other, there might be a way out.

But I couldn't stay there, not in that place, poisoned now by all that had happened there. I turned and made for the slope, scrambling up it.

Even as I went I knew I couldn't just run away; I'd have to turn back and face her. What was happening would have to be worked through; we couldn't go anywhere till this was settled. But still I climbed. Even when I heard her call my name. Even when I heard her voice get nearer as she scrambled after me, up the slope.

I was almost at the top when she caught my arm. I reacted without thinking; I almost lost my balance when she grabbed me, and I didn't want her intimacy, her touch, not any more. I spun, throwing her off with a sweep of my arm; I had time to catch one last glimpse of Ceridwen's tear-streaked face, the only emotions on it sorrow and pity. And then she fell.

"SHE BROUGHT THEM BACK HERE," SAID THOMAS. "SHE KILLED THEM, brought them back here."

"Who did?"

"You know. You know who."

"It can't be. She's dead. You know that."

"Then what the hell?" Thomas had a hand to his mouth; finally he managed to turn from that stinking chamber and put his back against the wall, looking away from it. "Oh, Jesus."

I shook my head. "Isaiah," I said. I couldn't take my eyes off the pieces hanging from the hooks. Dewi. Pete. Both had got on my nerves in their time, and there'd been no friendship between us for twenty years, since—*say it, if only to yourself*—since the day Ceridwen died.

"He's dead, too. He's definitely bloody dead. Saw him in the mortuary and then I saw them cremate the bastard. Isaiah Hughes is bloody well gone."

"Well, so's his daughter." I shook my head and managed to look away from Dewi's eyeless head, gripping the shotgun. "This is something he's set in motion, though. God knows how, but it's his work. Revenge."

"How did he know, then? How did the bastard know?"

I shook my head again. "Maybe he was watching the whole time. Who knows?"

"He wouldn't have just . . ."

"Well, it couldn't have been Ceridwen, could it?"

Thomas stared at the wall, lips moving.

"Can't be him and can't be her did this," I said. "You've seen them both go up in smoke."

He blinked and looked at me. "Shit."

"What?"

"No I haven't."

"What? What do you mean? Isaiah?"

"No. Ceridwen."

"But we—"

"They never found her," he said. "Couldn't tip them off, could I? Well, I could have, but—thought it was better to let things lie."

"You mean she's still—"

"Never went back to look," he said. "And even if I did, what's there to see?"

I stared at him. What he was saying started taking shape. "No," I said. "No."

And then I heard it. A scrape and clatter, from nearby.

We both turned, shotguns aiming down the tunnel. The torch beams probed the black, all the way back to the big cavern, but found nothing.

The sound came again, then a swift, light patter; something moving, quickly, over ground. Thomas's gun barrel swung sideways, the torchlight going with it, hunting, but found only bare stone.

After that, there was only silence. I thought, once, that I heard the faintest rustling sound from up ahead, but I couldn't be sure.

"There were two other tunnels," I said. "Could be in either of those."

"Or hiding in the main bloody cavern. Or could have been going up into the cellar. Christ—could even be hiding out in the house now, waiting for us to come out."

"We didn't hear the door."

"Might not. It was moving fast, whatever it was, to get ahead of us. Now it has, it can afford to go slow. Good at sneaking, isn't it? Aren't you?" he shouted down the corridor, aiming—but only echoes came back to him. "Good at sneaking around in the dark," he said. "Wonder how many times it watched Dewi before it took him? It watched and waited, and then it jumped him in that bastard alley. Cut his throat, most likely. Sneaked up to Pete's flat and broke a window, crept in and—" Thomas stole a glance back towards the smoking-chamber and what hung in there. "I reckon we should get out," he said. "Get out, figure out what the bloody hell we're going to do and then come back to finish this."

I liked the first part, at least; the second, I was willing to work on. "Okay," I said. My hands sweated on the shotgun's wooden grip and steel barrels, the torch's rubber grip. "What do we do?"

"I'll go first," he said. "You watch my back."

I looked at the twelve-bore I was holding, remembered the scarecrows. By the end of it I'd been at least able to hit roughly what I was aiming at, one barrel at a time. "Okay," I said. There wasn't likely to be anything creeping up behind us, not in this tunnel, at least, but I kept glancing backwards as we went, to the chamber holding Pete's and Dewi's remains.

I almost walked into Thomas when he stopped at the big cavern entrance, the pump gun at his shoulder, the torch's beam searching the darkness beyond. "What is it?" I whispered.

He shook his head. "Got to tell you," he said, "I'm scared to go in there."

I couldn't really say anything, not to an admission like that. No point telling him I was afraid, too—Christ, he'd know that. But if even he was frightened, that was worse still. Say whatever you liked about Thomas, he was good in a crisis. I knew that well.

"She's waiting," he said. "She's out there somewhere and she's bloody waiting for us."

I said nothing. Thomas's face was aglisten with sweat. "It's not like before, is it?" he shouted suddenly; I jumped. "Not like Dewi and Pete, didn't know what was going on till you were on top of them. They weren't armed. They didn't know. Well I bloody am, you bitch. I bloody know. So come on, then. Come and face us! Come and get it!"

"Thomas," I said.

"Shut up." He spat it through his teeth, breathed in and out through them hard. "Sick of this. Bloody sick of it, I am."

The gun and the torch moved back and forth. He took a deep breath at last, whispered, "Fuck it," swung the gun right and fired.

The blast of the gun going off in the clearing had been loud enough; this, in the confined space, it was as if someone had slammed my head between a pair of clashing cymbals. The muzzle flash lit the cave. Did I glimpse something in its momentary glare, or hear something almost lost under the roar? I could never be sure, then or later.

Dimly I heard the dull, thrilling *shucklack* of the gun's slide working, the empty cartridge case jumping from the breech as Thomas pivoted, firing again into the darkness, then again. Blast after blast, round after round, flung into the dark of the cave, till the gun clicked empty.

Thomas fell back against the wall, the gun pointing upwards, the torch lighting his face as he tugged cartridges from his bandolier and slotted them into the breech one by one. "Watch the cave!" he shouted, through the whining in my ears. He nodded at the side by side. "Watch the bloody cave with it—"

I brought the gun up, aiming the torch, just as Thomas turned back towards it. And a face swam out of the dark—ghost-white, vast eyes aglow with reflected torchlight, mouth a wet black shapeless scream. I heard him scream back at it.

I didn't fire, couldn't; the face had come round the edge of the tunnel, right next to Thomas's. It was all I could see and if I fired at it I'd likely take his head off, too. I tried to move sideways for a clearer shot; Thomas was trying to swing his gun around, but he was too close to the thing, and the gun was pointing upwards. In that confined space, he couldn't move in time.

White hands. One jerked the barrel of Thomas's gun aside while another snaked out of the darkness, towing a long white rope of grimy arm after it, to punch him in the throat. It screwed and twisted from side to side, then wrenched itself away. Black flew outwards, splattered me. It spurted from Thomas's throat, spilled from his mouth. It covered the thing's hand now, and the stubby knife it held.

I might have screamed. I don't recall. I pulled the shotgun's triggers, the barrels aimed at the silent, screaming face—I didn't think I'd hit Thomas now and doubted that it mattered—but as I did Thomas's gun fired, the flash lighting up the tunnel, and the wall beside me exploded. I lurched back and sideways and my gun swung up towards the ceiling; the triggers caved under the pressure and both barrels fired.

Stones and dust rained down, choking me; for a second I thought the triple blast was bringing the whole cave down. Bury us all.

I fell, hit the ground. The gun was gone. I couldn't hear, couldn't hear a thing except the low, constant *eeeeeeeeeeeeeeeeeeeeeeeeeeeee* sound in my ears. The dusk and pebbles stopped falling. I opened my eyes.

Mine and Thomas's torches, fallen, lit the cavern floor. My shotgun lay half-buried nearby under rubble and dust. Deep redness spread across the floor. Thomas lay on his side up ahead, eyes staring into mine, lips moving as blood-bubbles popped on them.

Then beside him, something moved, rising, and that white, vast-eyed face rose from behind him. Its body rose with it, on white, spider-thin limbs, and it crept across the cavern floor towards me.

I DON'T KNOW HOW LONG I SPENT, ON THAT HOT SEPTEMBER DAY, SITTING on the low wall and staring at Ceridwen's body.

The time passed in a numbed blur. When first she'd fallen I'd run to her side, tried to wake her, begged her to speak. I'd felt desperately in her wrist and throat for a pulse, listened for heartbeat, and found nothing. I was sure, so sure, that she was dead.

So after that, I just sat on the wall. I didn't know what to do next. Was there anything *to* do? Go to the police? I couldn't bring myself to do that. What would I say? Go back to my gran's and pretend nothing had happened? Yeah, that would work. Only a matter of time before the police came knocking. Wales wasn't *that* much of a foreign country.

I'd killed my girlfriend. There, I'd said it, if only to myself. And over what? If I told the truth, would I be believed? No—if I told the truth people would assume it was a self-serving lie, that I'd tried to rape her and it had gone wrong.

I buried my face in my hands and sobbed. It wasn't all self-pity, honestly. My life was over—and my mum, my dad, my gran, they'd all have to suffer this, too. And it was that sobbing that might have saved me, because it told Thomas and the others something was wrong.

I'd been due to meet up with them earlier, you see. And of course, I'd missed it; time seemed to have stopped with Ceridwen's death. But only for me, of course; for me and for her. For everyone else, it ticked on inexorably, and so they'd come looking. I'd promised to meet up with the lads one last time.

I heard my name called, distantly, and felt something close to relief, that the decision about what happened next had been made for me.

"Oh, Jesus," I heard Thomas say.

Dewi sniggered. Then stopped. Then realised, and said: "Fucking hell."

Pete said nothing, but I knew he was there. I couldn't look at any of them.

Footsteps crashed and slithered down the slope. Thomas knelt beside me shaking me, saying my name. "What happened?" he kept asking. "What happened here?"

I thought it was self-evident, but he kept asking, so I told him to make him stop. I wasn't crying anymore; I wasn't even frightened. I was . . . it's hard, even now, to describe exactly how I was. Disconnected might come close. None of this, nothing felt real. I was on the inside looking out at the rest of the world, or on the outside looking in. I just wanted a white room. I understood now why they put mad people in white rooms. Everything was still there, calm. Soothing. And the constant demands to know what had happened spoiled that, broke the calm. If I gave the voices what they wanted they might leave me alone. So I explained. Once I started, it was quite easy; after a while, it felt as if someone else was doing it. I heard my own voice, toneless and calm, telling Thomas what had happened. When it was done, it stopped. Now perhaps I'd be left alone.

"Jesus Christ," said Thomas. "Bloody, bloody hell." Dewi and Pete stood staring down at me as he paced up and down the dell, strayed towards its end, towards the thick grass and brambles beyond which lay open space and sunlight—

Was he going to look to see if anyone else was out there, or just trying to get out of that place, into fresh air and light, the better to think? Either way, I saw where he was going and remembered something. "Don't!" I shouted.

Dewi jumped, yelped; Pete took a step back, blinking. Thomas turned and stared. "What is it?" he said.

"Well," I said, and pointed to where it was. Thomas was okay; Thomas shouldn't die because of me, too. "Old well, there. You'll fall through."

Thomas looked to where I was pointing, then back at me. Then he went closer to the brambles and grass. I made a noise; he shushed me with an upraised hand. He crouched, peering down, then looked back at us: Dewi and Pete, looking to him for orders as usual, me sitting there like a zombie, Ceridwen lying in a broken, disordered huddle, her suitcase still lying in the cottage ruins. For a moment all our worlds and futures pivoted around him; I say a moment, but it could be minutes. There was no reckoning of time just then. And then he made his decision.

"Pete, Dewi," he said, "give me a hand here."

I half-rose; he pointed. "Not you. Bloody well stay where you are. Come on, lads."

It just seemed to get even more unreal; I watched as Pete and Thomas picked Ceridwen up and carried her to the well. Dewi, on Thomas's orders, picked up the suitcase and brought it over. Thomas nodded to him and Dewi chucked it forward; I heard a rush and clatter as it slid through the net of brambles, then the thump and splash as it hit the well's damp floor. Then he caught a leg that slid free of Pete's grip. I almost laughed, watching them holding her like that—Thomas had her under the shoulders, and Pete and Dewi, now, had a leg apiece. They shuffled round, ready to drop her.

"One," I heard Thomas say. They swung her back and forth over the well. "And two . . ." They swung again. "And thr—"

A soldier told me they call it bullet time; the way a moment can stretch out so that a second's work can seem to last forever. They swung her forward, hands already relaxing on her to let her go—

And Ceridwen opened her eyes.

She would have seen the three of them of course—seen them very clearly, holding her, swinging her. And in that last split-second before they let her go, her eyes found mine. She knew me, knew them; what she didn't know, couldn't understand, was what was happening—what *had* happened, and why.

She screamed. But their hands were already open, the act beyond recall. For an instant she hung suspended, arms and legs aflail in the air; I glimpsed the white of her knickers as her legs kicked. And then bullet time was over; real time came back, and she was gone, leaving only a scream that was cut off by the brutal, terminal sound of impact from below.

THOMAS—SOMEHOW, THOMAS GOT THE THREE OF US INTO SOME SEM-
blance of sanity again. A quartet of traumatised boys. Before, only one of
us had been a killer; now we all were.

But he told us, over and over, that everyone would think she'd run away.
With her crazy father, the missing case and the things she'd have packed
in it, who could doubt it? He was right, too, as it turned out.

The hardest part was acting normal for the remainder of the day and
the following morning, with my gran. I told her I was sorry to be leaving; I
think she believed that. She started to say something about being glad to
see my parents again, then stopped.

My dad picked me up the next day. On the journey home he told me,
haltingly, that he and Mum were getting a divorce. As I slumped under that
blow, I thought that the one good thing about it, the thing that made a part
of me—the cold, ancient part that had counselled murder back in the dell
the day before—actually glad of the news, was that now I had a reason to
be miserable.

The rest of the year . . . it's a bit of a blur, to be honest. I think I came as
close as it's possible for a human being to come to a complete breakdown and
still function. Kids, it seems, always feel guilt when their parents divorce;
add that to the very real guilt I had to hide and it was greater still. At times
I wondered if their divorce hadn't come as a punishment, divinely ordained;
for Ceridwen's death, or for the sexual adventures that had filled the weeks
before it.

The police came and spoke to me, albeit briefly. I stuck to the cover story
I'd agreed with Thomas; Ceridwen had been miserable at my going, said
she couldn't bear living with her father at Plas Merthyr any more. It wasn't
hard to stick to it; if nothing else, I owed it to Thomas, Dewi and Pete not
to land them in the shit. They seemed to accept it; they never came back.
If and when they found her body, they'd hopefully assume she'd met with
an accident while running away. As time passed, I assumed—wrongly, as
it turned out—that they'd found what little remained of Ceridwen, drawn
that conclusion and closed the case.

I spoke to Thomas very briefly, on a later visit to my gran. She was my
dad's mother and she and Mum had never really got along, so I saw less of
her after the divorce, as Mum got custody. But it made for a cheap holiday,
an easy treat for Dad to provide me with.

Thomas and I didn't speak much that time—or indeed, ever after that, till
that phone call twenty years later—but he told me that Isaiah had pretty
much disowned her *in absentia*. She was dead to him; he had no daughter,

et cetera. Funny—I'd only encountered the man once and as far as I knew he'd never even seen me, but I could imagine him saying that all too clearly. Ceridwen had told me often enough about his cold, loveless brand of fatherhood. From what I knew of Isaiah, I guessed he was secretly relieved, even pleased—no more daughter, no more product of his sin. He could devote himself to his farm and his cruel and bitter faith unhindered now.

On that, as it turned out, I was right and I was wrong.

And since then? Since then, I'd led a lonely, selfish life. There's no denying that. There'd been a few women, of course, but Ceridwen always got in the way. Even though I hadn't loved her, she was the ultimate bar to intimacy. There was always a section of me closed off to others, access denied. I could never completely share myself with another; so one by one, they drifted away.

And no real friends either; again, no one got that close. And with both friends and women, there was the fear, too; the fear of how it could all go cataclysmically wrong.

Thomas, Dewi, even Pete—each left, or would leave, a gap behind; people noticed, or would, when they disappeared. But me? Clients would puzzle over emails and phone calls that went unanswered, then shrug and go elsewhere. The bank would notice, when the mortgage payments stopped. And that was it. That was what I'd made of myself. Just that.

IT CRAWLED SLOWLY, STIFFLY, AS IF IN PAIN. ITS BREATH RASPED AND RAT-tled in its throat. Perhaps I should have moved, but I couldn't; my eyes were fixed on it.

Its body was smeared and caked in filth of one kind or another. There were bindings of some sort over the breasts and groin. Isaiah's work, I guessed. *Hide thy shame.* Beneath the dirt its skin was a horrible, mealy white, the colour of something that lived in the dark. Which, of course, it did.

Above the white face, the blackened mouth, was a jagged tangle of filthy, matted hair. Had Isaiah cut it? Or had it—*she*—done so herself, hacking at it with the stubby knife still gripped in one hand, clenched on the floor? It was still thick, anyway, but it didn't quite cover the shocking dent in her skull, part of which extended below the hairline to disfigure her forehead.

She reached me at least; she was above me, rank breath hissing in and out through her gritted, blackened teeth. Her knife hand rose; it was gloved in crusted, clotted filth that had been blood, and dripped with a fresh supply. The knife was thick and stubby, the knapped blade wide and razor sharp. Isaiah would have taught her that skill, I realised, as those pale grey eyes stared emptily into mine; if there was one thing that hateful bastard had known it was how to weaponise anything that came in reach. His Bible, his bereavement, even his daughter's love for him. And, finally, Ceridwen herself.

"Ceridwen," I whispered.

Ceridwen blinked and cocked her head, grunted. How much of her was left? Anything at all?

Her hand came up, opened. The knife dropped from her dirty fingers, swung from a little leather thong on her wrist. Her nails were long and sharp and clotted with dried blood. Her hand stank; but, gently, she stroked my cheek and let out the softest whining sound, before huddling against me, her head on my chest. After about a minute, her body started to shake with sobs.

I just lay there, not daring to move. Finally, Ceridwen lifted herself away from me and moved back, still on all fours. She jerked her head for me to follow, then crawled away. She got to her feet as she reached Thomas, and swayed; darkness glistened down her side. One of Thomas's blasts, or mine, must have injured her—how seriously I couldn't tell. At the cave entrance she looked back at me and jerked her head; at last, I followed, stopping as I reached Thomas. He was still, eyes open, unblinking; steam rose from the blood that had escaped him. The shotgun lay beside him, and his torch. I picked them up and followed her.

DOWN ONE OF THE OTHER TWO TUNNELS WAS HER LAIR; THE PASSAGE opened out into another, smaller chamber. In one corner was a filthy pile of reeking sheep and rabbit pelts; in another, the remains of a fire. I wondered what she'd made her makeshift candles from; decided it was better not to know.

On the walls were pictures. Dozens of them. Old photos of Thomas, of Dewi, of Pete, from back then and over the passing years. Right up to now.

And a smaller group of photos, which Ceridwen crouched by and gazed adoringly up at—smaller because, of course, I'd been there less.

How had Isaiah known? Had she been able to tell him? She didn't seem capable of speech. Perhaps there'd been more of her then. Or perhaps—the thought made me shudder—perhaps Isaiah had always known. Perhaps he'd even been watching, that day. Anything was possible.

But in any case, he'd found her. He'd fished her out of the well and nursed her back to health. But, self-evidently, he'd told no one. Why? *Hide thy shame*, of course.

O sinful woman, tainted in the fall of Man, author of that loss, all iniquities are due to thee. It was sex and sin, in his eyes, that had brought this about—that, and, perhaps, he'd suspected others would blame his treatment of Ceridwen for what had become of her. He'd always loathed her, blamed her; mightn't her death, or near-death, have seemed like her birth to him, another act devised to cause him pain?

Behold, thou hast brought shame upon thy house and grief upon thy Father's soul and behold how the retribution of the LORD has fallen on thy life. We'd made of her a cross for him to bear; that was how Isaiah would have seen it. Ceridwen had told me again and again how he'd seen himself as God's anointed and chosen; of course all things would be against him; of course every misfortune would be part of a greater plan.

There is but one sure token of thy repentance and that is blood. There is but one path to redemption in the eyes of the LORD and that path is to do His bidding and to work His will upon the earth.

So hid his shame down here—how long had he known about this place?— keeping the ruin that had been Ceridwen hidden in the dark and all this time schooling her. Training her.

Thou art the instrument of the LORD'S vengeance.

Not God's; Isaiah Hughes's. So that when he was dead, beyond shame's reach, his daughter, patiently and cruelly trained, would go out to destroy us. Was that why he'd left two wills? To ensure the house was left alone as long as possible, long enough for his revenge to be complete? Had he known Thomas would call me, or had he had another plan? Or had Ceridwen been supposed to set off from Barmouth and cross the country to seek me out?

She was whining again. She was touching the pictures of me, stroking them. I saw there was scoring and scratches across the pictures of the others, smears of filth. But not across mine.

I buckled and sank to my knees; distantly, I realised I was crying. Ceridwen crawled to me, rubbed her face against mine, then crawled to her bed of animal skins and slumped there. I stood, swaying; twenty years in this hellish place, and in one thing, still, Isaiah had failed. He'd been unable to teach her hatred for me. Why, I don't know. Perhaps because it had been an accident; perhaps she didn't remember the initial fall. Perhaps she only recalled Thomas and the others flinging her into the well, my face in the background. But she remembered what had gone before; remembered the closest thing to love she'd ever known.

Shame, remorse; I thought I'd known their meaning, until now.

In the fire's dull flicker I saw the fresh blood glistening. She'd been wounded by the spray of shot: in the left arm, across the ribs, the soft flesh above the hip. She lay there, slatted ribs heaving up and down.

I felt the shotgun's weight in my hand. It would be easy. She wouldn't fight.

It would be a mercy.

BUT I DIDN'T DO IT. I COULDN'T PULL THE TRIGGER; WASN'T THAT MUCH OF a killer. I went back to the other tunnel, instead, and searched Thomas's jacket till I found the bulky tin he'd thrust in there. It contained bandages, cotton wool, antiseptic; just in case either of us had needed it.

The shots that had wounded Ceridwen had gone straight through; she snarled and moaned as I cleaned the wounds, then dressed them, but she let me do it, and she swallowed the painkillers I gave her. And then she slept.

I think I slept, too; down there, it was hard to be sure. When I woke, I explored the last tunnel. It was the longest; at its end was sunlight, where it opened out onto a secluded part of the hillside. This must have been how she'd got out, to hunt the prey Isaiah had trained her for. Dawn was breaking; more time had passed than I'd thought.

I went back inside, then retraced my steps to the big chamber, the cellar, the kitchen. I replaced the false cellar wall, shut the cellar door and moved the fridge back into place, then slipped out of Plas Merthyr and back down the hillside in the silvery morning light, picking up Thomas's gun cases along the way.

And now, here I sit in Thomas's front room, typing this and watching the sun go down over Barmouth Bay. The cars go by on the road; on the horizon, there's a ship. Almost close enough to touch; and yet, it's another world.

Thomas said that I didn't know the meaning of friendship; said I didn't understand even something as basic as taking responsibility for my own actions. Perhaps he was right; perhaps I'm taking that responsibility at last, or I'm just finding a newer, costlier way to evade it. After all, fingers will point towards me when folk realise he's missing, too. I don't know; that's for someone else to decide, someone like you.

All that remains is to find a way to hide this account, but hide it in such a way that it'll one day be found. Somewhere far ahead, when Ceridwen and I are long gone, when she's past being hurt again.

I thought long and hard about it, of course. Ringing the police, being found guilty at long, long last, not having to carry the burden of my secrets and my guilt any more. But Mum and Dad are still alive, for one thing; there's the pain it'd cause them. And most of all, there's Ceridwen herself. What will become of her? She'll be a freak, an object of derision, of scientific curiosity or cloying pity. Or all three.

And so I'm going back to Plas Merthyr, and I'm not coming back. She's alone now, with Isaiah gone, and she's done what he trained her to do. He didn't care what happened to her after that; he expected her to be caught or shot out of hand like a mad dog. And she deserved better than that; she deserved, *deserves*, just for once in her life, to be cared for, not to be used selfishly.

And me? Well, the punishment is just. At least I won't be alone. And I'll have nothing more to hide.

After all these years, that might just be enough.

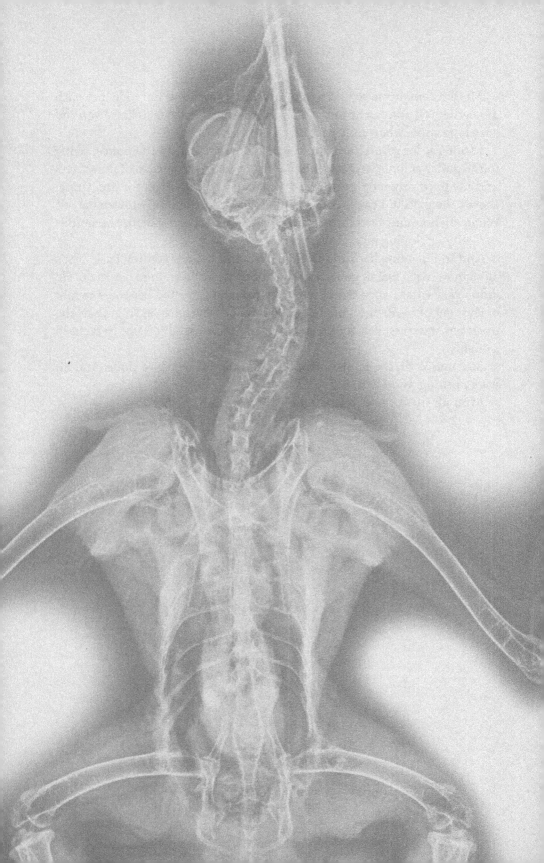

Afterword: Notes from the King of the Bastards

When I first met the author Lynda Rucker, she told me that I'd given her nightmares for a week.

Lynda is a very nice person, and an amazing writer—seriously, if you haven't already read her then you should. I liked her immediately. But I'd caused her a week's worth of horrible dreams with my story "The Narrows" and I was delighted to hear it.

Another friend, Laura Mauro (and yet another amazing writer you ought to be reading if you like the dark and the disturbing) who beta-read a couple of my novels, sent me a furious email halfway through one of them saying, "I CAN'T BELIEVE YOU KILLED [CHARACTER NAME REDACTED] YOU UTTER BASTARD." When something similar happened in the next book, I got another email, informing me that I was now the *King* of the Bastards.

Apart from "husband of Cate Gardner" (yet *another* brilliant writer you should all . . . look, you get the idea by now), I think that's the proudest title I've ever had bestowed on me.

Art should be a shock to the system: a crack in the world that shows us another. The axe that smashes the frozen sea within us, as Kafka said. At the very least, it should wring an emotion from its audience. T. B. Grover, one of the scriptwriters for the *Judge Dredd* comic strip in *2000 AD*, was once asked how he reacted to all the criticism he'd received for killing off so many of the strip's popular supporting characters. "Very favourably," he replied. "Readers criticise because they *care*."

So if they come away thinking you're a monster, you're probably doing something right.

Anyway, the show's over now. I hope you enjoyed the book, and I'm grateful to you for buying it. You can close it now if you want—or if, like me, you like looking behind the scenes and learning how the tricks are done, you can join me for a whistle-stop tour of the Kingdom of Bastardry—as long as you've read all the stories, since Here Be Spoilers. So if you *haven't* read the stories, go back and do so before continuing. Or you might find something scratching at your window later tonight.

Are you back now? Good. Hop aboard the Bastard Train, and hold on.

1. Dermot

I've never learned to drive, which can make getting around more complicated than I wish it was, but a lot of my stories owe their existence to my reliance on public transport. "Dermot" is a case in point.

When I lived in Swinton and caught the bus to Manchester via Salford, there was an odd-looking guy I saw a couple of times. When I wondered what his name might be, "Dermot" was the name that popped into my head. And when I wondered what kind of a *person* he might be . . . well, the answer wasn't too flattering. The only other question was how to turn that into a story. Once that was answered, it took an afternoon to write it.

I showed the manuscript to two friends. One loved it; the other, basically, said, "Meh." So I hesitated to send it out . . . for a couple of years, before sending it to *Black Static* magazine. Andy Cox accepted it within the week, and the story's proven popular since, having been reprinted twice in "Best Of" collections and broadcast on *Pseudopod*. Now and again you write something which strikes a chord—or hits a nerve—with a lot of people; like catching lightning in a bottle, it's impossible to predict or duplicate. "Dermot" was one of those tales.

2. Beneath the Sun

"Beneath the Sun" was written for *Acquainted with the Night*, one of Ash-Tree Press's anthologies of traditional supernatural fiction. My original title was "The Feasters," but Barbara Roden didn't think it was quite right; the present one was about the best I could do.

The original title—and the story—came out of listening to a couple of friends discuss John Metcalfe's classic supernatural novella *The Feasting Dead*, which I hadn't read at the time. I overheard the title, which gave me the image that eventually produced the story, plus some discussion of how the story revolved around a boy and his relationship with his father. It doesn't, I was glad to find out, bear any resemblance to Metcalfe's tale, which I can highly recommend to anyone who hasn't already had the pleasure.

3. THE MORAINE

"THE MORAINE" STARTED WITH THE TITLE, WHICH I THEN HAD TO GOOGLE in order to find out what a moraine was! (Read the story to find out.) I knew there was a story in it, but wasn't sure what. There had to be something *in* the moraine, and I knew that I wanted it to be something more substantial than a ghost—it had to be something physical, a creature of some kind. At the same time I wanted it to be scary rather than simply bloody, so it had to build tension and suspense. The nature of the setting helped determine that. And finally, of course, there had to be some actual real *people* in the story.

The final spur was an invitation to contribute to Paul Finch's anthology *Terror Tales of the Lake District*, the first in his series of *Terror Tales* anthologies. Originally I'd planned something with a bigger cast, but in the end—as is so often the case—simpler was better. Writing it, I imagined it as a short film or television play, which helped me focus on Steve and Diane. Making their relationship a troubled but not necessarily doomed one made them realer, too, and gave the story somewhere to go when the monster wasn't active. It's proven popular anyway, reprinted in *Best Horror of the Year* #4 (alongside "Dermot") and *Great Jones Street*, and read on the *Pseudopod* podcast in 2017. It was also included in the *Best of the Best Horror of the Year: 10 Years of Essential Short Fiction* in 2018.

4. COMFORT YOUR DEAD

THIS WASN'T MEANT TO BE A GHOST STORY. HERE'S HOW IT HAPPENED: one day—back when I lived in Swinton, once again—I set off to catch a bus and saw a divorcee I knew, with her young daughter, walking up the road with a man—a boyfriend, I assumed—and another young child. From that came the idea of writing a story about a relationship between two single parents; I decided to make one divorced and one a widower.

By the time I'd reached my destination—Lightoaks Park, which became the setting for "Comfort Your Dead"—the story had taken shape, and had decided it wanted to be a ghost story. I caught the first bus back home, grabbed a pen and exercise book, and wrote the whole thing out in a few hours.

But while the composition was easy enough, getting it published was rather more vexed. It went first to *All Hallows* magazine, which went onto a protracted hiatus. Unfortunately, because of the long delay I forgot about the story as new ones were written; eventually I withdrew "Comfort Your Dead" and sent it to a couple of other markets without success. For a time it was slated to be published as a chapbook with another tale, "The Climb," until the publisher changed their mind and replaced them both with a longer piece I'd sent them for a Christmas anthology. (*That* chapbook didn't happen either, but that's another story.) It was only when I was putting this collection together that I realised "Comfort Your Dead" had never seen print. I'm glad it's finally found a home.

5. The School House

BACK IN 2006, ON THE WAY BACK FROM A WEEKEND SPENT DRUNKENLY discussing horror fiction with my old friend Rob Kemp, the train passed a large Victorian building and the words *the school house* flitted through my head. I spent the next few months, on and off, turning that inspiration over and over and trying to decide what kind of a story it needed to be. As with "The Moraine," I decided I didn't want to write another ghost story (I've written a lot of those, and I still love them, but variety is the spice of life and so on); again, I wanted something more physical, where the house itself was a character in the tale; at the same time, there had to be more than just gore, an element of the supernatural. It needed to be a dream-like story—or a nightmare-like one.

The story fermented in my notebooks until the following year, when David Sutton invited me to write a novella for a BFS anthology he was editing called *Houses on the Borderland*. It was to be launched at the 2008 FantasyCon, but David was unable to attend and a number of key jobs changed hands at the BFS. In the confusion the anthology more or less sank without trace, much to the disappointment of the writers.

Not least me, as "The School House" is probably the most personal thing I've done. No, in case you were wondering, I wasn't happy at school. That said, Danny Denholm isn't me, and the basement scene is (thankfully) without any basis in reality. All the same, the story has its share of autobiographical elements. I also wrote it at a very difficult time—frantically trying to hunt down a new job while working full time *and* acting as board chairman for a small production company meant I was practically putting in sixteen or seventeen hours a day. Probably not the best circumstances in which to revisit some of the nastier memories of my youth. At one point I actually feared I was about to suffer a mental breakdown—I didn't, as it turned out, but the experience fed into "The School House," which tries, I think, to evoke the feel of someone going out of his mind as intensely as possible.

The story was reprinted in my novella collection, *The Condemned*, and again when David re-released the original anthology as *Haunts of Horror* from his own Shadow Publishing imprint. Despite—or perhaps because of—the place I was in when I wrote it, I'm very proud of it.

6. LEFT BEHIND

THE TITLE COMES FROM A SONG BY SLIPKNOT. THE STORY ITSELF BEGAN as a straight-up crime/noir story about a boy who commits a murder to gain entry to the Mob, but it wouldn't come to life. It only worked when I threw something weird into the mix. Story of my life, really. It first saw print in Trevor Denyer's magazine *Midnight Street*.

7. HUSHABYE

BETWEEN 2004 AND 2007 I WROTE HALF A DOZEN SHORT STORIES FEA-turing a sort of reluctant psychic detective by the name of Paul Hearn. A couple of them are still unpublished. He owes something to the likes of Algernon Blackwood's John Silence and William Hope Hodgson's Carnacki, but a lot more to the nameless protagonist of the supernatural police stories in the late Joel Lane's *Where Furnaces Burn*. Most of them are rooted in the Manchester and Salford area where I lived at the time; all the locations that appear in "Hushabye" are (or were: supernatural monsters have nothing on property developers when it comes to sheer rapacity) real.

"Hushabye" first appeared in *Inferno*, Ellen Datlow's first non-themed anthology. Ellen later reprinted it in *Nightmares: A New Decade of Modern Horror*, alongside work by Gene Wolfe, Caitlin R. Kiernan, Robert Shearman and Anna Taborska.

8. A SMALL COLD HAND

SOME STORIES COME TOGETHER SLOWLY AND PAINFULLY, WHILE OTHERS go from first inspiration to the finished article at speed. "Comfort Your Dead" was one of the second kind; "A Small Cold Hand" was another.

Written in 2006, it was inspired by a walk in my local cemetery, where a small, plain brown gravestone caught my eye, because of the bowl of fresh flowers in front of it. The stone was for a six-year-old girl who'd died in 1981. Twenty-five years later, I realised, someone was still grieving; someone was still in pain. Sometimes it takes a small detail to bring home the very obvious; in this case, how certain kinds of loss can never go away. The opening lines of the story came into my head as I walked home, and two hours later I'd finished the first draft. The story was published in the Ash-Tree Press anthology *At Ease with the Dead*.

9. THE PROVING GROUND

THE OPENING WAS INSPIRED BY PART OF A CONRAD WILLIAMS STORY; I thought I saw where it was going but in the end it went somewhere else entirely. "The Proving Ground" is basically the story I imagined. It appeared in my second story collection, *Pictures of the Dark*, and 'picture of the dark,' for me, describes this story perfectly:a glimpse of another, slightly crooked world.

10. ANGELS OF THE SILENCES

THE FIRST PAGE OF *ANGELS OF THE SILENCES* IS, ALMOST WORD-FOR-WORD, a real-life incident from my Salford days, and Emily and Biff are drawn from life. I was on the number 8 bus, stopping outside Chetham's Music School, when they and their friends all piled on, en route to an impromptu camping trip to Kearsley Mount. Where I lived, I'd run into far too many kids who were vicious, abusive little shits; it was great to meet some who were kind, funny and smart. I transcribed the scene as best I could from memory, and then Emily added the line "We've both been dead for nine months." After that, it very largely wrote itself. I loved writing it and spending time with the characters and in their world, especially after writing very dark, intense stories like "The Narrows" and "The School House."

Angels was originally submitted to Chris Teague's Pendragon Press, for their novella anthology *Triquorum*, but in the end saw print as a chapbook in 2011. It sold out quickly, and was reprinted in 2016 by Kate Jonez's Omnium Gatherum imprint.

Most of the locations in the story are real, or were, including the Moon Cafe (although not its special clientele). It was written in 2006, but by the time it came out five years later a lot of things had changed: Jilly's Rockworld had closed, and you could no longer smoke in cafes, clubs or bars in the UK.

Of all the stories I've written, "Angels" is one my personal favourites. I love the characters of Emily and Biff; I meant to return to them one day, but so far I never have. And it's a snapshot of a time and place I love, but isn't there anymore. Manchester is one of those cities that's always changing, always in flux. Every time I go back there now, another familiar place or landmark seems to have gone. But the city I remember still exists here.

11. . . . And Dream Of Avalon

This one owes its existence to Barbara Roden of Ash-Tree Press and *All Hallows* magazine. I originally wrote it as "The Boys of Summer" (no prizes for guessing where *that* title came from) and tried to shoehorn it into the form of a straightforward ghost story, where the character saw some ghosts and then ran away. Barbara quite rightly objected that there was, or should be, more to the story than I'd put in. And so a month or so later I sent it back to her, with a thousand more words and a new title—and hopefully all the better for both. It appeared in my first collection, *A Hazy Shade of Winter*, published by Ash-Tree. Glad to see it get another airing here.

12. Winter's End

Like "Hushabye," "Winter's End" was a Paul Hearn story, one that this time took him away from his usual Salford stamping ground and out to Dovestone Reservoir, at the edge of the Peak District. It's a beautiful and evocative area, but one that has hidden its share of dark secrets. The reservoir lies next to Saddleworth Moor, where the child-killers Ian Brady and Myra Hindley buried their victims in the 1960s, and in 2015, eight years after "Winter's End" was written, a man was found dead of strychnine poisoning in mysterious circumstances nearby. Carrying no identification, he was known only as 'Neil Dovestone' until two years later, when he was finally identified as David Lytton, a British expatriate who'd lived in Lahore, Pakistan, for the past decade. What had brought him to Dovestone Reservoir, how he came to be poisoned—and indeed, much of his life—remains a mystery.

Paul's love-life had been a pretty desultory affair in the preceding stories, and I decided it was time to give him a taste of happiness. Not that it lasted. The story was first published in the Gray Friar Press anthology *Where the Heart Is*. As a sidenote, I liked the name 'Helen Damnation' so much that I ended up using it as the protagonist of the Black Road novels, although she has no other connection to the character in this.

13. They Wait

Sometimes you discover what you want to write about by the process of writing, and this was one such case. "They Wait" began with not much more than the title, and developed into a meditation on old age and on the relationship between one generation's failures and those of the next. It was first published on Paul Kane's *Shadow Writer* website, and then in a print anthology compiling his guest authors' offerings.

14. The Children of Moloch

For many years Gary Fry ran the excellent small press publisher Gray Friar Press, bringing out collections and anthologies of quality short weird fiction. Well, and two of mine, but that's another story. Gray Friar also published the anti-fascist anthology *Never Again* and the anti-austerity anthology *Horror Uncut*, both of which I was proud to be a part of.

On a couple of occasions, Gary would have some extra credit with his printers, and he'd use it to put together an anthology at short notice, more for fun than anything else. *Home Is Where the Heart Is*, where "Winter's End" appeared, was one such project; another was *Death Rattles*.

The premise was simple enough: *Death Rattles* was a (fictitious) anthology series produced in the early days of Channel 4, aiming for cutting-edge, envelope-pushing horror. It was so controversial that it was never repeated, and the original recordings—and even the scripts—were lost. The contributors to the anthology would be trying to reconstruct the episodes they'd seen as best they could, in story form.

Gary put together a strong list of contributors, including John Llewellyn Probert, Gary McMahon, Thana Niveau and himself, together with an introduction by Stephen Volk, whose background in TV and film (not least as the author of *Ghostwatch*) added verisimilitude to the project.

I'd been going through a dry patch in terms of writing fiction, and *Death Rattles* helped get me out of it: I'd previously attempted a story based on the premise of "The Children of Moloch," but the result had been a bloated, overblown mess; as with "The Moraine," imagining the story in terms of a half-hour television play helped me visualise each scene and write it with the intensity it deserved. Nearly a decade on, I'm still pleased with the result; *Death Rattles* wasn't very widely read, so it's a real pleasure to present "The Children of Moloch." It's the first time it's been reprinted, although it was given an excellent reading by J. K. Shepler on the late Lawrence Santoro's *Tales to Terrify* podcast.

One final note: to help make the whole thing more convincing, all the authors contributed an anecdote about how they came to encounter *Death Rattles*. This was mine:

"Some things—like remembering *Dr. Who* being played by Tom Baker—make you feel your age. This is the opposite—I'm very much aware of being the baby of the group here, as there's no way I would've got to see *Death Rattles* on its original release. It was way past my bedtime for a start. . . .

"No, for my part of the story we've got to fast forward to 1999; and if things had gone just a little bit differently, this anthology might never have happened.

"Meet my friend Rick; we've been mates since primary school. Tall, broad-shouldered, long black hair and a goatee beard that either makes him look like Jesus or the other guy depending on how the light strikes him. Usually the latter option because of his penchant for black metal and matching t-shirts. But I digress.

"Rick, being a rebel by nature, loved horror films—everything from black and white classics like Lugosi's *Dracula*, through Hammer and Amicus, Italian *giallos (gialli?)* through to the latest stuff. He particularly liked anything that'd ever been banned or censored; if someone hadn't wanted us to see it, he was damned well going to watch it as a matter of principle. And if the only legally available version was cut, he would go to great lengths to track down the full-length uncensored version. And more often than not, I'd be watching it with him. Usually stoned. In this way I got to see the uncut *Suspiria*, *Deep Red*, *Nightmares in a Damaged Brain*, *Zombie Flesh Eaters*, *Oasis of the Living Dead* and many more besides. He even had *Child's Play 3*, although I never got to see that.

"Anyroad, one day I called round to find Rick in particularly jubilant mode. He'd made a huge haul of material at a car-boot sale; if memory serves, he'd picked up uncut versions of *The New York Ripper*, *The House by the Cemetery*, *The Beyond* and *Cannibal Holocaust*—stuff he'd been hunting down for months—all for a couple of quid apiece. The guy he'd bought them off also had a couple of battered VHS tapes, obviously home-recorded, which he was willing to throw in for a couple of extra quid.

"They were pretty good, he'd told Rick, if you liked that sort of thing. Two tapes, with stickers reading: *Death Rattles (1)—Scattered Ashes, Seen and Not Heard & Antlers*, and *Death Rattles (2)—Cow Castle, His Father's Son & The Children of Moloch*.

"For some reason I can't recall, we watched the second tape first. And we loved it. The first two stories were good, but then we got to the final one. . . .

 By the end, we were riveted. And shaking. Even Rick, who usually found the gore a laugh, was affected by what we'd seen. But there was no doubt that we'd found something bloody impressive.

"I left after that—I had to be up for work in five hours—but we arranged to meet up soon to watch the other tape, and Rick promised to record a copy of the cassettes for me.

But the week after, Rick was arrested for selling pirated copies of his video collection, which the police seized in its entirety. (They were particularly interested in where he'd got hold of *Child's Play 3*.) In the end he got off with a fine. Originally he was told he'd get them back—the legally available ones at least—but when he rang the police to enquire, they told him all the videos had been destroyed.

Rick is not overly fond of the police these days.

"So yes, you've guessed it—up in smoke went possibly the last surviving copy of *Death Rattles*. But if just one more week had elapsed before Rick had his collar felt, I might still have had those videotapes when we first started discussing the series. Then the talk would have turned to arranging a screening, rather than recreating the lost episodes from memory, and this book wouldn't be so much aborted as never even conceived.

"'The Children of Moloch' had the spare, gritty look of the kind of social realist dramas that were popular at the time: films like Alan Clarke's *Scum* or *Made in Britain*. It gave the play an intensity that made it at times almost impossible to watch, but equally impossible to look away from. That's how I recall it at least, but with shows like this you never know how good it'll be when you watch it again in the cold light of day. Here's the story as I remember it; if it wasn't really like this, it bloody should have been."

15. And Cannot Come Again

THE THEME OF THE PAST, AND HOW IT CAN BOTH POISON AND ENRICH THE present, is one I keep coming back to. It lends itself readily to the ghost story, but I'd long wanted to write something that had the feel and atmosphere of a supernatural tale while in fact being rooted entirely in the real and human (although no less horrifying for that).

Another inspiration was Denez Prigent's arrangement of the traditional Breton folk-song *"An Hini a Garan"* *(The One I Love)*, a plaintive and haunting evocation of lost love. Listening to the song on a long rainy bus trip gave me the image of the nameless protagonist's train journey through England and Wales (a lot longer in the first draft than it is here) and the rest of the novella's elements quickly came together around it, so that all that was left was to write the story.

"And Cannot Come Again" is also something of a love letter to one of my favourite places in the world: Barmouth in North Wales, where my dad grew up and where my family spent many weekends and half-term holidays staying with my grandmother.

While it isn't a love story as such—at least, not from the protagonist's point of view, although perhaps from Ceridwen's—it's very much about lost innocence, childhood and regret. So it's the perfect ending to this collection.

AND WITH THAT, THE TRAIN HAS COME TO A HALT, AND YOUR STAY IN THE Kingdom of Bastardry has come to an end. Out you get, and I hope you enjoyed the ride. Hopefully I'll see you again.

Don't forget to turn the lights out as you leave.

Or maybe, just for tonight, you might want to leave them on.

Simon Bestwick
King of the Bastards
Wallasey, March 2019

ACKNOWLEDGEMENTS

My thanks and gratitude to the following:

Editors and publishers: Andy Cox, Ellen Datlow, Christopher Teague, Kate Jonez, Barbara and Christopher Roden, Paul Finch, David Sutton, Paul Kane and Gary Fry.

Brett Savory and Sandra Kasturi at ChiZine Press for publishing this collection, and to my agent, Tom Witcomb. Also to ChiZine's Kari Embree, and to Greg Murphy and Jared Shapiro.

Reggie Oliver, S. P. Miskowski, Steve Duffy, Simon Strantzas, Alison Littlewood, Priya Sharma, Tim Major, Aliya Whiteley, Ralph Robert Moore, David Nickle, Erica L. Satifka, Angela Slatter, Colleen Anderson, Usman T. Malik and Gemma Files for their kind words about mine.

Love and gratitude to many friends: Priya Sharma (again!) and Mark Greenwood, Laura and Rob Mauro, Lynda E. Rucker and Sean Hogan, Sarah Pinborough (and Ted), Georgina Bruce, Anna Taborska, Ray Cluley and Jess Jordan, Ali Littlewood (again!) and Fergus Beadle, Ramsey and Jenny Campbell, Bernard, Claire and Cassie Nugent, Hannah Dennerly and Tom Collins, Michael Weaver, Paul and Cath Finch, Victoria Leslie, Vicky Morris, Roberta Lannes-Sealey, Carmel Reynolds and all the brilliant folk who support my Patreon page at *https://www.patreon.com/SimonBestwick*. If I've missed anyone out it's through forgetfulness and not any lack of appreciation.

Love and gratitude also to all at Ginger Nuts of Horror, This Is Horror, Black Static, Hellnotes and many other review sites. Thanks to anyone who's ever reviewed, shared, recommended or otherwise signal-boosted my stuff.

Love and gratitude to my parents, Judith and Roger Bestwick.

Profound gratitude and admiration to Ramsey Campbell once more, for his introduction. I'm greatly honoured, and can also cross an item off my personal bucket list.

And love, gratitude and so much more to Cate, without whom I would be nothing and nowhere.

Publishing History

Dermot (previously published in *Black Static* #24, ed. Andy Cox, 2011, and reprinted in *The Best Horror of the Year* #4, ed. Ellen Datlow, 2012)

Beneath the Sun (previously published in *Acquainted with the Night*, ed. Barbara and Christopher Roden, Ash-Tree Press, 2004)

The Moraine (previously published in *Terror Tales of the Lake District*, ed. Paul Finch, Gray Friar Press, 2011, and reprinted in *The Best Horror of the Year* #4 ed. Ellen Datlow, 2012)

Comfort Your Dead (previously unpublished)

The School House (previously published in *Houses on the Borderland*, ed. Dave Sutton 2008, and collected in *The Condemned*, Gray Friar Press, 2013)

Left Behind (previously published in *Midnight Street* #10, ed. Trevor Denyer, 2008)

Hushabye (previously published in *Inferno*, ed. Ellen Datlow, Tor Books, 2005)

A Small Cold Hand (previously published in *At Ease with the Dead*, ed. Barbara and Christopher Roden, Ash-Tree Press, 2007)

The Proving Ground (previously published and collected in *Pictures of the Dark*, Gray Friar Press, 2009)

Angels of the Silences (previously published as a chapbook by Pendragon Press, 2011; reissued by Omnium Gatherum Media, 2016)

. . . And Dream of Avalon (previously published and collected in *A Hazy Shade of Winter*, Ash-Tree Press, 2004)

Winter's End (previously published in *Where the Heart Is*, ed. Gary Fry, Gray Friar Press, 2010)

They Wait (previously published in *Shadow Writers 2*, ed. Paul Kane, 2003)

The Children of Moloch (previously published in *Death Rattles*, ed. Gary Fry, Gray Friar Press 2011)

And Cannot Come Again (previously unpublished)

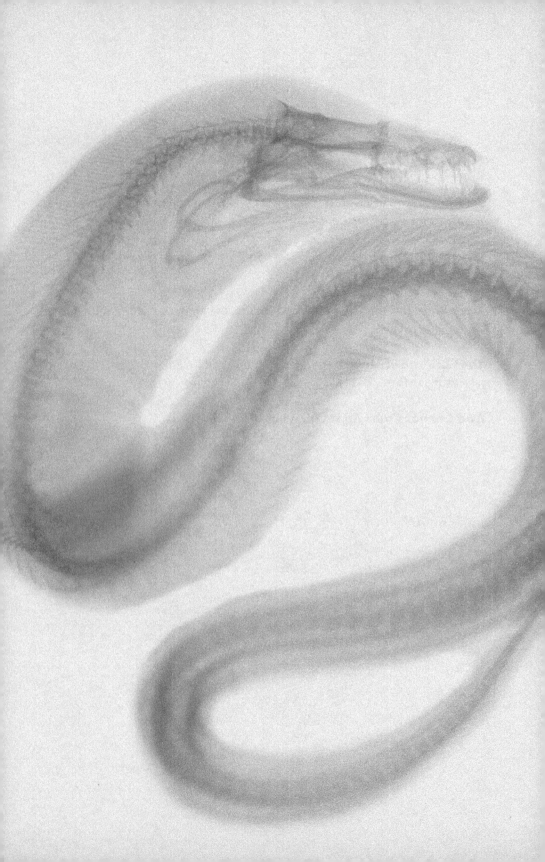

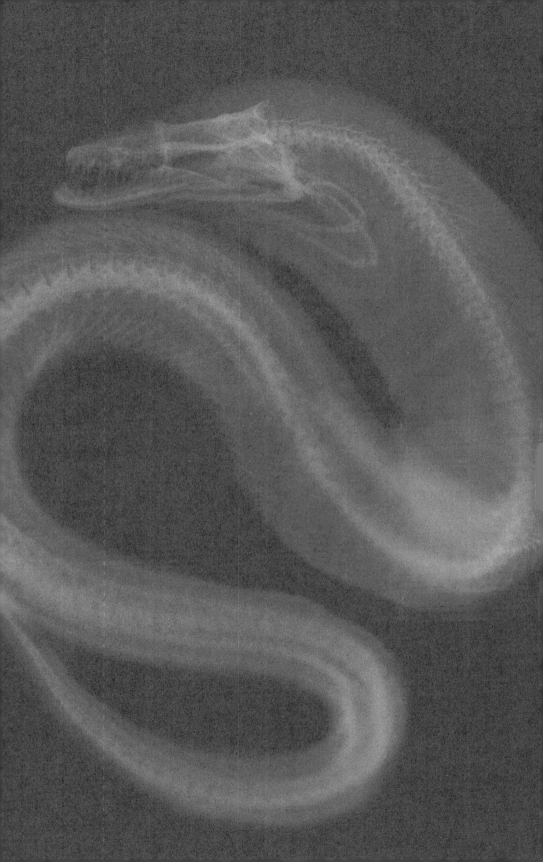